The Confessions of Sherlock Holmes

The Theological Odyssey of the Great Detective

Volume 2

The Abduction at Baskerville Hall

Thomas Mengert

Blue Forge Press
Port Orchard, Washington

Acknowledgements

The Confessions of Sherlock Holmes has, for all of its primary theological intent, a subtext that emerged in the course of the writing. That subtext is the decline and fall of the British Empire and of the imperial family structures that once supported it. The three Holmes brothers each manifest the end result of the system of primogeniture and the conflict present between art and reason in their blood. Each brother in his own way manifests the conflict entailed in finding a place and an identity in opposition to their father and his estate.

The character of the Holmes father remains distant and perhaps finally indecipherable. As the reader will discover in the course of reading the book the parental figure looks beyond his own sons in order to find an image of a substitute son that would meet the requirements and the pattern that the father needed each of them to represent. Unfortunately, each son manifested instead a diluted solution of traits that drew more from their artistic mother and her French heritage than from their stern father and his code. The individuality and character of the brothers manifests a freedom from convention that the father perhaps wished that he could have claimed for himself, but to see it present in his sons seemed both indulgent and a betrayal of his own strict principles. He valued rebellion, but not within his own house and among his own progeny. For this reason both Mycroft and Sherlock are comparative exiles, while Sherringford is saddled with maintaining Sigerside, the Holmes estate. If the Christian religion can be seen as the process of overcoming exile from God as Father through the sacrifice of a Son, the parallels will be immediately apparent.

I doubt that I would have been able to compose this book if it were not present as a reflection of the dynamics of my own family. So for this reason I dedicate this book as with all my efforts in life to my parents and grandparents and especially to my two grandmothers who each nurtured my early love for literature with their deep love and affirmation.

The support of my parents made my life possible in every way imaginable.

To my Father's mother, Tilly, who read me Longfellow's poetry on sunny afternoons.

To My Mother's mother, Gerda, who gave me the Doubleday Edition of The Complete Sherlock Holmes.

To my Father's father, Otto, who shared his library with me and taught me the value of family heritage.

To my Mother's father, Fred, who instilled in me a love of the sea and for his humor and love of stories.

To all of these my everlasting thanks.

"What is the meaning of it, Watson?" said Holmes, solemnly, as he laid down the paper. "What object is served by this circle of misery and violence and fear? It must tend to some end, or else our universe is ruled by chance, which is unthinkable. But what end? There is the great standing perennial problem to which human reason is as far from an answer as ever."

—From The Adventure of the Cardboard Box

"There is nothing in which deduction is as necessary as in religion," said he, leaning with his back against the shutters. "It can be built up as an exact science by the reasoner. Our highest assurance of the goodness of providence seems to me to rest in the flowers. All other things, our powers, our desires, our food, are really necessary for our existence in the first instance. But this rose is an extra. Its smell and its color are an embellishment of life, not a condition of it. It is only goodness which gives such extras, and so I say again that we have much to hope from the flowers."

—From The Adventure of the Naval Treaty

"The greatest schemer of all time, the organizer of every deviltry, the controlling brain of the underworld, a brain which might have made or marred the destiny of nations – that's the man!"

"Barker beat his head with his clenched fist in his impotent anger. 'Do not tell me that we have to sit down under this? Do you say that no one can ever get level with this king devil?' 'No, I don't say that,' said Holmes, and his eyes seemed to be looking far into the future. 'I don't say that he can't be beat. But you must give me time—you must give me time.' We all sat in silence for some minutes while those fateful eyes still strained to pierce the veil."

—From The Valley of Fear

Preface

It has seemed to me that a few words of preface should precede all else. My initial intention was to bring the book forward in a limited edition to be sold directly by the author to the purchaser after an appropriate lecture by way of introduction to prepare the reader for the unique demands of its content and length (over 800,000 words and some 2,000 pages) to explain my intentions in writing the book at all. The function of the present brief preface is to turn aside those readers who may imagine that a novel featuring Sherlock Holmes must of necessity be merely a tale of amusement and diversion rather than one probing into the very depths of the character of the man himself and the deeper mysteries of life. These readers may be distressed and disappointed if they expect only a vapid adventure tale and may attribute failure to the author, expecting him to have undertaken what he never undertook to do at all, simply to amuse and not challenge the reader.

The ideal reader of the following volume will be one who is willing to enter upon an intellectual adventure of no mean magnitude and to suspend his disbelief to the degree that he will find the Sherlock Holmes contained herein to be deeper in character and more worthy of esteem than any accolades ever afforded to him by Dr. John H. Watson might justify and to find herein a solution to many mysteries left unresolved in the original canonical tales. Since the present work exceeds the length of the entire corpus of the original tales, its existence may be very good news indeed to that ideal reader who wishes to hear more of Sherlock Holmes and Dr. Watson.

I shall here revive an old 19th century custom by greeting you dear reader. I trust that you will find a great intellectual adventure in reading the text that lies before you. It is no easy matter for an author to entrust his creation, formerly visited only by the mind which conceived it, to those he hopes will prove to be an indulgent public. A few introductory words before you begin seem in order. You are about to read a mystery that returns to the origin of all mysteries in the Mystery Plays of England, which attempted to explain the mysteries of the Christian religion by combining theology with popular entertainment and spectacle. The following story is told in two different voices with two different narrators: Sherlock Holmes and Doctor Watson. There are no chapter divisions. Instead there is a prologue, epilogue, and sixteen books. The span of time covered is from 1891 – 1899 with some short selections from 1914 through 1917 when both narratives were assembled by Doctor Watson. Together the two manuscripts constitute what may be called a discursive or picaresque narrative where ideas may be fully explored and examined. This type of book was quite common in the Victorian era but is less so today, though the need for such books is perhaps greater than ever before. I have long been concerned that with the decline of leisure, which is after all the basis of all that is most civilized within us, that we have forfeited as well the craft of the baroque prose of the 17th and succeeding centuries until the dawn of the contemporary literary scene. Even as late as the Victorian Age in England, some last vestiges of this sophistication and balance remained in the writings of men like Matthew Arnold and novelists such as Thackeray, Dickens, and Henry James. The work that you hold in your hand will I hope recall a vanished era, a more graceful period in the history of our common literature. Having made this brief apology for its ornate style I must move ahead to consider the extraordinary length of the complete book. Had this book been published in the 19th century, it would have been published in multiple volumes as was common for many of the books written by Charles Dickens and his friend Wilkie Collins, the originator of the modern detective story. I have often lamented the passing of that more discursive era when there was time and leisure to enter another world when reading a novel and to count on dwelling there for some time. I hope to have re-created something of that experience for the modern reader by writing this book in the fashion of an era, which I trust is not forever lost to us, when ideas might be fully explored to their furthest limits.

Any introduction should serve the purpose of explaining to the prospective reader the intentions of the author. It allows the author the liberty of an advance apologia, to deflect from the beginning any criticism for failing to achieve what was in fact never intended. Since the novel of ideas has become a rarity and since a didactic format has become unfashionable, I have thought it best to admit quite frankly that this novel is meant to take its inspiration from models whose several excellences have inspired my own effort. That a novel may include elements of the essay and extensively explore ideas is common in the Russian novels of Tolstoy and Dostoyevsky. The French also allow for the scope necessary to explore ideas in the works of Victor Hugo. English Literature is also not without models to inspire an endeavor such as the one that lies before you in this work. The primary genre or rather mix of genres, since I have taken instruction from several sources, includes the picaresque novels of Tobias Smollett, the writings of Samuel Johnson particularly *Rasselas*, and such unique works as *Tristram Shandy* by Sterne and *Vanity Fair* by Thackeray. The novel of ideas has been best represented however by the German writers. I have a special affection for two great German contributions to the novel of ideas: Thomas Mann's *The Magic Mountain* and Robert Musil's *The Man Without Qualities*.

To allow form to be flexible enough to allow for such content as I have intended here means to take liberties with the tradition of the novel of detection. Ordinarily the experience of the detective novel is considered to entail light entertainment or to be concentrated around adventure and romance. The appeal of Sherlock Holmes however exceeds both of these, for in the last analysis it is Holmes and Watson themselves who emerge from these narratives of Sir Arthur Conan Doyle as characters of such a unique and complete set of individual traits that the reader comes finally to have an affection for them far beyond perhaps any other protagonists in literature. It is for this reason that the focus of the present book is upon those very characters and the opinions and inner struggles that may have lain latent in the original tales, but that may now be explored in depth.

The present book is an effort to account for many problems of improbability or inconsistency in the original narratives of Sherlock Holmes. There are many cases that Doctor Watson mentions in his narratives of the great detective which he might have included in the annals of Holmes but never did. I have long thought it time for someone to attempt a grand synthesis using some of the brief and fragmentary hints provided by the established Canon. Although Sherlock Holmes appears occasionally as the narrator of a story we do not possess a sustained narrative in the Master's own hand until now.

Many readers of the Holmes saga may have wondered as much about the haunting character of Holmes himself as they have been curious about his untold cases. To round out the character of the man I thought it time that someone probed those moral obsessions and that hunger for the deepest meanings of life that evidently possessed him. Drawing on hints in the original stories I have therefore pieced out a narrative that I hope will reveal Sherlock Holmes in a deeper light and to solve mysteries that no previous chronicler has attempted to probe.

In writing this book I hoped to explore how Sherlock Holmes might have grappled with that most elusive problem posed by philosophy and by the many religions of the world, viz. how to account for the human condition and to explain the problem of evil. I thought it only appropriate that the greatest detective the world has ever known be given a chance to resolve these matters to the best of his ability and I thought it likely that he would have done so. What better time for him to have made this effort than during his long hiatus from London between the years of 1891 and 1894?

I have no desire to add mystification to mystery. This book presumes a certain knowledge of the original tales just as a symphony by Vaughan Williams depends upon a certain acquaintance with English folk melodies and the chromatic scale. For devotees who have loved Sherlock Holmes for years yet detect a certain mendacity and improbability in some of the endings as hitherto received, this narrative may pose some valuable answers. My desire is with this narrative to create a new unity where chaos and contradiction have reigned. May I not be thought presumptuous to undertake this task and may it serve to bring to rest the shade of the great detective who has no doubt asked why no one has yet followed up the clues so liberally sprinkled through the familiar accounts of Dr. John H. Watson. I hope that these will show how deeply imbedded in the original narratives is my own text, which growing from this fertile soil, will attempt to be true to the spirit and flavor of the original narratives and in addition serve as a substantial addition to the Canonical tales which with hopefully little effort of imagination on the part of my readers might be ascribed to the original characters brought to life by Sir Arthur Conan Doyle. If I appear to take liberties with the genre of the detective story by dwelling at length on matters of philosophy, of history, and of theology, then pray allow me to defend myself here before the bar.

Originally the mystery genre, of which the detective story is only one late example, referred to the religious mystery plays of the middle ages. These plays had a decidedly didactic purpose. Wonders and surprises were meant to widen the horizons of the audience to entertain the possibility of the miraculous and the wonderful. Are not these the very emotions we feel when we see Sherlock Holmes solving seemingly impenetrable puzzles? But more than this, the detective story has as its theme the struggle between good and evil. Nowhere is this dualism clearer than in the struggle between Sherlock Holmes and Professor Moriarty. I have taken the opportunity offered by these two icons of the moral struggle between good and evil to write a book in the ancient tradition of Christian apologetics to probe the nature of good and evil and explore in detail the Christian account for the origin of this struggle. In doing so, I have taken the model of the book of confessions such as that most famous example, *The Confessions of St. Augustine*, as my model. These confessions are meant to be the reflections of Holmes as recorded in his journal during his long sojourn of several years between 1891 and 1894 and continued in 1896 and 1897. Along with this account of what Sherlock Holmes scholars have termed, "the great hiatus," I have woven a tale told in the traditional manner by Doctor Watson that takes place primarily in the years 1897 and 1898. Together these twin narratives may answer some of the most perplexing problems left within the Canon of the original tales of Sir Arthur Conan Doyle. I have long been a devotee of those masterful stories and have wished to fill in certain lacunae that exist to complete the picture of Holmes' career. Sherlock Holmes is often spoken of as the most famous character in English fiction. The man who appears to wish to be thought of only as a scientific student of crime is fascinating because his own habits are so unusual. Does every detective study medieval music, ancient British charters, palimpsests, and do chemical research on coal-tar derivatives? Do they play the violin, attend concerts, and keep their tobacco in a Persian slipper? Are they beset with addictions, melancholia, and deep speculations upon the reason for human existence? Do they at once solve the crime and forgive the criminal in case after case? Do they enjoy the performing arts and masquerade? Do they have a sense of humor and enjoy teasing members of the upper crust? Do they enjoy horse-racing, fencing, single-stick, and boxing? If we eliminate these fascinating personal characteristics and the unique relationship with Dr. Watson, what would remain? Would the Master's immortal appeal be what it has been? Then why not, I asked myself, explore these ultimate questions of religious truth and ultimate meaning in a text written by the hand of Sherlock Holmes himself in the form of a journal accounting for the years spent on what has become known as the great hiatus, those years between 1891 and 1894, while not denying the pleasure of an old-fashioned Watson narrative at the same time in a parallel text occurring in 1897 and 1898? The result is the twin-narrative that now lies before you. It is my hope that the reader will find within this book not only a revival of the lost discipline of Christian apologetics but also that by meditating on the challenging thoughts and feelings of both Holmes and Watson this book may explore the deepest dimensions of human experience wrestling with the eternal problems. To use characters of fiction, well-known perhaps beyond all others, to enunciate and give form to life itself would surely be within the ambit of Sherlock Holmes, the greatest detective of all time. I also desired to explore the parameters of Holmes' relationships, the better to vindicate him from easy charges of vanity and if anything to make him more beloved when his unique personality is shown in greater clarity than ever before by revealing the hidden facts of his life, now hopefully revealed through the interlocked cases that lie before the reader in this long-suppressed account.

The reader will note that many ideas will throng these pages and it would be surprising if every reader agreed with the opinions that I have portrayed as existing in Holmes or in Dr. Watson. I have tried not to place opinions within them that would contradict what we already know of their established characters but I do admit to a didactic purpose in many of their discourses. This account may then be considered a fantasia of my own construction upon the essential themes provided by Sir Arthur Conan Doyle. That gentleman was known for the courage of his convictions that often led him to espouse extreme opinions in his own day and I claim similar latitude in exploring my own characterization of Holmes and Watson. It is the prerogative of the author to write his own book and to set before the reader only what the author possesses. If it be too much to hope that the graft will take in the original body of work, I shall be content if the indulgent reader will treat this account as a mere suggestion of what might have been and not what was. There will remain Sherlockian fundamentalists who will always look askance at the temerity of any additions to the Canon. For this reason all additions must be seen as what they are, an attempt to gratify the hunger of those who would wish for true immortality to descend upon the great detective so that there will always be another tale to read. May you enjoy reading this tale then as much as I have enjoyed writing it and hearing again, as if I were merely a channel for them, the old voices and feel again that sense of adventure known first to me in my youth when I feared to read the last Sherlock Holmes mystery and to know irrevocably that there would be no more.

Here again then, the curtain rises upon what I trust will reward the discerning reader of the old tales who has hungered for more, not merely of the stage props of Holmes and Watson in new and improbable adventures, but to find instead an answer and a completion in this addition to what has become the larger Holmes peripheral canon. May this contribution attempt an answer to the deeper mysteries posed by the original tales themselves. It is for the ideal reader who having read with a discerning eye the original tales and also for those specialists known as Sherlockians, but also for new readers, who will take this work as a useful hypothesis for what may have actually happened, that I have the pleasure to announce in that immortal phrase: the game is afoot!

The Abduction at Baskerville Hall

Thomas Mengert

Book Four

Afghanistan
and
Persia

Dr. Watson's Narrative Continues

Upon disembarking from the train at Grimpen after a comparatively short journey, we caught a wagon that would take us home to the rural environs of Baskerville Hall. I have not yet spoken in detail about Coomb Tracey or the village of Grimpen, both of which connect Tavistock to the larger Devonshire town of Exeter. The west of England possesses an austere but unique beauty and a heritage that predates England as we know it in its present dominance of the united islands of Britania, that constitute primarily the lands of Scotland, Wales, and Ireland. This humble confederation governs a significant part of the world, a fact that reassures those nations that see England as a great civilizing influence in world affairs while troubling other nations that resent the British Empire. Grimpen, the nearest village to the home that Sherlock Holmes chose as his retreat from the great city of London has its charms. Local craftspeople and even a small professional class have raised it above most rural towns in England and having Sir and now Baronet Henry Baskerville nearby to provide a source of education and culture to what otherwise might have been a backward and impoverished corner of England has been a great benefit to Grimpen and the surrounding hamlets that dot the desolate moors.

But to proceed immediately to my story, my readers may imagine my surprise when after our train journey and many adventures Holmes directed that the wagon was to take us immediately to Baskerville Hall. It had been some years since I had last seen Sir Henry Baskerville. After the death of the man known as Stapleton, the very man who had intended, as I have recounted in my book, "The Hound of the Baskervilles," to murder Sir Henry and to take his place as a distant heir to the estate his wife had spent time in a sanitarium in Exeter before eventually marrying Sir Henry. This unusual state of affairs owed much to the forgiving nature of the man who had become one of Sherlock Holmes' closest friends. The woman in question, although originally of a fiery Latin temperment had once been totally dominated by the strange man who had kept his true identity as Rodger Baskerville hidden even from her. Such cases of a beautiful and intelligent woman deliberately deluding herself as to the true character of her husband are unfortunately quite common.

As with so many young women of the upper-class in South America, she had led a sheltered life. Stapleton's wife had once been the beautiful Beryl Garcia of Costa Rica. She was raised in a convent so that her concepts of romance were nurtured upon the hidden romance novels that passed from hand to hand among the young denizens of the convent school where she resided throughout her formative years. Her knowledge of the real world of men and affairs had thus only begun when she was of marriageable age. Her debut was considered an event of great national importance, since her father was among the chief ministers of the government of her small country in what is often called Central America. As an honest man his career was doomed though, for in the government of Don Juan Murillo, known to history as the Tiger of San Pedro, honesty and honor were seen as sins fatal to a man of ambition to power.

Once he was fully established in power, Don Juan Murillo might have sought her hand himself, but by then young Beryl was already married. She had been captivated from the very first meeting, which she had at an embassy ball with a young man of English extraction, Stapleton. It was true that his family had lived in South America throughout his early youth and he might have been considered a native Costa Rican, but the lad had received a proper British schooling at a Public School in the North of England after reaching the age of twelve. It was later in England that his remarkable ability as an entomologist made him a man of wide fame even while he was still in university studies. That he chose such an obscure science in which to excel was not the sole peculiarity of the man. His fascination with the delicate beauty of moths and butterflies and their kin including spiders and insects was later mirrored by his desire to capture and to retain as his sole possession a lovely wife, young Beryl Garcia. Her story recalls to my mind the famous poem by Robert Browning entitled, "My Last Duchess," in which an Italian nobleman consumes the very soul of his young and innocent wife due to his jealousy.

There are men who will gladly destroy what they cannot totally possess. This is often a matter of a hereditary disposition. Mental aberration in a family often extends over generations. The boy's father had also been named Rodger Baskerville. He was the youngest of the three Baskerville Brothers, two of which had left England in their youth to seek their fortunes abroad. This original Rodger Baskerville had left under a cloud only to prosper in his new country of Costa Rica. In the tropical climate of violence and intrigue that prevailed in Central America at the time, he had worked his way up from being an overseer in a silver mine to finally becoming one of the richest men in Costa Rica. How many native Indian miners met their deaths to purchase his fortune will never be known.

Baskerville Senior later used his position in Costa Rica at the proper time to purchase a ministry post of some delicacy in the Treasury of Costa Rica for his only son. Young Baskerville held that post under Don Juan Murillo until after years of tyrannical rule the dictator was finally forced to flee the country after a successful revolution to depose him. After years of the most appalling atrocities Murillo and his immediate entourage managed to abscond in the general confusion of the times with considerable private fortunes. By that time young Rodger Baskerville had wooed and married the young Beryl Garcia over the most strenuous objections of both her brother and father.

Her father, alas, was but a broken man by this time, serving as best he could the people of Costa Rica and ameliorating as much as he could that tyranny that had blighted the lives of the native population of the country. Hoping for the best he had finally consented to the union perhaps imagining that in England in their married life his daughter might escape the intrigue and violence of her native land. He could not know that in the person of the blond young man to whom he was entrusting his daughter there was a man every bit as brutal and resourceful as the tyrant Don Juan Murillo whom he abhorred. Alas, her father's foresight for his daughter's welfare had only betrayed her to future years of degradation and servitude. As the years passed the gallant spirit of the young woman was beaten down until she became at last in every way the mental slave of the man now known in England by the name of Vandeleur and later Stapleton. After his theft from the people's treasury Rodger Baskerville managed to escape from Costa Rica and the wrath of an outraged people to return to England where he hoped that after some years of obscurity all traces of him might become cold with time. It was in pursuit of this aim that he purchased a boy's school located in the North Riding of Yorkshire. It was there that the true nature of the man finally revealed itself.

I can still recall the broken confession of his wife at the time of the conclusion of the case that I have recorded as, "The Hound of the Baskervilles." I can still see her in the private library at Baskerville Hall where, sitting in a high-backed chair, she recounted the story of her life with the man Stapleton in the presence of Holmes and me. Sir Henry meanwhile, out of that innate delicacy and nobility that are not among the least of his estimable characteristics, chose not to attend that interrogation so that she might speak more freely without the constaint imposed by the presense of the man that her husband had intended to murder.

Sir Henry it appears had grown to love the woman at first sight, in spite of her silent complicity in a plan that had almost brought about his death through the agency of Stapleton's demonic hound, the fulfillment of the legend of an ancient curse upon the entire family of Baskervilles. I can still see her sitting, proud and erect in her chair before the fire, though the fine hands that reposed in her lap frequently wrung themselves together and now and again she would grasp the arms of the chair for support. During the entire interview Holmes had shown alternately his most severe demeanor and then again that tender compassion that had manifested itself so often during the many cases he had handled where human character must confront the strain of the implacable forces of life. I will report her testimony on that day as well as I can reconstruct it from memory.

"You must understand my hopes, Mr. Holmes. I had been raised in a tropical land and you might imagine that I would have been appalled at the starkness of the Yorkshire moors when my husband first brought me to England, but I was struck instead by their beauty. I can still see the waves of heather with their purple blooms. We arrived in summer you see and the bleak winter at that season seemed far away. The heather would toss beneath the wind in great waves like the sea. I was still almost a girl myself and I imagined that I would work as a teacher among the younger pupils while my husband and his assistant Mr. Frazier took on the boys in the higher forms. I would teach art and my husband and his assistant the more academic subjects. I can still recall my joy as the first term started and the boys, mostly from middle-class homes, whose families were seeking a higher station in life for their sons, began to arrive. I was given some measure of authority at the time. It was I who hired several young women of the neighborhood to act as staff or housemothers for the boys, to prepare meals in the kitchen, and to act in a domestic capacity in keeping the dormitories clean. All began so well you see, but it was not to last. That fall a most dreadful plague of dysentery, perhaps even cholara broke out in the school and before it could be arrested, several boys were dead. The school never recovered from the blow and many of the parents blamed my husband for what they felt was his neglect in the incipient stages of the illness."

"And was he at fault?" Holmes inquired.

The beautiful young woman shifted in her chair and it was with downcast eyes that she answered, "My late husband was not a man who it is easy to describe, Mr. Holmes. Why even your companion, Dr. Watson, has had several conversations with him and I dare say noticed nothing strikingly amiss in his character. He was a man of immense enthusiasms that carried all before them. He had the capacity to move men. It is to that capacity that he owed his former influence in the life of my native Costa Rica. It is not too much to say that the finances of the government were once left in his hands alone. He had elaborated a vast taxing structure that bled the country for years. Don Juan Murillo was a mere brute. He was cunning, but beyond sheer cruelty, he could never have held on against the patriots of my country for the horrible twelve years of Don Juan Murillo's rule. No, it was my husband who kept some order and structure in the country. He insisted that the money extracted would be used for the most noble of purposes, to raise our nation beyond being a mere vassal state dependent upon American pleasure. The United States had claimed, since the promulgation of the Monroe Doctrine, all of South America as its zone of influence. The silver mine once controlled by my husband's father was largely American sponsored. Did the stockholders know that the dividends that they received were purchased by blood? Rodger claimed to be different from his father. He imagined running the nation as a laboratory for his grand designs. He would build roads, harbors, and a small domestic fleet and cast off at once and forever the subtle Yankee bonds that held the country. The years passed and the great and noble families were gradually reduced to penury under his scheme of taxation and still the great developments that had been promised were delayed on some pretext or other. A rail line was laid to transport goods across the swamps and the mountains and it was during that time of hope that I married Rodger. Finally, at the end of those twelve years, Don Juan Murillo, noting with all of his animal cunning that a revolution was afoot, absconded with the man Lopez, who was his personal secretary, and his two children. His wife had succumbed to brutal treatment and yellow fever in the last years of his reign. I can say nothing of his whereabouts now and no official word has ever emerged as to his new domicile. Such was the anger of the people that my husband and I were forced to flee also. We took a boat for England and changed our name to Vandeleur. We met a consumptive tutor named Frazier on the boat and instantly my husband was all alive to form a school that would advance the fortunes of young middle-class lads. It was called St. Oliver's Private School and you may recall from the newspaper accounts at the time that it was involved in a most hideous scandal."

"Yes, I do recall the matter," Holmes answered. "There were several deaths I believe and the school was closed soon after by order of the authorities."

"That is true, but I would have you know that at first matters did not so appear to me. I believed that we were making a fresh start in a new country and that our institution would become a model of its kind. Rodger, my husband, spoke only in the most glowing terms of his new educational methods. It was the same story once again as it had been in Costa Rica. His great promises and enthusiasms carried me quite away. I am sad to say that the school was run really as a vast laboratory for his pet theories. Little actual education really took place. In order that the school might pay for itself the food was poor and there was inadequate heat. The brutal Yorkshire climate that dreadful winter worked its malice upon the poor boys. That might not by itself have done such damage but there was human cruelty as well. The man Frazier was soon drunk with power and I can still hear the cries from the brutal beatings given to the few boys who had spirit enough to protest their neglect and abuse. Letters from the school were forbidden. The parents were to place their sons entirely into my husband's hands for one year. School loyalty was to overbear all natural ties the better to breed a hearty group loyalty. Oh, he was most persuasive in the written descriptions of the place and the new theory of education he proposed!"

"At long last, one of the lads succeeded in escaping. He appeared a week later in Whitby, half-starved and ill with a most virulent fever. Upon his word an investigation order issued and our remote location became a subject of official inquiry. By then a plague of cholera had spread, three boys had died. For a month the newspapers made the name of Vandeleur loathsome to the entire county. My husband succeeded in placing most of the blame upon his second in command, the man Frazier. He claimed that his scientific studies in the field of entomology left little time for the details of the school. He had been led astray by the man's references from some of the finest families of England, though they were later discovered to be forged. Even I who saw once again the evidence of his coldness and calculation in terms of the lives of others found myself again confused and undecided. In the event I did not leave him. We changed our name again and came to Devonshire in the extreme south and west of the country."

"Rodger had heard by then of the immense plans of his cousin, Sir Charles, who proposed to use his South African fortune to improve conditions among the farmers of Devonshire. Sir Charles had retired for reasons of health. He was no longer the vital man who had dominated the search for South African gold with brutal men like Cecil Rhodes. Having made his fortune, he now desired to somewhat redeem himself and to cast an aura of Christian beneficence over his former cruelties among the native miners of the Transvaal. He was very like Rodger's own father. Both had been miners but on separate continents. I do not know if my husband intended to kill Sir Charles right from the start. It would have been like him to imagine some good reason for his intrigue. Sir Charles was slow and methodical. His heart ailment would not allow of excess. Excess though was in my husband's very nature. Instant enthusiasm and immediate results were all that he cared about in any task that he undertook. Perhaps he persuaded himself that he could better employ Sir Charles' money than Sir Charles himself would have been able to do. I can see now that he eventually intended to murder both Sir Charles and later his heir, Sir Henry, as well so as to gain control of the Baskerville estate and property as the only remaining member of the family. I had suspected as much but could not be certain. Rodger had claimed that our change of name to Stapleton was only to elude our former notoriety and that he would take Sir Charles into his confidence as to the family relationship that existed between them when the time was right. Alas, that time never came! I stand before you today as a woman who has tolerated everything and even in my own way advanced his schemes, always hoping for that initial love that he once showed me in my youth, futilely hoping that it might return at last. Instead he had grown to view me with contempt and ever and again would mock my own fidelity as the measure of my stupidity as a woman."

She broke into the most piteous sobs then and wrung her hands together in her despair. Holmes looked at her with severity tempered and modulated by the understanding of how readily isolation can deprive a woman of resistance and perspective when dealing with a man such as her husband had been.

"You have indeed much to answer for, Mrs. Stapleton, but I do not believe that that this answer will be made before a court of law. There now, try and bear up if only for Sir Henry's sake. What will you do now?"

The beautiful face of the woman emerged from behind the veil she had worn that day in deference to the husband, unworthy though he had been of her loyalty, who was now presumptively lost in the Great Grimpen Mire, which had been the scoundrel's last retreat when his plot to murder Sir Henry had failed and the great hound that had been his instrument was killed. "I shall return to Costa Rica, Mr. Holmes, for my brother is still alive there. I shall take the money that I still possess and return it to the people by some act of service and reparation. That is the least that I can do and perhaps it may assuage my own complicity in these terrible affairs."

From that day the lady was as good as her word. After some years had passed, spent in good works in her native land, she was sought out again by Sir Henry who had never ceased to love her. She was able at last it appeared to find that happiness in married life that had so long eluded her. The curse that had so long beset the Baskervilles, the curse that had started with an abduction of a wild daughter of the moors in the 16th century, now found at last a healing in true love centuries later. Slowly indeed does the burden of family sin find a resolution at last! It is not in the individual, but in the maturity of the clan and of the tribe that civilization emerges. I wonder did the stone huts of Neolithic man harbor more brutal passions than those of the elegant drawing rooms of England today. Will we escape our natures before they destroy us with our own brutal armaments? Even the great Sherlock Holmes might find the solution to that question beyond his abilities.

All of these events were resolved some years ago, but are events ever really finished? Each action sets in train a series of ripples moving in all directions. Who can foretell what trivial incident of today may in the course of its many permutations result in the greatest and most irreparable results to the fortunes of tomorrow? Far on the periphery of events forces gather that await only the slightest trigger to set them into motion. A teacup falls to the floor and shatters in Piccadilly and a man is killed in Lisbon. A writer crosses out a paragraph in his novel and a vessel sinks off Trieste. A love letter is crumpled and thrown away and a chain of lives remains unborn. If we knew the full ramifications of every action, would we dare to do anything at all? Would we not remain still and silent, afraid that the earth might shift from its axis should we alter our position? What then of those men who instigate wars, revolutions, or who bear the burdens of fame? How do they dare to assert their own egos against the tides of history, to consciously affect the lives of millions? To be a spectator of history, even if that history be only one's own, is therefore to view a fearful prospect.

Though I am a man who has been at times somewhat skeptical of the claims of religion, I have always thought that each thinking man must remain ever on his knees with a single prayer: that my many errors and sins—conscious, but more fearful still, unconscious—might, through the great tuning of the Divine Conductor of the universe, somehow tend to the good and that all events may cycle finally into that greater plan that would justify all creation, so that even God Himself might be vindicated and that He might not repent of what he has done by calling me into being. I suppose that any man who has witnessed death as a soldier as I have done or faced the dramas of life and death as a doctor must think in some such manner from time to time...

But, to return to my present narrative, we had at last

arrived at Baskerville Hall after our adventure on the sea at Ilfracomb and our railway journey across the moors. The fog and storm of the past days had lifted and the prospect of the moor had all of the beauty of early autumn which seemed to have arrived overnight. Drifting leaves already littered the sodden pathway over the moor that our wagon had followed. The great twin towers of Baskerville Hall had emerged even at some distance and the scenic lime alley had appeared. The gardens that had made Baskerville Hall a showplace in the southwest of England were heavy with the last blooms of the year. Great rhododendron hedges surrounded the gardens. Even the grim granite walls had been cleaned and the ivy, no longer growing wild, was now tamed to a milder incursion upon the trees and walls. The household staff had grown, but was still modest by the standards of the times for a man of Sir Henry's wealth. He had ended the ancient entailments of the farms of High Tor and of Foulmire and those families who had been tenant farmers through the generations now held the land in fee simple. Mr. Frankland had been somewhat reunited to his daughter, Laura Lyons, who now owned clear title to Merripit House. Laura Lyons had received Merripit House as a gift from Sir Henry's wife showing that abiding characteristic of reconciliation that is perhaps the only hope of humankind. When Beryl and her actual husband, Rodger Stapleton, had first moved to the moors (my readers will recall) they had claimed to be brother and sister and hidden the fact of their marriage. After Stapleton's death in the Grimpen Mire as he tried to make his escape after the attempted murder of Sir Henry, the true state of his affairs was revealed. Since Laura Lyons, who had been wooed by Stapleton, was innocent of any wrongdoing, Beryl Baskerville both forgave her and relieved her precarious situation in life by doing what she could to help her. This charity was in keeping with the benevolence that Sir Charles had pursued when he was master of the Baskerville Estate. Indeed, Sir Henry and his wife had attempted to pursue the many efforts for improving the life of the community that had once been planned by Sir Henry's uncle, Sir Charles Baskerville, prior to the latter's untimely death.

We were admitted that day to the hall by the man, Perkins, who had succeeded Barrymore and his wife as the primary servant at the Hall. The rest of the present staff had been hired from the nearby villages of Fernworthy and Grimpen. Perkins led us back to the library where Sir Henry rose to greet us heartily as we entered. You can imagine my surprise when I saw sitting at the fireside the figure of Professor Moriarty who rose from his chair to greet us with a swift nod as we entered. We were all soon seated and Perkins brought in a bottle of old port and several elegant crystal glasses. He served each of us and then withdrew. Sir Henry spoke first.

"I have been waiting anxiously to hear the results of your expedition, my dear friends. Professor Moriarty joined me yesterday from his estate at Kings Pyland and has informed me of the great issues at stake. I can only hope that you have been successful in your endeavors."

Holmes took a sip of his port before replying, "Yes, Sir Henry, our expedition has averted the danger that I had anticipated for some time. It is a most amazing story and normally I would rely upon Watson to tell it. It was the final act concluding an ancient wager between the Professor and myself. I should never have known all the details had it not been for the Professor, for the entire plan was made at his instigation but held in abeyance until such time as I should return from my travels in Asia. We had both agreed at that time to lay our cards face-up upon the table and to compare hands once and for all in this year of 1897. It was a most extraordinary meeting and it is recorded at the end of the manuscript that Watson has been reading in recent days and I will not spoil the symmetry of that narrative by revealing it now. All that is essential for present purposes is that the Professor agreed to terms in Switzerland and that he fulfilled in due season his promise by giving me the information necessary to interdict this fiendish attempt to land upon our shores a most virulent agent of pestilence and destruction. Watson and I have been able to prevent this for now, but our task is not yet complete. By no means is it complete. There is still the matter of arresting the principals of this plot: the man Baron Maupertuis of Amsterdam and Mr. James Tweed of the Bank of London, without whose efforts this affair's most essential elements to be enacted after the plague, those elements involved in matters of public finance, could not have been completed. Their first step has now been foiled. These men, both of the most adamantine outer respectability, are the two greatest criminals at large today in the world and they will soon be brought before the bar of justice."

I interrupted Holmes here. "Then the matter is still not settled with the sinking of a single vessel."

"No, for our foes need only attempt the same thing again or they may rely upon some other mode of contagion or of terror. We must capture them and see that they are made incapable of furthering their schemes. But it will not be easy. We have, after all, destroyed the very evidence of their crimes by sinking the ship Friesland without trace. We must then set a trap for them of our own. We must go on to the offensive. I fear that it will make great demands upon us, but if we four might this day pledge ourselves to that end, I believe that we will succeed. Shall we then, my friends, enter upon that pledge to one another?"

The Professor spoke up first and with more vigor than I had thought might reside in his shrunken frame. "Very well for as Tennyson once said, 'old age has yet its honor and its toil.'"

Then I spoke up in turn by saying, "You need hardly ask me, Holmes, for I am always at your side."

"Bravo Watson!"

"And I, Holmes, for surely without your aid I should long since have fallen victim to that infernal hound."

"Bravo, Sir Henry!"

We all turned then to Professor Moriarty as the most senior among us and the man who had himself hatched the extensive plot before now doing all in his power to thwart it. He looked up at us younger men and smiled. "Ah, the enthusiasm of the young, I fear that you do not know the power of the man with whom we will have to deal."

"We not callow youths, Professor, for we are all men in our

fifth decade of life," Holmes remarked smiling before going on in his turn to quote Tennyson. 'Some work of noble note may yet be done not unbecoming men who strove with Gods.'"

e four sat that evening at the great dining table in Baskerville Hall. The meal that was set before us then recalled the grand repasts of days gone by. There was something of Elizabethan grandeur in the roast venison and the pheasants cooked in Old Madeira. Did the ghost of Sir Hugo Baskerville, of infamous memory, stir in his ashes and wonder who now found solace and joyful company in his great dining hall. The fire roared in the huge chimney and our glasses were filled many times with a vintage from Provence. Mrs. Baskerville, who still carried on her labors of mercy, was visiting the home of a cottager whose wife was ill that evening and could not join us. This left us free to discuss the matters that lay before us, matters of some danger, without alarming her with the prospect of what was to come. At last the meal was ended and we repaired to the warm library to discuss, over our port, the prospects of our campaign.

We were just about to rise from the comfortable chairs in the library to seek our beds when Sir Henry surprised us by asking, "Mr. Holmes, do not think me mad but have you by any chance in recent weeks heard at times in the silence of the night...the baying of a hound?"

I recalled instantly that strange sound that Holmes and I had heard on the day of our journey up to Ilfracomb and of the most unpleasant recollections that sound had induced and the tremor that had run down my spine.

Holmes answered at once, "I have, Sir Henry."

"Well what does it mean?"

Holmes looked fixedly at the old briar pipe in his hands before answering, "It probably means nothing. After all, there are hounds upon the moor to help run down small game as this is a rural district and many working dogs abound. Still, I must admit that I feel that something strange may be afoot. I can give no reasons and that alone is troubling to me. But we are pressed for time and to look into the matter now may distract us from our larger purpose. In any case, Sir Henry, I trust that you will accompany us to Amsterdam and so be beyond reach of any former ghost that may be haunting the moor."

Sir Henry at once agreed to lend us his support. I urged Holmes to retire early after the physical strain of our recent adventure at sea. Events were rushing us onwards to encounter dangers such as we had not faced even during the days of Moriarty's control of the criminal underworld. How strange, I still felt it was, to have him working for us and not as our most urgent antagonist.

The next day found us enroute for London via Exeter. Having spent so much time severed from the vast metropolis, I had lost those habits peculiar to the denizens of great cities of blunting the senses to nature. How dear now to me were the open airs of the moorland and the great open wonders of the seacoast. I had grown accustomed to daily walks by the echoing shore and to gathering each day those unique treasures cast up by the waves onto the glistening strand. Now the great coal-choked air of London would embrace me once again. I would feel the press of humanity close about me. All of those desires and so often-thwarted aspirations for some measure of happiness, security, or property forming its own grim sea of insurgent humanity would envelop me once more. In a city, each person is but a droplet flung about by forces beyond his or her control; each is like a small human mollusk seeking somewhere to attach a slender tendril upon the reef in order to survive and not be washed away by events. Does not the urban environment, despite its many varieties and attractions, finally distort the soul? Where is to be found the community of common fellowship and the simple comfort of one's natal soil in all of this turmoil and unrest? In cities our creations dwarf our sense of our own being. Perhaps this is why the great novelist, Thomas Hardy, so often sets his narratives in remote Somerset, there to seek out natural man. As in Shakespeare's plays, it is in country districts that the human reaches epic proportions and fate, physical and brutal, is made clear in its operations. In the great cities of the world, all is mere force of trivial and accidental circumstances. Our stature barely exists as human when compared against the fate of the multitude. If wars are ever fought from the point of view of mere cities, there will be no battlefields, no soldiers, and finally no noble victory. There will only be a mass-slaughter of women and children and other non-combatants by the great machines of man.

The world of finance has already paved the way for this. Swift transactions cause money to fly from hand to hand and the shares of corporations also are but packets of money passing onward before any true sense of ownership may even emerge. This practice of ever swifter exchanges will, in the end, leave a vast vacuum of responsibility within corporate structures. Men will arise who will know how to exploit the money of others to attain greater powers then any mere men have ever exercised over their fellow human beings. These men will act like parasites and will finally convert the great machinery of corporations into tools to serve their own personal ends rather than the public good. The result will be that the mass of men will live lives dictated by larger structural imperatives while the few will be exalted to the status of demi-Gods! I can already see this dynamic at work. Mr. Herbert Spencer in his book, "Social Statics," explains the dwarfing of ethical man in the face of economic forces. Mr. Friedrich Nietzsche, with his exaltation of a will-to-power as the essence of morality, will only ensure that a new barbarism will envelop mankind. What those men will be like who will control the great agglomerative structures of politics and of economics if not Hun-like marauders? And what will be the fate of those who will be encased in these vast economic structures as mere ad to a series of anarchist attacks or revolutions in order to restore balance to mankind and preserve the dignity of the common man? I recalled the writings of the great reformers of the 19th century, of men like Henry Ward Beecher, and wondered if mild reforms would ever be adequate to subdue the cunning and the rapacious qualities of mankind. These melancholy thoughts filled my head, no doubt brought on by the deep nature of my reading of Holmes' manuscript with its own far-flung interpretations of the fate of the human enterprise. Meanwhile, Holmes was evidently in the highest spirits as we neared London. He was engaged in talking with animation to Sir Henry. I had caught fragments of their discourse, but now I listened with greater care as Holmes laid before us his plans for our London adventure.

"We will begin by making a call on Mr. James Tweed who is the managing director of the London Branch of the East Indies Mercantile Bank. By now the Friesland will have been reported missing and I anticipate that there will be an investigation. We will need to be on the scene and in communication with the principals. Our basis of inquiry will be that we are stockholders in the bank and that we are anticipating bringing a stockholders derivative suit to mandate disclosure of any dealings with the Netherlands-Sumatra Company. We will apply for an injunction as part of this suit to freeze all funds that have been channeled through the bank to that company. I anticipate that substantial funds have already been deposited, funds that were to be used to purchase shares in British Companies as soon as the threat of the plague took a firm hold on the public mind and prices dropped. These purchases may not be in the Baron's own name or even in that of the Netherlands-Sumatra Company by name. No doubt a series of trusts or shadow entities have been established in order to hide the trail. Stock purchases could be made over time in small quantities so as not to cause prices to rise unduly, but the net result would be to gain control of the assets of key British companies. Do you have any questions gentlemen?"

Sir Henry spoke up. "Mr. Holmes, if I get your drift, excuse me, I am not entirely free yet of American slang, that is if I understand you correctly, this entire plan was originated in the head of Professor Moriarty who now sits before us. The scheme was part of the wager between the two of you at the time of your journey to the east. If you could convince him that his methods and his general theory of existence were wrong, then he would in turn suspend his operations and yield the key to that enterprise to you. He has now done so with the result that we are aboard this train to capture his confederates. Is what I have said accurate?"

Holmes smiled. "Ah the directness of living on the frontier has not abandoned you, Sir Henry. Your summary is quite accurate, although it omits details which our current enterprise will reveal in time. Let me say merely that the outline of the method has been revealed and that we now know the principals. What we do not know is all of the mechanics involved. The Professor's role was merely to introduce the idea and bring the principals together. He then collected his fee in advance, which I understand has been rather substantial. It should be adequate to supply all of the Professor's wants during the remainder of his life. This matter has been, if I may so characterize it, his last bow to the criminal world. I believe that he has many more lawful projects in hand to occupy the rest of his days; do you not Professor?"

Professor Moriarty had been silent and pre-occupied during our journey thus far, but he now spoke up. "I do indeed. I am currently engaged in a study of repetitive patterns, of replicating forms in crystallography. I have turned from the macrocosm to the microcosm and I hope to create a theory to explain molecular crystal formation. Furthermore, my stable of horses at King's Pyland promise well and I believe that we will certainly win this year's Wessex Cup!"

"Quite so Professor, but before you gather that honor we shall I hope gather other laurels by seeing to the arrest and the prosecution, with your aid of course, of as pretty a collection of villains as any that may exist in the world. Ah can you smell it gentlemen? The first familiar scent of fog and coal smoke, we are entering the outlying regions of London."

We were indeed. Even as he spoke the green of the surrounding countryside yielded to the furthest outer tentacles of the great city. A city is in many ways like a great cephalopod or jellyfish. We were being drawn closer to its mouth as our train neared Paddington Station. In Westminster all of the strands of empire have come together. From palace, from parliament, and from the clubs of Pall Mall come the directives that determine the lives and deaths of millions of people in every corner of the globe. Obscure ideas in the minds of the few will in their furthest permutations reach into the intimate hopes and sorrows of obscure denizens of the Ganges in India, of the Pampas of Argentina, or to an opium den in Hong Kong.

The tangle of politics and of finance might prove inscrutable to even the greatest of detectives. At such levels can one even speak of motivation? Is there not instead a mere pattern of physics or blind forces? Where is the morality in the sudden storms that may emerge to swamp economies in contractions of credit or the glacial and irresistible movements of industrial expansion that grind the workers into oblivion? In our modern world even currencies are unstable and nations both gather arms and enact tariff legislation to secure some relative advantage over each other. Everywhere a vast duplicity disguises human discourse. Power, is it not Satan itself? Can virtue exist then only in obscurity?

Such did my brooding thoughts continue until we descended from the train at Paddington Station and caught a brougham that would take us to the impressive marble columns that were the façade of the East Indies Mercantile Bank. After disembarking, we entered beneath the great portico. A huge amphitheater opened before us as we entered the building, one filled with desks with at one end a great division of the room into an area behind which stood yellow-faced bank-tellers. They were separated from the public area and stood behind an impressive oak and bronze grill-work.

Holmes went to a substantial and centrally-placed desk and spoke to a severe and self-important individual of middle-age. Holmes laconically presented him with a paper which he drew from the copious pocket of his caped overcoat. The man first looked at it with an air of boredom and then leaped to his feet. In a moment he was all obsequiousness. He bowed to my friend and to our small company where we stood just behind Holmes. We were led at once back through high arched corridors to a large office in the very bowels of the bank. The official knocked on the door and was admitted. A short time later he re-emerged and bid us to enter. Upon doing so we discovered that we were in a huge room with a great walnut desk at its center. A substantial coal fire burned in the grate of a large fireplace. Oil paintings covered the walls and a few velvet-lined chairs found refuge, more as decoration than as objects of occupancy, against the walls. It was in these though that we were soon seated as they were drawn up to the desk by our guide.

As he stood up to greet us, I had a chance to observe carefully the physiognomy, and to try and read the character of Mr. James Tweed, the managing director of the London branch of the bank. He was indeed a remarkable individual. He was a large red-headed man who, once he stood up, was equally tall in stature. He was exceedingly well, if conservatively dressed but sported a great gold watch that he consulted frequently during our interview. It was clear that he followed the old adage that time is money and that any period, however short, ought to bear its weight of interest or of dividends.

Holmes began the interview in a most direct manner. "We have come to discuss with you the loss of the vessel Friesland chartered by Baron Maupertuis of the Netherlands-Sumatra Company."

Mr. Tweed looked at Holmes with some distain. "The commercial dealings of the bank's depositors are matters of some confidence, Mr. Holmes. If you have any interest in the matter, you must go to the authorities."

"Mr. Tweed," said Holmes sternly, "it will not do. It will not do at all. I must warn you that any attempt to brazen this matter out will result in the most severe reprisals. You may see by this paper that that the Prime Minister and the Home Secretary are already highly interested in the cargo of the vessel and that some account must be given. Do you deny knowing anything about the nature of that cargo?"

"I do, Sir. This bank has merely acted as the agent for payment and to obtain insurance on the vessel in the case of loss. We intend to forward the full indemnity to the chartering party and that should be an end of the matter."

Holmes shook his head. "Why then was not the charter open and above board? Why this long chain of fictitious entities if not to keep secret the involvement of the Netherlands-Sumatra Company and of Baron Maupertuis? Why the transfer of a sum to your private account from the Zurich Creditanstalt at the time of the charter? Why the brokerage account opened in the name of the Exeter-Orient Investment Trust at the behest of Professor James Moriarty, its trustee, who stands before you and can identify the other principals?"

Mr. Tweed leaped up from behind his desk. A ghastly pallor had taken the place of his former expression of bland professionalism. "Mr. Holmes!"

Holmes spoke in his most quiet manner while gazing at the fire. "Do you deny any of it? I assure you that I can explain the entire course of the enterprise before these gentlemen as witnesses if necessary."

The bank director sat back in his chair, or rather it might be said that he collapsed. He took out a great monogrammed handkerchief and mopped his brow. At last he reluctantly spoke up. "I do not deny it. There may have been some slight irregularity about the shipment. I was given to understand that certain unique investment opportunities might appear in the future for well-placed individuals, and that several investment companies were to be formed to pursue those investment possibilities. All of this I knew, but the details were only to emerge in due course. It was to be my task to put the financial machinery in place and to sanction the whole and to further the processes involved. The East Indies Mercantile Bank is an old established firm with ties into every area of commerce, both in the home isles and throughout the orient. Since huge sums and foreign-currency exchanges would be involved in the transaction, I considered it a unique opportunity for the bank and as its managing director I considered it to be my duty to pursue the matter. There were no actual illegal transactions involved to my knowledge, but merely an elaborate series of sub-entities to handle the transactions. I did not consider it to be my province to enquire too deeply into matters pertaining to our client's interests. Should future events result in actual illegalities, I would of course have been forced to take the matter to the authorities."

"You have admirably circled your wagons, Mr. Tweed. But, I must ask you why the personal payment was made to your own private account? Were you to be one of the principals in this venture?"

"The payment was in the nature of a bonus for services rendered."

"And does your fiduciary duty to the bank's officers allow for the acceptance of such gratuities?" asked Holmes.

Mr. Tweed looked abashed. "No, Sir, the bank's trustees generally frown upon such payments. But I assure you that I did nothing that I would not have done in the bank's best interests even apart from any benefit to me. The payment to me was in no way a quid pro quo."

"No," said Holmes sternly. "But, was it not in a way an insurance premium paid to you in advance so that should you notice irregularities in any patterns of trade or timing that you would overlook them? Had you not been previously sounded out on the matter and given assurances?"

"You seem to be privy to my private conversations, Mr. Holmes," the man croaked.

"Let us say that I have ties to one of the principals. He has wisely abandoned the project in a most timely fashion. I assure you Mr. Tweed that this entire scheme will not succeed. You may abandon any hope of that. The reason that we have called upon you today is to enlist your aid, possibly in lieu of prosecution. I assure you that had this conspiracy (for a conspiracy it was) succeeded, most grave damage would have been done to the interests of this nation. The Home Secretary has retained me in the matter and it is my intent to bring Baron Maupertuis to justice. It is my further intention to enlist your aid, which if it is not immediately rendered will ensure that from its omission a most dire fate will await you. I assure you that your life is in the greatest danger at this very moment."

The bank director apparently wished to protest but instead inquired, "From whence, will this danger that you speak of come?"

Holmes placed his finger-tips together before offering the following discourse. "Form over substance. Truly that is the nature of the age. If the forms of civility are followed, then we imagine that all is well. Mr. Tweed, you have been placed in possession, by virtue of your position, of a great public trust. The influence of the machinery at your command can work great good or great evil. In this case that machinery has been co-opted by a man who will stop at nothing. The sinking of the vessel Friesland will indefinitely delay his ill-intentions and he must abort the machinery and its agents that would have furthered his schemes. You are more than expendable, my dear sir, you stand condemned at this hour. It is only our protection that will save you. Will you consent or will you face it out alone and await the time of your visitation by the angel of death?"

Mr. Tweed paused but the pause was short. "Very well, Mr. Holmes, I consent. I will contact my subordinate Abel Crosby in Exeter and have him deliver all of the necessary papers and..."

Holmes quietly handed over to the director a newspaper that he had purchased that morning in Exeter on the station platform. The banker looked at Holmes with a puzzled air before putting on and adjusting his pince-nez and reading. He immediately dropped the paper and stared aghast at my friend. Holmes bent down and retrieved the paper from where it had fallen to the desk and passed it over to me. I read the following headlines: "Banker Found Slain on Leaving His Club." The article went on to say that Mr. Abel Crosby of the East Indies Mercantile Bank of London had met with foul-play on the preceding evening on his way home. The body was found horribly mangled in an Exeter alley and that the death must have been one caused in a particularly horrible manner. The article stated that he had not called out for help. The whole affair was a great mystery, as there had been no witnesses, and the local constabulary was utterly puzzled by the crime. The local authorities were debating whether

Scotland Yard had not better be called in to investigate. I handed the paper silently to Sir Henry. Mr. James Tweed sat in his great chair mopping his brow where a clammy sweat had re-appeared. At last he spoke.

"But, why Abel Crosby? He knows very little of the affair. It was merely his task to purchase certain securities at my bidding over the course of the next year and to deposit the proceeds in accounts to be maintained in the branch of our bank located in Exeter. Certain funds would then be transferred to a Swiss bank account and a local trust in a periodic fashion in order to keep the remittances small so as not to invite undue comment and attention. Professor Moriarty, who I see before me today, was to have special drawing rights to one of the trust accounts. The remainder of the funds, once they reached Switzerland, was to be the sole property of Baron Maupertuis. Beyond the names of these two principals, Crosby knew nothing."

"He knew enough," said Holmes grimly. "But in any case his death was meant as a warning to you. The Baron is even now engaged in covering his tracks. If you are still spared, it is only because he will need a highly-placed confederate to guard the records and correspondence involved in setting up his elaborate investment mechanism. The Baron wished to have all in place so that when prices began to fall he could make select purchases of securities and equities. Once your function was completed and the trail back to him was obscured I assure you that you would have shared Abel Crosby's fate."

"What can I do then, Mr. Holmes?" asked the banker in the voice of despair.

"First, we must have the entire correspondence between you and the Baron with any supporting documents," Holmes demanded.

"Yes, but if the Baron thinks that I no longer have them, then my fate is sealed!" cried the terrified banker.

"That very fact is in your favor. As I said, if you were not needed, you would already be dead, Sir. Your justified fear must be your excuse for refusing to surrender the documents. The Baron will therefore be convinced that you still possess them. He will therefore try and reassure you. He will point out that immense profits may even yet materialize. He may even go so far as to attempt another shipment of his noxious agent from the orient to spread panic in our markets."

"But what was the nature of that shipment," asked the banker with evidently complete honesty. "I was never clear on that matter. What goods could be so valuable or of such wide appeal that so many stocks would rise upon the marketing of these items?"

Holmes could not repress some amusement. "So that was your conclusion? You thought that valuable goods or objects d`art were being smuggled into the country? No my dear sir. Precisely the opposite was the case. The goods aboard the Friesland had no intrinsic value; rather, they were noxious in the most extreme degree and would have caused a general deflation in the country. That was the Baron's plan and one that you have so far aided. You may, however, even now make partial reparation to your country and perhaps, only perhaps, and depending upon a mercy that it is not my prerogative to bestow, save both your life and perhaps your freedom from prosecution."

"But I did not know—" the banker insisted.

Holmes held up his hand. "That is immaterial. You acted for a foreign-agent and in a manner that would have manipulated the markets of this country. This you knew."

"But within the letter of the law. There are matters of a confidential nature that..."

"Do not speak to me of confidence," interrupted Holmes sternly. "The indicia were there and you chose to ignore them. If you insist upon retaining some hope in maintaining a false dignity and hope in any way to bluster through this affair, I assure you that you are lost. Work with me and, though I can make no promises, you may have a chance of escaping. Will you do so then?"

Mr. James Tweed sat silently in his chair where he had appeared to shrink throughout the course of this exchange. At last he spoke, but in a most subdued manner, "Yes, Mr. Holmes, I will do as you suggest. All of the papers touching upon this affair shall be delivered to you at once before you leave the bank today, but what if I am contacted by the Baron?"

"You will prevaricate, delay, and if necessary quibble. You will weave such a web of procedural delays that we may have time to seek the spider out in his lair and destroy him."

"When may I contact you?"

"You may not. Any instructions will be delivered to you through normal banking channels and you will obey them immediately is that clear?" Holmes advised.

"It is, Sir," answered the banker with alacrity.

"Then I think that we will conclude this interview," said Holmes.

"Watson, you have the briefcase that I gave you?" he asked of me.

I reached down to the floor where the briefcase lay and surrendered it to Holmes. I had wondered what its function was to be. Holmes handed it to Mr. Tweed who disappeared with it. He went down to the vault and returned within fifteen minutes with the now full briefcase which he handed to Holmes.

"That is everything, Mr. Holmes. It is in sequential order and I am sure that your abilities will enable you to complete your case with their aid. I included copies of my own correspondence also so that both sides of the affair would be represented. I can do no more."

Holmes stood up and Sir Henry, Professor Moriarty, and I rose also. Holmes nodded briefly and we withdrew from that august chamber to seek the streets of London once again. We had decided to stay for old time's sake at the Northumberland Hotel where we had both first met Sir Henry Baskerville some years ago. It was there by a fine fire in the best suite of rooms that we discussed how we were to pursue our quest upon the continent for it was there that we were evidently now headed.

olmes proceeded to lay before us his plan of campaign. The source of Holmes' knowledge of the mission of the Friesland must be kept secret, the better to confound our foe. The Baron must not realize the full extent of our knowledge. He must be kept off balance. Time was of the essence in the matter, so by acting swiftly we could take advantage of the confusion that must exist in his mind knowing that the plans of years had been opposed and foiled by the sinking of the Friesland. "We will leave on the boat from Dover to Ostend and proceed from there to Amsterdam," Sherlock Holmes stated as he paced before the fire. "The Baron is unlikely to give us an interview, but he cannot refuse to meet with his former confederate, Professor Moriarty. He will hope that you, my dear Professor, may suggest a way out of his present difficulties."

Holmes then turned to me. "Watson, you will go also to the Baron in the guise of the Professor's personal physician. Your name for the occasion shall be Dr. Nathaniel Withers and you will explain that this entire matter has been a great strain upon the Professor. As his confidential physician you must be at hand constantly to treat certain heart palpitations which manifest themselves under strain. Your actual function will be to act as a bodyguard to the Professor, for we cannot be sure what steps the Baron might now take even in regard to the Professor in the Baron's present state of chagrin and desperation and how far he already suspects some betrayal. The Professor will pretend complete ignorance of course and will ask, with some asperity I may add, how the Baron has managed to botch the whole affair. In this way we may extract valuable confidences and other valuable information as the Baron attempts to defend his actions before his confederate. Armed with additional information we may then be able to affect an arrest of the Baron or at least some of his own subordinates. We will leave on the boat-train for Dover tomorrow morning, but for now I suggest that we partake of some of the last of our hearty English fare in the dining room below and then that we all get a good night's sleep for there are strenuous days ahead for us all."

On another matter I had been reading, with great interest, the unique manuscript of Holmes' Journal during our trip across the English Channel to Oostende on the Belgian coast. The channel was foggy and our passage across to the continent was therefore slower than usual. This gave me time to consider the role that I was to play before one of the most ruthless men in Europe. I must say that I wondered if I could play my part adequately as outlined by Holmes. The Baron was undoubtedly a man of some resource and should he see through our ruse my life and that of Professor Moriarty would not be worth two farthings. Where would Holmes be during this time? How would he bring his vast skills to bear to confront perhaps the most dangerous man in Europe? I could only await events.

Upon our arrival in Belgium we were soon through customs. We caught the train from Oostende to Amsterdam and were immediately flying through the lush green fields. I felt that sense of order and frugality that stands behind the role that these regions have played European history. We arrived in Amsterdam, that quaint city of canals and of commerce. The Dutch are a practical people with few illusions and this quality of mind appears also in their architecture. There is little feast for the eyes in the low dark buildings, as simple and grim in their way as a Calvinist sermon. There is nothing of the spring of the human spirit that one feels in looking at the bright colors of Florence. Amsterdam is as practical and down to earth as a banker's ledger or a cake of soap. There is something stifling to the human spirit in the presence of commercialism and finance. Mere numbers on a balance-sheet cannot express human creativity and enterprise. Credit should ideally be a sign of trust and of hope in the future, but all too often it is an excuse for usury. We made arrangements for our lodging and then proceeded with the business at hand. Baron Maupertuis apparently acted in a dual capacity: as the Chairman of the great Netherlands-Sumatra Company and as the President of the East Indies Mercantile Bank. It was at the address of the latter institution that we sought to obtain an interview with the Baron.

The offices of the Amsterdam branch of the East Indies

Mercantile Bank were somber and modest. There was no need to impress the public here by the presence of great marble columns. No ordinary depositors kept their money here but only businesses accustomed to risk and a corresponding higher rate of return. These principals needed no stage-props to designate and display the bank's vast resources. Holmes and Sir Henry Baskerville had arranged for rooms in a separate hotel from that in which Professor Moriarty and I were to stay. This would allow Holmes freedom to work. As we entered the bank I took a retiring position as befitted my role as a mere accompanying physician and it was the Professor who announced his name and requested admission to see Baron Maupertuis, the Director General.

The man who received this request looked somewhat skeptically at the worn tweeds and scholarly manner of the Professor, but one look into those piercing eyes was adequate, and he disappeared to convey our request. He returned almost instantly and we were shuttled up to the second floor and down a long hallway into an adjoining building where we were admitted to a large room covered with maps and furnished in a heavy manner with Dutch Walnut furnishings. From behind a great desk the Baron rose. He was a heavy man with great sagging jowls and a most unpleasant expression, as though he had just swallowed a sour oyster. The door was closed behind us and the Baron waited some moments before speaking.

"Is this wise, Professor? Our agreement was that no outward connection was ever to be made between us, yet I find you in my chambers. Who is this man?" he asked, referring to myself.

The professor spoke. "This man is Dr. Nathaniel Withers, my personal physician and companion, a man in my sole employ, and before whom you may speak freely. I assure you that I in turn am not pleased to be here. I do not enjoy channel-crossings at my age and I would not be here now if matters had reached the conclusion that I believed I had clearly outlined for you. The ship Friesland has been reported missing, as you no doubt are aware, and I have come here to find out how you have succeeded in bungling this affair."

The Professor had assumed a most truculent air and I could easily see how in past times he had intimidated some of the most dangerous men in London's criminal circles. I could see that even the Baron was disconcerted by the nature of this frontal attack. The Professor immediately pressed his advantage. "All of the machinery was in place for the investments to begin and now I hear that Abel Crosby has been the victim of an attack and has perished at my very doorstep in Devonshire!"

The Baron looked surprised at the state of the Professor's knowledge but asked for no immediate explanation. "That is so," said the Baron grimly. "I am equally appalled by this untoward event. I suggest though that any failing in this matter lies not on this side of the water. I depended upon your contact in the east, Colonel Sebastian Moran, to hire a captain capable of getting the cargo safely to its destination. Surely, the failing is yours and not mine, in recommending Colonel Moran."

"I assure you that I have every confidence in Colonel Moran," said the Professor bristling. "If this affair has miscarried, it is not from poor seamanship on the part of the crew selected by Colonel Moran. There is evidence that the ship was lost, not on the high seas, but in the Bristol Channel at the very moment when success seemed most assured. There has been a leak. Information has been divulged, and since I work alone, then it must be somewhere in your organization that the leak has occurred."

"That possibility has occurred to me and inquiries are even now being made. I have already seen to the most probable source of the leak and silenced it forever."

"You are speaking then of Abel Crosby?"

"I am."

"You realize of course that by silencing him you have prevented him from giving us perhaps vital information."

The Baron smiled and it was if anything a more hideous version of the face than the one he had presented when we first entered. It was unnatural in the extreme. "Oh he gave what information he could before he died, I assure you. A man in mortal terror spares nothing. Alas, he could not name the source of the leak and so was of no further use to me. Of course he could not know who had ordered his death, so your name did not appear in anything that he said nor of course did mine. That was fortunate of course but not conclusive."

"Do you mean to imply..." bristled the Professor.

"Well there are two of us here Professor, and when you accuse my organization you accuse me, and I am not one to be thwarted easily. You can hardly blame me then, if knowing that the failing was not on my side, I conclude that it was upon yours."

The Professor did not blanch, as anyone else might have done, but like a fierce terrier pounced home. "Nonsense, you mistake our roles. It was my role to invent the scheme and it was yours to execute it, the risk was entirely in your hands and you might have minimized it. I assure you that during my days as the head of a similar vast organization no such failing occurred in a matter of this great importance."

"Except once, my dear Professor, except once, and it led I believe, to your premature retirement. What are you now but a small country squire and part-time lecturer at a minor university? Yet you dare come here and demand of me an explanation, of all the infernal effrontery!" The Baron rose from behind his desk. "If I should discover..."

"Sit down, Sir!" commanded the Professor in a ringing tone. "Do you suppose that you may adopt such a tone with me? The failing is yours and that is an end to it! Someone in your network has gone to the British Authorities. Perhaps in your selling of the investment vehicles to your many investors, you let something slip, some extravagant promise of expected returns perhaps. Just how many people knew of this matter?"

The Baron had sat back down and was breathing heavily. His anger seemed distracted for the moment. "In England at this juncture there was only Abel Crosby and James Tweed while on the Continent I have many contacts in Zurich and even in Rome."

"Then I suggest that the leak is most likely to have occurred where the number of potential informants is greater," said the Professor smoothly. "What did you tell them?"

"Only that I expected values of British equities to plunge during this next year and that certain unique buying opportunities would soon emerge."

"And on your word alone, in spite of excellent business conditions in the empire, vast sums of money from investors would come forth as if by magic? You must have said more. Come now, some hint perhaps of the mechanism of the fall in values?"

"I said nothing."

"It is a lie!"

"Very well, I told Cardinal Tosca."

"And why him, was he to pray that the values would fall?" asked the Professor with evident contempt.

"Cardinal Tosca has ties with some of the greatest fortunes in Italy. He is an expert in art and he handles many of the financial dealings of the Papacy. He is a man who understands that in this world, the Church must adapt to the powers that be, and he is an expert in rendering to Caesar the things that are Caesar's."

"And you spoke to no one in Zurich?"

"My contacts there are purely professional. The Swiss have long ago learned not to ask awkward questions as to the source of their funds. It is one of the great wonders of money that it is clean once it has changed hands. No matter how steeped in blood or in human suffering, money in its very coldness does not absorb the personality or circumstances of the owner."

"True. Gold and silver are indeed hard and beautiful," stated the Professor quietly.

Baron Maupertuis seemed to object to something of the tone in the Professor's words. "Come, Professor Moriarty, gold and silver are not money. They are mere symbols of power."

The Professor smiled grimly, but asked patiently, "What is money then? I ask this for the benefit of my physician here, who may enjoy this little excursion into economic theory. Since your practical talents seem to have gone so awry, perhaps you can impress us with your theoretical acumen."

Baron Maupertuis sat back in his chair. When next he spoke, it was with the aura of an oracle, a vast sphinx. He was no doubt reciting the very creed around which his life was oriented. "Money is ultimately an idea. Think gentlemen of the many forms that money has taken throughout the centuries. How might anything take so many forms and yet be one? Surely such mutability indicates that we are in the presence of nature's supreme chameleon. Money is born of man's great denial regarding time and mortality. Everything ages, passes away, and even perishes but money? Never! It may be transferred, but in itself it is immortal. Why? It is because the very nature of money is to embody the conservation of value. If it loses that ability, then it is no longer money, it becomes worthless. But how I ask you can it lose its value?"

"By inflation or by debasement of the currency," stated the Professor.

"Hah, you are in error Professor! Currency is exactly that, a mere current of supply and velocity of exchange! It is the creature of an hour, largely built upon a pyramid of hopes and promises. Currency, yes even the British Pound itself, may represent power as a symbol, but in itself it is not power but only its symbol. Money is the functional link between currency and power."

"Gold and silver then, surely these are money," said the Professor growing impatient.

"No, they are merely commodities for which one may pay currency and after that they may in turn become symbols and be used in exchange or to retain value but they are not strictly speaking money. No Professor, money is an idea; it is an act of faith. It is the god of this world. It begins in our trust in our common nature and in human need, but as with all things human it only exists among us by consent and common usage just as language does. A wolf would nose about a fortune in gold or diamonds for a bit of meat and ignore them while a man will suffer the loss of his soul for an account in a ledger representing his wealth. Why? Because just as men need language to survive and to carry on the business of life, so they need money or else they exist only in the moment, the poor paltry present. This is why we also have the idea of credit and of debt. The first exchanges a present good for a future promise of repayment and the second is that promise which may serve as though the promise was itself a present currency. What are all promises finally but wagers based upon a naked assertion coupled with trust and perhaps the ability to foreclose on securities thereby put at risk? Destroy or tamper with that fundamental trust and you destroy the entire human enterprise and the entire economy grinds to a halt. Money, my dear sirs, rests finally upon human needs and human desires for a substitute and that thing is money. These are essential human traits: need and desire are the parents of an idea. They are a constant element of all societies. So therefore is money."

Though it was not my place, I could not resist speaking up at this point. I could not forget that this cocksure man had almost cost Holmes and I our very lives and that he had planned the deaths of countless innocents merely to advance his schemes. "You speak of trust, Sir, and yet, if I understand you correctly, you and my patient are discussing the manipulation of these ultimate values for your own gain. What then is to become of the very social faith that sustains the system from which you hope to benefit?"

The Baron turned his cold and glittering eyes upon me. "I had thought it was your function, Sir, to deal with the very opposite of money as a physician, one who is concerned with the all too material human body. As a banker I am concerned with the future of the human race which is the growth of money over time. You on the other hand are limited by the mortality of the human organism stuck in time. Your stock in trade is flesh, that poor creation of God that barely endures three score and ten years. We wrinkle and die like so many prunes in the sun. Are we then God's vintage that he so avidly drinks our blood and delights in our ashes?"

"I take it you are not a man of religion," I said drily.

"No, I leave that to men like Cardinal Tosca. He knew the worth of ideas you see ... as do I," stated the Baron. "

"But you are wrong in saying that I have no religion for mine is the most popular religion on earth. I am a Priest of the only true religion and this is my temple," cried the Baron with an expansive gesture. "I am besides an honest man, for I speak the truth. I do not as you, doctor though you are, promise health to a dying animal. Why do people come to you but to be healed? You send them forth with the illusion of futurity and for this they pay you a handsome reward. They look to you with hope in their eyes to grant them only a few more short days of frost and sun when it is all irrelevant. Man dies, period! What matter then if he whiles away his time for days, months, or even years? Men breed like moths to flit about mindlessly. All look busy and purposeful, but it is but the flutter of useless wings over a flame. Look to the great charnel house of history! Where are the kings of yesterday? Where is the great beauty of a woman's flesh that only yesterday set the loins of men aflame and today is like a withered and stale parchment, and then, poof, not even that. Who would open a grave a month hence to assess its contents? Doctors, bah! You promise to relieve human suffering, but can you relieve the human condition? Can even priests do that? They send us forth in a cloud of incense; they seal our tombs; they forgive our sins; but had we but a few more days and hours, behold we would revive our sins again. What is our secret desire but to sin and still know immortality?"

I was astonished at this insight into the man's very soul. He continued. "The story of Adam and Eve and the tree of the knowledge of good and evil; the entire story is surely nonsense. The primal couple never cared about good or evil anymore than I do. What they really wanted all along was the Tree of Life! The serpent spoke the truth of human nature as we still find it. Man and woman resent limits; it is our nature. It took no serpent of course to tell them that, some wretched snake whose only crime was to crawl lazily through Eden and become an accessory of Eve's desire. Do even men of religion reflect upon the origins of all that they say they believe in order to discover its true meaning? Was the snake not on its belly to begin with and if not was it a snake at all? Are we to believe that it hopped about on the point of its tail before being condemned by God to crawl on its belly for the rest of its days? But this is a minor point. The key thing is that Adam and Eve wanted life. They wanted to endure. They wanted to seize the day, *carpe diem*, as does all life. What drew us from the primal slime if not that very hunger to be as gods enjoying immortality?"

"I tell you gentlemen," he continued, "what religion condemns, science applauds. It is the long sustained tale of the great human struggle for life! In that struggle there will be winners and losers. All shall die, but those who lose most who die first. Did God think that He could fill Eden with so many delights and that we would then someday lie down in the dust in subservience to our own contingency and relinquish everything without a gasping struggle for breath? Was that fair? Was not God the true tempter of man through bestowing so many gifts upon us? Why walk about with us familiarly in Eden and not expect us to look at him across no gap between creature and creator? We coveted more than intimacy; we demanded equality! Were we to blame for this?"

It was clear to me that Baron Maupertuis was a man of no mean intellect and that his own cynical corruption might have begun with an extraordinary propensity to faith in his now distant youth. He gazed into the vast reaches of the room that symbolized his own particular kingdom as he went on with his extraordinary discourse.

"God saw that it was all good and he was pleased and he rested. But do we ever rest? Simply to stay alive we must crawl over each other in a vast swarm until we come to loathe each other as obstacles to our own fulfillment and survival. Thus is bred mistrust in man; thus is bred fear of each other! And what have we to hold against this fear that is finally the fear of death itself? Only the one great immortal idea, the one that has brought far more happiness to mankind than religion ever has managed to do; yes money is the one true religion and I am its Priest!"

He hesitated to draw breath and then concluded, "Or if you don't mind another comparison, what is religion but a credit transaction drawn on a fictitious account maintained in heaven? Why the bank of heaven has been in receivership since Voltaire! You might have asked Cardinal Tosca if this was not true! We have spoken even as I am speaking to you now on many occasions."

Here I interrupted him. "But if you are right, then your

schemes are also futile for they must terminate also," I said quietly.

"But I am at home in my despair; I expect nothing." growled the Baron.

"Then you will undoubtedly receive nothing from life," I said in response. The room was silent for a moment before Professor Moriarty spoke up.

"Banker or physician, which profession bestows the best benefits upon mankind?" queried the Professor. "I fortunately have both upon retainer and a barrister as well! Mine is the comfort of science, which abstracting from the human point of view entirely looks to a value-free universe. What is more immortal then mathematics? If money is one idea and religion another, then surely physics and its language of mathematics is the most noble of all because it is the most disinterested. To pursue science of course, I must have money, but not as an end but as a means. Where is that money Baron, to return to the subject at hand?" he demanded.

"You have received a substantial partial payment on account as a down-payment for your idea," stated the Baron. "It should be sufficient for several years of chalk and ink."

"But the rest was to come with the fruition of the plan, which you or a member of your organization has now betrayed."

"Risk," the Baron smiled unpleasantly. "All of human life is risk. And what is faith even in money but the greatest risk of all."

Again I spoke up unbidden. "I should have thought not having faith was the greatest risk of all, for surely to abandon the possible fruition of our deepest desires should require complete certainty and that we will never possess. You think of the physician's task as that of a mere mechanic, mending the flesh, but this is not so. Our task is to sustain hope in the human condition, even in the face of those things that would seem to deny its dignity and its purpose. We are at one with the Priests. We surrender to them when we have done all that we can. We are comforters and what is nobler than to give comfort, to know the reality of compassion? It is you who are the purveyor of illusions with your religion of money as an idea."

"I shall remember that nobility the next time I get a medical bill from my own doctor," said the Baron. "I am sure that he will relish your views. But no more of this, I am still making inquiries Professor. That is all that I can do. There will undoubtedly be more changes in personnel and associates if I discover anything. I think that we may both agree that the final disclosure of our former plans would be embarrassing for us both and that Abel Crosby may soon have company."

The Professor stood up. "We will leave you then to tend to your own affairs as you think best. I shall remain a week in Amsterdam and I will call upon you again when I hope you will have something more concrete to report. We cannot afford to launch another vessel only to have it meet a similar fate."

"I quite agree with you there Professor; something clearly must be done. Good day gentlemen." With that we both bowed and left the august presence of Baron Maupertuis. It had been a most interesting interview touching upon matters that I would return to often in the days and weeks that followed.

An hour later we were sitting in a bistro in a suburban annex of Amsterdam discussing the matter with Sherlock Holmes. He had listened with the greatest attention to our mutual account with only an occasional exclamation. When we had concluded he turned to me.

"Well Doctor Nathaniel Withers, you have hardly proven to be the laconic doctor I had thought to send in as a witness. Apparently you took a most active part in the discussion."

I looked down in some embarrassment. "I could hardly allow him so to disparage my calling."

"No, perhaps not, but I should have rather preferred that you delayed in your editorial comments until we have the man in custody. Then you might have lectured him at will. As it is, I hope that he did not penetrate your assumed role. It could be most dangerous. Still..."

"Holmes?" I asked.

"Well, perhaps you have inadvertently baited our trap,"

said Sherlock Holmes. "In any case we know that the Baron has already taken immediate actions to cover his trail. He would not have acted so precipitately so as to bring about the death of Abel Crosby if he was not frightened."

"He did not seem so to me," I stated. "In fact he treated us to a rather extensive treatise upon values and religion."

"It is a peculiarity of this type of man that he must exercise power on all occasions, and that he must feel justified in doing so. It is also possible of course that his entire discourse was meant to test the Professor. What was your demeanor during his exposition, Professor?"

Professor Moriarty thought for a moment before answering. "I can only tell you my thought processes. He seemed to be calling a stray sheep back to the fold. He assumed the same cohesiveness and unanimity in evil that actually is only to be found in the exercise of goodness. Nothing can exist without a center of attraction. But any center pretending to be present in the realm of evil associations must reckon with the dispersive quality of individual selfishness. There is then no mirrored correlative of the good in the realm of evil. Evilness cannot be worshipped because to be converted to evil is really to wish to be one's own center. Any loyalty must then be merely disguised self-interest and any actual love must be non-existent. This is the reigning characteristic in hell. Still, evil will always attempt to clothe itself in the aspect of purloined characteristics from the good that it can never possess."

Professor Moriarty turned and addressed me. "You see, Doctor Watson, that I have learned my lessons well from your friend. But to return to the aspect that I assumed before the Baron; I flatter myself that I betrayed few of my inner thoughts and we must hope that the Baron is therefore confused."

Holmes looked at both of us with concern as he said, "Confusion leads to fear, and fear in the Baron's case is quite clearly a prologue to violence. I fear that we may expect further deaths."

At this a grim silence possessed the room. Holmes requested two telegraph forms and filled them out quickly before handing them to the pageboy who had brought them with a tip. After the boy left Holmes said, "I have just wired to Mr. James Tweed and also to my brother Mycroft. Tomorrow morning Mr. Tweed will leave his lodgings, pretend to have forgotten his umbrella, and thus to enter his house again. He will at that time be taken into custody by the British Government."

"But if he refuses?" I asked.

"Then Mr. James Tweed will I fear be dead before nightfall. He already knows about the death of Abel Crosby and we may assume that Baron Maupertuis is extinguishing first the minor links in the chain before proceeding higher. He may still need the Professor and may have been convinced that the Professor's indignation was genuine. Mr. Tweed's testimony may be essential later, not perhaps in a court of law, for the criminal act was not completed, but rather so that the principals in this affair may be kept for years under surveillance with a ready witness in the wings, in order to prevent any renewed attempts. That will be the Baron's view of the matter and it will mean that Mr. Tweed must die."

After this discussion, we separated to go to our respective hotels. We had agreed to meet on the following day to discuss any further actions to be taken. It was on the morrow however that we heard of two events that threw even Holmes into confusion and forced us to abandon, for the time being, our role as the pursuers of Baron Maupertuis.

I had spent the previous evening regretting my own precipitous comments to the Baron. I had not thought that I had such deep theological convictions and I wondered whether my intensive reading of Holmes' manuscript and consideration of the questions that it raised was beginning to tell upon me. Of course, like all doctors I was concerned with questions of life and death, but my own religious opinions had been at most strictly conventional and more of a matter of form and respectability than of actual conviction and commitment. I had found my primary religion in my loyalty to the Crown and my pro forma membership in the Church of England. As for the rest, I admired above all else the sense of duty in each heart and the ever-questing spirit of mankind. It now appeared though that I was more concerned with religious matters than I had hitherto suspected. Perhaps advancing age may account for this fact. As one reaches the end of life, one seeks for some significance in having been present at all upon the earth, some justification for the many days and nights, so many of which seem to have been exercises in futility or spent in the mere commonplaces of existence.

How few people after all play any significant role in history? The great seething mass of humanity progresses upon its natal course and the individual life is but a fragmentary part of that larger whole. Yet we are all individuals before everything else and the fate of one is the fate of all. "Do not seek therefore to know for whom the bell tolls it tolls for thee," to quote John Donne. That sentiment may be very natural when contemplating the lives of others, but what of one's own? It is here that the great primordial disgust and disillusionment at the human condition sets in. Has my life meant anything at all really? Have I followed that path that perhaps has lain latent in the mind of God all along while remaining still unreadable to me? Is everything in our lives finally accidental as well as incidental? What force chose the persons who were to become dear to me? Were my enemies foreordained or might I have avoided them by the slightest interposition of fate? Is my death in prospect of great moment, the result of great forces, or will it come by some slight clot somewhere, some cell mutating and soon determining the fate of my entire body? Why is there no democracy among cells to overrule the insurrection mounted by some purposeless cancer? Should not the brain have access to the files kept in some dusty corner of our bodies to expunge these rebellious cells because they contain some fatal infection to the whole?

And what of death and decay as the twin specters that betoken the final indignity of man? Should not life ebb gradually like the sea and the body dissolve slowly like a rusting piece of iron over years rather than decline so swiftly into its constituent elements? But perhaps that is the nature of age, and not of death, for once death actually descends upon us even the hours matter for time itself is foreshortened. In prospect of death how much is even a further minute precious for in the one is life and in the other death with its eternal embrace of silence, one that shall never be interrupted begins!

Such is death and it is horrifying enough, but then decay begins. In a matter of days some putrid liquefaction blurs our features into one sodden mass of the organic matter that composes us. I have seen this process upon the fields of battle in Afghanistan. How soon the witness of a heroic end is mocked by decay. Against this horror what have we as a remedy but the witness of the empty tomb of Christ?

It was with thoughts such as these that I was oppressed the night before our next joint meeting and it was further news of death that greeted me upon my entry to our meeting room before the arrival of the others for I wished a private word with Holmes. At my entry he tossed me a foreign copy of the London Times with an article circled. The headline read "Cardinal Found Dead in Rome under Mysterious Circumstances."

I proceeded to read it. It ran as follows: Our correspondent in Rome has wired of the death of Cardinal Tosca who supervised the Vatican branch of the national bank of Italy. His body was found last evening and the initial opinion of the authorities was death by poison. The Cardinal was a man of some importance in international circles who traveled widely upon Vatican business. He was a man renowned for his worldly sagacity while not of course neglecting his spiritual duties as a Prince of the Church. Intensive inquiries are being made as to the person or persons involved in the Cardinal's death. Suicide is out of the question in such a case. The Vatican desires to prevent any scandal. An intensive audit of the bank accounts may yield some illumination should any irregularities be found."

"Well Watson, the Baron has played his hand swiftly. There is no going back now. I have received word from Mycroft that James Tweed is in custody and the Professor is in our protection here. We can make no arrest of the Baron however at this time so our continued presence here in Amsterdam serves no purpose. I think it best that we take the Professor back to England at once."

"What then shall we do," I asked.

To that question Holmes answered by handing me a telegram. It came from Grimpen, the village nearest Baskerville Hall. It was from the Perkins, the butler and estate manager, and it stated: "To Sir Henry Baskerville—Amsterdam—Sir, Lady Beryl has disappeared, we are in great distress, please return at once—Perkins."

I looked up shocked. "Sir Henry...?"

"He left by the early boat this morning. We will of course follow at once. I am afraid that the affair with the Baron will have to be deferred in light of this terrible event. Come Watson, for the boat-train to Ostend leaves within the hour!"

I returned to my hotel room and packed immediately for our departure and with the Professor, paid our bill, and caught a cab for the boat terminal. I had developed something of Holmes' unique sensitivity through the years of our association and it seemed to me that our departure was observed although as far as I could ascertain we were not followed. No doubt we have been kept under surveillance by agents of Baron Maupertuis. I resolved to tell Holmes of my apprehensions on the boat. We arrived just in time. Soon the boat was out in the foggy channel waters and the quaint city of Ostend with its quiet bustle was behind us. The Professor preferred to stay in the warm salon of the vessel with a whiskey and soda. Holmes beckoned me and we went outside to pace the decks together. I immediately mentioned that I thought that our swift departure had been observed. I had thought that Holmes might be disturbed at the news but he looked instead grimly satisfied.

"It is just as well Watson. The death of Cardinal Tosca shows that the Baron has already made up his mind to completely withdraw from the affair, to cut his losses, and turn to one of the other many ways that a man of power can insure large returns on his capital by more legal means. Beyond the initial conception,

Professor Moriarty has nothing more to contribute to the Baron's scheme and he is finding his own way out. The Professor has already received the initial payment and it is safely deposited. It will, no doubt, ensure that the Professor will have ample funds for life. I always doubted whether the Professor would ever receive any future remuneration as promised and I gave him my opinion that his life was always at great risk. The Professor has placed his future safety entirely in my hands. The only reason he has been safe to this day is that the Baron may fear that the Professor has provided for the dissemination of critical information and evidence to be released to the authorities in case of his death or incapacitation. It was, in any case, imperative that the plague's spread be well-advanced before the Baron could safely take any action against the Professor, even had the plan succeeded, for the Professor alone could be depended upon to handle the scientific end of the entire enterprise. But now that the entire plan has been aborted, the Professor's life is of no consequence to the Baron. The fact that Baron Maupertuis would eliminate a man of the renown of Cardinal Tosca shows that the he will stop at nothing. What is the death after all of an obscure Professor in Devonshire who may readily be made to appear to die of natural causes? What a shock then it must have been to the Baron when you and Professor Moriarty, the very man he had determined to kill walked into his very lair? No doubt that shock was one of the reasons that he went into his lengthy discourse upon the nature of money. He gave you his philosophy for there was really nothing else to say. It confused him and his confusion caused sufficient hesitation so that we are now safely aboard a boat bound for England."

"But surely," I said, "the Baron will not allow matters to remain so. He will give orders. The Professor is not safe."

"Nor are any of us," Holmes replied grimly. "If I do not mistake my man, the Baron has already penetrated your disguise, which I tried to make as transparent as possible..."

"What?" I protested.

"My dear fellow, acting is not one of your best talents. I chose the improbable name of Dr. Nathaniel Withers on purpose. I must have my little jokes even in matters that are most serious. I wanted to see how this man, so accustomed to barter with the lives of thousands, would react to having his beard pulled. I marched the bait right past his nose. He believes that he is so subtle, but he is really at one with the other brutes that people this world that is so beset with crime."

"But Holmes, why then did you say nothing? We were in great danger throughout our last night in Amsterdam!"

"As you already knew you were. This is why I told you to never leave the Professor's side for an instant."

"But what if my own guardianship had proved insufficient?"

Holmes shook his head. "Your doubts are painful to me Watson. Do you imagine for an instant that I and Sir Henry were not at hand? You no doubt noted the young Austrian Count and his decrepit elderly servant with the room just down the hall from you."

"Then it was..."

"Exactly, it was Sir Henry and I in disguise. Sir Henry quite enjoyed the whole masquerade. His assumed Austrian accent was superb. He really should consider joining a local group of players at the next village holiday treat. The locals would be quite amused. Alas though, poor fellow, times of amusement may be distant for him."

"Do you think the Baron is behind this kidnapping of Lady Beryl?" I asked, appalled at the prospect.

"No Watson, I do not. The timing might cause one to assume that the events are related and one might immediately jump to the conclusion that the Baron knows about Sir Henry, but mere propinquity in time does not mean that the two events are related. On the other hand, I do believe that your own disguise was penetrated, as I designed that it should be. If you are involved with the Professor, then can the Baron doubt for an instant that I am on his trail as well? It is my hope that this alone will cause the Baron to be cautious and refrain from any attempt on the life of Professor Moriarty."

"But will he not then cover his other traces as well to prevent prosecution?" I asked.

"He is already doing so with these swift deaths of his nearest accomplices. It will not avail him though for I shall have my man brought up by the heels at last—even if not in a court of law."

I took some time to assimilate these views of our situation. "Where are we going when we get to England?" I asked, still retaining a sense of our danger.

"I think Devonshire is as safe for us as anyplace," Holmes replied.

"But surely we would be safer in London where the entire police force of Scotland Yard could act as our protection."

"It would only put off the inevitable. No, I prefer to encounter any danger that threatens us upon open ground. Let the Baron assume that we are confident and have simply returned to await developments."

"What if he does nothing?" I asked somewhat reassured by Holmes' manner.

"Oh I think he will do something; we must be on our guard at least. He has already played his most important cards. That really was quite careless of him. You see, up until now he was a mere investor. The importation of the plague was arranged by his agent. He was quite safe. It shows the degree of panic in the man. A reckless man is in many ways more dangerous than a calm one because his actions are unpredictable."

"This agent you speak of is Colonel Sebastian Moran."

"Colonel Moran was in fact our agent in the east. He tried to prevent the shipment, but he was unable to do so. He then wired us with the dates of the probable arrival of the Friesland and its proposed destination."

"But the Baron believes that..."

"It was essential that Professor Moriarty convince the Baron that he had the very man to arrange the details in the east, Colonel Sebastian Moran, a man with some experience in dealing with the disease on his plantation in the Malayan archipelago."

"Yes Holmes, but if the Colonel was in fact not able to stop the voyage, then how and by whom was the voyage actually arranged?"

"Clearly Watson, the Baron preferred to take another course at the last minute and hired his own agent in the east which means that he distrusted the Professor from the beginning. It only shows the cleverness and infinite caution of our foe. It is that very caution that will now lead him to try to cover his traces. We are all still in very grave danger, I assure you. I will be very much mistaken if an assassin is not even now on our heels."

"But this is intolerable! Can we not simply have the Baron arrested? Surely, Mycroft could communicate with the Dutch government," I suggested.

"Ah, but these are delicate matters of state in play, Watson, where national sovereignty is concerned. We have an insufficient chain of evidence, not yet at any rate. No, the Baron will not be extradited by the Dutch government on any slim proof that we might provide. The Baron's importance and connections make him immune. These precipitate murders were decided under duress; he may already see how foolish he has been. This may show him that killing the Professor as well would be a great mistake. Still we must not assume that he is brighter than he has thus far proven himself to be. We must keep up our guard of the Professor."

"Unless we are to be killed as well," I said ruefully.

"Well, it shall be our fault if we are. From this hour we must all be upon our guard. But it is not merely to draw the Baron out that we return to Devonshire, forcing him to act upon our own ground; but rather we return to investigate the scene of the possible kidnapping of Lady Beryl. If nothing else we must be there to comfort Sir Henry. I believe that he may himself be the reason for this bold action and for an independent reason with no connection to the Maupertuis affair at all. His own noble nature may cause him to risk all to obtain the safe return of his wife and we must be there at his side to guide and to temper any impetuous actions that he may take. But we must return now to the Professor in the salon, as I do not like leaving him alone. Come Watson!"

We returned to the Salon and found the Professor deep in a book on astrophysics. We soon after returned to our staterooms so rest. In an effort to distract my mind from our many difficulties, I took up again Holmes' journal of his travels to the east.

From the Journal of Sherlock Holmes

August 31, 1891
Farewell to Tibet

Today we began our journey to Persia. I can tell that Colonel Moran is happy once again to be in transit. There are men who can never rest content with any home and he is one. He is a hunter by nature. I have often thought of writing a monograph on the two great divisions of men. First there is the agriculturalist, the man rooted to the land and its local inhabitants; from this class we have created the great estates of England. My own people were of this sort and one need look no further than to my eldest Brother Sherringford who never leaves the family estate in Yorkshire or my second brother Mycroft who never leaves the ambit of his rooms or his chair at the Diogenes Club to see the force of this heredity disposition. Even I have at times revealed this strain in the blood. One need only recall Watson's descriptions of me slumped in my arm-chair playing my violin for days at a time in Baker Street to see that I am not immune to the family influence. Yet here am I beyond any of my previous habits in faraway Tibet! But then my character is not without its contradictions.

Then there is that second great type of mankind, the Homo Viator. Men of this type seek always for that further vista that never ceases to beckon to them to seek a higher hill. From among them mankind draws its great acquisitors, the collectors of art, the men of travel and adventure, those who pursue a thousand women, yet never find a mate; for them all the world is always too little and time too short. To quote Tennyson they profess a creed in words such as these: "Ever roving with a hungry heart much have I seen and known of men, cities, climates, councils, governments, myself not least but honored of them all and sought delight of battle with my peers far on the ringing plains of windy Troy."

To which sort does mankind owe the most: to those who have cultivated one square plot of land, built cities, taken time to write or paint; or rather to those who have explored and extended the borders of future empires? Would mankind have advanced without the tyranny of the exploiters of their fellow men? Without them would we still exist in that comparatively mute silence that existed before the great civilizations destroyed the peace and tranquility of local tribal groups and merged them into linguistic groups that could act as the basis for the great epic poems that seek to express the widest parameters of human aspirations?

Even the Bible is not immune to these sentiments of blood and slaughter. What is the Old Testament but one long narrative of conquests? This seems to even involve even God in our hunger for glory and subjugation and to favor warfare and the slaughter of our enemies. Did God then so prefer one people over another so that he should abandon all solicitude and all care for the Hittites and Amorites? Did not Hittite mothers care for their children? Was the slaughter of the first-born of the Egyptians just? Were these children responsible for their father's sins so that they must pay the ultimate price? Is it not a more likely explanation that a fortuitous plague may have struck the houses of Egypt and that the Israelites fled the stricken country and that a flood tide along the way made any pursuit a difficult matter? Is the Exodus event as Biblically recorded a miraculous event or is it the product of later accounts that over time were written down as a stylized exaltation of a people? Is the Bible to be read as accurate renditions of historical events in the way that we write history today or is it a series of heroic tales meant to convey God's abiding care for his people in exalted and stylized language meant to celebrate great events in the national heritage of the Jewish people?

Is it likely that the Hebrews would wander for forty years in Sinai rather than traverse the few intervening miles northward to enter the promised- land? If Genghis Khan could traverse Asia like the wind, what force so paralyzed the footsteps of the Israelites in the ultimate conquest of Canaan? Is it not more likely that this wandering people migrated gradually northwards and that the narrative compressed or extended the telling of events in order to reinforce theologically based conclusions of the ultimate meaning of those events in the formation of a people?

This would make the great drama of deliverance in Exodus another poetic example of the compression of events into a meaningful theological form just as the story of our origins with Adam and Eve addresses in stylized form the mysterious and unsolved paradoxes of human life. One must not mistake theology for history. They serve different purposes. Theology exists to tell an inner truth of human nature in relation to God, while history is the cold and objective account of what occurred in time. Theology is open-ended and symbolic while history is linear and concrete.

The religions of the eastern world seem far less impressed by history than those of the west. There is no apocalyptic end of the world and therefore no progress towards such an end. The eastern mind-set is one that seeks to enable the individual to adjust to the nature of things as a constant state. If man is dissatisfied, then the problem rests with man and not with the world in which he finds himself. Man in Eastern thinking is not the center of things or the purpose of creation. Even his ability to debate the nature of things is not a unique gift but rather a sign of man's pride and lack of attunement to what is. Who can quarrel with the humility and soundness of this position?

Compare this attitude to that of Western thought as embodied in Christianity which teaches that God is crucified for our sins! By placing man at the center of the cosmos rather than as one more species on an obscure planet with an idiosyncratic habit of questioning and seeking patterns to justify his own pride in himself, Western man distorts all things. But then even Scripture asks of God, "What is man that thou should be mindful of him?" If any part of Holy Scripture shows an evolution of consciousness beyond the bounds of the artificially heroic it is this passage. Of course this raises the dreadful possibility that we have been in the habit of reading scripture as though it is immune from human influences and limitations in its composition.

The Bible seems to share the spirit of the restless man, for what is heaven but a projection of our dissatisfaction with our human limitations and what is the hunger for eternal life but an unwillingness to finally accept our brief span of time and our small plot of allotted ground at our burial? Yet as the great poet Robert Browning says, "Man's reach must exceed his grasp else what's a heaven for?"

The course of this year must then be my first grasp at heaven, for never have I so far exceeded my own grasp in daring to entertain such thoughts as these! I am become a wanderer and I seek now the lands where the great Western religions were born. In those once fertile lands, now desert, I may find the further answers that I seek.

September 7, 1891
Crossing Pakistan

We have left the highest of the Himalayas behind and with them that clarity of vision that seemed to come upon me in those isolated regions bordering on China and India. As we near centers of population again, I feel again the press of humanity. I recall standing once by the sea and looking down at the sands. I gathered some of the coarse grains into my hand and looked down into a graveyard. Amidst the rocks were countless crushed shells. These skeletal remains were as a great clock telling of endless days on ancient seas, all existing aeons before my birth. Each life-form is tossed into a common oblivion, the delicate tissues, the tiny gills, the phosphorescent and vestigial hunger of mollusk and crab, of urchin and crustacean, all reduced to the pumice of life.

Who then is Sherlock Holmes to probe beyond the present? In what inscrutable depths lie God's purposes? Ever there is the great moaning of the sea and that wind just before dusk when the night chill takes its place. How fearful is that bleak hour when the tides seem to draw the sun into the depths and with it all of life. The sun sinks and after that fire a pale and silvery light embraces all. There is a great peace. The wind that had been so violent begins to abate, canceled by the opposing breeze from the heated land and all grows still. It is then that beach fires are kindled on the shore and far out on the horizon lonely ship lights appear. Even so must be death: first a pale, silver light and then and then....

What will you be then, Sherlock Holmes? What will your vast reasoning be? Will not God laugh? How very earnest I have become, how convinced that I could probe by mere travel into the workings of the universe. What stars light our way through these vast desert regions that lie beneath the barren snows? What did these people of the mountains believe before the light of Mohammed shown upon them? Even now they are savage fighters. The entire might of the British Empire has not been sufficient to finally subdue them. Violence here is as harsh and omnipresent as the dry and barren highlands that are their home. This region will never be a place for stable nations. If Europe has never known an enduring peace even under Christianity, then how much less is peace likely in these fractured lands of Pakistan and Afghanistan? The high mountains and deep valleys breed a tribal isolation. All is a striving for borders; all is war; it cannot be otherwise!

These lands cannot ever be dominated; they can only be avoided by the vain paths of empires. The imperial mind can never comprehend that there are ways of conceiving the world different than its own. The assertion of power must destroy first the culture, the religion, and finally even the language of the conquered regions and their civilizations. The imperial attempt is always to create a mirror image of the dominant race or region and to hold in contempt the conquered people. This of course creates resistance among them which is interpreted as stubborn rebellion and a blind adherence to an outdated way of life. It becomes necessary then to kill the body to save the soul as it were.

This is the source of all tyranny and proves that the true savage is the conqueror and not his victim. How shall we separate religion then from its role in greasing the wheels of conquest? We kill bodies in order to save the souls of those who remain. The problem with Christianity is not then with Christ but with his professed followers. When will a general reassessment of Christian history allow for that much overdue critique that might reunite all Christians again under the Prince of Peace to the joy and admiration of the world?

Dr. Watson's Narrative Continues

ere I placed the manuscript of Sherlock Holmes down and turned for a moment to the scar left from my old wound, received in Afghanistan so many years ago. The residual pain of it has often oppressed me. I could not but concur with Holmes' sentiments. Truly it has always been madness to reach from afar into the cauldron of the Asian tribal turmoil.

Our boat was drawing into Dover. How good it felt to be in England once again with the white chalk-cliffs towering over the channel and the great sentinel of Dover Castle on the hill above the town. There is a unique freshness to the English coast and the familiar sound of the gulls, curlews, and cormorants must always be welcome to any Englishman's ears. Shortly after going through customs we caught the boat-train for London where Holmes intended to meet briefly with Mycroft before proceeding to Devonshire to aid Sir Henry. We caught a hansom cab at Waterloo station in London and Holmes and I proceeded to Whitehall where Mycroft was to meet us, while the Professor proceeded to engage rooms for all of us at the Northumberland Hotel. We arrived at the austere center of the British government and were soon shown in to a small but elegant room which was retained for Mycroft to use as a sitting room and study. Adjoining it was a vast chamber littered with tables, bookcases, and papers. A small, wizened individual sat at a telegraph key transcribing messages from all over the Empire. This was the very center of operations, the obscure heart of policy formation where it could accumulate layer by layer in the mind of one great intellectual resource, the brother of Sherlock Holmes. The slow pulse of empire passed through this room. Mycroft was able to keep up with all events and yet to seek repose in his comfortable sitting room where even now he rose to receive us. "Ah Sherlock, Doctor Watson, pray take a seat by the fire. Your wire from Amsterdam has had me perplexed. But I have been in constant contact with the Scotland Yard over the matter at hand and the Emissary from the Vatican has been contacted for any news he might provide."

We sat down by the fire and Holmes, after lighting the briar pipe that was his favorite traveling companion began. "We are at a most inconclusive state of this investigation, Mycroft. Not because we do not know the principal agents but because we must devise a means to apprehend him if that is possible. You know of course of the deaths of Abel Crosby and of Cardinal Tosca. What has become of James Tweed?"

"We have taken the course that you suggested, Sherlock. He followed his usual routine. He came down from his residence to his carriage; then told the driver that he had forgotten his umbrella. He went back inside and from that moment to this he has not been seen by man or woman. He was unceremoniously helped over his back garden fence, down between the hedges, and ceremoniously conveyed to Scotland Yard in a Black Mariah."

"He is under arrest then?" I inquired.

"Say rather in protective custody," Holmes answered. "He put up no resistance?"

"Not after the news of the death of Cardinal Tosca was conveyed to him. He knew that he would be next. He was glad to accept the solution that we offered him," answered Mycroft. "He has told us what he knows of the matter and given us a list of the foreign contributors of capital. How much they in turn knew of the details is of course a matter of some uncertainty. I fear that we will never be able to bring charges against them. They are merely of the class that asks the rate of return and not how it is to be obtained. Even James Tweed seems to have had his areas of blindness; it is a requirement of his profession."

"There is the eastern connection of course," said Holmes grimly. "I have sent a message by ship to Colonel Sebastian Moran promising the aid of the British government in your name, Mycroft, to apprehend those involved in the shipment. I believe that we can count on the Colonel's tenacity to bring them to the bar. Islamic justice in such matters is swift and decisive. There will be no further shipments made. It therefore remains for us to concentrate on Baron Maupertuis himself, which I would do personally, but now there is this Baskerville affair that has arisen."

"We are ready to aid you in that matter also," said Mycroft. "Why do you believe that Beryl Baskerville was kidnapped, if indeed she was?"

"Well there can be no doubt of that. The lady is devoted to her husband. She was clearly abducted, but since no ransom note has surfaced, we cannot assume that it is an ordinary kidnapping. Something more is at play here."

"Have you no ideas?" Mycroft asked.

Holmes smiled. "When in our lives Mycroft have I not had ideas? But it is a capital mistake, as I have so often said, to theorize without data. However, we have at least her background as a foundation for supposition. Who is Beryl Baskerville? She is, to begin with, the former Beryl Garcia, one of the beauties of Costa Rica. Her father was one of the highest dignitaries of the country and her brother was killed years after the case involving the Hound of the Baskervilles in attempting to bring justice to Juan Merillo the dictator, also known as the Tiger of San Pedro. We know further that she married young and was for a time subject mind, body, and spirit to the second Rodger Baskerville whose aliases included: a school master named Vandeleur and the naturalist Stapleton. We know that after Stapleton's death in the Great Grimpen Mire, that she later married his cousin, Sir Henry Baskerville, and that since then she has lived in wedded happiness and engaged in many charitable activities as outlined by Sir Charles Baskerville but never completed due to his murder by that same Rodger. It was Sir Charles who preceded Sir Henry as the Lord of the Baskerville estate. He fell, a victim to the deadly hound that had been long reputed to have plagued the family. That is the state of our knowledge at present."

"I promised Sir Henry that he might finally enjoy the good fortune of his inheritance yet here again, we have misfortune and misery and a problem to solve. What has happened to Lady Baskerville and why has she been abducted?" concluded Holmes.

"Have you no possible theory," I inquired. Holmes paused and I received in what followed, a further insight into his methods, which always fascinated me.

"Well, we must begin with what we know. This woman has ties to two sources of crime and of violence, to Rodger Baskerville, who is dead, and to President Juan Murillo, who is also dead along with his assistant Lopez. This latter event occurred in Spain in the city of Madrid after his escape from England following the assassination attempt by Beryl's brother and several others was foiled. So what have we? Those who might wish her harm are now dead. Then there is the matter of timing. The events involving the hound occurred in 1888 and it is now 1896. How are we to account for the delay in vengeance if vengeance is involved from that quarter?"

"What of Laura Lyons, Stapleton's mistress?" I inquired. "Might she not bear some grievance against her former rival?"

"I hardly think that likely. You will recall, Watson, that it was her own profound disillusion upon hearing that Stapleton was in fact married to Beryl who was not his sister but rather his wife, that led to our solution of the problem of the Hound of the Baskervilles. She no doubt relished the death of the man known then as Stapleton with that peculiar relish that is present when a woman's love turns to hatred. Besides, Beryl has been most kind to the lady who, thanks to her and her husband's generosity, still lives in the area but is no longer living under straitened circumstances. Sir Charles's kindness to her has been brought to fruition by Beryl and Sir Henry. No, I think that we may dismiss her as a suspect."

"But then what remains?" asked Mycroft.

"Precisely, my dear brother, what indeed remains? You will recall my dictum, Watson, that when one has eliminated the impossible that whatever remains, however improbable, must be the truth."

"I do," I stated.

"Well then, what have we here? Those who would wish her

harm or through her to harm her husband are dead. We must always allow for the possibility of a new enemy for some outside reason, such as the distraction posed by presenting this domestic problem to us at this particularly urgent time when our efforts might be better employed elsewhere, but I doubt that Baron Maupertuis knows every detail of the Baskerville affair and would, in such short order, strike in that direction to get at me. The chain is too attenuated. So once again we are thrown back into the past where we find that the principals are dead. We are faced with a great improbability."

"Holmes, can it be that you are suggesting?" I stammered.

"When one has eliminated the impossible, whatever remains, however improbable must be the truth. Either Ex-president Juan Murillo and his assistant Lopez are alive or..."

I finished the sentence for him. "Rodger Baskerville, alias Stapleton, is alive and well!"

"Precisely, Watson," said Holmes with some satisfaction. "I fear that our old foe has arisen from his supposed grave in the Great Grimpen Mire!"

"But Holmes, how can that be? And why, even assuming that he did not die on that terrible night, should he only now reappear? Besides, what evidence do we have that this is true?"

"These are the very questions that I have asked myself, Watson. But let us do a short retrospect to see if our past conclusions about Stapleton's death may withstand a more minute inquiry. You will recall that we reached the conclusion at the time that he had met his death, based on finding some indications that he had passed that night to at least that point in the marshland where we were forced to abandon the search. We concluded that he had gone further because we refused to admit the possibility that, like ourselves, he had realized the madness of further penetration into the mire by night, and because we believed that he had no other avenue of escape. Think though! Was such an avenue as penetrating to the center of the mire, where an island awaited him, ever a practical means to a real escape? We might have simply encamped and waited for him to emerge from his retreat.

Surely such a bright and resourceful opponent must have long since prepared another avenue of retreat should his plans fail. We may not say what that avenue was, but certainly there are indications. He may have prevailed upon his friends on the moor to provide a night's cover and thereafter remain silent. He may have even gone overland and avoided the mire entirely. In any case, that he would seek refuge on an island, from whence there could be no passage to freedom, would have been like marching into a cell and closing the door behind him."

"Why then, were you ready to accept that solution at the time, Holmes?" I asked incredulously.

"I didn't. I immediately wired all train stations in the neighborhood to keep watch for a man meeting our opponent's description, but we must remember that he had assumed a convincing disguise on at least one other occasion. When no word was heard of him and the trail was cold, I accepted a solution that was at least possible and that would enable you to conclude your narrative on a successful note. I do not like to fail, Watson, it is one of my small vanities."

"Then why is he only now re-surfacing, Holmes?"

"We cannot be certain of the reason. He no doubt found our conclusion as to his death, convenient for some years. There must therefore be a compelling reason for him to encounter us once again."

"Perhaps he intends to mock us? Perhaps he is still seeking a latter-day vengeance?" I suggested.

"No, I do not think that either one is an adequate explanation. It must involve some prospect of decisive gain of which he has only recently become aware. Otherwise, why wait almost ten years? But there is mockery in play here that is characteristic of the man; I admit that. You will recall those sounds that we heard upon the moor as we travelled up to Ilfracomb? They made a most unpleasant impression upon me at the time. I found its supposition fantastic though and so shook off the impression that we might soon be facing again this spectral hound and his phantom-like master. But all too often, Watson, the fantastic becomes the truth. I have long suspected, though I could not prove, that Stapleton was still alive."

In our discussion we had quite forgotten Mycroft's presence. He now spoke up. "Ahem, if we may return to the matter at hand… Sherlock, what are your next steps to be regarding Baron Maupertuis?" Holmes was silent for a time and I could see that he had not yet reached a definitive conclusion. His eyes were piercing, but they lacked that luster and suppressed excitement that came when the solution was at hand.

At last he spoke. "We must see the matter from the Baron's point of view and deduce, not the actions that we would take, but rather what actions he may take, that grow naturally out of the type of man that he is. It is a pity, but there is no single rationality for the human species. Human nature can take us only so far, for are there not many human natures? If that were not so, then there would be no use for Shakespeare. For every Hamlet who hesitates, there is an Iago or a Richard the Third who does not. The Baron has shown us that he is prepared to act and to act swiftly, not in remorse, but in order to re-group his forces for another assault. Such men are never happy. Happiness is always just beyond their reach. Power is an end in itself for them and money mere counters in the game. He has been exposed by a shaft of light, so that he desires to draw into the darkness again, to cover all traces, and to break all associations. So we must ask ourselves the question of what associations in the furtherance of this plot remain to be traced. There are two primary links to his foiled plans, Professor James Moriarty and the banker, James Tweed. Both of these lie within our protection at present. So long as either or both exist though, the Baron will not know that he is safe. Uncertainty to such a man is intolerable. Uncertainty demands trust and such a man trusts no one but himself. He will therefore come for them, but in his own time and in his own way. His initial burst of activity was meant for surprise and two were indeed surprised. Before they realized their peril, Abel Crosby and Cardinal Tosca were already beyond it; they were dead. The others have escaped. I believe that the first period of our case is over. There will now come a quiet latency period. The great toxicity will gather its forces; the arms of the octopus will be hidden in a cloud of ink. He will bide his time. He knows now that we are aware of his plans, but he also knows that we cannot bring the crimes home to him, not now at least. He will withdraw into the cover provided by his image, his dignified position, and his foreign nationality and dare us to come for him. He will not make the same easy mistakes again, but he will I trust, make different ones. We will attempt to aid him in that direction. We will use his force but provide the direction as the ancient discipline of Aikido trains its practitioners to do. Our task then is to sense that force before it is deployed. Our eyes must see all sides and our ears listen for the smallest whisper of movement, and our skin must sense the air before the blow is struck."

Mycroft nodded and then asked, "But in the meantime?"

"Well, we will not be idle. Our friend, Sir Henry, requires us and if our new opponent is the man that I believe he is, then here also dark deeds and remote ends are afoot whose malice and repercussions we have yet to grasp."

Holmes stood up. "Well Mycroft, we are off for Devonshire before the trail becomes too cold. Farewell."

We returned to our hotel for the night. Events were crowding swiftly upon us. Our peaceful autumn had been transformed in a matter of weeks into one of the most strenuous periods of our time together. The next day we all departed for the train from Paddington Station to take us to Devon. Holmes and Moriarty engaged in desultory conversation on the journey while I returned once again to my reading of Holmes' journal. I found its thoughts and speculations were proving to be a comforting counterpoint to the strenuous tasks that I knew now lay before us.

From the Journal of Sherlock Holmes

September 12, 1891
Afghanistan

We have now crossed the border into that contentious region of fluid borders referred to as Afghanistan. We emerged briefly from the mountains and spent two days on the coast looking at the great Indian Ocean. Dhows and skiffs of all descriptions dotted the bay engaged in trade or in fishing. Like great birds they spread the feathers of their wings to fly over the surrounding blue. How pleasant it is again to have fresh fruit after the dried meats and lentil diet of the mountains and fresh fish are a veritable ecstasy. I do not thrive far from the sea. For all of its bitterness and cruel force it is the giver of life as well as of death. If it is Kali, it is also Shiva. Its many arms, the waves, carry each their own light in the tropic sun.

Now the sea is far behind. Daily our small expedition climbs deeper into the dry mountain gorges. The entire aspect is monumental. I have seldom seen a land grander or more intolerant of human habitation. The people's faces, both men and women, are seamed like old cracked leather. The years of harsh winds, bitter cold, and the remorseless summer suns has baked them like old clay. They are a silent people but with a deep inner dignity. The message of their lives seems to be merely a witness to survival rather than to any elaboration or grace or ever a celebration of spring. Even the young here show a grimness that betokens an early knowledge of what life will have in store for them.

The opium poppy is everywhere and what trade there is takes place with the British who manage to smuggle this deadly substance from here into China. China gives us tea and silk and we in turn deprave their population with this noxious and seductive substance that they may better bear the unequal burdens of our imposed trade. As I travel I see more clearly that the injustice meted out to the Irish, our more domestic colony, is only a shadow to what exists further afield on the periphery of our empire, not that the French or the Germans are much in advance of us in humanity. I sometimes feel that any real civilization that would deserve the name lies hundreds of years in the future. What we have now is mere dressed- up savagery. We hide our clubs and knives beneath our robes. The victims never live to build their monuments. The result is that all of our tombs and arches are celebrations of the crimes of humanity whereby the victors hide their guilt under a guise of grandeur and empire.

The vast majority of the human race lives a life of imposed slavery in various forms. They have greased the wheels of the chariots of the conquerors because they have not the means to resist us. Their bones have paved the streets over which have marched the soldiers. It is not that the masses are a herd; it is rather that in their attempt to live they have not possessed the same comprehensive vision that we call history. For what has daily life to do with the subjects of history? Are there in the pangs of birth or in the tilled fields or the stories told around the domestic fire on winter nights matters of glory and conquest sufficient to merit historical significance? Even in the Bible we have violence and slaughter portrayed as supposedly mandated by God himself.

What are we to make of this entire idea of a chosen people? Is it not the very foundation of all injustices practiced since by Christian peoples? Once any people assume that they are chosen or of the elect, then any atrocity or suspension of the ordinary ethical rules becomes, not only possible, but are even seen as acts of virtue. They are held to include a right or even a mandate to slaughter, to execute, to steal from, to enslave, and God Himself will supposedly nod in stern-faced approval at the murder and rapaciousness of all that Christians have done in His name.

At last the victims, in sheer despair and weary at wailing over the blood of their children, strike back, and by so doing the defender becomes a renegade and a rebel and this in turn justifies any means to be used against him. This is the story of history as it has been written for three thousand years and the prayers of all nations have been tainted with it. Even the concept of a blood sacrifice implies that God Himself favors blood. Surely the halls of the heavenly choirs are not made sweeter by the stench of burned animals. Do the cries of slaughtered beasts ever disrupt those sacred harmonies among celestial choirs? Is it ever possible to fight in a just way in defense of God or of Allah? Do not even the unbelievers deserve mercy? Why should a God who might reveal himself stand coyly behind the curtain of creation and witness such atrocities?

To merely appear as God in one manifest instant and belief and unbelief would become irrelevant in the face of what would then be clearly manifest! A gentle Jesus could never suffice to convince even Christians. The ascension was in this regard a great benefit because it was then possible to construct a savior to our liking. We demand trumpet blasts and ruined cities. If God presented in this manner then battles over doctrines would become irrelevant when faced with direct knowledge.

If we would seek for God in truth would we not do better to cease believing doctrines forged out of our primitive intuitions and instead honor what of God we actually know from deep inside ourselves in our more tender moments, from those moments when we excel ourselves and through our limited visions grasp in the most alien of peoples a common humanity? Would this not end all religious slaughter once and for all? Might God then stand before us and say, "Now is your original sin purged; now you can see me, for you have ceased to shed one another's blood in order to honor me?"

Is this suggestion blasphemy or is it akin to the words of the great American philosopher Henry David Thoreau, who after a lifetime of studying nature was asked on his deathbed if he had made his peace with God, to which question he answered that he was not aware that they had ever quarreled. Such are the words of an individual who, even knowing that the God of sun and stars might with a breath incinerate him, dares to say words such as these. "If I was made so that I may not question you, then why give me the capacity to do so? If you require my worship to be God, then what is there to worship in the first place? Can my worship increase your glory? Is creation a mere whim with you and might you gather it up at last as a child gathers his toys when his nurse bids him to come in at night from play? Are you not weary finally of your own definition as Great repeated endlessly? Did you not always know this about your own being and if so, then what does it matter that lesser beings, not merely derivative from you, but of such lower orders in view of your infiniteness should praise you? Must they now mutter Amen to add their small vindication to your limitless prerogatives? The very nature of worship is finally blasphemous, because it requires a God who would require or even appreciate such a petty return from so insignificant a source. Unless that is that the true God does not as we do revel in His Greatness, but instead acts rather as a Mother who would sacrifice everything for her dear children. Unless that is that God has been crying out not merely from the Cross but even in the birth pangs of Creation that have never ceased. Unless God does not exist apart from us but lies within, around, about, and through us, believers and unbelievers alike and that our incomprehension of this is His agony. When shall the human race show compassion to God and hear the prayers of the Deity to us? That voice cries out, 'I beg you to modify your definitions and to see me at last as I am!'"

This would be a God most worthy of worship and not the sanguinary God, distilled out of select passages of Scripture to create a rendition more acceptable to those persons who adore power. Such a portrayal would be worthy of Jesus on the Cross and the type of a Father that He would have had, for did Jesus not say that, "He who sees me sees the Father? Do you not know that I am in the Father and the Father is in me?"

It is no small matter to step into a text, or into a series of texts now presumed to make an integrated whole, and from them to assemble not only a clear image of the unseen God but simultaneously to deduce an outline for events that were yet to emerge under social conditions and economic structures that could not have been perceived let alone communicated within the conceptions of the audience that first received these writings. Are we the first generation to dare to ask questions such as these, not to deny the possibility of miraculous intervention, if no other possibility remains, but rather to allow for the possibility that human writings are human events and thus may be subject to human limitations? Oh, Sherlock Holmes, how bold your inquiries have become! Yet, I believe that I am correct in these musings and theological perambulations. I shall take them before the Pope if I arrive in Rome, for I hope that he will grant me an audience.

September 15, 1891
Afghanistan

Our progress has slowed to a crawl. Each day we climb dry mountain ranges but no plain is seen from the top but only a deep and treacherous valley with another range beyond. Here the force that sent the Himalayas skyward dissipated itself creating endless waves of land like a great storm at sea. The land is wrinkled and old. Everywhere there are marauding bands of armed men. At the border we were given a small escort of British troops, but I wonder whether they increase our security or only make us retributive targets for native patriots.

Colonel Moran seems alert but untroubled by our danger. He is again in his element. There are men for whom action is their only contemplation. I am no stranger to this feeling and have often found in the thrill of some of my more exacting and dangerous cases that my native melancholy would subside. Then there was no need for the artificial stimulant of cocaine and my life would seem to focus to a hard gem-like point and have a purpose. But ever and again there would come those long days and nights in Baker Street. I would look over at Watson reading one of his collections of sea-tales and absently rubbing his wounded leg. The smell of cooking would filter up the stairs from Mrs. Hudson's kitchen below, a stale wet smell of British boiled beef. (Thank God that I managed to get her to cook a few French dishes over the years).

I would grasp then the latest edition of the Times and scan the agony columns for some suggestive hint that crime was somewhere afoot and find only the usual melancholy advertisements of governesses looking for a position or items like, "Henry, will you please come home, all is forgiven, Maude." At such times the entire human enterprise would seem to me to be the heart of vanity. Why these meanderings and woes, why waste our few brief and bitter days on such drivel of the ever-disappointed human heart? Everyone is seeking love, self-respect, and some measure of dignity and everywhere these basic needs are crushed by pettiness or by the scarcity that plagues even the great British Empire. How can Great Britain, which is the destination of most of the world's goods, still maintain such a large gin-soaked lower class? Why does plenty not spread wider so that we at least might claim to have escaped the squalor of human existence? But alas, even our upper classes have a dowdy aspect. Beneath their soiled tweeds how many Lords and beneath their feathered hats and velvet dresses how many great Ladies of the realm bustle about like disgruntled water-fowl complaining of the state of the drains. The entire empire seems to be at such times a vast cesspool without grace or dignity or charm. If one seeks a weekend in Brighton or Bath or goes across the channel to Deauville or Biarritz one finds only the endless string of seedy Hotels and villas and encounters shop-girls giggling or some young fellow attempting liberties under the pier with an all-to-willing ladies-maid. Squalor is piled upon squalor.

Thus the cycle of want and disillusionment continues generation after generation. Youth demands its brief spasm of joy, which brings more relief than happiness and then follow the endless days of raising children on insufficient income: the quarrels, the tears, the recriminations, and finally an early death from drink. At least here in these isolated Moslem lands the poverty of the people is naked before the glaring sun. Here at least the women have the dignity of being shrouded from the leering eye and human lusts are governed by the ever present restrictions of the Prophet. There may be brutality here, but not the squalor of home. This breeds a pride in the people that we British may never know. Perhaps this is why this Pashtun race has proven unconquerable through the ages. What they lack in industrial production they make up for by village trades to meet their most immediate needs. No one is unemployed for there is no employment relationship. Instead there is only naked physical need and the tribe must cooperate to ensure the survival of all.

Need is the great creator of egalitarianism and perhaps when some disaster forces the whole human race to recognize its common needs, then wars will cease and all people will form one great tribe of the spirit. Is this not the dream of the One Holy Catholic and Apostolic Church? That one great tribe of believers might be purified as the Bride of Christ and presented to God the Father on the final day as is the Church's announced mission. But just so is it not the dream of Islam also that at the last day the believers, those who have submitted to God and followed the path laid out for them by the Prophet Mohammed will enter the gardens of delight?

The desire for unity in human life is perhaps humanity's oldest dream, yet everywhere disunity reigns. If there is one great constant in human life it is conflict. At the early Church Councils men came to blows. Look at the disunity in Islam between Shiites and Sunnis or in Christianity between Roman Catholics and the Protestant movement that emerged from within Catholicism or the even earlier split between the Roman Church and the Eastern Orthodox Churches. Look at the splits between Hinduism and the later emergence from it of Buddhism and Jainism. But look above all else at the wars of tribes and nations throughout the entire earth. All have been guilty of atrocities that memory cannot expunge. Who can separate justified vengeance from merely a new offense? Thus the great cycle of bloodshed continues. There is conflict, and often most bitter quarrels of all, even within the confines of marriage and its outgrowth, the family. Where may one seek peace at last except within the portals of death where the mouth is stopped and the grasping arms are stilled? Even those who seek to withdraw to the desert, to mountain tops, or to islands find that they are pursued.

Tongues have been cut from the silent mouths of men, who if they spoke at all, did so only in praise of God, or to confess the inner impulses of the heart. The mind itself has been raped by interrogators who demanded to know what thoughts of heresy or discontent may repose within the soul. Must religious triumph breed the terrors of the Inquisition? He who knows history must despair!

Yet all begin alike. Who may look at a babe-in-arms and not imagine a better life for it than its parents ever knew, yet expectation always fails when the child encounters life where victim and oppressor struggle in the very eyes of God. Are their roles pre-assigned, I wonder at times? What of the great duality represented by my struggle with Professor Moriarty? Which of us is the villain of the piece? Is not the certainty that I hope to possess upon my return: to possess the answer that will convince the Professor to join me and to take upon himself my vision of how things ought to be? Or will I return to see the universe as the same chaos of forces and brutality that may justify any self-interested action with worldly triumph as the only measure of justice? Isn't that what Moriarty possesses in his philosophy? Does the murderer consider his crime only as proof that he is a successful wolf? Does the lamb deserve the slaughter by simply being a lamb? If so, then there is no hope but for continued bloodshed. Futurity will only bring heightened weaponry to aid the wolves among us until the earth runs out of lambs. When the wolves then fall upon each other, what then? Who can bear to listen until the snarling ceases in one great common death for all?

September 21, 1891
On the Frontiers of Persia

We are descending again from the bitter highlands of Afghanistan. Those barren regions did not agree with me as my last entry must bear witness. It is not easy to glimpse so sparse a condition for human life. There was besides the constant danger of attack. Even Colonel Moran showed by his alertness that he realized that we were traversing dangerous regions. Our small escort was more pro forma than anything else. It meant that any attack upon our party would invite British retribution. That fact combined with an occasional gift of tobacco and jeweled knives upon the way as tribute to the local warlords may have ensured that we have escaped harm thus far in safety. Will Persia be safer or will a more complex set of tensions demand a more sophisticated bribery in order to survive, and what of the great Arabian lands beyond? We have at least escaped one source of danger. What a race it has been to stay ahead of the coming snows that have even now fastened their iron-grip upon these mountain regions. From here on, it is a race to Tehran and to those low-lands and fertile valleys that Persia possesses.

It is always in the valleys, where food and commerce are combined, where civilizations arise. The human race must have a measure of comfort and of leisure before men may speculate upon their condition and dream of the gods. Suffering breeds a pinched and sterile life when it affects whole peoples. Asceticism must be a choice and not an accident of straightened circumstances in order to be fruitful. Any culture that relies upon punitive measures to ensure compliance rather than a feeling of loyalty from its citizens must finally fail. The measure of injustice is the force that must be used simply to sustain social order.

A large per-capita prison population in a nation is the very best evidence that exploitation is depriving the masses of what they need to live: a life of order and of social contribution, all of which come from the legitimate satisfaction of material needs. There is no lasting advantage to any nation in having great gaps between the social classes. The fruit of such arrangements is always criminal violence and finally revolution, unless some great central tyranny, which is itself criminal in nature, attempts for a time to keep the boiler of indignation from exploding. The rights of man are not a privilege but a destiny and the man or the group who opposes this great fact cannot hope to rule for long nor can fear silence forever the pulse of dignity that beats in the heart of all human beings.

Dr. Watson's Narrative Continues

We are out upon the legendary moors once again. Our train arrived in Coombe Tracey after a late night train journey from London. We had spent the previous day at the Northumberland Hotel to regain our strength and paid a brief call at Scotland Yard where we had encountered our old companion-in-arms Inspector Lestrade. He is taking only a minor personal role in the matter of the abduction. He is now in a senior position at the Yard and only came in occasionally in order to instruct some of the younger members of the force and to assess the case so as to follow its progress. He was satisfied that we had escaped unharmed and promised that he would send a guard along with us who would establish a small advance presence upon the moor. These men would not be in uniform, but would aid the local force of the county constabulary. Lestrade himself promised to run down within the week to Devonshire and parted with us warmly as an old friend. Afterwards we took the train with Professor Moriarty who was anxious to return to his horses and to hear how their training was progressing for the Wessex Cup. Holmes advised him to keep up his guard and to use all caution. We left him at the station where his personal carriage awaited him. We in turn took a dog-cart to Holmes' cottage on the moor where we were able to unpack and to refresh ourselves before setting off at once in Holmes' own conveyance to Baskerville Hall.

Perkins admitted us and we repaired to the drawing room where we found Sir Henry pacing the floor before a great log blaze in the ancient fireplace. He came up eagerly to greet us. I could see instantly the wear that had been wrought upon his visage in the short time since we had parted from him and it was evident that he was at his wits end with the worry induced by his wife's abduction.

"Holmes and Watson, thank God you've arrived at last! I've had no rest and precious little sleep since this thing has happened. It's just sitting here that gets me. I could face any danger, bear any burden, but she has vanished without a trace and..." He was quite overcome so that we sat down unbidden by the fire before he could continue.

"There has been no communication then?" Holmes inquired.

"There has been nothing."

"Dear me, that is surprising; I should have thought...but then it is in character with what we know of the man. I should have expected it." He was silent for a time and Sir Henry looked at me with questioning eyes behind which there was just a flash of hope. I shrugged my shoulders. I could not fathom what thoughts had so occupied my companion, but I had learned through the years that all would be revealed in due time.

At last the distraught husband could bear it no longer. Sir Henry spoke. "In God's name, Holmes, have you any ideas at all regarding this matter. Anything would at least be for me a cause of hope, something to allay the twisting of my mind over the most remote and maddening possibilities."

Holmes answered him gravely. "Ah that is precisely where your thoughts should be, Sir Henry, on the most remote of possibilities for it is there that the solution lies I fear. Let us consider the matter. A woman whose husband is of great wealth is abducted. The abduction has been a success and we must assume that we have no leads since the local constabularies, which have been quietly alerted throughout the county, have discovered nothing. What would we then expect in the normal course of affairs? A ransom note would appear. But there is none and a reasonable time has passed. What then? Has Lady Beryl left of her own accord? No, for it is not in the Lady's character to do so. She is devoted to her husband and to the community where she takes great pleasure in her philanthropic work. An accident then; again the answer is no. Tracking dogs have searched and there is evidence that her scent led briefly over the moor to an isolated area, where she evidently climbed aboard a conveyance of some sort, for the trail stops abruptly. This fact is highly indicative, is it not? She went at least this far on foot and therefore willingly. What does that indicate to you?"

I spoke up. "That Lady Beryl had made an assignation."

"Excellent, Watson, she had agreed to meet someone. Now then, what was her frame of mind at the time? I think that we must inquire as to that. Will you summon Perkins, Sir Henry?"

Sir Henry proceeded to the bell-pull and a short time later, Perkins appeared.

"Ah Perkins," said Holmes. "We are investigating this most distressing affair of the disappearance of your mistress Lady Beryl and I believe that you may be of some aid."

"Anything that I can do, Sir, I will do gladly." Perkins replied.

"I must ask you to recall with great exactness everything that occurred on the day of her disappearance. I trust that you have yourself spoken with the other servants?"

"I have, Sir, and so has Sir Henry of course. There is little to tell; Sir Henry has always followed the same frugal practices as his Uncle, Sir Charles. He maintains a modest staff. There is the cook, a chamber-maid, a housekeeper, a groom, and myself. The housekeeper does double-duty by acting as a secretary for Lady Beryl."

"Then it would be she, the housekeeper, who would keep track of Lady Beryl's correspondence?"

"Yes, Sir."

"Then perhaps she should be present also. Will you bring her here? Thank you."

A short time later Perkins returned with a stout, maternal woman who stood nervously before us. She showed evidence also of the distress that her mistress's disappearance had wrought upon the entire household. She was introduced as Mrs. Maria Castillo.

Holmes at once raised his eyebrows. "Ah, you are of Spanish extraction, Madam."

"I am a native of Columbia, Sir."

"How did you come into Lady Beryl's employ?"

"She advertised, Sir, for a secretary and housekeeper who spoke Spanish. I was working for an export firm in Plymouth in a capacity as a clerk and translator of foreign commercial letters. I had always wished to live in the countryside, so I answered the advertisement. Lady Beryl offered to double my salary and I accepted at once. I have been with Lady Beryl and Sir Henry now for some years and have had no cause to regret my decision. All has been well until, until... Forgive me, Sir, but I was much attached to Lady Beryl."

"And I trust that you shall see her again soon," said Holmes who had always had the ability to reassure and comfort members of the fair sex. "Now then, knowing your mistress as you do and her habits I will ask you to cast your mind back and describe her actions and manner on the day in question. Leave nothing out; the slightest apparent triviality may be of decisive importance."

"Well then, Sir, I will try. Lady Beryl is a woman of regular habits. After breakfast that day she repaired to the morning room where it was customary for her to answer her correspondence before venturing out upon any visits to the tenants upon the moorlands or doing any personal items such as going to the village or spending time in visits to friends. Her visits to the larger towns of Tavistock or Exeter were rare occasions and usually Sir Henry accompanied her."

"She had made no new acquaintances that you knew of," Holmes inquired.

"None, Sir, My Lady led a most restrained and quiet life," the housekeeper answered with some dignity.

"What about at Mass in the course of fulfilling her religious commitments?"

"We are both Catholic and I accompany Lady Beryl to Mass. There is a small chapel in the village to serve the few Catholics of the region. We have had no new members of the parish and such visitors as there have been have been relatives of members of the congregation."

"Thank you; now let us consider other matters. How did

Lady Beryl receive her letters?"

"We are quite informal about that, anyone from the estate who goes into the village brings what correspondence there is. I review it and discard irrelevant circulars and then give the remainder to Lady Beryl."

"Did any letter come at that time that may have made an impression upon you for any reason such as being from an unknown party?"

"Lady Beryl is a most charitable Lady and she receives many solicitations for aid from strangers. It would not be unusual for her to hear from an unknown party."

"Precisely, but then she would show no sign of upset. Was Lady Beryl in any way disturbed before her disappearance?"

The Housekeeper was silent for some time and was evidently attempting to see again the day in question. We waited for her reply. "Lady Beryl seemed distracted, Sir, and was more than usually quiet on the day of her disappearance."

"At what time of day?"

"That morning, Sir, I had taken in her correspondence as usual after breakfast. She opened the first few letters and finally came to a large envelope without any return address. She looked at the handwriting and appeared to freeze for a moment. Then she opened it all at once with trembling fingers. She read the contents and allowed the letter to drop from her hands. I inquired at once of course if it was bad news. She said that it brought news of the death of an acquaintance. I did not like to disturb her, so I said nothing more. Lady Beryl pushed the letter aside and she opened the rest of that day's correspondence, but I could see that the heart had gone out of her. Finally, she pushed them aside and bade me to answer them, as I often did, sometimes enclosing small sums. She asked that I leave her then and I recall that she was staring out of the window across the moors towards the Great Grimpen Mire as I left."

"Why did you not bring this matter up before?" Holmes inquired.

"I did not like to, Sir, it seemed a private matter to My Lady and I did not wish to betray any confidence that had inadvertently been placed in me by my witnessing of the scene."

"This is not a time for delicacy your mistress's life is at stake. I must bid you to abandon any further reservations and tell us all that you know. What happened next?" Holmes demanded.

The woman looked up briefly with a show of spirit appropriate to her Latin antecedents before yielding to Holmes' commanding presence.

"Very well, Sir. There is in any case little more to tell. Lady Beryl spent the morning and early afternoon in seclusion. She skipped lunch, but I brought her a tray with tea and some biscuits about two in the afternoon. She looked up at me then with haunted eyes and thanked me. In the short time since that morning I saw the years written in every line upon her beautiful face and sorry I was to witness her distress. I left her at once however and shortly afterward Mr. Perkins told me that she had asked for her heavy cloak and that she intended to take a turn about the grounds. She walked off then along the quiet moorland paths, which she often did in perfect safety, for we are a quiet neighborhood, but this time she did not return. At five o'clock a search was made as the evening mists were drawing down and we feared that she had turned an ankle. The constable was called at once as a precaution and a thorough search was made for her even after darkness had set in, but from that hour to this, there has been no sign or word as to her fate."

"Thank you Madam, but what became of the letter that had so upset her?" asked Holmes.

"I have not read it. I considered it to be a private matter," answered Mrs. Castillo.

"But surely, her husband—" Holmes began. "And in the light of her disappearance...."

"It has troubled me greatly," the woman answered stiffly. "But I was in a position of trust to Lady Beryl. She is a strong woman and knows her own mind and even a married woman is entitled to some secrets of the heart."

"You did not dispose of the letter though?" Holmes

inquired with a severe glance.

"No Sir, as far as I know it still remains among her papers awaiting her return."

"Thank you, Mrs. Castillo, that will be all," said Holmes. He waited until she had left before asking Perkins if he could confirm or supplement the woman's account in any way. Perkins could only say that he had not observed Lady Beryl's demeanor in any great detail that day, but that she had seemed subdued. It was not unusual for her to walk out upon the grounds, but that the hour and the rising mists had caused him to caution her and that when she did not return in a timely manner that he suspected the worst and acted with dispatch to summon aid. Perkins was also then dismissed by Holmes and only we three remained by the crackling fire as the great logs shifted on the ancestral hearth of the great hall.

"What does it mean, Holmes," cried Sir Henry. "If you have any thoughts, however grave, please take me into your confidence, for it is having no idea at all that tortures me."

"Take courage, Sir Henry," said Holmes looking up with his piercing grey eyes. "We must first review the contents of this letter, since it was the occasion that clearly precipitated what has followed. Have you reviewed your wife's correspondence?"

"No, I simply assumed that she had been kidnapped for ransom and it did not appear likely that her kidnapper would announce his intentions beforehand. Everything has been preserved as she left it."

"We must go then to the morning room at once where I trust that we may still find the letter. Her correspondent no doubt wished her to keep the existence of the letter a secret and even to bring it with her but we may hope that in her distraction at the time she failed to follow his instructions as given and that the letter remains among her papers. If so we have our explanation why there has been no communication from her abductor. He assumes that we have found the letter already, know its contents, and are only taking time to deliberate a course of action. He has been waiting for us to move and we have in turn been waiting for him.

These past days have been wasted and I can only hope that we may repair the delay immediately!"

We returned to the great central reception hall that ran the length of the great 17th century edifice of Baskerville Hall and went down a small passageway leading to the morning room. It was as Lady Beryl had left it. The letters had been gathered up, presumably by her housekeeper and secretary and placed into an unlocked box to which we turned immediately. We spilled out its contents and with all three of us searching we soon located the envelope in question that was somewhat larger than the rest. Holmes opened it with a quick glance at Sir Henry for permission. Sir Henry nodded and Holmes proceeded to read the letter with some care. At last he set it down on the walnut desk and turning to us he said, "It is as I suspected, our great foe has returned. Rodger Baskerville, your cousin Sir Henry, still lives. It is he who has abducted Lady Beryl."

Sir Henry seemed about to collapse and I sprang forward to grasp him before he fell. I placed my flask of brandy to his pale lips and led him to a nearby chair. Holmes looked out of the window towards the moors. At last Sir Henry spoke from behind Holmes in a weak voice. "But how, Holmes, can this be? Is this all a matter of revenge? What does he want of us?"

Holmes turned to face Sir Henry. "A question of revenge, yes so it may be, but it is more, far more, Sir Henry. He desires the papers of ex-President Murillo, the Tiger of San Pedro!"

I cast my mind back to the case that I have published as "The Adventure of Wisteria Lodge," a case involving the attempted assassination of the former dictator of Costa Rica by Beryl Baskerville nee Garcia's brother Aloysius who was killed in the attempt. He and several fellow patriots of that nation had attempted to serve a belated justice upon the man who had looted the country and absconded with his henchman, a man named Lopez, and a voodoo-practicing mulatto manservant. They had been traced to England at last and the attempt had been made with the help of a Mrs. Victor Durando who alerted the assassins of Murillo's presence in England. Her husband had been the ambassador to England during the Murillo dictatorship and his death had been ordered by Murillo. Afterwards, Murillo and Lopez had sought refuge in Spain for a time but were killed in Madrid and their assassins were never apprehended. Attempts to trace the money, which represented in many ways a large proportion of the savings of the entire nation, had thus far failed.

Holmes and I had, at the conclusion of the case of the Hound of the Baskervilles, made a report through Mycroft that the man Stapleton, who was actually Rodger Baskerville, was now dead. All of his property then passed to his widow, Beryl Stapleton. Since no will was ever found, after the statutory period, her husband was presumed to be dead. Thus after the death-certificate was issued, all of Rodger Baskerville's property passed by intestate succession to Beryl Baskerville. Stapleton had maintained a bank account in Exeter, but the sum on the account was rather less than might have been expected since Stapleton had made large cash withdrawals during that last month of his life. Where those funds were now, it was impossible to trace. He may have opened other bank accounts under assumed names or placed the funds in safety-deposit boxes in London during his trip there to intercept Sir Henry upon his arrival from Canada to claim his inheritance as recounted in my account of the Baskerville case. The remainder then was quite small but still adequate to meet his former wife's needs during the year of (to my mind at least) unnecessary mourning for the deceased villain after which she married Sir Henry Baskerville. With the death of Rodger Baskerville it was unnecessary to inform the public or the authorities of the cousin relationship existing between Rodger Baskerville and Sir Henry since Sir Henry was descended from an older brother than Rodger's father.

In addition to the bank account there was the cottage on the moors which was paid for in full with its small surrounding acreage. This had been turned into a small county museum displaying artifacts of the region and charging a small admission price to tourists upon the moor. The excess funds were used to maintain a school for village children in the same building. Finally, as I will soon relate, there proved to be a box found behind a sliding panel in the upstairs study that contained her husband's papers, a few items of jewelry, and a few artifacts such as a hand-carved wooden box and a testament from a naturalist society commending Stapleton for his discovery of a unique species of moth during his period in Yorkshire. This was all that remained to the man who had once occupied a position of high public trust in Costa Rica under the Murillo regime. He had imitated his former President by himself absconding with a share of the public funds that had been under his control and it was those funds that had enabled him to first run a public school in Yorkshire under the assumed name of Vandeleur and then, when it failed, to seek refuge with his wife, now under the assumed name of Stapleton, on the moors of Devonshire where he had attempted to kill his cousin, Sir Henry Baskerville, in order to inherit the family fortune. Instead he had only inherited the family curse.

Sir Henry sat in his chair looking pale and Holmes took the liberty of walking to the sideboard and pouring him a brandy which he accepted gratefully. At last he spoke. "But Holmes, Dr. Watson's own account of our mutual adventure in 1888 describes how we had all come to the conclusion that Rodger Baskerville had died on the very night of his attempt upon my life. How is it then that he still lives?"

Holmes smiled. "We must I am afraid separate literature, Sir Henry, with its needs for symmetry and for cohesiveness from life, which is alas, often far from simple or symmetrical. An open-ended narrative simply does not work, particularly if one is celebrating the seemingly infinite gifts of one Sherlock Holmes before an adoring public. That is not to say that I had not taken precautions that night against his possible escape. I had alerted the local constabulary; the roads were watched and there was an official at the railroad station to apprehend our man if he sought escape by means of that conveyance, yet somehow he must have managed to slip beyond our grip. I had suspected that perhaps an unknowing accomplice might exist who could aid him at the time, but there has been nothing conclusive and no one has stepped forward to confess. Of course it is not beyond conjecture that Rodger Baskerville had long anticipated the possibility of failure and had provided a ready avenue of escape even without an accomplice. It would be within what we know of the character of the man. If he has emerged now, it must be either to regain his wife, which is unlikely considering his former treatment of her and his affair with Laura Lyons, or else it is the remnants of his estate sitting here before us that he seeks. The content of these Murillo papers may be nothing or everything. "

"But then why has he delayed so long in coming forward to pursue the trail of these possessions?" I asked.

"Ah there Watson, you place your finger upon the very issue and the fact of his long delay is the only clear indication that we have to show us the trail. Two possibilities suggest themselves immediately. First, he may have never recognized the significance of the papers even though they were in his possession ever since he left Costa Rica. But then, why take them in the first place? To answer that question we need to know something of the nature of the papers and how they came into his possession. The second possibility is that the papers may have served a dual purpose. They were worth something at the time to Rodger Baskerville, but that importance was deemed to be minor and hardly worth the risk that would be entailed in attempting to regain possession of them should they ever pass out of his hands. Since then ... in fact I would suggest recently, something must have changed so that now the papers are quite valuable and therefore worth the risk of contacting Lady Beryl on the supposition that she knows where they are and can help him in obtaining them. We must seek the nature of that changing event which we cannot do without some hint as to their nature. Of what nature are these papers? Are they a diary, a series of compromising letters, or are these papers stock certificates or deeds? Many possibilities suggest themselves but without data..." Holmes made a gesture of futility.

I gazed out of the window. Somewhere out there, perhaps in some not too distant retreat on the moors lurked our opponent and his captive, Lady Beryl Baskerville. It was as though he mocked us with his silence, his patience, leaving the first move in the game to us. If as Holmes had stated, he had assumed that we knew of the letter that he had sent to Lady Beryl and that he was only awaiting our first move, then what should that move be. Where were the documents in question now? Had Lady Beryl been so indiscreet as to take them with her? No, for the letter specified only that Rodger desired to meet with her. She would naturally suppose a trick and would not risk her very life by bringing them with her if she had any idea of their value. The papers were her security. How surprised she must have been then when she was detained without them. So assuming that we were in possession of the papers and Rodger was in possession of Lady Beryl, then an exchange might be made at some point. That was as far as I was able to reason upon the matter.

Sir Henry spoke up after shaking his head in perplexity. "I am very grateful that you are here, Holmes. Even after hearing you explain the matter it is still difficult for me to grasp. This Rodger Baskerville who we knew in 1888 as the man Stapleton is then alive. He has now abducted my wife who was, prior to his presumed death, married to him. He is holding her now in order to obtain certain papers of Juan Murillo that we have possessed all of these years in ignorance of their true nature. They have now become so valuable that this Rodger Baskerville has resurfaced to claim them."

"An excellent summary, Sir Henry," Holmes exclaimed. "But we must still account for his silence."

"Perhaps, he came back only to re-claim Beryl. She married me of course in good faith, believing her husband to be dead, but now she may feel duty-bound to return to him since she is Roman Catholic and marriage is until death. Perhaps she returned to him out of duty and the pair has now left England." Sir Henry said these words in great distress.

"I hardly think that likely," said Holmes. "Lady Beryl is in possession of the true facts of his character and his hold over her affections has long since ceased. She would not leave the house without leaving at least a note for you to explain her actions in going back to her former husband. Also, our knowledge of the man's character combined with his long abandonment argues that he has little residual affection for his wife. What becomes then of his silence? He is merely waiting for us to reach such a fever of anxiety that when he does communicate with us, we will do as he says without delay. I must however ask you a question, Sir Henry. Have you any notion as to the location of the papers in question?"

"I have not. I only know that she once spoke of some papers preserved from the regime. Over the years I have often suggested to my wife that she dispose of the possessions of her late husband since they are linked with the unhappy memories of her past with him, but she has always refused. When I pressed her for a reason, she would not, or perhaps could not, answer me. Perhaps in her own way, maybe by observing the value that her former husband once placed upon them, she realized their latent value and felt that someday they might be useful."

"If that is so, she was correct in her appraisal, Sir Henry. They may now be all that stands between her and death. We must find them at all costs. Do you keep these remnants of Rodger's estate in the house, Sir Henry?"

"I do. They are in a locked chest behind a sliding panel in my bedroom."

I spoke up. "Have there been any attempts to break into the house?"

"No, there has not, Dr. Watson. In any case, my bedroom is on the second floor and to access it from without is impossible. I have always seen that the house is secure at night. I have never you see entirely lost by terror of the moors. Even though the hound is long dead, I have feared that perhaps a real specter might still exist. I have never known complete peace here, but I have remained to fulfill my obligations to the tenants of my lands."

"Let us go then at once and examine these items left behind," said Holmes, and we proceeded upstairs with Sir Henry in the lead. Much of Baskerville Hall was made of quarried stone and the roughness of its 17th century origins was evident. The inner English Oak and Walnut construction added a soft glow to the interiors. The great bedroom to which Sir Henry led us was an excellent example of the substantial design of Tudor conceptions of comfort. The great and heavy bed might have been designed to hold one who was the size of King Henry VIII. It was surmounted by a great canopy of damask and silk. The room also contained heavy maple cabinets and chests. Any intruder would have a great deal of trouble knowing where to look first for the papers that we sought. Sir Henry walked directly to an obscure corner of the room decorated with knobs of wood. He pulled upon three of those in succession. There was a low grinding sound and a panel opened. Within as I peered I was able to discern several dusty shelves with room on the floor for a larger chest. It was to this latter receptacle that Sir Henry addressed his efforts.

He raised the lid and removed several items which he handed to Holmes and to me. We in turn took them to a table in what was evidently the chamber's breakfast-nook where the light streamed in from outside to illuminate the items in question. There was a stack of papers, a small notebook, a testimonial document, a few personal items, and an intricate smaller carved-box. It was to the latter that Holmes directed his most minute attention, while I took up the papers and began to read them. Most were mere bills from the village. There was a deed of title to the cottage on the moors, a few bankers' statements, and a correspondence with a naturalist society. The notebook contained entries on a daily basis of his observations of the Lepidoptera of the moorlands. Evidently, the man's passion for moths and butterflies was quite real. How strange that he should be fascinated by such delicate creatures while being so brutal in his own nature. Holmes had often remarked on the study of contrasts in the criminal mind. While I was thus engaged, Holmes had been turning the box over in his hands. It was evidently quite heavy for its size. He shook it forcefully close to his ear and gave an exclamation of satisfaction.

"Has this box ever been opened, Sir Henry?"

"I was not aware that it could be opened," he answered. "I

had always imagined it to be merely a sample of intricate woodcarving, an object d'art."

Holmes was looking intently at the box. "A not unlikely supposition since there is no evident space between the lid and the body of the box. But under a severe shaking such as the one that I have just applied there is a discernible motion inside. It is quite slight. The box is evidently quite full. But it clearly has contents of some sort. Watson, have you found anything among your own set of papers?"

I answered that I had not found anything of significance.

"Then gentlemen, I believe that this box may very well contain the papers in question, which we may quickly ascertain if we can manage to open it." As he said this, Holmes had taken out his strong magnifying glass and was carefully observing every detail of the box. He placed the glass down at last and began a systematic process of pushing on various surfaces of the box. "I am familiar with the intricacy of Chinese puzzle-boxes and have considered writing a small monograph upon the subject. This box though displays several unique features and is evidently of a Mayan design. Witness the unique figures that appear. They definitely show a Mayan influence. This box alone would likely grace a gallery of the land from whence it came and no doubt fetch by itself a pretty price."

"Holmes I am ready to consign it to the axe within the hour if it will help us," exclaimed Sir Henry.

"Oh I don't think that so crude a measure will be necessary! Just give me a few...holloa! You see that one side shifts, now if, hmm, yes so does the other, now by pressing upward, ah, it opens! Well the Mayan's have yet to surpass the Chinese for intricacy, but knowing where to press, that was somewhat challenging. But let us observe the contents without delay. Shall we divide them? Here Watson, and here, Sir Henry, while I will examine the first few from the top. Please keep them in strict order."

Holmes proceeded to divide the contents upon removing them from the box and I bent eagerly to the batch entrusted to me as did Sir Henry. We each took a chair at the table and soon its ample expanse was covered. We were all silent for some fifteen minutes with each reading samples from the pile in our care. After a short time I looked up at Holmes. His face was a study in concentration and suppressed excitement. Clearly he was seeing something in the documents that was escaping me. I bent down again to my own pile and attempted to read faster, scanning the documents for any clue that they might present to me. The language was English for the most part which surprised me. They were evidently dispatches to many different individuals. When I came upon one in Spanish I passed it to Sir Henry who was now fluent in the language. He nodded and gave it his immediate attention. At last he threw up his hands in frustration.

"What does it all mean Holmes? I can't read any further without knowing if we have anything here of value. What do all these papers have to do with my wife's kidnapping? It must be mere vengeance that is the chief motive after all."

Holmes looked up, the light of excitement still on his face, but coupled now with some impatience. "Well then, we must take a break in our examination. The whole series must of course be set out later and an extract formed. I see that you have both broken my admonition to keep the papers in order, but it does not matter in this case. They were evidently thrown together in some hurry and never sorted chronologically. The drift of the little that I have read is clear though and sufficient to provide a motive for Lady Beryl's abduction."

"Good heavens!" I cried. "If you can make anything of this jumble of contracts, diplomatic papers, jotted-notes, names, and references please tell us."

Sir Henry looked up at Holmes with a forlorn hopefulness.

Holmes smiled. "Surely a theme emerges. Think of what lies before you with all of its cacophony as though it was like American jazz music. There is always a thread within, which if not melody, yet sets a motif that appears recognizable at last. What we have here is a series of memoranda from the American Department of State and from various American business-interests seeking concessions of various sorts within the nation of Costa

Rica. Immense sums have been paid over several years. These sums enabled Don Juan Murillo to maintain his security-forces and to strengthen the army that was the seat of his power in his country. This man was essentially a paid-employee of the American government in order to grant concessions to American financiers at his own country's expense. He betrayed his own people and compromised his own national interests in order to please American business interests. Do your own readings square with this initial assessment?"

Both Sir Henry and I nodded, however I inquired, "But Holmes, this is all history, of what value is it today?"

"The value is in blackmail, my dear fellow, in fact blackmail so great in its potential, that it might be conducted upon an international scale by a man with the wit and determination to do so. One must remember that these papers cover a significant period in American history. It was not a pleasant period; after the idealism of the American Civil War America descended into a period of intense venality and corruption under the Grant administration. After the financial panic of 1873 and the disastrous years of Reconstruction, the country was attempting to put itself together again and to restore public confidence in the possibility of a democratic union of the once sundered states. America was also waking up to the severe class-divisions existing in the nation and the power wielded by the great, new industrial combinations. There was talk of anarchists and of various and sundry revolutionaries. You will recall how matters came to a head in the further financial Panic of 1893 of recent memory. It is now 1897 and America's posture in South America is tenuous indeed. There is even talk of a great canal that would open the entire Pacific to American trade, which would have a decided effect on the balance of trade of England and our own domination of China. The French as well have ambitions in Southeast Asia and the Pacific islands and Germany is not far behind while the Dutch are involved in the Indonesian islands."

"These papers show America in the worst possible light and there exist any number of international buyers who would pay for even a selection of these documents. Evidently, Juan Murillo intended something of the sort and managed to acquire and preserve them over several years. How the man Stapleton, for I will not insult your name Sir Henry by calling him by his real name of Baskerville, came by them I cannot say. We know that he occupied a position of some trust in the Murillo treasury and managed, in the chaos attendant upon the ousting of the president, to get to these papers before anyone else. Perhaps Lopez the Secretary was careless in a discussion over a drinking and gambling session, or perhaps he was bragging to show Stapleton that he knew of matters that were beyond Stapleton's knowledge. There was undoubtedly some jealousy between the men of the regime. Stapleton was a rising force in the government. Lopez was also growing in power. Juan Murillo may have feared a betrayal. It is part of the nature of powerful men that they distrust power in others. As a result they often rely upon mutual jealousies in those below them to make sure that no man may rely upon any other and form an alliance. This means that each minion owes his position solely to the leader and to his patronage alone. By this means leaders create a loyalty bred out of self-interest rather than out of virtue. It is the only security possessed by men of power, for they have no real friends. Stapleton then no doubt bent all of his efforts towards discovering the location of these papers. He kept quiet until the fatal hour, when, in a preemptive fashion, he stole them for profit and security against reprisal and absconded to England. It is quite possible that the later presence in England of Juan Murillo and Lopez, at the time of the attempt upon his life by Beryl's brother at Wisteria Lodge, was due to the fact that they were attempting to trace these very papers by locating the man, Stapleton. It also indicates why Stapleton attempted to keep on the move and kept changing his name."

"But why," asked Sir Henry, "did he not simply play his hand at once?"

"Ah," Holmes smiled. "Because we are dealing with a man of infinite patience and resource. I remarked once in 1888 to Watson that we were dealing with an opponent worthy of our steel.

His very scientific nature led him to play his more immediate hand first while the papers mellowed slowly like a fine wine. He would use them at a time calculated to cause maximum embarrassment to the American government and business titans and by doing so fetch a higher price from the buyer or buyers. In the meantime he needed funds, since he had settled in for a long siege to eliminate the heirs of the Baskerville fortune so that he could claim it as the son of the original Rodger Baskerville who had emigrated to South America where he later died an outcast, but not before leaving a son with his own name, an heir who might inherit the Baskerville riches someday.”

“But could it be otherwise?” I remonstrated. “What if the note from Stapleton to Lady Beryl is a forgery? What if Juan Murillo and his secretary, Lopez, were not killed in Spain after all? Rather than lying dead in Madrid, they may be masquerading as Rodger Baskerville. Might they not have used the ruse of their deaths to put the authorities off the track and are even now themselves trying to recapture President Murillo’s papers?”

“That would be possible, Watson, but it is precisely here that proper deductive method is required. First, we must look at relative probabilities. We have the witness of the reports, scanty though they are, from Madrid. And the vessel that took them to Spain left its own traces. The customs-records and the boat-log that was checked by the authorities at the time of departure from England indicated that President Murillo and Lopez boarded the vessel that took them to Spain. The log was found when the boat was salvaged after a storm, since it sank in shallow waters. That imposters boarded it is a possibility, but we must consider that Murillo and Lopez were boarding the ship in order to put further distance between them and any pursuit by other vengeful assassins. Also there is the matter of the passport photographs. One mistake is possible, but that the authorities could mistake two photos is unlikely upon boarding the vessel. Then, would Lady Beryl have trusted the man who had been responsible for the death of her brother and had ruined the health of her father? No, the letter to her must indicate to her by its tone or choice of words that it did indeed come from her husband and not from the only two other men who would know of the existence and nature of the papers."

I recalled, having since perused the brief document arranging the assignation, the intimate tone of the letter to Lady Beryl, its cajoling language, and the familiar Spanish term of affection that indicated that it might have been a nickname for the Lady during her early marriage to Stapleton. "But Holmes," I replied, "For the same reason, why should she meet with the man who had attempted the life of Sir Henry, the man she now loves and to whom she is now married?"

"Because Watson, she no doubt believes that she may still influence him in some way. They were after all once married and some faint faith may yet remain in the woman that he cannot be the complete scoundrel that we know him to be. It is one of the charms of women that once they truly love, they love forever. It is the great comfort of unworthy men that it should be so."

"But what would she expect him to do, to renounce a fortune?" asked Sir Henry.

"No, Sir Henry, but she may even imagine that she is protecting you from some further assault. She would attempt to convince him that she had long since destroyed the papers as a sorry reminder of their now lost love. He may even believe her, but we must hope that he does not, if this is the ruse she has adopted, for if he feels that she can be of no more use to him, well..."

"Surely, he would let her go," cried Sir Henry turning white. "Holmes you can't mean that..."

"Do not distress yourself unduly, Sir Henry. We have at least the assurance that Stapleton is a kidnapper and the kidnapper does not so easily destroy the means of obtaining a ransom. If not the Murillo papers then ransom money may be better to him than disposing of Lady Beryl and receiving nothing for all of his efforts and expectations. We may now on our part expect a communication from him. The man is playing with our nerves. Witness of this presupposition is offered by the somewhat theatrical device of again purchasing some sort of hound to recall to our minds the horror of the past. He will not try again that means to kill you, but the sound alone cannot but add to the pressures that he desires to place upon us. It is a war of nerves. We are indeed fortunate in possessing the papers. Why did your wife never destroy them I wonder?"

Sir Henry smiled. "She had a horror of disposing of anything. Even now one entire room is filled with small gifts from the local people, scraps of poetry that she has written, and other items. I always found it an endearing trait with her and was determined not to oppose it if it gave her pleasure."

"In this case that habit may save her life, for we will not part with any of these papers until we have her returned safely. I am afraid that a hard-line is indicated, Sir Henry. We must risk all in order to obtain all. Trying days lie ahead for all of us, but I believe that we need not fear that a communication will soon arrive. May that time come for all of our sakes! For now let us gather these papers and restore them to their place of rest. No, I do not think the box need be closed again. He knows its secret contents and the way to get at them if the box is in his hand. The box itself though may be useful and we need not guarantee its contents to a rogue such as he is."

After this hint as to our future conduct Holmes would say no more and we placed the papers behind the sliding panel and descended to the dining-room below.

We each spent the rest of the day on our own pursuits. Holmes went into the village of Grimpen. Sir Henry was given a mild sedative at my orders. I in turn returned to Holmes' manuscript, the slow and concentrated reading of which had grown upon me as I attempted to follow his daring theological speculations. I could see that Holmes had chosen his Catholicism, not through a process of easy capitulation as is true for so many, but rather in the face of a thorough examination of the other candidates for his commitment to an ultimate faith.

From the Journal of Sherlock Holmes

October 4, 1891
Tehran, Persia

Summer has passed and I believe that I have found the ideal spot in which to spend a month recuperating from our strenuous travels and to put my notes thus far in order. We have arrived in Tehran and have found a hotel that caters to the English. I have grown a beard in the course of my travels and have registered as one "Knut Sigerson" of Norway. Mycroft was able to obtain, through the Norwegian Consulate in London, an alternate Norwegian Passport, which was forwarded to me, care of the British consulate in Tehran. It can be perilous to carry two passports, but as my travels progress it may be of use occasionally to be able to invoke different national recognition and protections at will. Not everyone is fond of the English. We have not yet reached a view that all persons from whatever nation are of innate value. The rights that are recognized in the case of any individual depend upon one's citizenship. There is no real equality among nations, but only a balance of forces. It is this fact that makes the arms trade necessary. Borders are merely temporary indications that represent a consensus that war, at least for the moment, is not advantageous to either party so as to change those borders. Borders then finally represent merely the status-quo of power-relations between nations.

Perhaps the best example of this phenomenon is found in

the Americas. In one hundred short years, the American nation has managed to push the British north into Canada, to annex Texas from Mexico, to eliminate Russia as a threat by purchasing Alaska, and through fraud and warfare to eliminate most of the original inhabitants of the land. One speaks of the Mongolian hoards of Genghis Khan, but no period of history has witnessed such depredations as that visited upon the native dwellers of America by a society claiming to exist under a rule of law. How strange that the same nation that fought a civil war in an effort to free the Negro slaves should have spent the 1870's and the 1880's destroying the means of life essential for the continued survival of the red man. Only recently at Wounded Knee, South Dakota, the last remnants of a starving people were slaughtered by U.S. troops. I fear that America will always be a land of violence and terror; its hunger for great wealth, since it recognizes no other nobility but the dollar, will lead it to despoil the nations of the world in order to fuel its industrial capacity. If only its oceans may contain it, the world may be safe.

My own dealings with America have been confined to only two or three cases. I can still recall that major early case memorialized, in his usual lurid terms, by Dr. Watson as, "A Study in Scarlet," and the equally lurid manuscript that he intends to call, "The Valley of Fear," whenever it is published. Both cases reveal the violence of America and its desire to break from all past civilizations in order to enthrone mere gain as the principle of living. There is no noblesse oblige abiding in America's wealthy class, but only relative advantage in the marketplace. There are no titled gentry in America; the rawness of the land will not allow for the ideal of the gentleman. All of this is better explained of course by that most excellent writer, Henry James, who I met in London last year. The density of the man's writing style is impenetrable at times, but he is insightful as to the true relations between the old world and the new. I think often of this strange urge of Americans to collect the spoils of the creativity of other nations.

Even in religion this is so! Who can read of the tenets of Mormonism without seeing in that strange book of Joseph Smith how Americans can rely upon misunderstanding to create an entirely new religion. In one step Mormonism has moved Israel to America, created two fictional tribes to replace what we know of the anthropology of the Americas, and endowed God the Father with a human body so as to eliminate any transcendent notion of God as a creator and as the utterly other, the spiritual source of all and every creation. Instead Mormon belief substitutes a succession of gods and tells its adherents that (at least the males) will someday be gods themselves in turn and will people new realms with spirit children who will someday assume flesh in their turn before in their turn becoming gods. This belief in the deification of man of course completely denies the traditional Christian understanding of the uniqueness of Jesus Christ as the pre-existent Word of God and the Second Person of the Blessed Trinity, begotten but not made, for whom and through whom alone creation was made.

The participation in divine life offered the Christian must always be derivative of his sharing in the life of Christ as part of creation and through Divine Grace. This new American faith of Mormonism, which is consistent with the national apotheosis of the individual, cannot rest with the idea of empowering the citizen politically but must go so far as to dislodge the Trinity and imagine that we ourselves can become Gods. The whole process violates that most basic teaching of St. Thomas Aquinas that the mind cannot tolerate an infinite regress but must posit finally, an unmoved-mover or final-cause of all things. God is an absolute point of origin, a great singularity. Still, if religion is to function as merely the glue of a social organization, then the Mormon tribe is as valid as the many American Indian beliefs that trace the tribe's creation to a mythological point of origin.

Perhaps religion is best understood as a function rather than as a collection of doctrines. One may witness that even in Christianity and Judaism there is this perpetual need for a blood sacrifice. What is the purpose to be served by slaughtering beasts and finally even God Himself upon a cross? Who demands such behavior? Does retribution finally restore anything? Is that not merely disguised revenge, one of the less attractive motivations for human conduct? Does the same God who created the seas and peopled the deeps with sharks demand blood, even now from mankind, the summit of his earthly creation? Shall we never escape this shark-like view of the world but must needs devour one another in perpetuity? Must our highest sacramental action be the devouring of God Himself? Why should God cater to our voraciousness in this way? But did we perhaps in Eden make ourselves so hungry for life that even death must be fought rather than merely humbly accepted? Whatever plunged us into this rash desire to be immortal? How strange it is that what the devout follower of Buddha views as a curse the Christian views as a blessing, eternal life!

To read the legend of Tiresias as immortalized by Alfred Lord Tennyson is to know the agony of indefinite futurity! When I think of hell, I need only imagine human life as we know it indefinitely prolonged. Think of the weight of ancient jealousies and hatreds that have brewed, not merely for decades but for centuries! Walk into any gambling den and look at the bloated faces of those bent over their cards or a spinning roulette-wheel or gaze into an opium-den and see the sleepers frozen into fantastic attitudes of despair. Watch as the crawling fingers reach out to grasp again the opium pipe in order to suck the noxious fumes into hacking lungs. Go to the great laundries of London and see the gin-soaked women plunging their great, rosy arms into the sullen grey water and cackling over their witches-brew of the stench and odor of man. I turn in relief at times to Schopenhauer and my only quarrel is that the man paints too dignified a vision.

All too often I find mankind to be unworthy of redemption. I find in myself even sympathy at times with the Moslem belief that God would never assume human nature or beget a Son. The Moslem at least keeps the proper distance between man and God. He confines God's relations to man as one of compassion and mercy, but not of identification, even with a sinless man let alone the rest of us. There is something absolute in this. Perhaps Islam is the greatest Monism that has ever existed. But is there not also a slight taint of Calvinism in it also? Every Monism eventually becomes deterministic for if God is to be all-in-all, then He finally absorbs even His creation itself. When the only writing is God's, then he must write also even if indirectly in the left-hand script of evil, and who is to question that writing, least of all the believer. So, unless God does assume human nature and take our evil upon Himself, then Monism would give us a God who is occasionally evil or evil to some but not to others.

Still even in my hours of greatest disgust and despair at mankind, I return to the figure of Christ upon the cross begging forgiveness for his enemies and I sink again to my knees in the inevitable dualism of the two natures of Jesus Christ as both God and man in a hypostatic union. But I confess to also exploring the beliefs of other cultures as well. I nourish my Christian beliefs by looking at the other visions of God: the wisdom of the I-Ching that tries only to tell the man of virtue how to proceed. The Chinese mind rebels at metaphysics and revelation. Rather, like the American Indian religions, the religion of China is based upon observation of the nature of "The Way." It bows before the unexplained and attempts no final answer to the problem of evil. Above all, it avoids asking questions about the nature of God. God is Waken-Tanka to the Lakota Sioux, the great Om of the Upanishads to the Hindus, the union of the forces of Yin and Yang to the Chinese. Perhaps every culture and individual gets the gods that they deserve. But this implies that it is we who create images of God rather than God who creates us. Is God then merely an extrapolation of our own highest conception of ourselves? We feel powerless, therefore we make God powerful. We live our lives in ignorance and frustration, so we imagine that God knows everything and that He even determines our fate by that fore-knowing. We live our lives encased in vain desires, so we define God's impassibility: He is immune to desires, yet the Old Testament still speaks of a jealous God, one who desires worship and defines in detail its parameters. Yet this same Old Testament says that God also desires mercy, not sacrifice. Are the writings then part of an innate dialogue of God with man through our own imaginations, whereby God purifies our conceptions of His nature over time? If this is so, then we look in vain for God when we gaze outward at the stars and the heavens. God's voice and revelation will only be found within us.

But what if it is only within us that God's origin lies? If so, then the concept of God comes cascading downward until it inhabits only our small brain-pans. Must God echo always within the tiny cathedrals of our skulls? When will God emerge: resplendent, pure, as in God's own nature God actually is? For this reason St. John ends his Book of Revelation with a plea that the Lord Jesus may come quickly and that history (and even our own sorry lives) may find an end on that day, one both dreaded and embraced, when all will be revealed at last.

If this desire that is within us is only human desire and that is all, if God is only a conception, a projection of our own condition and its inevitable frustrations, then may our species soon die out and be supplanted by another, one that is at peace with the accidental universe that gave it birth for no other purpose than merely to live for a time and then to pass on into the mindless elements again.

To believe in God for the Christian means first of all: believing in ourselves, that we matter and that our actions are significant, that even the angelic orders mirror and serve our strivings, that we are above all else not alone, for solitude, both as individuals and as a species, is what we fear the most. We beg that someone will notice us from the moment of our birth for we know in our very being that we are not self-sufficient, but are creatures. Whether there is a God or not, this much is certain: no one can be a God unto himself and for himself for longer than the short hours when our vain powers persuade us that we are supreme. Finally, the sleeper must awaken and see himself as he really is; then, oh the horror, if on the vast and empty plains of existence, he does not descry the arms of God reaching towards him in eternal embrace.

Dr. Watson's Narrative Continues

I fell asleep last night with a strange feeling after reading Holmes' last entry. I felt that his journey to the high places of Asia and through these sites of ancient empires had so enlarged his views that thereafter our own British belief systems must appear as trivial. I must admit that my own world is confined to a desire for comfort. I ask merely that my copy of the Times be ready on my breakfast table in the morning and that my housekeeper shall bring me a banger sausage and a plate of kippers in the morning, and that she will not burn my toast or forget that I like a Scottish bramble-preserve with my crumpets. I like to take a brief walk along the sea cliffs in my Norfolk jacket in the morning after breakfast. I may thereafter stop in at the village library to return a few books and then have a pear-cider and a steak-and-kidney pie or a Cornish pasty at the local pub for lunch. I usually take a brief nap in the afternoons and then when the winter light is fading I have the blinds drawn, the fire built up, and have a whisky and soda before my dinner, followed perhaps by an evening of whist at the club. The storms of passion and the dreams of a Harley Street practice are no more for me. I place my own claim to significance in the lives that I have helped as a medical man and to my long and intimate association with Sherlock Holmes. For the rest I simply ask that my mind shall be at peace.

I am glad that I did not die of my wounds in my military youth. I am grateful for the two women who successively shared my life and when I gaze at the mirror I do not frown or smile but only say, "Ah Watson, old fellow, there you are again." I do not know whether it is possible to live a life confined to the immediacy of simply living though for a man constituted like Sherlock Holmes. During the years of our friendship I could not but remark how he turned aside from all of the usual comforts of life. He did not seem, for instance, to care about success in a monetary way, often taking the most extraordinary pains to solve a mystery involving what appeared to be trivial or at least highly private matters while neglecting investigations that, though prosaic in nature, might have netted him generous fees. Mycroft, his brother, of course drew a huge salary from the British government and it is possible that Mycroft in turn kept Holmes on a retainer, but we seldom spoke of money and Holmes never seemed to lack the funds necessary to attend concerts and to meet his simple needs. His taste in dining, when he chose to indulge it with an evening out, was often elaborate it is true. His wardrobe was that of a gentleman and though of the highest quality not excessive in quantity. He kept for years his old ear-flapped hunting cap and it became something of a trademark with the man.

But what of the comforts that might be provided by a wife and children? On the few occasions when I was indiscreet enough to inquire about his ideas in this direction, he looked up at first with mild remonstrance, and then smiling might remark that procreation was the business of the lower-classes and an activity of which they seemed never to tire. When I once suggested that it would be a pity if the Holmes-line were to be broken, since Mycroft was also a bachelor, Holmes said that I need not fear for his Brother Sherringford had married and that the name would continue from that quarter and that as the eldest brother under the rule of primogeniture he was in the best position to raise a family.

"Besides, Watson," he had said, "I could hardly face the dangers of my life if I had to fear that my demise would devastate my children and leave a grieving wife behind. I believe that love would so curtail my freedom that I would be useless in my present line of work. And Watson, need I remind you that you have no children either."

That subject was indeed painful to me and we did not long dwell upon it. So Holmes cared not for money, nor for love, and as for fame, well, there he may have had some slight vanity, for though he spoke of them deprecatingly, he seemed to enjoy my accounts of his exploits and would read them avidly before sniffing and tossing them aside carelessly upon the old and stained deal-table in our common lodgings in Baker Street. This attitude sometimes nettled me and Holmes would be immediately apologetic and might treat me to dinner that night in recompense for his apparent callousness. I believed though that it was only to hide his own pleasure at being celebrated, that he acted thus towards my efforts to make his name famous throughout England and even as far as distant Russia.

His use of cocaine appeared to be his only vice and that habit ebbed with the years and under a course of my own medical treatment. I was often called upon to minister to him in a medical capacity, not merely to treat wounds sustained in battle with the ruder elements of London, but also in order to restore him to health after periods of more than usual exertion when his overall condition was near to collapse before the excessive demands that he made upon his resources. He tended to treat his body with contempt and his eating habits were irregular at best. He abhorred vegetables and seemed to live upon bread and beef. When I suggested that he might be lacking in the necessary variety of foods and that his health might suffer in consequence, he would state that he was not a forager and though he might ratiocinate at times he did not ruminate. His tobacco use was appalling, but at least it was preferable to cocaine, so I said little about it. He drank only Irish whiskey and the best French Cognac and occasionally some Amontillado or Madeira, but these not to excess. He abhorred the vices of intoxication and sexual excesses. He was as abstemious and feline as a cat in all that he did.

If he had any true vice it would seem to be his occasional extreme melancholy when he would withdraw from all communication, even with me, for days at a time. During these periods he would appear to indulge in certain extreme and morbid doubts as to the value of all human existence. He was too aware of all that surrounded him to ignore the social conditions of the British Empire. He had, for instance, a perfect horror of Liverpool with its ghastly slums and on the few occasions when I urged him to take a holiday in Ireland, he insisted upon departing from Holyhead in Wales instead. He seldom traveled to Yorkshire where he was born, and though he corresponded with his brother, Sherringford, their relations were not warm and were usually confined to Christmas remembrances and similar occasions.

Holmes preferred to take his holidays in France. He was fond of the coast of Brittany and was quite fond of the oysters served in Quimper, a quiet town that acted as a base for excursions north and south along the French coast. We once spent a week in St. Malo and walked the lovely bay at low-tide. It was on occasions such as this that he might unbend a bit and confide in me his religious doubts and fears that were often at the bottom of his melancholy. All of this of course might have given me advance notice that he might someday break away to pursue his religious quest among the great religions and cultures of the east. Reading his present journal was therefore a welcome experience for me for I was able to trace how his great mind had grappled with the most essential questions of life and death and the great purpose of it all. I could see the vacillations and the way that he would find seeming clarity only to lose it once again as new doubts assailed him. He had no high opinion of churchmen and even bishops were often for him occasions for ridicule or at least for gentle chiding. For some men faith is not an easy possibility. They do not accept God out of convention or social convenience but only after the long agony of doubt and exploration. I fear that Sherlock Holmes was such a man.

I have often remarked that the men and women who have advanced the great thoughts of the world might be contained in Covent Garden Theater, whereas all who have lived and died and known the human condition are countless. Many have died before sustained habits of thought were even a possibility. Others caught up in the daily struggle to earn a living, to raise crops, or to hunt have never known or entertained abstract possibilities. Even the great engineers and builders of this world are caught within the webs of various design imperatives and the concrete functionality of things.

Then there are men, such as Immanuel Kant, who lay the entire human condition before them and try and arrive at fixed principles for all of thought and knowledge and also the great religious prophets who reach beyond the human condition to ask if it is of any value to a higher order of being. Can these men be described as detectives who sift clues, or are they rather, originators, who leave clues for others to follow? Much depends upon this question, for if they are detectives, then they follow a path laid out by another that in this case might be God Himself. If they are originators, then they are the creators of images of what a God might be if there really is one.

How then is one to judge such religious claimants? Do we not judge them when we decide which faith to adhere to? If there is a God, then perhaps He has an inner image written in our hearts. We compare the outer-teaching of the various religious claimants with our own inner-desire and intuition of what a God would be. When a match takes place, then we decide to adhere to that creed. Does that mean then that there are many gods and one picks one as one would choose a desert from the tray at Simpsons? No, for this choice must determine one's entire stance to existence. The choice of a creed is the most important decision that one will ever make. Yet men of good will choose different creeds. Are religions then mere lenses with which we focus our attention on a reality that is too great for us to grasp and will God have mercy, not merely on all men, but upon all religions as well for their deficiencies, and pity our earnest striving to bridge an impassible gulf between God and humankind?

Truly I hope that this may be the case, for I am no fond follower of those elite cults that claim the unique salvation of an elect. If we are not all elect, then God would be like a fickle, rich uncle who favors his nephews according to his whims. Surely God does not indulge in trivialities and petty jealousies. But then, if it is truly God, can anything in his immensity ever be petty? Does God not determine the rules of engagement before his creation is ever manifested so that the human must always utter a Job-like amen to the Divine Prerogatives? Certainly John Calvin thought so. But just as Abraham dared to question God, and Jacob wrestled with his angel, so perhaps God allows us to complain and to question as a mother allows her child to cry and even at times to push her away. Reading Holmes' manuscript brought forth many of my own long latent religious questions. To truly think about such matters is a fearful thing! No wonder that we for the most part live our lives in quiet and routine tasks so as to avoid the full demands of being a conscious being!

I must say that I was, after entertaining thoughts such as these, grateful for the return of Holmes from the village. Sir Henry still slept. The evening shadows were drawing down over the barren moors and a light late autumn wind was driving the leaves before it. Holmes came into the library where I had been reading and musing before the fire. He walked over to the great table that was littered with various items and tossed down his portmanteau that was filled with papers and books and came over to join me at the fire. He gazed deeply into the blaze in silence and rubbed his hands briskly together to restore their circulation.

At last he spoke. "It has come, Watson, a letter for Sir Henry postmarked from Tavistock. I did not open it. I felt that Sir Henry must be the only one to do so. The writing was similar to the message to Lady Beryl. I think that you will need to awaken him, though I hate to disturb the few hours of peace that he has known after many nights of unrest."

I rose to my feet and ascended to Sir Henry's room leaving Holmes standing tall, lean, and as energetic as ever before the library fire. I proceeded down the ancient corridor to his room and knocked gently before entering. Sir Henry was breathing regularly. I went forward and lightly touched his arm. He was awake instantly and blinking upwards at me through the gloom.

"What is it, Dr. Watson? Has something happened?" he asked.

"Holmes sent to me to fetch you," I answered. "A letter has come."

In an instant the man was on his feet and clothed in a warm

dressing gown. We descended together and entered the library where Holmes awaited us. He walked to the table and picking up the letter in question handed it to Sir Henry who took it eagerly. He proceeded to rip it open and to read it slowly before handling the letter to Holmes and collapsing in a chair by the fire. Holmes then proceeded to read the missive and then handed it to me. The contents were as follows:

Sir Henry—

We appear, each of us, to have succeeded to the property of the other. If you have the man at your side that I believe you do, then it will not be necessary for me to inform you that I am alive. You have succeeded to the Estate of the Baskervilles that might have been mine and you are welcome to it and to blazes with you. But taking my wife also as part of the legacy may have been going a bit far. In any case, she has been restored to me for the present. Whether I will keep her and how depends upon you. I have a bone or two to pick with the lady. I have refrained to date from any well-deserved chastisements and she sits silently before me as I write this with that dear doe-eyed expression that I recall so well. She no doubt frets that her absence is causing you pain and well it might for she is still quite tempting, though somewhat weathered since she came into your possession; but enough of that. I shall come directly to the point. You possess, perhaps inadvertently, some papers and other items that I would like to obtain. They are of course of little use to you, but I advise you to guard them carefully for it is by their means alone that Beryl might be restored to you. You may or may not know why they are important to me, but I trust that as a gentleman you will not withhold property that is rightfully mine. I alone know their true value and how to obtain it. Perhaps also it is you alone who know the value of Beryl, for she has little anymore for me. What can therefore be more natural than an exchange? Do not disappoint me in this or you may imagine your lady pinned like a butterfly in my one of my collections. I am not a common kidnapper and quite within my rights in this matter, so I will not be the one to dictate

I put the note down. Sir Henry was shaking his head and muttering, "The cad, the foul cad!"

"Cad he may be, cunning devil he is, Sir Henry," said Holmes. "But we shall have the better of him, never fear."

"He will not return her safely; I know it."

"You know nothing of the sort. I have already considered his character and made allowances for it. He will act in his own interest and that interest depends upon the continued safety of Lady Beryl. He will preserve it I assure you, for he will obtain nothing until we see her again well and whole."

"But can we dictate terms?" asked Sir Henry.

"The man is desperate." Holmes answered.

"No less so than I, and he knows it," cried Sir Henry

"But he is the weaker in character. You must be firm, Sir Henry, or all is lost. We will of course respond immediately and it is we who will dictate the terms. The papers will be placed in a vault in a bank in Exeter to which his legal counsel will have access. His counselor will be admitted to the vault and take possession only upon the safe release of Lady Beryl. His solicitors will then deliver the papers to their principal, Rodger Baskerville."

"But will he relinquish her until he knows that all is safe and that the papers are there?"

"They will be there. We will have them examined by his counsel and then they will be returned securely to the vault. Access to the vault will remain with the bank director with instructions that the vault may not be opened again until a transfer and notarized signing takes place. Rodger Baskerville's solicitor will be instructed to deliver Lady Beryl to sign over these documents to him so that we will both take possession of her and sign over the documents at the bank simultaneously. When Lady Beryl is quite safe, we will transfer the right of access to the vault and its contents per the contract," said Holmes.

"But Holmes," I protested, "think of the use that will be made of them!"

"I have done so. He will blackmail some of the wealthiest men in America who stood by the Murillo regime in order to obtain trade concessions. It is not that which troubles me, for they deserve whatever comes to them at his hands. It is the fear of what Rodger Baskerville will do with the money that concerns me. He would no doubt be a man similar to Baron Maupertuis if he had the means. We cannot leave him at large. He must be apprehended if possible, but after he obtains the papers. We shall have other shots at our quarry, never fear. For the present, we are in a difficult position and as the I-Ching states so well: to proceed rashly in time of danger is not to prosper. We must await our hour. It will come. Now, Sir Henry, if you and Dr. Watson will leave me alone for a time I will draft the response. You will of course review it and sign it, which I beg you to do, I am afraid that it is our only practical course at this time."

Sir Henry assented and went upstairs to change into some warm tweeds for a proposed walk upon the moors leaving Holmes and I alone.

"This is a bad business, Watson. Did you note the insolence of the fellow? It is a mistake to allow emotions to come into play, for they cloud the judgment, but the fellow has come as close as any of the opponents we have met to touching the latent chords of vengeance within me. The man is a cad of the first order, a callous brute. There are men of evil, not principled evil as in the case of Professor Moriarty, who are finally amenable to reason, but men who have left the human order behind entirely. These men are truly diabolical and against them force and even death is justified if they can be stopped in no other way."

"You have made a decision then?" I inquired.

"I have done so. I have, as it were, prepared my own Hound of the Baskervilles and I intend to set it upon him. The trap set for others will now entwine the feet of the man who set it. It is not easy to stand upon the very abyss of evil, Watson, and not to be drawn into it. The tendrils and roots send runners out to grasp our feet. To touch evil is in a way to become evil. For this reason the great Saint Philip Neri had a simple formula for dealing with evil. He advised his followers to simply flee. Evil cannot be understood, nor can it be fought directly. It is only by turning to the source of all good and dwelling securely within it that we have any hope at all. We are led constantly to the test and are usually found wanting. For this reason we are bid to forgive constantly and to ask to be forgiven. God alone can deliver us from evil and He has done so, not by fighting it, but by taking it upon Himself, for God alone is impermeable to evil, for in Him evil has no part. I often think that the real wisdom of the saints lay in their proper fear of evil. It led them to seek shelter in God. The timid, the humble, and the innocent are close to God, not because of their great efforts, but because they allow the force of Divine Grace to operate unhindered within them. They do not grasp for the knowledge of good and evil, but rather await God's will in quiet and utter mirroring of the sublime consent of Our Lady the Virgin Mary. Recall her words, 'Let it be done unto me according to Thy word.'"

"But what of the words of Jesus: 'The kingdom of heaven suffers violence and the violent bear it away?'" I asked, for these words had always puzzled me.

"Those are words of exhortation to single-mindedness, Watson. The violent man is single-minded. He is obsessed by something that becomes for him at the moment an ultimate goal. He will spare no pains to obtain it. He loses all vision for the peripheral. In this world no partial good, not even respect and honor, deserve this absolute commitment. Think only of Jesus who did not shield his face from buffets and spitting, nor claim the honor and vindication due to Him as God, even finally accepting death and the degradation of the tomb, not a sleep but a real death, that foul thing that haunts our days."

"You may recall that St. Francis Borgia prior to being the General of the Jesuit Order was appalled with what rapidity flesh turns to corruption when deprived of the divine spark of life. The fire dies and all is ashes. One would think that our destiny of the grave would breed humility in all men and women, but it is not so. We revel in our tattered garments of flesh and adorn our mortality with possessions, and yet all the while we draw closer to what will finally receive our charnel bones. Evil, knows this and preying upon our fears awakens pride. In this way and only this way do we know the difference between good and evil, not as God knows it; for with God evil always wears its own blank face of empty promise, but as willing participants in evil, we do not always see this."

"Men and women indeed do know evil in a way when they fall into it, but in so doing they really know it not, for to them it is the good of an hour, a comfort on the desolate road of solitude without God. Evil is tolerated by God because it alone can both defeat us and also save us by showing us itself at last in all of its naked horror. At the moment of death each soul is granted by God one last vision of Grace whereby the soul sees its entire life and all things from the point of view of God. That vision is the final test spoken of in the Gospels. We are to pray that we not be put to the test, for it will be a horrible vision to those who have made of evil their good. They will wish to hide themselves from the light, and some perhaps fearing the light of God, will run from that light even into the depths of hell itself. For others this revelation will also show them the true home that they have always desired. That is the judgment of God."

We both fell into silence then. The ashes ticked in the grate and outside the great hall the winds blew the dead leaves of a late autumn afternoon to bank up against the trees in the yew alley. Sir Henry found us smoking in silence upon his return and we both quietly withdrew and left Holmes to write the missive to obtain the release of Lady Beryl from Rodger Baskerville, our most deadly foe.

We both left the house soon after and the great hall door closed behind us with its studded oak that fit perfectly into the ancient stone archway. The long yew alley stretched before us interrupted at intervals with vistas of open terraces. I could feel the soft carpet of the sodden leaves beneath my boots. I reached into my pocket for my pipe and soon the comforting taste of my favorite Cavendish mixture filled the air and drifted with the breeze. Sir Henry walked quietly by my side carrying his heavy walking-stick that he had carried for years since the night of the attack by the great hound. I do not know that he had ever really recovered from the horror of that night, nor could I blame him. It was enough that he still chose to live upon the moors with their ancient legends and the remains all about of neo-lithic man.

The furze had turned brown with the waning year and each night brought its visitor of hoarfrost to the higher tors. How strange that King Arthur should have chosen this place for romantic Camelot. Of course our English legends have borrowed heavily from Celtic France and the tradition of courtly love that brought some charm to the longings of the flesh and helped to cast aside the bleakness of the 12th and the 13th century. It was a time when men were rejecting the world and finding solace in the mendicant orders, the Franciscans and the Dominicans. It was also the days of crusaders who combined greed for plunder with a misplaced ardor for the spread of a Christianity that owed little to the Carpenter of Galilee. Pope Innocent III had brought papal temporal power to its maximum and all over Europe the spirit of the age began the triumphal raising of the great cathedrals. The complete cultural dominance of Christianity over all of Europe will perhaps never be known again. If there is a similar guiding spirit today it is the lust for colonial possessions that cannot but lead finally to a great European conflict. Power can brook no rivals.

Sir Henry in contrast, though a man of wealth, had turned it to improving the lot of his neighbors. The village of Grimpen had spread and new cottages dotted the moors which we could see from the yew alley. A new herd of dairy cattle, owned in combination by local farmers, had created a base for a local creamery and Baskerville Cheese now was exported to both America and to the continent. There was also a biscuit factory partially owned by the workers themselves. The salaries supported the local merchants, a tobacconist, a book store, a community library, a local grammar school, and even an agricultural institute was planned. The brutality of mere survival had yielded to a hardy domestic yeomanry and Sir Henry demonstrated that attitude of social obligation without which the so-called higher classes are mere parasites and vultures. We could see the clean, white, workers cottages down in the dale, but our way took us to the higher ground and the picturesque rock formations that convey such interest to a moorland walk.

To walk on the moors at any season can be enchanting. The odd stone formations create a natural park-like setting and the gorse and heather are interwoven with countless paths. Now and again the bleak landscape is interrupted by copses and groves of trees. These trees now almost bare of leaves made a type of wind-harp that moaned with the rushing wind. It was as though the moor had its own music, a bleak soprano, wailing of lost loves and vanished lives. Holmes has always decried observations such as these as examples of the pathetic fallacy, but I always counter that nature may be more sympathetic to us then we know and may reflect back upon us our feelings and our passions. At this he would usually shake his head and resume some chemical experiment of his own. He would always say that experience that cannot be replicated is only individual and as such subject to error. I would then counter that all typology must be arrived at by degrees, that nature creates change first by individual variation. All real growth and creation exist primarily at the individual level, while the sentiments of the madding crowd are watered-down and derivative. Only the tree that stands taller than its fellows is ever noticed.

What is history then but a record of time's exceptions? Think only of the many lives that leave no trace behind them. These existed only to fulfill the temporary mandate of the species. We recall only the exceptions, the explorers, the statesmen, and the poets. Nor is power all, for yesterday's heroes may be swiftly forgotten while an obscure poet may become immortal. Great fortunes run to rust; while poverty, if coupled with literary or artistic abilities, may well shine through the ages. The surface of humanity bubbles while the deep brew beneath merely exists to support the surface where history is finally observed and recorded.

But then I must agree also that the individual soon loses himself in the typical. Think of the strangeness of genealogy. How swiftly are we as individuals lost beneath the storm of life! Our parents add fifty percent of our heritage while our grandparents add only twenty-five percent. Two becomes four. Our great-grandparents add as individuals but one-eighth of our heritage and our great-great grandparents one-sixteenth. If we allow twenty five years between the generations then within a single century only one sixteenth of oneself remains in one's distant progeny. In this way the individual decays even in that fragmentary remnant that might be deemed immortal, the genetic train of his life. No life really leaves a dynasty then, but it has really only a short impact upon the ever-widening sphere of life. The compass of relationship grows always and with it variation. Life twists about a widening circle. It is a great fountain throwing off spray into the sun. It is a spiral nebula whose distant light is but a reflection of the source of all light.

But to return to the individual, to the level of uniqueness, here unpredictability reigns. Think even of the brain with its competing hemispheres that so often divide a face. Look at a portrait and cover one side of the face, then view the other side alone in quick succession. Why even the individual is divided and in that lifelong colloquy attempts finally to find the union of the self! Or if we turn from the individual to cultures, races, religions, or ideas: what emerges but variations striving toward unity? Surely to impose the views of one race or culture upon all, even if war is the price and the result, is the height of folly!

Sir Henry interrupted my meditations. "Why, Dr. Watson, look who approaches us, our old friend Dr. Mortimer!"

It was indeed the good doctor who had played so central a role in our lives when he first brought to us the case of the legendary hound that had so oppressed the Baskerville family through the ages. Dr. Mortimer had aged with the years, but still carried that same walking-stick, the one presented to him by the faculty of Charing Cross Hospital in his youth. The ferule had no doubt been replaced many times through the years. His habit of walking on his rounds to his scattered moorland patients had preserved his health. Nor had he lost that particular enthusiasm for his own unique anthropological interests. As was usual upon meeting him, he began without prelude.

"Ah Doctor Watson, I must see your friend at once. I have found it. Mr. Holmes alone will appreciate the significance...it will surely have the greatest impact...the anthropology of these isles will need to reflect what may be the greatest discovery in the history of Devonshire excavations!"

Then, noticing my companion, as if for the first time, he said, "Oh hello, Sir Henry!"

Sir Henry and I smiled at each other. We were accustomed to the man's strange manner and on this occasion could not but fall in with his enthusiasm. "You are to be congratulated," I said. "But what, pray, have you discovered?"

"Ah, that I must only reveal to Mr. Holmes, for he alone will appreciate the full implications... Where may I find him?"

"He is at Baskerville hall," I replied. "But I must beg you to defer your news for the present. Mr. Holmes is much occupied at present with two cases of the greatest moment and..."

"Cases, cases, what are cases!" exclaimed Dr. Mortimer. "When the mists are parting and the earth at last yields its secrets? I must see him at once."

The man hopped from one foot to the other in his excitement. There could be no putting him off I could see, so we consented that he should return with us to Baskerville Hall. I was aware that Holmes had on occasion enjoyed an afternoon with Dr. Mortimer and that both enjoyed walks over the moors and speculation about the original inhabitants. I could only assume that Dr. Mortimer had found some unique item, an ancient shield perhaps, or the fragment of a skull. Holmes would know how to put the man off in a courteous way so that we might concentrate all of our energies upon the significant tasks that lay before us.

We were soon at the hall. Even the chill of the great central reception hall seemed warm to us after the cold of our walk. The evening shadows were drawing down and I could just discern the scent of roast-pheasant wafting from the great kitchen in the rear of the mansion with that heightened sense of smell that comes to us after a walk in the cold air of autumn. We entered the library to find Holmes seated before the fire and smoking a blend of Persian Latakia. He rose at once and showed surprise and also a mild annoyance at the entrance of our visitor, but quickly he subsided into his usual manner of courtesy, but still with a rueful smile to me of acquiescence to the inevitable.

"Ah, Dr. Mortimer, it has been some time. Pray take a seat. I trust that your researches are going well. No, you need not withdraw, Watson, nor you Sir Henry. I have had Perkins prepare a spiced-rum punch awaiting your return from your autumn stroll. It may act as a restorative after your brisk walk upon the moors."

We gladly assented to his invitation and each took a comfortable seat by the fire after reaching a ladle into a pewter bowl to fill our respective flagons with the mixture. Dr. Mortimer had already begun enthusiastically.

"It is the find of finds, Mr. Holmes, unless I am very much mistaken. It is an ancient British barrow located southwest of Grimpen on the very borders of Cornwall. It is on the coast in a deep crevasse that forms a natural bowl or hollow. On the cliffs above there are the remnants of a monastery from the sixth century. The area has of course been well-explored and its artifacts catalogued and documented long since, but the clues were not connected. It appears to have been an early site of both learning and of commerce. The very variety of materials indicated to me that extensive trade was once carried on with Africa and even with the regions of Phoenicia and of Asia Minor. There can be little doubt that it represents one of the earliest Christian settlements in Pagan Britain, for there are also some objects of a decidedly Celtic design. It is evident that we have here a meeting of the two great cultures of the age, Roman and Celtic."

He rubbed his hands briskly together in his enthusiasm. "My first clue was the sheer sparseness of remaining items at a place that clearly supported at one time a significant population of perhaps five thousand persons, which was for the time quite a dense population. The monastery had long since been raided during the Norman Conquest and perhaps before, which of course made it impossible that any illuminated manuscripts would remain. There were only homely domestic objects for the most part. This made the site of little interest to scholars and our remote location has rendered it forgotten and obscure. It was with some audacity therefore that I took it upon myself to try some excavations in the chasm nearby, after obtaining from a local landowner a yearlong option on the property, paid for by myself and by Mr. Franklin as equal partners in whatever we might find."

"Congratulations, Dr. Mortimer, your tale is indeed remarkable," said Holmes. "Have you found anything significant to date?"

"There are evidences, my dear Sir, evidences that there may have once been an even more ancient Druid settlement in the chasm below the monastery. I have found shards with unique designs that show distinct Druid antecedents. The items found thus far that are, when combined with the items found in the monastery located above the site, quite consistent with my supposition that more is to be found by excavating deeper. The findings also confirm your own theory, Mr. Holmes, that Chaldean tin-traders did indeed once visit these shores. You must drop everything and come at once to Cornwall. I am sure that Mr. Franklin would consent to our sharing the find with you and offering you a third and equal share in the property. Your aid would be invaluable."

"That is very generous of you, Dr. Mortimer, and I assure you that I will look into the matter as soon as occasion permits, but I am much engaged at the present in two rather significant cases that unfortunately demand all of my time and energy. I may be able to spare Watson for a few days, but I really cannot do better at the present."

It was both painful and comic to see the disappointment written on the face of Dr. Mortimer who, like all arcane enthusiasts, can imagine little to exist beyond their unique specialties. He did at once look up at Sir Henry though and nodded a reluctant consent.

"You are of course helping Sir Henry in the case of his wife's tragic disappearance. My sympathies, my dear Sir, are with you. I regret that in my enthusiasm I was so remiss as to have forgotten your troubles. We of the neighborhood have been deeply troubled by the mystery and both trust and pray that Lady Beryl shall soon be restored to you in good health. As for you, Dr. Watson, I should be most happy should you be able to slip away. Mr. Franklin is of little use due to his advanced age. Indeed, I believe that he only wished to be part of the quest in hopes that some litigation might result. He has, as you know, a passion for lawsuits that raise unique points of English law. I dare not hire local laborers for fear of stimulating an unhealthy curiosity regarding my intentions. The steep declivities of the land are of poor farming quality and the chasm is seen as a useless appendage to the fertile lands nearby. Only a few walls remain standing of the monastery, and were it not for an occasional visitor to a shop and a small museum on the high road, the land would be of little value. The present owner is a young man-about-town and resides in France. Upon my application for permission to dig upon the site, I received only a short note to be presented to the overseer. It said only that I might dig to China for all that he cared. My option money, he said, was welcome and he trusted that in due time a complete sale might be contemplated."

"He has no awareness of the possible value of your find

then?" asked Holmes.

"I tried to point that out to him, as I am a man of honor, but it was evidently a rather tenuous prospect from his point of view. He quite prefers ready cash as his expenses are great and his manner of living is reputed to be characterized by dissipation."

"His indolent attitude may not remain so for long should you find the barrow to be a treasure trove and begin to sell certain items. Mr. Franklin may have his litigation after all. But that is for the future. You have done all that you can for now and I assure you, Dr. Mortimer, that I will turn my attentions to the matter at my very first opportunity."

"Thank you, Mr. Holmes. I will bid you gentlemen goodbye, since my wife will have dinner prepared for me at home. No, I really cannot stay for dinner. I do beg you though to advise me at your earliest opportunity how we may proceed and if Doctor Watson, should you still be engaged for some time, might be able to slip away now and again to aid me in my explorations."

We accompanied Dr. Mortimer to the door and parted from him as he entered the bleak autumn night that had already enveloped the bronze colors of the setting sun upon the moor. He had fortunately brought a lantern with him to light his way home over the treacherous ground. He soon gathered his muffler about him and plunged into the windy darkness. A few last glimmers in the west were all that now remained of the autumn day. We three who remained then proceeded to the dining room where a sumptuous repast awaited us.

After dinner we took our port to the library and it was then that Holmes read us the letter that he intended to dispatch on the morrow if its contents met Sir Henry's approval. Dr. Mortimer's visit had, along with our walk, acted as a stimulant to the spirits of Sir Henry. That, combined with the sureness demonstrated by Holmes in his wording of the missive, gave the English Lord perhaps the first hope that he had been able to entertain since the abduction of Lady Beryl. The private letter stated that the contents of a safety deposit box in a vault at the bank in Exeter could be inspected by Rodger Baskerville's solicitors prior to the release of Lady Beryl. The sole key would pass to those solicitors, but the title to the box's contents and the opportunity to use the key or to remove the contents would only happen on condition that Lady Beryl co-sign the document of transfer at the bank on a date certain. This would force the man, who I will still refer to as Stapleton, to surrender Lady Beryl to us at that time. She would come in the company of his solicitors to sign and would then be placed in immediate protective custody by the police. The solicitors would then be admitted to the vault and the title to the contents of the box now perfected, they would be at liberty to withdraw the box and its contents. They would also be free to leave and to communicate with their client.

To my objection that Stapleton would naturally fear that his representatives would be arrested upon presenting themselves at the bank, Holmes assured me that the solicitors would be guilty of no crime. All communication with their client, Stapleton, would be privileged and the production of Lady Beryl at the proper time would argue for their good faith and ignorance of the fact that she had ever been detained against her will. Therefore, it could not be proven that they were accessories after the fact to a kidnapping. No blackmail had yet occurred, so there was no crime in simply possessing the papers under the conditions specified. The papers themselves, though initially stolen, have passed to Stapleton by long possession and he had as good a title as anyone to them. The signature of Lady Beryl as the former Beryl Stapleton became then, a mere matter of form based upon the community property laws of her native Costa Rica, and would arouse no suspicion at the bank, which would view the entire matter as a formal business transaction, perhaps a little unusual, but undertaken to please the depositor who would be Sir Henry acting for his wife. Sir Henry was to be on hand, to be sure that it was indeed his wife and not an imposter who will be presented to co-sign for the transfer of the documents.

"But Holmes!" I cried, when he had finished his reading of

the letter and presenting his explanations. "The guilty man will escape a second time!"

Holmes spoke solemnly. "We must bear in mind, Watson, our order of priorities. Lady Beryl is irreplaceable and her welfare is non-negotiable. We must first assure her safety at any cost. We will then bend all of our efforts to the problem at hand which, briefly stated, is that a dangerous man is in possession of papers that are compromising to well-placed individuals in American business and to the government of the United States. I have taken the liberty of having transcripts made of the papers in question by a local solicitor in Grimpen, who has acted for me in other matters. He should arrive shortly to do so and he will carry on his task under the watchful eye of the Scotland Yard appointed constable who as Lestrade promised us has been keeping guard over us. I expect both men to arrive presently. We will take no chances that the papers will leave the house. I expect that the task will take all night and we will dispatch this letter tomorrow afternoon to the place on High Tor mentioned in the letter. The letter will of course not be picked up by Stapleton himself, but he will receive it in due course, I am sure. We will not have the messenger traced as we will do nothing that might imperil Lady Beryl or antagonize Rodger Baskerville. The copies of the Murillo papers that we will possess will be of use to us later."

"But they will not be originals," I protested.

"That is irrelevant; their contents alone are their bona fides. The authors of the correspondence and the state documents will recognize their actions and see immediately the damage that might be done by their presentation in their original and authentic form. We may offer to aid them in their recovery. This course of action will naturally make it imperative that we visit America, but that eventuality may be unavoidable," said Holmes.

"And Baron Maupertuis, what shall we do about pursuing him? Can we handle two such dangerous men as Maupertuis and the man we knew as Stapleton at the same time?" I expostulated. "I must protest, Holmes, your health has not been up to the mark lately."

"Well, we have no other choice, do we? Events have moved swiftly in upon us, but we shall not be alone. We have Mycroft and Scotland Yard to aid us and I shall be surprised if we do not find a way to flush our adversaries out of their lairs," Holmes re-assured me.

A short time later the representative of the Grimpen legal firm arrived with the Constable. The constable greeted Holmes with awe to be in the presence of the great master of the art of criminal detection. Holmes' reputation had grown during the 1890's as more of my accounts of his exploits appeared in the Strand Magazine. Offers of new cases streamed in from all quarters. This fact had made the years 1895 and 1896 the busiest years of his career. There were also individuals who had scanned the back numbers of periodicals in order to read again the dispatches from the east and from Africa published under the name of Sigerson, who had become a cause célèbre in his own right.

The accounts had aroused some interest at the time, particularly in official quarters. It was seldom that such accurate reports from the frontier, written by a European of obvious insight and erudition, had appeared before the public. They were written with an insight and an awareness of the equivocal nature of the European attempt to spread its own civilization that was unique. The writer managed to convey that peoples and nations that we had been taught to hold in contempt had civilizations far older than our own and that their views of the human condition did not mirror ours. I had heard at the time in certain clubs comments like, "This man Sigerson is an upstart," and, "The opinions of this bounder should not be published in England."

Holmes of course had escaped such opprobrium in Norway, which had its own experience of being a semi-colonial possession of Denmark. For any people to find its own voice and to celebrate its own culture is a general contribution to mankind as a whole. There is nothing more boring than a successful domination of others. I have often thought it strange that the fall of the Roman Empire is treated as a decline from a period of a higher culture. Surely there was something of a new vigor in the Barbarian tribes that explained the conquest of Rome as the legions expended the last of their strength seeking to extend the frontiers of the empire. It was to the mixture of races and the spread of Christianity among them that we owe all later progress. Had Rome survived and its own monolithic and self-indulgent domestic cruelty continued would we not today still be celebrating gladiators and the bleak spectacle of death as entertainment and would not crosses with mounted slaves still adorn the land? There are times when chaos restores a voice to the silent and when to tear down a temple is the only way forward.

This message of support for insurrection ran through all of the dispatches of Sigerson. His writings were discussed at many a dinner table in Pall Mall. Some society hostesses of the time professed to find the writer romantic and clothed him in the guise of a new George Gordon Lord Byron who once set out to free the Greeks from Turkish rule. Had Holmes during that time had a return address, he might have received many a scented handkerchief as a token of esteem. I found this all highly amusing and would occasionally chafe Holmes a bit by reminding him of his anonymous feminine followers. He would look up at me over his books and say, "You are developing a certain pawky humor, Watson, against which I must learn to guard myself."

How I longed for that humor now as I watched Holmes ascend the great stairway with Sir Henry and the two other gentlemen to retrieve the Murillo papers. They would all hopefully be copied by morning and we should have two witnesses that they were accurate and authentic as to their contents. I could only imagine whether their use in the future would lead to the capture of Stapleton and whether we might prevent scandal in the highest quarters of American finance. I was troubled by the strain that all of this might be to Holmes' still precarious health. I had intended the coming year of 1898 to be a time of rest for him. I had hoped that he would abandon all strenuous activity and feared that the progress of recent months would soon be dissipated. I feared most that the excitement of the two cases at hand would bring on a period of collapse.

Though he was descended from stout Yorkshire landowners, Holmes also had the delicate blood of the French aristocrats in his lineage. The same hands that rejoiced in boxing and fencing played the violin. The long nervous fingers could as well hold a test-tube steady and arrange specimens on a slide in the laboratory. It was this dual nature that created a constant warfare within him and I often wondered if I as his resident physician had not been present through the years, if Holmes would not long since have burned himself out and perished through the sheer abundance of his expenditure of energy.

There are elements that grow more brightly just before they fail entirely, as the American, Thomas Edison, discovered when inventing his electric source of illumination. I had heard from Holmes that his travels, particularly in Africa, had brought him to just such a pass and it was due to this fact that he had devoted at least a year of recovery in France, engaged in quiet study, before returning home to England in early 1894. In his brief account to me at the time he had mentioned his various destinations during his long hiatus, but the account was somewhat inaccurate. His visit to Tibet had not been one of years, nor had he proceeded as far as Lhassa as he once claimed to me. I could only assume that the manuscript that I had been reading would account for the details of his journey and perhaps provide a motive for his distortions of the duration of the time that he had spent in any one place.

I returned now to that manuscript recording his travels as Sigerson. A long evening lay before me. We could do no more at the present. The wind had risen again with the night and a bitter rain rattled against the windows of the library as I read. Perkins had returned to build-up the fire and I sat in a cozy nook surrounded by the great shelves of leather-clad volumes with a snifter of brandy within easy reach and opened the manuscript to where I had left Holmes and Colonel Sebastian Moran in Tehran, Persia and began to read.

From the Journal of Sherlock Holmes

October 12, 1891
Tehran, Persia

We have definitively settled in for the winter. We have rented a delightful villa located above the town and I am now for the first time able to send dispatches of my travels home to England. I shall now have time to reflect upon what I have learned thus far in my journey and best of all I am now capable of wiring and getting word out to Mycroft and to hear how things are with Watson. I have been often troubled by the pain that I must be causing him by my supposed death, but I am still in hope that upon reflection he has been able to see that any solution of the mystery posed at Reichenbach must have had a different outcome from any spontaneous conclusions that he may have reached on that first day. I hope also to hear from Mycroft if Professor Moriarty has kept his bargain with me and thus far abstaining from any criminal activities until my return. My travels have given me a sense of the sheer size and variety represented by the Asian landmass and for the first time I can see how the doctrines of the message of Mohammed could have spread here with such rapidity.

To read the Koran is to be initiated into an oral poetry and a literature as well as to a religion. There is simplicity in the essential message that must grasp the mind at once. There is but one God, so immediately the complexities inherent in the doctrine of the Trinity disappear. There is only one final and supreme prophet and all other men and women are only believers, so the distinction between clergy and the lay-Christian disappears. There are no sacraments, so the questions that touch on the operative nature of Divine Grace disappear. There is no sacrifice, so that the nature of atonement for sin and the reason for and the efficacy of the Passion and Death of the Savior and its relation to original sin vanish.

Almost 2000 years of theological Christian disputation are made irrelevant to a God who remains an ultimate mystery, as in the belief structure of Islam. The vast distance between this vision of God and mankind is bridged only by His compassion and by the fullness of the final revelation to Mohammed. The endless complexities required by the Jewish law of Torah are reduced to the Pillars of Islam so that the endless complexity of the Talmudic laws is avoided. Yet such is the complexity in the heart of man that even this simple message has been convoluted over mere questions of succession and Sunni and Shiite still divide the world through the accident of events that have occurred since the death of the Prophet who believed that God had given him the means to unite all of mankind in a simple and common and final belief system. The circular processions at Mecca, which I hope to visit, where the pilgrims are stripped of every measure of divergence manifest the essential commonality of the human race.

The trappings of religion show an infusion of distinctly human touches. The mind of man generates both language and religious divergence I fear with equal avidity. History shows not unification over time but rather an ongoing diffusion of all religious beliefs. There is a principle of both fragmentation and yet perhaps some degree of evolution in all things and perhaps this is appropriate, for do not the great land masses of the continents flow over the great molten sea of lava that lies beneath. Humanity is never finally grounded because the earth itself shifts beneath our feet. Each human meaning structure is impregnated with our own presuppositions even in the moment of its first formulation. What shall human creation finally achieve? Shall we someday break through the great categories of all human thought and escape forever the punitive and dubious nature of things that has haunted the drama of human life within recorded time? Are we still in the primal beginnings so that a true human nature and nobility still lies in visions that are now inconceivable because they are blocked by our own premature conclusions? Must the mind escape first from its own duality and fragment into colonies and multiple identities even within the one individual in order to really understand the purposes and conditions of life and of death? Perhaps the visions of those that we call mad manifest more accurate disclosures of the true nature of reality than our vaunted reason with its linear chains of causality.

Already mathematics is reaching beyond experience into numerical concepts that are as far from simple counting in real numbers as the stars are from the earth. Perhaps only this non-linear mathematics will explain the courses of the stars in the infinity of the heavens. If by the gods we mean only another link in the vast string of causes then we must ask always what lies beyond God. To assume that there are a series of Gods is never to reach God at all. But on the other hand to simply call God what lies at the remote end of the string of causality as the first mover is to so attenuate His acts as to make our own existence trivial. A God so removed could never relate to us nor could we relate to Him. Shall we than place God's existence primarily within the human heart? But if we bring God too close to us, then what is to prevent Him from becoming only one more reflection of our own instincts, one more poor concept in the great sea of our conceptions, or worse an occasional nervous storm of religious enthusiasm.

Where then shall we locate God? For Islam there is the Glorious Koran that is said to exist in the very mind of God and is only transcribed by the prophet. This solves of course the problem of bridging into that mind of God, but shall we assume that anything as crude as mere human verbiage exists in the celestial halls? Does God speak with throat and vocal chords or is God to be found in pure ideas alone where neither metaphor nor allegory can ever reach? But can any idea exist without verbal or numerical symbols to record it? Surely, heaven has no bookcases nor has it even one great pedestal to hold this example of jeweled and transcendent discourse, the Koran. Can anything so physical traverse the bounds of eternity? Does the mind of God even think in words and sentences?

The bridge between an infinite and unknowable God the

nature of which can only be known by analogy is to some extent bridged by Christianity and the Incarnation of Jesus Christ. Christianity holds that Jesus Christ is the very embodiment of the creative will of God and that all things were made both for Him and through Him. The humanity of Christ is but the lens through which we grasp unseen ages when the Son lodged in the very bosom of the Father in a primordial embrace before the dawn of time. To believe otherwise is to fall into heresy and to believe that Jesus was once only a man but was later exalted to his present ascendant position, as a Divine favor due to the life and death of Jesus embodying the characteristics of the Suffering Servant of Isaiah.

It took some time for the Church to address and formulate a clear awareness as to how Jesus could be both the pre-existent Son of God and simultaneously the man, Jesus the prophetic teacher and healer from Nazareth. In Christianity salvation is a bridge made from man to God, which dispenses Divine Life through Grace. The death and Resurrection of Jesus opens again the free flow of intercourse between fallen mankind and God. This in turn opens a radical new possibility for what would otherwise be the fate of each individual human being, a chance to dwell intimately with God as an heir of heaven through the mediating action provided by Jesus who is both Son of God and the quintessential Son of Man. So radical is this claim that it even led over time to the triumph of an obscure Jewish sect over the might of Rome itself and the marriage between the remnant of the Roman Empire and the Catholic faith under the successor to Peter, the head of the Apostles, with the Bishop of Rome as Sovereign Pontiff.

The three great Abrahamic faiths of Judaism, Islam, and Christianity have, since the death of Mohammed, lived in an uneasy state of co-existence, with each claiming to be the exclusive channel and modality of God's relations with the human race. Shall I find, I wonder, an answer to questions such as these here in modern Persia, which is all that remains of the glory of Babylon? Is an answer reachable by means of mere human thought at all?

Perhaps religions simply grasp us as madness does and suddenly one awakes to find that he has been long committed to one particular asylum or another. It then becomes impossible to return to that time when one was not mad. We become our madness finally. The mind once stretched around the concept of God loses its primal elasticity. It shall never again be lean and tight and capable of taking in data with no preconceived categories.

Thereafter we cannot follow Descartes back to the simple and unfettered ideas, for there never were any such ideas. All ideas are already complex and mixed into a string of prior mental relationships. There is no such thing as the *tabula rasa* of the philosopher John Locke. The mind sees in clumps and forms before it can be said to see at all. Otherwise all would be mere sensation, sets of uncoordinated nerve impulses, and we would be little more than reflexive creatures, mere mollusks, or echinoderms. To conceive ideas is already to reason from them and in no time an entire web is formed and somewhere in the center of that web there is the need of a God. We feel this need before any discipline of a particular religion or community as we first conceive of ourselves, as part of yet separate from the rest of things. The individual seldom has the luxury though of reaching to unfettered contact with the actual God, because the community soon saturates us with the historical conceptions attendant upon a particular faith. Few can leave all behind of this and enter the desert, there to strip away the detritus and to seek a direct vision of God. For most of the human race these communal ideas become all they will ever know of God and religion then becomes a mere social attunement to a set of strictures and structures that form the doctrines and dogmas mandated by the divine reality. This in turn creates a religious myopia that denies the very nature of God in that God is now dwarfed to the measure of our conceptions. An example is the fate of the Torah after the advent of Christianity. After Christ the Torah no longer leads to God, but becomes an end in itself. Meanwhile in Christianity the cross often became a deification of suffering rather than an act of love extended to us from a Divine Person, a member of an inseparable Trinity.

For the Jews of the exile what mattered most was that land and the songs of God were irrevocably linked. How could they sing the songs of God in a foreign land? God could only be God in Israel and among His own people. If they were not chosen but abandoned to exile, then the Jewish people as Jewish could not even claim to exist. For this reason they hung up their lyres. Only the end of captivity brought a return to Jerusalem; and with that return God Himself showed a hitherto unimaginable concern and mercy for God cared for Israel and so was recognized as God. In this manner we see that the Jewish conception of God is almost maternal and is rooted in our deepest need for primal survival and for community. To fall from this special concern was, for the Jewish mind, to face obliteration.

The legend of the Wandering Jew is really about the need of the abandoned ones to find God once again. But surely, if God does not first look for us, then He shall never be found. God must come to us; he cannot be excavated out of creation, nor simply posited as the cause of all causes as the cold and heartless philosophers conceived of God. Either God is among us and within us or there is no God at all. God must be for us or all will stand against us, alien, harsh, and worst of all indifferent to our fate. No stoic pride may stand against the harshness of a sentence like, "Depart from me, you evil doers." To depart from God is to enter the whirlwind of chaos and ultimate emptiness. This would truly be what we mean by hell. Yet we are by definition evil-doers. To be left then in ourselves is already to know hell. We hang from the thread of the mercy of God over an abyss of terminal isolation ... only the Saints seem ever have known the full extent of the anguish that this realization can engender within us and simultaneously the hope that it also enkindles within us for salvation.

October 14, 1891
Tehran, Persia

I have written and dispatched the first of my papers as the Norwegian explorer, Sigerson. I have also received word from Mycroft by paying a visit to the British consulate. He has agreed to forward my submissions to the Times. My first submission described our journey through the Kashmir region and I developed what I believe to be the interesting thesis that there are political fault lines between various places that are analogous to the earth's tectonic plates. Just as stresses build along fault lines due to pressures exerted, which must finally result in either heat or in the kinetic energy of an earthquake, so do political stresses build when divergent cultures or peoples meet along border regions.

This phenomenon makes wars predictable but also renders them preventable. International trade acts as an energy exchange that is preferable to war. The parties agree to form a trade-bond which creates avenues for cultural exchange as well. Each nation or region may then develop an incentive to avoid war in order to preserve the benefits of orderly trade between nations. Wars are after all disruptive and expensive. Even in the case of actual conquest the resulting destruction and disturbance of the life-patterns and organic structures of daily human domestic economies are such that wars seldom pay a significant benefit even to the victor when balanced against the costs incurred in their prosecution.

In order to avoid wars however it is essential that some form of energy exchange shall take place in order to avoid conditions where nations prosper to such a degree that they become a military threat to their neighboring regions. This observation is particularly relevant in the case of Asia because of the sheer physical proximity of various ethnic and religious groups. Isolation in Asia is impossible. The historical flow of peoples over this great land-mass has never ceased, nor is it likely that population migrations and the domination of local powers will ever cease. In the absence of a great central power around which smaller sultanates or dynasties can orbit a general condition of equality would need to prevail based upon shared principles such as is the case in America; although even there a great civil war proved what can happen when divergent regions cease to see a mutual advantage in the exchange of goods where neither side predominates and thus poses a threat to the other.

In contrast to this principle of equal exchange is that of hegemony and isolationism. The effort of the Chinese to build a great wall in China to keep the barbarians out was finally a failure because it sought to make a present set of relations in trade and even in culture a permanent physical fixture. Even isolationist Japan, since the barrier of trade with America and later with the rest of the world at large have fallen, has not managed to sustain its isolationist mentality and to sustain an internal culture that could withstand all incursions from the outer world. Particularly in the present day the growth of industrial production and the ready supply of raw materials from colonial possessions have made the supply of goods such that they threaten to outstrip demand. This creates a constant search for new markets in order to prevent deflation.

This poses a great threat that war may someday break out between the dominant colonial powers. All wars begin as trade wars. The mere military occupation of large areas of land ceases to have value when compared to the benefits of peace and of open trading policies. Military conquest's only result is to burden the conqueror with a larger area to police. This is why certain dry and barren regions such as Afghanistan are seldom successfully conquered; it is simply not worth the effort, particularly when stern resistance is encountered. Sheer land mass is of less value than human development that can only occur where people are not concerned with daily survival. The real prizes are the rich river valleys or mineral-rich lands. Lands that will not produce are not coveted. People who will later purchase manufactured goods from a centralizing power are best left free to do so rather than being physically absorbed into a dominant empire. Conquest then is finally a matter more of an archaic to control rather than of a real need to assimilate and subdue, which is always an ill-advised policy. The costs of maintaining domineering governments will always be prohibitive because they are not strictly, speaking, involved in the actual production and consumption of goods and services. This is why Russia will always tend to be a bloated and backward nation filled with sorrowing and discontented subjects.

For this reason the laws that are the natural result of actual trade practices and that simplify and guide them will always be superior to any imposed code or command-structure that comes from above. Centralization cannot adapt swiftly enough to changing markets and emerging technical resources. For this reason it is the destiny of most empires to be finally tested in Asia and found to be wanting. Asia is the great steaming population caldron of the world. Its peoples mingle and flow freely over this great land-mass. How foolish it is then for England to think that it may dominate such a large area from its own small island. It is also unlikely that the great unwieldy possessions of the Russian Czar can long endure. When the age of Empires has finally passed perhaps even India and China as we know them will be no more. If Tibet for instance is not free to act as a lubricating disk between China and India then will not these regions finally know a great destructive war? Two such great centers of mass and of peoples must finally clash if there are not other sovereign regions between them to insulate and to prevent actual physical contact. These areas must not though be so weak as to invite invasion. The vast forbidding mountains of Tibet make it the perfect wall between the great cultures of China and of India. May it always be free!

But does not Europe have similar zones of contention? What of those regions that separate the Germans from the French? There are, for instance, the Belgian Ardennes Forest and the Alsace and Lorraine regions. I fear that they will someday be the grounds for the most horrible conflicts because they are not mountainous and armies can sweep over them at will. Or take the case of Africa and the Levant. Will not the bordering Sinai region from whence the Ten Commandments of God was bestowed upon savage mankind always be contentious? Will the regions of Egypt,

Ethiopia, and the Sudan ever know lasting peace? Take the case of the region of the Sudan. Will not its very centrality be its weakness as it can always be invaded from all sides at once? Thus, as I said in my article, wars will come not only from the dark heart of man but by the sheer determinism of regions built into geographical features of the land itself. Only an international legal-order of some sort, based upon mutual trade advantages, will create a lasting peace among nations.

I allowed Colonel Moran to read my first papers in which I elaborated this thesis. He looked both interested and amused. Upon my inquiring of him his opinion he merely stated, "It will always come down to superior arms, Mr. Holmes, and to logistical support-capability. The task of war is to destroy the will to fight on in one's opponent and then to extract concessions in the negotiations for peace. Most nations will fight far longer than they should. They allow outrage to exceed good sense. War is mere diplomacy with material force added. It always has in mind the negotiation for terms of peace. A nation that is well enough armed can dictate the terms of settlement without even using the means for warfare at its disposal. Fear and mistrust are the primal instincts of mankind."

At my urging to develop his thoughts further he went on to say, "A dominant nation is at the same time itself impervious to attack. This logic explains why there will always be a race to obtain more arms in order to secure a strategic advantage over other nations. The margin of supremacy must however be quite large to avoid challenge. Yet as it builds its arsenal, fear among its rivals may finally cause a weaker nation to attack rather than to continue a race that is draining its economy and destroying the quality of life of its people. This test of arms may also breed strange alliances between former foes. If they wish to attack this course should be embraced early, since as the years pass an inevitable war will only become more costly for all parties and the price of defeat will therefore be greater and the war will last longer in consequence. A war to be waged among the several great powers of today would be unimaginably costly."

"The logic of war is thus to fight early, rather than to fight late. There is no greater danger to nations then a long term of peace for then, should war come finally, the damage will be all the greater and no nation will emerge a true victor. This is why the smaller regions of the world and the more primitive enclaves such as Afghanistan have never known peace. They know that they cannot afford long periods of material growth and saving. They know that they cannot long protect their surplus of goods. They live then merely for the day and have no illusions of growth and prosperity. They leave these illusions to the great Empires. Only empires and the citizens of them have ever known conditions of security and plenty, which are the fruits of the peaceful periods between great conflicts. Only they have ever known peace at all, for they impose it upon the weaker peoples of the earth, but always upon terms that favor the Empires. For this reason, Mr. Holmes, a general and equal prosperity among all peoples of the earth will never be possible. The best that we can hope for is that regional equity may exist in small tribal areas. I have myself long hoped someday to own a plantation in the islands of Indonesia or Malaya. I believe that a small feudal-holding is the best hope for peace. I shall so administer matters on my estate that my tenants will be happy. I will take the best of native culture but supplement it with a quality of health-care that may prevent diseases such as Malaria and Leprosy and Plague. I believe that a healthy primitivism is closer to human nature than our hopes for a universal literacy and technical progress. Why, we have not achieved these goals even in England! The progress of industry is not advisable for all peoples. The world will always require its innocents and its savages."

I remarked that it was strange that if he desired a return to innocence, that he had spent his life in card rooms and in furthering the schemes of Professor Moriarty. He looked at me fiercely as he replied, "I only gambled among men who could afford to lose to me. It is true I have put my heart and sinew into games that depend upon sheer will more than the face value of the cards, for more in life is achieved by threat than by performance. I have long known you see that only a fearless willingness to lose everything will allow one to prevail at the games that I have played. It is fear that makes a man lose and his opponents will scent it at the gaming table. I have known the danger of imminent death on the field of battle. What then was the mere loss of money to me? I was unafraid and being so, I always have that edge. The cards themselves are finally distributed fairly equally if one plays long enough. This means that the winner is finally the one who plays best and he will always be the man who has no fear."

"But I you ask again, what of your service to Professor Moriarty?" I inquired. "Surely a man of your confidence and mettle did not need to partner up with a mere scholar!"

The Colonel smiled. "Perhaps if I tell you a story, you will understand. The Professor and I first met in the great casino at Monte Carlo. He saw that I was winning against stronger hands. This intrigued him. The Professor never played against others. For him it was always roulette with its static odds. He was the scientist and I was the artist. It was the Professor who would evolve a scheme, but I would execute it. His was the music but he left the playing role to me. You smile, Mr. Holmes, but there is an elegance to crime."

"It is not merely the task of not being apprehended, but in choosing one's victim. We of course chose carefully. We preyed not upon the weak but upon the strong, not upon the poor, but upon the wealthy. We assumed at the outset that our gain must be worth the loss of another and perhaps inadvertently serve a greater social good. We tried when possible to leave our victims bled but still standing and able to go on. The imposition of death was for us an inconvenience and we found ways in most cases to avoid it but when this was not so we accepted it as a cost of doing business. Do you think that death is not a part of life? Most businesses grind the life out of their employees in a far more heartless manner than the Professor and I ever displayed. We were the lions that follow the herd, but unlike lions we did not cull the weak, but took instead the great ones. Why, because they were strangers to the role of victim and as a result had not learned to hide in the herd. They did not know how to elude, how to be humble, how to endure defeat. No, they would go up against us, and in their pride they were inevitably defeated. In addition we were able to coordinate our own group of criminals who would otherwise have preyed upon people less able to bear the loss. We directed them upwards. Crime, my dear Mr. Sherlock Holmes, is a constant, and to that fact you owe your own livelihood. We took one of the great constants of human nature and turned it to our own use. Was this evil? Very well, but we did not create the world. If there is a moral order we have yet to glimpse it. Are there not great statesmen with the blood of thousands upon them yet they fancy themselves to be Christian gentlemen? Are not these the greatest criminals of all? Even the great Abraham Lincoln in his determination to save the American Union cost the nation a vast civil war. Had he not paid the ultimate price in his own death would he still be revered as a hero?"

"Slavery and the cotton-harvest that required it were already a dying industrial mode by the 1860's. British cotton goods from India would soon have made African slavery in America obsolete with the falling price of textiles. Look at the condition of the defeated southern states today! The former slaves are still there but what are they to do to earn a living. A dying economy in the south would have caused a successful confederacy to seek reunion with the prosperous cities of the north. The great growth in the lands west of the Mississippi would soon dwarf the economies of the eastern states anyway. America has always existed on the very threshold of ruin because of its sheer profligacy! Already the sun of future economic growth has moved westward to Japan and to China. The southern agrarian states that naively thought of forming a confederacy against the superior population of the north existed in shadow and twilight, but rather than gracefully surrendering its pretensions to aristocracy, it made the colossal error of secession. It fought not for the future but to preserve its past! Wars are so often fought over decayed ideas and outworn fashions, even religious ones. Man is never more absurd then when he pretends to a status of nobility that he does not possess. The Professor and I, we merely looked about us and found that even in England in the 19th century that jungle-law prevailed.

We adapted to this fact and we prospered, and in doing so I might add, we even provided a reputation for the eccentric recluse and former drug addict, Mr. Sherlock Holmes of Baker Street and his redoubtable companion and guardian, Dr. Watson."

"Watson is my Guardian!" I exclaimed in indignation.

"Why of course, Mr. Holmes, did you think that your indiscretions were unknown to us? Take your cocaine habit as an example. This alone told us that you craved excitement before all else. We led you for years to cases that provided excitement while we pursued mundane targets that were far more remunerative. You could not be bothered by them, because they had to point of interest for the scientific investigator that you fancied yourself to be. You in fact only caught up with us when we were ready that you should do so. We each had enough money by then to retire in comfort, but our line of business does not lend itself to easy terms of retirement. We needed someone to rid us of our adherents who might otherwise have exposed us. You provided that means. The Professor's slip betraying his entire organization into your hands was of course intentional."

"I was aware of that," I said quietly. "You are correct Colonel, that I had my weaknesses and that you played into them, but they were displayed for you so that you would not go underground. The cases that you fed to me kept you visible through the years. It was the constant pull upon the line that let me know that my fish was still there. Could I have done as well as I did if I had to wait only for a mere chance crime to betray your presence? I furthered your career as well, the better to keep you before my eyes and I took what cases I could in the meantime to keep my steel bright and sharp. I knew that I could not defeat you, so I in turn bled you as best I could."

Colonel Moran smiled. "We are more alike than you are prepared to admit, Mr. Holmes. If we were criminals and parasites, were you not doubly so for preying upon us? Is your art-form of detection anything beyond a self-indulgent hobby? In spite of your successes have you turned the tide of history or are you not a mere relic of England during the complacent reign of Queen Victoria?

And what is Mycroft, your esteemed brother, but a lackey of British foreign policy?"

"Would you then have me serve France or Germany instead?" I protested.

"I would have you serve those who cannot serve themselves," Colonel Moran returned vehemently. "You were on the wrong side in that matter of Vermissa and the Scrowers Society when you went up against the Professor and me. Sir Douglas deserved death! How many miners have died in the coal mines which are located in one of the most attractive regions of America? The miners leave each day the green forests and fields to descend into the earth. They spend their lives as worse than slaves and cough their lives away with consumption and black-lung and all so that Douglas and men like him can grow richer. There are cases you should have left unsolved. May the day soon come when you leave aside your belief in a stable society and see the jungle that exists at your very door! You should seek solace not in religion or in the music of Sarasate but in action. If you had put in with us you would not have required a guardian to protect you from yourself and your precious ennui would have yielded to a sustained purpose for your life. Where are you now for all of your metaphysics? If you adapt to the world, you will know just how far good is attainable, and when it must be sacrificed as the price of survival. You will abandon those fixed ethical principles that have always bred chaos and unhappiness among men for the law of expediency, knowing that the paths of power do not keep fixed schedules or display drawing-room etiquette."

This and more we discussed that day, but I have transcribed the essence. It shows a fundamental difference between us and I can see clearly that without a transcendent base in God that his reasoning could be persuasive. Still, I must adhere to a higher hope for human life than this world may ever provide and I believe also in the sometimes superfluous beauty of art and of music, for man does not live by bread alone. Life must be more than mere survival, yet I must admit that survival is the occupation of the majority of mankind. Is the mere possession of sufficient time to debate religious truths and the nature of existence by philosophers the greatest of luxuries; or is it not rather the task that is most basic to being human: to turn about and ask something of our origins and not to be plunged always into the great issues of the current of affairs?

In all of my years in Baker Street I always felt as though I had created what is most rare in life, a place of stasis, a calm place amidst the storm. Out of that storm though and through the year's supply of clients with their mysteries and problems there would emerge opportunities to be of some use in this sorry world. These opportunities would arise as though they were treasures thrown up by great waves upon my beach. Whether passion had brought them there, or some great and insupportable loss had occurred, or a great crime had been committed, I always believed that a solution might be found. But then I would send them back into the storm and always there remained the question of why that storm even existed. Why was it, I would ask, that scarcity so plagued us: scarcity of time, scarcity of resources? Where might men discover that rarest of finds, the opposite of scarcity, the fullness and the security to stand back from creation, and to find a purpose, not a mere goal amidst of sea of goals, but a final purpose, one that would resolve and distil all human effort into one concentrated and irrevocable essence of eternal meaning? What is the high point of the Catholic Mass but simply that? The presentation of the host at the end of the Canon is that moment when the Priest says in effect: that here before us is that point of unity between God and man. The communion host is the very lens through which God sees us and where we in turn can glimpse our God! For just a moment, time stops. Man reaches up to God in praise and thanksgiving, and God reaches down to create out of many the great central unity of the Church. Sin and the great sea of disorders are calmed before this great sign to which the participants in the name of all the men and women of the earth cry amen, amen, amen!

Through the years I sought that very certitude, that moment of stasis, so that what reason might not conjure, faith might finally supply. Always, with Watson at my side, I was demanding this certitude in life. Was Watson my guardian as Colonel Moran implied? Was I so mad that I needed a guardian? It is after all the delicate orchid that needs the greatest care. It is the complex composition that is most difficult to play. To make demands upon the universe, to shake the stars and demand an answer, is that not the goal of all religions? Is not religion the ultimate guardian of the spirit of man, without which, we would wither and die? If the world does not come out to meet us we fall back into the abyss. The Gospels say that even the hairs upon our heads are numbered, that we in fact exist before God in His constant care and that we never exist beyond the radiance of God. We are assured as Christians that even a personal guardian chosen specifically out of the angelic orders is assigned to us so that we need never be alone to face our lives unaided. Compare this creed to that of the jungle concept of Hobbes' bleak war of all against all. For what end does this struggle for faith exist but to add a small margin of comfort to our brief and bitter days and our storm-tossed nights? Human life is simply unacceptable upon its own terms. Either we exist for God or we do not exist at all!

Later—This far do my reflections take me to date as I take up my residence here in this ancient Persian city from whence King Cyrus once ruled an empire. I exist here in a strange land, one that is far from London and far from the power of British rule. For the first time I am able to look back upon my own certitudes without the support provided by residing within Christendom. Religions are, to an extent, geographical phenomena. One drinks in one's faith as a legacy of mere existence in the particular soil provided by the tradition sustained means of nation and language. Religion is the legacy of the cultic and ritualistic roots of simply being human. Humans punctuate the primal experiences of life with image and enactment. In a sense then all religions partake of idolatry to the extent that man must form some concept of God if only to know how to worship at all. This then leads to the formulation of laws and doctrines, which tend over time to substitute an illusory certainty for the very substance of God as He is in Himself. There is a mindset that can come to prefer the idea over the reality, so that God becomes immanent in what was initially meant as a mere way to encounter Him. The end result of this is a book such as the Mishna portion of the Talmud which would be inhuman if not for the commentary provided by the Gemara and the experiences of the Hasidic rabbis, such as the Baal Shem Tov.

In order to test this geographic theory of the general origins of the religious impulse, I know now that I must go to Mecca. I must see if it is places that are holy or whether holiness lies in the heart, so that every real pilgrimage must be made within our own selves. I wonder if the Catholic Church is held as a sometime hostage to Italian politics. Far from uniting all the peoples of the earth into one Mystical Body of Christ, recent history indicates that the Church can no longer seem to hold onto even Italy within the ambit of its governance. The Pope exists as a prisoner of the Vatican while the Italians have, alas, preferred becoming a secular state to being the holy seat of God's Kingdom here on earth. The entire question of the development of republican sentiments, in Italy of all places, is surprising. Italy, by its sheer proximity to the center of Christendom, would presumably have all of its wants satisfied by being on the shortest track to heaven and to attaining a measure of justice upon this earth.

Perhaps temporal power is inconsistent with spiritual authority. I feel that I shall find little solace here in Tehran in any case, for here and soon in Mecca, there will be only the Prophet and the Koran and as to these my own beliefs are heresy and an affront to Allah. Yet I shall go to Mecca anyway in spite of the dangers posed and there depend upon this savage man and former enemy, Colonel Sebastian Moran, for my security. In order to survive in the Arabic regions we will soon traverse, I must depend upon his rough instincts and determination to survive at all costs. Whether Watson was my guardian I know not, but at least for now my life depends upon Colonel Sebastian Moran. How strange this may be, but his very antipathy towards me gives me reason to trust him because he refuses to hide his malice and scorn for all that I believe.

October 21, 1891
Tehran

I just have heard from Mycroft. He has been in contact throughout these months with Watson. The dear fellow still persists in his view that I died that day at the Reichenbach Falls and has written an account, a copy of which was forwarded to me here, entitled "The Final Problem." It is a most kind and touching valediction and I am almost inclined to oblige him by disappearing from the scene forever if only to be worthy of his words. I appreciated the final sentence that elevates me to the same status as Socrates. The intention of Watson to overestimate my small abilities apparently remains constant.

The story of my demise and that of Professor Moriarty has been of great use however. All attempts to trace me by the few members of the Moriarty organization who may be still at large have ceased and the various miscreants have gradually acclimatized to a world without the Professor. The Professor in turn has managed to establish himself under a pseudonym as a stable owner in Devonshire. The eremitic manner of his former life and the lack of any known pictures of him appear to have made it possible for him to purchase the stables and estate at Kings Pyland and to go about the nearby villages without fear of recognition.

My own enemies have celebrated my death by trying the temper of the steel of the many Scotland Yard Inspectors whom I have done my best to educate through the years in the art of scientific detection. They have done well and have apprehended many already. I do not know that I am glad to hear that my presence in London is superfluous and that the world can manage quite well without me, but there it is. The wounds of the world heal swiftly and even the most important men leave only a gap of short duration by their demise. History continues on its own bitter and irrevocable course though dynasties fall and new follies embrace the daily news. The great idealists will continue to invent new schemes for the amelioration of the human condition. The builders and contractors will erect monuments to growth and change. The military strategists will devise plans to blow them all up again. Young lovers will walk in Hyde Park and dream of undying love, while on a few park benches a few old couples will celebrate having come very close to achieving it. Children will laugh as their nannies escort them to the round-about and they will dream of stallions and riding to glory alongside King Arthur. A few tattered men will sleep on the grass to escape the gin-soaked dreams of the night before and a bobby on patrol will tap at their boots with his nightstick telling them to move along. The poor and derelict are always asked to move along, but they are never told where they are to move along. Is that all that life is, simply to move along?

Then surely I am doing well and the bobby would smile and say, "Be ye like that detective feller, Mr. Sheerlock Holmes. Why he has so moved along that 'ee isn't even 'ere anymore. He be out there in them Persian lands where them long haired cats come from and looken into the religions of the world for to quiet down his doubts and fears. Me, I be just happy with my place on the force. I'm respected for I represent the laws of England I do. I represent social stability. Sure every man may have 'is say and stand on a soap box, long 'as 'ee don't be disturbin of the peace. But I don't hold with none of this talk of revolution and them what throws little black bombs at folks. Anarchists they call them. Me and the missus have tried and raise our kids right and believin in the Church of England and our daughters is respectable and our sons knows how to do a day's work fer a day's pay. The queens on 'er thrown and say what you will about me I'm an Englishman and that makes me one on the elect and better than any Frog or Proosian you may care to name."

There it is; that is life ... and for most people these burning questions that haunt me so draw not a bit of interest and why? Because they are doing as the bobby says, they are just moving along. Life is a vast funeral cortege from birth to grave and for those who early on accept this view of things, perhaps some happiness is possible. They do not expect to change the course of events but yet hope not to be ground down too early by dying young. They flock into the vulgar music halls and laugh at the ribald antics as they did as children when it was all Punch and Judy shows. They will cry at cheap tragedy and laugh at a cheaper farce. They have withal, their own nobility though and from among these are peopled the Kingdom of Heaven. The Second Person of the Trinity descended from heaven so that they might have life and have it more abundantly. I try and believe this and to gaze into the faces of all people, even in this foreign land, and to see in them the potential for eternal life that is present in all men and women whatever their circumstances may be.

In some ways this practice is easier here than in London. There is still some remnant of the glory of Babylon here. The men go about with pride in their walk and even the women, so closely garmented, seem to manifest a dignity that they are worthy of their shrouds. Someone cares about their virginity. They are not mere offerings to the first drunken lout who will tell them what they want to hear. They are never without a male caretaker who in turn knows that the wives he takes must be his care. This leaves little room for the squalid extra-marital couplings so common in Christian nations. The fear of hell seldom curtails the lusts of men in any case, nor does the fear of the agony of birth restrain the passions of women. The great fetid channel of life continues to produce more people, and daily Thomas Malthus awaits his vindication in the slums of the great capitals of Europe. Can the inevitable vast dying-off of people and nations be avoided indefinitely?

Capital after all migrates wherever it must to support industrial development and from this development more products result, made by ever cheaper labor. The members of the industrial masses cannot afford to purchase what they have just made with their own labor. The result of this process is inevitable deflation. The world economy constantly seeks new markets, when there would be one at home if a rule of just and equitable wages was to prevail. When new markets are not found, wars break out and those who might have been purchasers are killed so that the nation-states will not have to forfeit the colonies that supply the cheap raw materials and so that they will not need to forfeit the power that allows the rulers to consume and to invest. The result of all of this is what we term history and what is history but the story of rapine and conquest in age after age?

The men and women who can best testify to the inequities of history never live to write it. There are instead only the palaces and the castles of those who had the strength to rob their neighbors that remain to testify to the distant past. The only justification of titles of nobility is to stimulate the consciences of the powerful to protect the common people from still greater robbers. These are they who commission the great works of art and commerce. These robbers pass on to their progeny a sense of their own nobility. Finally a time comes when a few make some small return to the masses and these we call benefactors.

All men must tip their hats to someone. Even in America there is little of the equality dreamed of in their great Declaration of Independence. Indeed the slums of New York rival those of India. Great wealth only gives the scandal to the poverty that surrounds it. The greater wealth of America only makes its failures more inexcusable. A civil war was fought to free the slaves only to leave the Negroes destitute, vote-less, and without masters, scratching at whatever piece of land they may acquire as sharecroppers.

We in England of course never have claimed to honor equality. We are still a feudo-capital society, if I may coin a term, and the French, for all their talk of Liberty, Equality, and Fraternity are a nation of grubby shop- keepers and grasping peasants, while Russia has yet to even emerge from the Middle-ages. The mass of humanity lies below the surface of a decent life so that a tiny splinter as of an iceberg may rise, crystalline and blue, into the freshness of the surrounding air. The great tides of events sweep over mankind but leave the dominant minority largely untouched.

What to the surviving few are famines or the terrors of war? These noble ones exist at the nexus of the great inventions of money, trade, and the law (and what is the law but that which protects money and trade). The study of property is the study of estates, but the poor have no estate but what is spent daily merely to sustain life. They never have a foothold upon the shore but the currents and tides sweep them again out to sea where they can only tread water and try and keep their heads above the surface. Generations pass and they do not emerge from this condition and the life of the son is like his father's was before him.

The plight of the women is even worse. Their sole possession is their virtue and this they must bargain to obtain the support of life. Their lives are spent in pain and labor and how soon their beauty passes under the twin-threats of labor and of pain. Their children soon forget them in the storms of the struggle for survival. The vast chasm to a decent life is never bridged for so many of our fellow human beings. Christianity and Islam both counsel payment of alms and charity and pray for a day of judgment that has yet to come when all shall be equal before God. But turn from religion and ask the rulers to adopt a voluntary charity on the basis of reason and the rights of men and women and the odds of success in the venture become even less.

Which of us is willing, having once achieved a measure of security, to sacrifice his own good fortune, knowing that his own small margin of safety lies in his property? What possible difference will his drop of charity finally make among the vast ocean of need and want of the human race? If he gives all that he owns, he shall be naked before nightfall and the evening will still witness the same dark spectacle of those who arrived too late for his largess though it cost him everything. Yet Christ urges us to make that sacrifice.

Unless a society changes simultaneously there is no change at all. Equality must come from the laws and from the state that enforces it. The growth of a nation, if it is not to be based upon taking from another, must rise from a common belief and from coordinated actions. These will increase the national wealth. But alas no sooner does a nation grow in strength then it spends its surplus on arms to protect what it in turn has amassed. War soon follows and the surplus is gone. The society arises from the ruins and the great struggle must begin again. The futility of the individual life then is matched and exceeded only by that of the nations. One does well to have lived in one of those brief periods of peace between wars and the times of economic decline.

I have lived in just such a period in the history of England during most of the reign of Queen Victoria. A remittance has come to me from my London bank forwarded as a note to the British Embassy by Mycroft. It will allow me to continue my travels when I go to Mecca and beyond. The Sigerson Expedition may cut through this time and place of world history without taking time for labor or for trade even to support itself. What seems ordinary to me and in due course must appear miraculous to the people of the lands that I am passing through. They will remain among the monuments of a longer history. Yet they still have pride and their eyes show a deeper wisdom in the course of their ordinary daily duties that I have yet to plumb. They are as much a part of the land as the mountains and desert sands, while I as a privileged exile, alone feel the nakedness of the human condition as represented in their lives.

Ah well, it is time to abandon these reflections for now. The afternoon is waning. I believe I shall go out to the marketplace and also make a visit to the Grand Mosque. The British Ambassador has kindly provided several introductions to men of note here and I hope to discuss with them my observations and to be taken to view local sites of beauty and of historical significance.

Dr. Watson's Narrative Continues

The fire had burned low and Holmes and Sir Henry had both retired to sleep. I closed the manuscript that I had been reading. The winds still howled about the great hall and I seemed to hear in them the great ineluctable forces of time that Holmes had described in his journal. It was amazing to watch his great intellect wrestling with problems that have yet to find a solution. How natural it was that a man like Holmes would turn to these problems someday and to at least attempt a solution in words, if not their completion in action. These are after all the great eternal questions that beset us as human beings. It is not surprising that they resist definitive solution for is not our existence itself the greatest mystery?

It was necessary however for me now I reflected that I set such speculations aside; we certainly had sufficient immediate tasks at hand. I could not imagine how Holmes would manage to defeat his two greatest adversaries, one from the past and one from the present, Rodger Stapleton and Baron Maupertuis. Yet Holmes would soon be spreading the nets for his fish, of that I was certain. I turned to the oil lamp that burned at my side. My eyes were weary with reading. Sir Henry had yet to have electricity laid-on in the house the better to keep the great hall as a monument to the past. He had made few concessions to modernity and his own long habits of camping in the wilds of Canada had accustomed him to the lack of comforts. Though built of limestone and basalt to withstand the elements, the great mansion was often drafty. The great oak doors could not stop the ghostlike drafts and the flagstone passages seemed to be alive with the wraiths of the past. Outside the wind still blew with ferocity. It made a howling sound about the eves and I could imagine that the legendary Hound of the Baskervilles did in fact still exist and roamed the bleak moorlands by night. The household staff had already retired for the night. Only a dim light below the door of the study showed where the copyist and his guard were still awake and avidly engaged in their task.

I was about to ascend the great stairway to my room when suddenly Holmes was at my side. I am afraid that I started and almost dropped the lamp. "Steady, Watson," he said, grasping my arm firmly. "There is a light upon the moor."

"What can it be?" I cried.

"Come and you shall see for yourself. It is just visible from my room, but we will see it more clearly from one of the two towers."

He led me up the grand staircase to the second floor from whence we proceeded down the wide hall past our rooms to the end. There a second, narrower stairway led to a square tower that looked down upon the yew alley and the country beyond. The towers were primarily decorative in nature and had been added on at a later period to the main hall. They were from that neo-gothic period when estates like Fonthill had captured the English imagination. From the top, the view was magnificent on a clear day.

The winds of the storm had blown aside the usual fogs that rose from the boggy peat-lands of Grimpen that often shrouded the estate in mist and the night was for once extraordinarily clear. The boughs of the now barren trees tossed before us. We could see where the carriage drive ended on the high road that snaked its sinuous way over the moors, first to Grimpen, and then onwards towards Coombe Tracy where it widened and proceeded south to Tavistock. I could just see along the road the two lights of what must be a carriage. It was proceeding slowly and carefully for already the road from Grimpen was rutted and mired from the autumn rains. Clearly, the carriage must pass our drive before going on to the villas and cottages of our neighbors. We could intercept it as it passed, should we care to do so, or were we the destination of this excursion upon so wild a night?

"Come, Watson," said Holmes. "I think that this calls for great-coats and mufflers. We must go out to the road and discover, if we may, the motive for this midnight journey."

We were soon both prepared and descended the stairs. We were forced to awaken Perkins and to instruct him that he was to guard the front door carefully and to re-admit us upon our return. We then plunged into the windy night. I had seldom been abroad on so tempestuous a night. The wind from the sea met little resistance as it blew over the hills and seemed if anything to grow in strength as it was funneled through the deep valleys and clefts of the moors. The yew trees made a deep moaning sound as the wind blew through the sere and barren branches. One might imagine that Sir Charles, who had fallen as a victim to the hound in that very yew alley, was still crying for help as he ran from the spectral vision that had brought ruin through the ages to the male members of his family. I put off such fanciful visions however, for I needed all of my fortitude to resist the blast and to keep up with my friend who had already advanced some paces beyond me. We had so timed our departure as to intercept the carriage and to minimize any useless exposure to the effects of the storm. The carriage was soon before us and the horses pulled to a stop as the driver encountered the commanding figure of Holmes, who stood in its path with his arm raised.

The driver called out, "Is that you, Mr. Holmes? We hardly hoped to find you awake, let alone out on such a night as this. I have the Professor aboard. There has been some unpleasantness over at Kings Pyland. The head trainer, Addleton, has been killed and the great horse, the pride of our stables, Silverstar, has been abducted. But the Professor will explain all. Shall I follow you inside?"

We directed the driver at once to follow the round-about carriage path, while we in turn re-traced our steps up the yew alley which was shorter for us on foot as we were. We soon arrived at the front door. The steam from the nostrils of the horses showed the great effort that they had made and the speed of the journey. We directed the driver to take the carriage round to the stables and barns after depositing his burden. Perkins would see to the coachman's comfort and awaken the groom to bed-down the horses. We opened the door and helped Professor Moriarty to disembark. We each then grasped an arm and led him to the steps and to the great door where we were soon admitted by Perkins.

How silent the hall seemed after our exertions. Even its cold and drafty corridors seemed warm after the bitter chill of the night. The Professor said nothing at first but allowed us to minister to his immediate needs. We placed him in a chair by the fire and Holmes soon had a restorative brandy in his hands. I in turn checked his pulse which was somewhat threaded and placed a warm woven wool-quilt over his legs. It was some moments before he rallied and Holmes and I looked at each other with concern. Events were crowding in swiftly upon us. I insisted that Holmes also take off his wet tweed outer garments and that he help himself to a brandy. I feared for his health, which might suffer a relapse from just such an untimely exposure as this.

At last the Professor spoke. "He is gone, gone, Holmes; Silverstar, my hope for the third winning of the Wessex Cup, and Addleton poor fellow. He gave his life rather than allow his charge to be taken from him without a struggle. I have never known a more patient and devoted trainer. He knew the horse like no other and never asked anything of Silverstar that the horse would not accomplish. They were a pair and now both are gone."

He placed his head between his hands and was lost for a time in his despair. I had not thought the Professor would be able to show such emotion, but I was witnessing again a proof of Holmes' theory that the individual is but a replication of the family story and for the Moriarty family the ancestral tie to horses had been existent for generations and bred a resulting tenderness for the great beasts.

"This is indeed distressing Professor, please accept my most heartfelt commiseration at the loss of your trainer. I remember him of course from my prior visits to Kings Pyland. Let me assure you that his loss will not go unavenged. Pray give me the details and we will see if even now there is some action that we may take to restore him to you."

Professor Moriarty looked up at my companion and I could not but note the strangeness of the series of events that now brought this man to Holmes, not as an enemy, but as a client. He began, "The event must have occurred in the early evening. I was down to see Silverstar in the last hour before dusk. I could see that we would have a storm tonight and I wanted to ensure that all was well."

"You have had some prior trepidation then?" questioned Holmes.

"My dear Sir, there are always reasons to become nervous as a great race-day approaches. So much depends upon the most trivial matters. These great animals run on nervous energy and the will to win. The slightest thing may put them off their form. One must consider their feed, their surroundings, their usual company and routine. A storm is always a disturbing influence. But it was not that alone. I have felt a dark shadow hanging over us lately. It is not something that I can define. I have of course taken all precautions as to my person as you advised me to do. I am careful never to stand long at an open window. My food is brought from Coombe Tracey and always from a different grocer or butcher or at least at irregular intervals. The house is secure and I myself am always armed as is the constable who has been assigned to me. Yet I feared, despite these precautions, that some untoward event would transpire. The precautions that were lavished upon me gave me a false sense that all had been prepared for any invasion or attempt. In my concern for myself, I forgot however that which alone makes for my joy in life, my horses and particularly, for Silverstar. I imagined that the constant presence of the trainer, who was a stout and resourceful man and utterly devoted to Silverstar, would be adequate security. Alas, it was not. How shall he be recovered? How..."

Holmes reflected for some moments before answering. "There are of course two principle motives that may account for the loss of the horse. First, there is the question of Silverstar's value to a competitive stable. If he can be kept from running in the

Wessex Cup, it cannot but improve the odds for the other competitors. There is also the possibility of envy, that someone does not wish Silverstar to assume that place in history that will surely be his if he should win a third time. The second great possibility is that the horse has been taken as a surety to procure your silence in this Maupertuis affair. Since you have not been killed as has Crosby the Banker and Cardinal Tosca and since the Baron must be aware that you are guarded night and day, he may have struck at your one Achilles Heel. The horse then becomes the equivalent of your death. He knows that you will never speak out against him as long as he possesses the animal, but he must then know also that should anything happen to it, you will not rest until he is convicted. It is that factor, my dear Professor, which must be your comfort now."

"But how does one spirit a horse away, particularly on such a night. I assure you that Silverstar is not easily led."

"He has undoubtedly been sedated then. We can unfortunately do nothing tonight. The darkness and storm are prohibitive and our foes have already several hours head-start upon us. We shall wait then for the dawn in order to reconnoiter the land and see what it has to tell us. Until then, we can but wait and grasp what sleep we may. I must ask though how you discovered that the horse was missing."

"One of the grooms came running to the door of the manor house at about ten. I was just about to retire for the night. The lad said that Silverstar was not in his stall. I of course alerted the household at once and the entire staff made an immediate search of the area. We found the poor trainer within a quarter mile of the house. He was dead and his limbs had already begun to stiffen, indicating that he had met his end some hours before. Of Silverstar, there were no indications. I asked that the men continue to search, ordered my carriage, and came directly to you. It has taken me at least two hours to reach you on these wretched roads and with the darkness and the storm it was difficult even to stay upon the road at all. Several times we were off and in the mire. Can you not return with me at once?"

"It will not avail, Professor. These men have too long a start upon us and the early rains will have obliterated all tracks. But we shall go to Kings Pyland immediately in the morning I promise. I must also tell you, Professor, that I have another matter in hand here that is of some moment. The matter of Lady Beryl has reached a most critical stage and you must forgive me if I must divide my efforts. Watson, will you summon Perkins? I think that it will be as well if we lay our plans tonight and give all necessary instructions."

I summoned Perkins who came at once. He had yet to retire after admitting us again to the hall after our walk in the storm. He had even been so efficient as to prepare a small cold meal of thin sliced-beef and some scones in order to restore the Professor and to fortify Holmes and myself as well. He brought in the meal and a fine bottle of claret with three glasses.

"Ah Perkins, you anticipate our every need. Watson and I have been called forth I fear tomorrow and I must leave it to you to explain matters to Sir Henry. I have prepared a series of documents that you must deliver personally to High Tor tomorrow morning. I desire that they be placed in this hollow metal cylinder. You will place it in plain sight and in addition place this staff in an up-ended position in the ground alongside it to mark the place. You will then return to the hall immediately and not stay there to await the messenger. I desire that you be eminently visible throughout this operation, so please wear something of a bright color that will contrast with the dark greens and browns of the moor. Tell Sir Henry when he awakens that all is well in hand and that we shall return after noon. You will please instruct the grooms to ready the Professor's carriage for our departure at dawn. Watson and I will accompany Professor Moriarty to Kings Pyland. I think that will be all for now Perkins. Will you see that a room is prepared at once for the Professor next door to Watson? Excellent! Thank you Perkins."

Perkins bowed and left. We both looked at the Professor who seemed more confident now that he knew that we would begin the investigation by first daylight. We then proceeded to the meal that lay before us. I could witness its immediate restorative effect upon the Professor. Holmes was speaking. "We shall go upstairs after this welcome repast and see how the copying progresses so that we may be assured that all shall be in order for tomorrow. After that, I advise a few hours of sleep, for the morrow shall no doubt have many trying tasks for us all."

It was a stern gray dawn that broke over the moors the next morning. The storm had abated, but a grim chill embraced the land. Hoarfrost glistened upon the gorse and heather and we could see the steam from the nostrils of our horses as the carriage proceeded along our way to Kings Pyland. Holmes seemed remarkably rested in the few short hours since we had parted. He had left a note to Sir Henry explaining our absence and assuring him that all was in hand. We would soon have accurate copies of the documents that constituted collectively the Murillo papers. Our notice to Stapleton would be delivered to High Tor, as he had instructed us in his ransom note.

On the other matter we also had evidence that Baron Maupertuis had now made a choice of how to proceed with regard to the special knowledge of his activities that was possessed by the Professor. It was evident that the Baron was becoming more cautious. He was now purchasing silence from his former confederates not by summary death but by theft and blackmail. He would undoubtedly soon have to prove to the Professor that his horse was alive and well, lest the Professor in turn should become desperate and reveal all to the authorities in spite of any consequences to himself. This proof might take the form of a photograph. I doubted though that this ruse could be long continued for could the horse not then be destroyed shortly afterward? How would he keep the horse from the Professor and yet assure him of its eventual safe return? Was the Baron merely playing for time and if so what were his real intentions? Or had the horse been abducted by other parties whose sole intent was to prevent the running of Silverstar in the Wessex Cup? To these questions I had no answer and as Holmes always repeated, it is a capital mistake to theorize without data.

We were at precisely that point in these cases when all seemed to have reached a point of maximum disorder. The threads of the pattern were pulling apart and I could not imagine how Holmes could reassemble them and provide, not simply a single solution, but one that would encompass all of the many threats by which we were beset. He had certainly seldom encountered foes with such complete resources at their disposal. Baron Maupertuis, as the head of the Netherland Sumatra Company, was one of the richest men in Europe. He occupied the same role on the continent that J.P. Morgan occupied in New York. At his word speculative interest in securities might appear overnight or vanish just as quickly. The extent of his company's trade with the East Indies encompassed hardwoods, spices, and textiles. His great personal estates I was to learn included a villa in Trieste and a dacha above the Black Sea in Odessa. So great was his power that he had risked, within days of the collapse of his scheme, one worked out over several years with Professor Moriarty, an assassination of a Prince of the Church, Cardinal Tosca. Since then, Holmes had received word from the Pope himself requesting a quiet investigation of the circumstances of that death. Holmes had reassured him that he was even now doing so. Scotland Yard in turn had sent no less a man than Inspector Lestrade to contact the Italian authorities and return to London with any findings of significance.

All of this of course involved questions of the most delicate international relations and as such Mycroft Holmes was acting as a central point of coordination. The man's capacity to sift data from many sources and to weigh each incoming bit of information and to assign it its appropriate significance may have even exceeded that of Sherlock Holmes himself, as my companion would readily admit. Sherlock Holmes was rather like a great sight-hound whose function was to bring down the prey and who would run until his heart might burst once having spotted his quarry. Mycroft was a man more of the temper of Baron Maupertuis. He was an executive by nature whose mere gesture might set events in motion among his many subordinates in a far flung net that might encompass the earth, for the sun could not set upon lands untouched by the British Empire.

What then of our other foe, Rodger Baskerville, alias Stapleton? Holmes had once referred to him as a man worthy of our steel. He had occupied a station of trust and power exceeded only by Murillo and his Secretary of State, Lopez, in the former dictatorship of Costa Rica. The three men had used the front of respectability provided by Lady Beryl's father, one of the highest dignitaries of the former state, to hide activities that had stripped that green and lovely land of its resources. A corrupt government is the worst of all calamities to an industrious people. It had left Costa Rica burdened in debt and in foreign control by some of the largest companies in the United States. I had read at the time of the incursions upon its national sovereignty made by these entities and of the elaborate nature of the developments planned there and of how they would supposedly benefit the people of Costa Rica.

These promises of course were never kept. Instead the people had known terror, poverty, and the importation of foreign labor from as far as Italy in order to complete a railroad from Limon on the Caribbean Coast to the capital city of San Juan and then on to Puntarenas on the Pacific coast. The American company that built the railroad gained from the state thousands of acres of land adjoining the tracks including some of the most fertile and beautiful land in Costa Rica. The native people were in turn left with small farms on the steep hillsides which were often eroded by the tropical rains. The people then had no recourse but to work in the mines and soon streams of gold and silver were diverted to the north. The mines and the railroad worked together, as is so often the case in the American western states of America, to the detriment of local interests. A few highly-placed men reap the benefits of these extractions from the common wealth of the nation. These men become demi-gods in lands that claim to be democracies. By understanding the means whereby wealth may be obtained in this manner they use these very laws to further consolidate their control. Finally, when the game is almost up and the victim, the nation itself, is brought close to death, they abscond with their mobile wealth even as Stapleton had done. The people are of course left to pay the debts of the national loans incurred, while the benefits that had been promised to them by this foreign aid and investment evaporate like mists over the mountains. Such is the mechanism of international rapine that leaves the native population worse than slaves. But now it appeared that even Stapleton's ill-obtained funds had been so diminished that he was forced to turn again to his past and to seek these long abandoned papers that might only now be used to blackmail some of the conspirators, who had in the intervening years been long ensconced in an aura of respectability. These men might not care to have it noted how and by what means they had, in their youth, acquired their vast sums of money, of how they had betrayed the interests of even the people of America to obtain them.

The same techniques of domestic acquisition have worked only too well when applied abroad, where there was less oversight by an educated populace. The fragile democracy of Haiti, for instance, had been drained of resources by sugar-barons and the lands of Central America, that might have become one nation, had been fractured and fragmented and entrusted to local dictators like Don Juan Murillo, the better to enslave the Indians and the peasant farmers. When even that labor source proved to be insufficient, due to the losses from hunger and disease, then foreign conscript-laborers from China, the Philippines, or from southern Italy was brought in by the ship-load, only to further swell the ranks of the dead workers. Over 4000 men were lost in building the Greater San Juan Rail Company. The remainder stayed on after the railroad was built to serve as virtual slaves on the great banana plantations and the cattle ranches of the few wealthy men of the nation. Such was the story of Costa Rica under Don Juan Murillo, of infamous memory, known familiarly as the Tiger of San Pedro, which place was the small village where he was born.

Are some men simply born to be tyrants? Does some evil seed take root in their youth or some grim hunger for power possess them in the cradle from which they are never cured? Such is the mystery of evil. Even my reading of Holmes' journal of his travels during his long absence from England from 1891 to 1894 has not yet enabled me to resolve the many questions that it has raised in my mind? At times I found myself agreeing with Colonel Sebastian Moran's position, as recorded therein, that we live in a jungle still and the world that seems best described as in the words of the great poet Matthew Arnold, "So various, so beautiful, no new has really neither love, nor light, nor certitude, nor peace, nor help for pain, and we are here as on a darkening plain, swept with confused alarms of trouble and flight, where ignorant armies clash by night."

I put these grim reflections aside though as we arrived at the gates of the great horse-training establishment of Kings Pyland. Ahead of us stretched lovely pastures and a training track for the horses. Many well-maintained barns and stables lay along the margin of the road and a comfortable manor house lay in a small copse of trees. The drive, ringed with rhododendrons, ended at a circle before the house. We disembarked and were met by the head-groom who led us at once to the scene of the night's tragedy. The body of the slain trainer had been removed and the rain had indeed erased most of what might have been discovered by Holmes. He bent down anyway to examine an area at the side of the road, where the grass appeared to be trampled.

"There is but little here I am afraid," said Holmes as he straightened up. "There are however one or two indications. Clearly the horse was led this far by someone from the stables. There are a few areas of higher ground and the sandy soil has retained several footprints of a square-toed boot on an unusually small foot. The horse evidently followed on the lead well enough but there are several areas where he appeared to shy and to stamp about. When we arrive at where we now stand we see that the horse has made a virtual mire of the ground. Perhaps he sensed the death of his trainer nearby. The horse was undoubtedly hooded throughout the process to prevent him from bolting and so that he could be led up a gangway to a wagon. That wagon was evidently quite a heavy affair. You will see that the water has filled some unusually deep ruts in the road. The horse may then have been sedated to calm him down. I fear that we shall have no luck in attempting to follow the trail; for once the wagon reached the comparative hardness of the high-road all traces will be effaced. The horse is too well-known in the area to not draw note and therefore I expect that he was taken to Tavistock or north to Barnstaple. We will of course make inquiries. Now then, as to who led the horse out, we need only look for a man with this very square-toed boot and to discover who may have paid him to aid in the abduction of Silverstar."

"A small foot you say?" inquired the Professor. "That would be young Slattery. He is a feeder and groom and the horse knew him well. He had a light touch with the curry comb. He has not been here long, but he came well-recommended from the Brighton stables where he had worked since he was a lad. As it is, he cannot yet be over twenty."

"Not a cold blooded killer then. He probably did not know that he would be followed by the trainer who no doubt surprised the lad and his more brutal confederates leading to the death of the trainer at their hands while the groom attempted to quiet the horse, thus the trodden ground. Ah well, we may well return to the house and send out a description, but I doubt that we shall find the groom. He has no doubt fled with his money but...halloa, what is that?"

Holmes pointed. His unusually sharp eye had caught a glimpse of a blue coat at some little distance. We had soon traversed the ground and discovered what proved to be the body of the young groom. He had been stabbed repeatedly and had evidently attempted to run for help or to escape from his pursuers. His body had tumbled backwards as he made a great effort to climb a small stile over a fence after being stabbed for it was there that he had evidently breathed his last after making a final futile effort to regain his feet.. Several great wounds showed the ferocity of the attack made upon him. A quick search of his pockets revealed the ten-pound note that he must have received in payment for his service in the matter. It had not been retrieved by the malefactors.

Holmes shook his head. "You see Watson that money was not of any importance here to the thieves. The important thing was to get away quickly with the horse. These men knew that ready money was available that could make up for any losses that they might entail in obtaining the animal so long as they were successful in their mission. You see the pattern again. No witness is left to bridge the gap. I see the Baron's peculiar ruthlessness in this and I believe that we can dismiss from our minds the thought that some other parties are responsible for the theft of Silverstar. Since it is the Baron with whom we are dealing, we may also presume that he has made plans to preserve the horse if he may, if only for its value alone. He is not the man to throw away profits. The horse will not be killed unless the Baron is apprehended or unless we press him too closely. I believe that is all that we may discover here gentlemen. Let us return to the house. I trust, Professor that you have several telegraph forms on hand. I will send wires by one of your servants to Tavistock and to Barnstaple to alert the authorities there of the theft, though I regret that I cannot predict success there in our search. They can watch the trains and boats for the shipment of a horse matching Silverstar's description. For the present I believe that you should return with us to Baskerville Hall, as Sir Henry will require our presence and I should prefer that you remain under our protection in light of these recent events."

"You believe that an attempt may still be made upon me then?" asked the Professor.

"Well, we must not tempt fate. This very atrocity may be a guise to fool us into thinking that no worse event may be in the offing," said Holmes. "I believe that we must increase our defenses and precautions. It is time that we mount an offensive of our own. This man has had the first few sets all his way, but the game shall be ours in the end."

"You have outlined your campaign then?" I inquired with excitement.

"Say rather that my forces are gathering. We shall leave

tactics to the future, but a strategy begins to suggest itself," replied Holmes grimly. He would say no more.

We returned to the house where we were served a quick breakfast. Holmes had soon prepared the telegrams and dispatched them to the local telegraph office by a swift rider. We in turn took the carriage back to Baskerville Hall. We dismissed it at the front door after the Professor's sparse luggage had been unloaded. His valet carried this into the house with us where we were met by Sir Henry who had heard the sound of our approach and come out to meet us. He had already heard of course of the events of the night before. Perkins had given him the note from Holmes assuring him that all would be well and that our morning adventure would not prevent the delivery of the note to High Tor.

We all proceeded to the library where Holmes was able to relate quickly our discoveries at Kings Pyland and to assure Sir Henry that we would now devote our full attention to completing the measures necessary to return Lady Beryl safely to her home. He was reassured by this promise of ours, for the hours of waiting without word from her still weighed heavily upon him. Holmes began the outline of his strategy of dealing with the Baron, surprising me at this point by suggesting, what at the time seemed to me to be a pointless excursion from our course of action. He requested that we should read a selection from the Iliad by the Greek poet Homer, which he had marked and set upon the library table when we each should have a chance to review it that afternoon. He then proceeded with a disquisition which I will attempt, as well as memory serves, to re-create here.

We can never learn too much from the classics, Gentlemen. It is wisely said that all that is has occurred before. We walk in the paths of vanished ages; yet the heart of man remains always the same. There are but few gambits upon the chess-board of life. True originality is very rare and we may safely assume that it is not present here. Evil men lack imagination. Their techniques are as dreary and forlorn as their occupations. This was why the former works of Professor

Moriarty and Colonel Sebastian Moran were of such value to me as a student of crime. They alone seemed to me to be inventors. You will forgive me please, Professor, for referring to your old occupation. I thought though that I might divert you a bit and thereby distract us from our present woes this afternoon, since we have done all that we may for the moment to achieve our ends.

The capacity of the mind to re-direct itself from exhausting its resources before the time of action is much to be cultivated. I recommend to your ardent perusal on this topic the writings of the I-Ching. The Chinese are the very best of strategists and tacticians. It is said for instance that there is no disgrace in retreating before a superior force. The advantage of a temporarily superior position reverses at exactly the moment of the seeming victory of the opponent. His pride and the anticipation of the fruits of victory, before they are securely within his grasp, lead him to overstep his bounds. He fails therefore in the time where perseverance and fortitude are most necessary. This leads him to disgrace and defeat. The wise man waits for the forces that guide all things to change and by combining his energy with the currents that pervade of all things he wins though to victory at last. Good fortune is his end."

"So to apply this mode of thought to our present situation, we are dealing now with two particularly evil men. There is no admixture of good in them; therefore there is no artistry in their evil ways. Brutality leads to the most predictable of events. Its only advantage is speed and ruthlessness. It forgets to guard its rear. It depends always on the mode of attack, for its pride leads it never to expect defeat, particularly if the attack comes from a quarter that it regards as insignificant."

"Our enemies will assume that the force that we must mount against them will be of a high order to match what they imagine to be their great cunning and power. They will look as it were for a massing of our troops upon the plain from their ensconced citadel. We shall in turn gratify that expectation. We shall stage a great scene before them with much sound and fury. While they look down from their height upon our martial display on the plain below, we will be acting with the strategy of the tiny things that whisper about us."

"This is why I suggest that we each consult the Iliad and take note of ruse of the Trojan horse. We shall act even thus with our foes. We shall slip through their defenses by adjusting ourselves to our opponents rather than opposing them. We will lead them in the path to which they have already committed their energies; but we shall gradually re-direct it, just as a heavy falling object that cannot be stopped can at least be deflected. I ask that you recall, Gentlemen, your elementary physics and the study of vectors. I have often read with great interest that remarkable treatise by Professor Moriarty here entitled 'Dynamics of an Asteroid.' I have even tried on occasion to summarize its arguments and translate its insights into my own more common language. The manuscript of my travels to the east that Dr. Watson has been recently reading mentions a wager that existed, and one may say still exists, between the Professor and myself."

The Professor smiled and nodded and Holmes continued. "The results of that wager may be said to have created a new configuration of agreement between the forces of the Professor and my own forces. A new pattern resulted out of what might be described as a chaotic condition maintained between two polarities. Disorder tends to finally create its own order, but the process and steps to be followed in reaching that new configuration are not predictable. That is I think, Professor, a fair estimate of one aspect of your theory is it not?"

Professor Moriarty had carefully followed this disquisition. I could see that Holmes was attempting in his own kind way to lead the two stricken men before him to train their minds upon a distracting influence, the better to restore them to peace of mind. I could also see though that he was preparing us for what lay ahead for us all. He was instructing us in the theoretic base from which his actions would flow in thwarting and apprehending these most dangerous foes. Holmes had often said that my own accounts of his cases lacked that cool presentation of principles that might have made them more instructive to students in the art of detection. Of course, he assumed that my readers would be detectives or students of crime and not common readers seeking entertainment alone.

I knew that my readers, though curious to solve the puzzles presented, would also include many who read my tales precisely for the romance that Holmes so decried. I could not but note that a certain knight-errantry ran through my heroes for instance who often speak in my narratives with outrage and noble gallantry as they save the women that they love. The women in turn often display a fire and spirit not usually glimpsed in accounts of the fair sex in accounts written by other authors during this proper Victorian age. Though they may not have the passion of an Emma Bovary or that of the rather lurid females in the stories by Guy de Maupassant, I flatter myself that the women in my tales show a remarkable courage that often shows them to be the more dangerous sex. What my stories lack in scientific rigor they make up for in being a portrait of strong personalities. I trust that they shall not soon lose their appeal to future readers and that the personality of Holmes himself will remain burnished by the glamour of my pen.

Professor Moriarty continued the disquisition from where Holmes had left off. "It is true that Holmes and I had a wager and that he may in the time prior to its resolution have used against me the very strategy of deflection that he has just presented to you. He already knew of course of my devotion to mathematics. Mathematics after all is the purest of all languages. Numbers have the advantage of arbitrary assignment to any qualitative item. What are gears in an engine really but the embodiment of mathematical proportions set into motion? I fancy that inventors will continue to apply numbers to substances until man devises some sort of thinking machine that will deal with numbers alone. In any case we need not turn to the creations of mankind when nature itself is the greatest of machines."

"All that we see around us embodies the formula of some great underlying thought process. There is a harmony, what the ancients called the music of the spheres, in the heavens. Even one who might not hear sounds might imagine the concepts of harmony and of dissonance as the underlying nature of all physical events. Music is the relation of vibrations produced by various objects upon the air. The air in turn conducts these vibrations to the ear which carries the patterns to the brain of man. The brain in turn interprets these patterns and finds pleasure or emotive content in their apprehension. But what if one was deaf, would music cease to exist? No, for music in the last analysis is an idea, a relation of numbers just as mathematics is. Music is a language as is mathematics, the purer and the more perfect in that it possesses a unique syntax. It matches patterns that already exist in the brain, prior to the ear, as innate possibilities."

"There is something about music that is always a state of recognition. A gripping melody is such that one feels that one has already heard it before upon some occasion. From this idea Plato evolved his entire philosophy: that all knowledge is a remembrance of a pre-existing state of being when we knew all things. He could not otherwise account for the immediate recognition of truth and beauty when they are first presented before us. Surely he felt, these matters were already familiar to us. Our very certainty was the guarantee of this. We could not doubt truth or beauty, for they gripped us immediately upon presentation. The mind turns to them innately as a plant turns to the sun. Even as a youth I hungered for the perfect certitude that I could find only in mathematics and in music. Metaphysics in contrast seemed to me to fall afoul of words with their endless burden of connotations. Even the physical objects that surrounded me seemed to be less things of substance than they were embodiments of universal formulae for their construction and maintenance. It was this particular bent of my mind that Mr. Sherlock Holmes played upon and it was by this means that he won, in a fashion, our wager. I had of course read the writings of Pascal and of Spinoza for instance, but I had not found a bridge adequate to spring from their religious aspirations to the concreteness of actual doctrine. Holmes succeeded eventually in providing that bridge for me. But this is all better dealt with in

Holmes' own manuscript and I will leave its exposition there for your perusal in due time. As to my own theory of astral motion though, I remain the best witness, so I will lay it before you now."

He settled back in his chair. "I hope that as an old instructor I do not bore you gentlemen. It is no easy matter to speak of the principles that move us. Most men and women are like the asteroids; they are in motion but mindless as to their penultimate course. Few take the time necessary to probe those forces that create or influence their movement and direction. Socrates says that the unexamined life is not worth living and I trust that should Dr. Watson ever give an account of these days and events that his readers may rediscover that apothem and apply it to their own lives. My first insight then vis-a-vis asteroids was this: I could not trace their courses backwards in time to the point of impact or origin when they were first set into motion. I was faced only with an arbitrary period assigned by my birth and the observations made of them in the 19th century in order to begin to describe their motions. Time is for man the great and ineluctable reality for it moves in one direction only. The ultimate past forever escapes us, yet one may imagine a point of singularity and ultimate simplicity—oneness."

"As I made my observations of asteroids, I discovered that each gravitational body deflected the motion of the asteroid as it passed them. The motion of each then was not a straight line but rather a path of indeterminate nature based upon the multitude of forces acting upon the object at each instant plotted against time. I assumed of course that the measuring stick of time was a constant and unaffected by the speed or mass of the asteroids. As I sought to describe this process to myself an analogy of this process dawned upon me. It was as though each asteroid was engaged in a celestial dance upon a dance floor or field and was deflected in turn by all of the whirling partners about it. Its path or trajectory was predictable only by making certain unwarranted assumptions that belied the amount of data at hand for in each instant a new deflection occurred and I would have to begin my calculations all over again. From this I concluded that certainty was only possible by freezing time, which is to say no more than to imagine a condition of absolute stasis in the universe, which of course belies all observation, for observations themselves must occur over time and require duration. Time itself cannot be made to grind to a halt. This means that if I was to obtain any regularity in the motion of the asteroids, it became necessary to imagine how the movement of the asteroids might appear from the vantage point of an infinite distance. As distance increased the motions of deflection would seem to be cancelled out and a greater order would appear than what was obtainable from minute observations. I posited that if one might imagine an absolute perspective, one engaged in viewing every motion of every object in the heavens from outside as it were, one might then further imagine a perfect order to exist as seen from the vantage point of that absolute perspective. From all of the above observations I developed my general theory, which, stated briefly, was that of the innate unpredictability of events to the degree that we are close to them.”

“The actual location of an object in motion could at best be assigned a probability value in terms of the next motion occurring in a small segment of time. The shorter the arc of motion chosen the greater the predictability became as time would then for all practical purposes appear to stand still and the higher mathematical probability of accuracy would be reflected due primarily to this arbitrary condition placed upon the scope of observation. The aesthetic problem for me was that such observations become trivial if they are dependent upon merely stating the object’s position in space which says nothing of its velocity in passing through time. My own position in other words doomed me to approximations rather than to ever achieving my goal of certainty. In other words I was brought face to face with the innate problem of achieving any certitude even with regard to the motion of physical objects; how much less then could I achieve any certainty regarding other matters.”

“However, at an infinite distance one might imagine complete predictability, because from that perspective all influences might be not only tallied-up but actually observed in operation. This means that all events must have a deterministic base as seen from the point of view of an absolute observer. I was led thus willy-nilly plunged back into the world of metaphysics and I emerged with the same confidence as Leibnitz with his monads coordinated by God into the best of all possible worlds."

"This was no great comfort to me though, for I had always lived by my own will and imagined that I was free! I was the unmoved-mover, at least towards the objects acted upon by my own will. I was the God of my own nature. To find a metaphysical source for all things then was no comfort to me. Therefore I left my nascent metaphysical speculations where perhaps a scientist must always leave them if he is to remain a scientist and not become a theologian. I found that I had probed too far and only succeeded in the annihilation of my own existence as I actually experienced it, viz. as free. If my being is contingent upon not only God but to a universe of determined motions, however unpredictable they might be at the micro-level, they still seemed to be utterly predictable at the macro-level. Once sum up all the influences and complete knowledge would be theoretically possible but not obtainable by any observer whatsoever existing within the system to be measured!"

Professor Moriarty paused here to allow us to catch up with the train of his thoughts. At last, he continued. "There was only one possible way that I could see beyond this lamentable conclusion: If God or the absolute wished to do so, He might create a small gap in the order of visible creation. Within that gap we would be free to act. There were of course two other possibilities remaining, but these would make all knowledge impossible and so I rejected them out of hand."

"What were those possibilities?" I inquired after a minute.

"They both went to the nature of God," Professor Moriarty answered. "The first was derived from the observation of Descartes where he stated that he could only be sure of one thing and that was that he was thinking. Applying that observation to my own case I was forced to inquire whether my thinking might be some vast illusion or dream where I myself was God unaware that I had created anything at all and that I would someday awaken in some vast solitude alone with all of my perfections intact startled at a strange dream wherein I had imagined suffering and sin and a stooped and aged Professor seeking to understand the heavens."

"And what was the second possibility?" I enquired.

"Ah, the second severed the contingent and the absolute perspectives and made my own efforts at theorizing pointless. It was a variation on Leibnitz. It was the possibility that the entire universe has within its smallest particles a principle of freedom and unpredictability. This meant of course that though the great forces might be orderly and irreversible that at the smallest scale of events in time and space the universe was entirely spontaneous. At any given point the entire universe could then burst asunder! This would mean that granted infinite time that any and all permutations also might occur. In other words, there was a principle of evolution not merely in life but in the inorganic universe also. It might be tending towards some purpose but by blind chance and random variation. In this sense the God of Spinoza might not yet exist because the totality had yet to be realized!"

"You will see at once the further paradox. If the order of the universe and of my own being is fixed and determined by physical events, then I do not choose to discover (as a scientist) the laws of nature; I am rather, compelled to do so and my heroic search for knowledge becomes nothing more than a mathematical mirror of what could just as well exist without my own efforts at mimesis of its functions in knowledge. I in short become only one more assimilated part of the great whole and my privilege and dignity as an observer disappears."

"Any assumption of relativity is even worse; that truths are many. Knowledge is then impossible because the canvas as it were of my mimetic function is itself changing even as I paint; then to observe, and to calculate as a scientist are not only pointless endeavors but they are illusory in nature as well! I myself may be the source of change rather than anything that is occurring in my model of reality! If this is true then complete knowledge becomes impossible even in theory. The scientific enterprise is doomed from the start, for all that we can know are local conditions as measured by a contingent observer in time and no statement can be made that conditions that are local prevail universally. Thus reason itself collapses in upon itself. We might of course still assign probability values to immediate events, but certainty would escape us, and science is ultimately based on either/or principles. The principle of exclusion is at the basis of the experimental method on which all science has rested since the days of Sir Francis Bacon. The scientist attempts to choose between two carefully constructed alternatives by setting up carefully a set of controls. The appeal is always to nature to affirm or to deny our provisional assertions as to the nature of things. Go back and read Parmenides, Anaximander, or Anaximenes and you will see how early the impulse of scientific certainty grasped the minds of thinking men."

"Heraclitus on the other hand embraced change as the only absolute and by so doing created the schools of skepticism and of the sophists, a school of thought that reached its conclusion in the philosophy of David Hume and of Immanuel Kant. If certainty becomes impossible, then all things remain conceivable. This of course means that faith, though of its nature metaphorical and incomplete, becomes a distinct possibility and atheism as such becomes impossible! If we cannot know the universe directly, even in principle, then we cannot know God unless God chooses to reveal Himself. Behold! Religion has just come in through the back door of philosophy! This throws the sophisticated mind of man back upon religion with its claims that God or the gods of various sorts have intervened from beyond nature in order to tell us the purpose of nature. I was, you see, already opened to the distinct possibility of a God even prior to the wager with Sherlock Holmes!"

Sherlock Holmes smiled at this diatribe of Professor Moriarty and now spoke up in his turn. "This confession of the Professor shows you see why he was at the precise point in his career when he would be amenable to our joint wager and why he gave up crime when he did. He had made a slip as I had always contended. That slip of course that betrayed his organization into my hands was deliberate and preceded by an even greater slip which I had stumbled upon when reading his own account of the motion of asteroids. His theory left him in a metaphysical quandary. He must either abandon science or enlarge its parameters. He was up against that terrible dictum, "I believe in order that I may understand." That dictum of course has always been interpreted as a provisional position of one who suffers merely from insufficient data. Professor Moriarty had reached the point where he could see that even if all data were to be known, then the Absolute Mind would itself have only two alternatives. Either all events are determined and the freedom of the mind of man is only an illusion, in which case the universe is but a mimetic reflection of the mind of God's prior intentions, or we have the second alternative, which is that the universe admits of freedom in both the mind of man and perhaps even in all events through a universal indeterminacy. Final knowledge then becomes impossible, except from the standpoint of the Absolute Mind of God and even God has chosen apparently to allow freedom."

"In the first alternative, the universe that we know is as it were sucked back into the mind of God and our sense of separation becomes illusory. The entire universe becomes a mere toy spun by God without either surprises or the possibility of opposition. If we as human beings are not separate from the rest of creation we could not study it; for in that case our very study would become itself an order of nature. It would be as though one were in a hall of mirrors each reflecting only its own reflection which in turn is a reflection of a previous reflection. Such knowledge becomes futile, for it never arrives at the thing-itself that it attempts to study, the ding-an-sich of Kant."

"If we take the second alternative, science again becomes incomplete, but for a different reason. If the universe is changing and if we are changing also, then the universe may change beneath our observations even as we record them and try to express them systemically. Just as a globule of mercury breaks into innumerable smaller balls when pressed upon, so would the possibility of definitive knowledge escape us. Even worse, what we now call scientific knowledge may only reflect our choices of modalities with which we approach and observe phenomena and our conclusions may only be true because of the present state of the mind's evolution. It finds that device or modality of thought persuasive and thus it extends whatever metaphor is most attractive at that historical moment of time. Thus would the universe of knowledge and reason descend into mere metaphor and all knowledge would be reducible at last to the laws of logic and linguistic constructions alone."

"This would mean that even mathematics, for all of its supposed exactness, could not ultimately do anything but mirror the universe, translate its operations from one language into another, but never probe beneath supposed causal relations, never prove that actual contact was ever made with a world of independent phenomena. We might even be dreaming the universe unawares. Observations may themselves be only spot-samples of the changing behavior of things that alter too slowly for our instruments to record those changes. The physics of today would then not be the same as the physics of a million years hence, for the very principles that now seem most indubitable might no longer be applicable."

Holmes smiled and ceased speaking and Professor Moriarty continued the discussion.

"I was indeed in a quandary, gentlemen," said the Professor shaking his head. "I could not leave the mystery unresolved. There was simply no time left to waste upon crime. I had funds that would last me the remainder of my life and I determined to devote every second to solving the problem that I had encountered. I had already gone so far and decided to betray and dissolve my own criminal organization, sparing only my friend Colonel Sebastian Moran, when my mind turned to Sherlock Holmes. What should I do with my continuing nemesis? I decided that he would be a continual nuisance in my retirement, so he must be destroyed. I still maintained that position, even on the day when we met at the

Reichenbach Falls. I had even brought along Colonel Sebastian Moran as a second should I fail in my duel with Holmes."

"I was actually speculating upon the manner of approaching him on that ledge when it suddenly occurred to me that the entire drama that I was enacting was absurd. I was about to kill the one man who might extend my own life. If I could add the resources of his mind to my own, perhaps we could jointly solve this problem in metaphysics that now so obsessed me. Besides, I had come to enjoy his company by proxy. I was always aware of his presence on the scene. He was a constant stimulus to my own creativity. I would always reflect, 'Will this plan pass the test of an inquiry by Sherlock Holmes?' Sherlock Holmes was my insurance policy. If the crime could be easily solved by that man who is even now smiling at me, then I would simply turn down the business at once. His mind was the whetstone against which I sharpened the blade of my own mind. I could not, frankly, imagine the world without him. I had reached that conclusion before I was even close enough for him to feel my presence behind him and to turn about with his usual cocksure and insolent manner and address me. You may imagine my surprise to discover that his thoughts on that day paralleled my own. I chose another course instantly with the results that we are both here today in a library in Baskerville Hall in Devonshire rather than, one of us at least, at the bottom of the falls in far off Switzerland."

I recall that I interrupted this extraordinary joint narrative at this point. "But what of the results of the wager, Professor? How did Holmes convince you upon his return so that you have now thrown your lot in with us in our present adventure?"

"I will refer that question to be answered in due course in the manuscript that you are now reading, Dr. Watson. You had best hear the conclusion there because that conclusion would be entirely superfluous without the steps by which it was reached. I will say this much however, we in a sense convinced each other, for Holmes began his quest in much the same confusion as I. The journey to faith, if it is to be authentic, is not an easy one. Though some may merely yield to Grace, others are condemned to go the long way round the mountain and to climb laboriously to its summit. When Sherlock Holmes returned from his travels, he asked that I read his journal and he also thrust into my hands two books by an obscure Danish philosopher named Soren Kierkegaard, one entitled "Either/Or" and also a volume entitled "An Unscientific Post-script to the Philosophical Fragments;" both were written under the device of pseudonyms of Kierkegaard. The result of perusing them was that I adopted a different point of view, one that did not deny the validity of much that I had believed before, but rather completed it. That in brief is my story, Gentlemen, as a man held prisoner by his own intellect, a story told here today from my side of the events at the Falls of Reichenbach."

Such was our conversation in the library at Baskerville Hall on that momentous autumn afternoon. It may be too much to say that abstruse metaphysics is a stimulant to the appetite, but I can say that we all ate heartily of the late lunch that Perkins had ordered to be prepared for us as we talked. There was a fine halibut cooked in a white crème sauce with dill and thin-sliced cuts of a rare London-Broil just touched with rosemary with an accompaniment of a most excellent Yorkshire pudding and some of the local Devonshire butter served with Scottish Bramble Preserves from Dundee. The meal terminated with a custard-cup with a melted top of molasses and Demerara rum. The meal revived our spirits and put us in the frame of mind to enjoy even the grim pleasures offered by a late autumn day in England.

After lunch we each went our separate way. The Professor went up to his chamber to seek some restoration from the events of the night before in sleep. Sir Henry went to the library to read the passage from the Iliad that Holmes had indicated. Holmes in turn put his cloth cap upon his head and asked that Perkins drive him to Coombe Tracey so that he could catch the train for Exeter. I offered to accompany him, but Holmes demurred, "I place these two gentlemen under your care, Watson. Guard the papers well. You will not be alone for the servants are all well-armed. I will try and return this evening by the train, which should arrive from

Coombe Tracey in time for us to share an evening meal."

It was with some reluctance that I consented, for the responsibility was a great one, though it was gratifying to know that Holmes reposed so much trust in my abilities. We parted and I went up to the second floor to my own room where I sat down by the window. I could see below me the great flagstone terrace and I caught a glimpse of the carriage with Holmes inside as it swept down the drive to the lane that connected to the highroad to Grimpen and beyond. The Murillo Papers lay securely in their hiding-place a few doors down from me. The window would reveal any approach and I had instructed the servants to patrol the house and to cooperate with any instructions given by an additional constable requested from the village patrolling the grounds. He was in turn to report to me at regular intervals and to secure the bottom floor and the grounds surrounding the Hall. At last, feeling quite secure, I opened Holmes' journal and returned to where I had left him in his account, in the gardens of Persia. The winds still buffeted at my window as I traversed the years, only now realizing the fullness of the life that had gone on in far distant lands, while I and those who had mourned his death, indeed all of England, had supposed that Sherlock Holmes was dead.

From the Journal of Sherlock Holmes

October 25, 1891
Tehran, Persia

It has been a most interesting few days after settling into our winter quarters. I have paid several visits to the central Mosque in company with a gentleman who is a Mohammedan who works as a translator at the British Embassy here. He has given me many insights into the mood of the inhabitants of the city. The weight of the British Empire is felt intensely here and it has created an atmosphere of both tension and resentment. It may seem strange to the British mind but these people feel that they can do quite well without us. Our supposed contributions in opening the country to trade are felt as an imposition upon an entirely satisfactory way of life.

There has grown to be a balance of forces in Asia through the centuries that has little to do with our concepts of property and of national sovereignty. Indeed I would say that national borders in this region are of less political significance than the great cities where trade acts as a counterbalance to insular belief systems. These are the centers of trade, of art, and of opulence. Beyond the outer limits of the city there is only the semi-nomadic life of the great mass of believers in the unifying message of the Prophet. Collectively, they are part of the Umayyad, the cohesive mass of those who follow the teachings. The effect of Islam is to create a uniform rhythm to life in obedience and obeisance to Allah. Religion knows a centrality here that we have not seen in the west since the building of the great cathedrals in the 12th and 13th centuries. Life here is still seen as a preparation for eternity and all things are subordinated to a proper order. There is luxury of course, but it is disciplined and directed as are the various appetites of man. The supervision of women is so rigid and defined that sexual vice is virtually unknown here and as for theft the maiming of the malefactor acts as an obvious if overly symbolic deterrent to future offenses.

The Moslem heaven of course is depicted with a specificity of sensuality that would shock any denizen of a Methodist or Society of Friends Meeting House. The protestant mind as opposed to the Catholic mind has selectively sterilized the sensuality still seen in Rome in the great paintings of Michelangelo and Raphael. In protestant thinking the body is seen as always antithetical to the soul. Anglicanism represents a middle position in this regard. The Church of England's spirit is perhaps best represented by the image of a well-dressed, middle-class solicitor, who, if he is pious, may wear a cross on his watch fob. Christianity in Britain is becoming merely a matter of commercial good behavior, a union of state and church. One is first of all an Englishman and his Christianity is then simply included as an adjunct to good manners.

There is little sense of the supernatural in this. Charity becomes a proportionate tax upon the electorate levied by God. One need not expect heroic virtues and the works of religion are increasingly consigned to those exercised by the female members of the flock. A man in England would compromise his social status by being too aggressively Christian in his behavior. It would be seen as bad form. The upper classes at least enjoy proper music and ceremony in the Church of England although they have foregone the elements of enthusiasm seen in the more evangelical sects. The sterility of middle-class and working-class Methodism and the grim hysteria of the Baptists and Pentecostals has succeed to the grandeur of the great English cathedrals with their fine choirs as is still seen in the grand architecture of the York Minster.

Great art and great music are a bridge to the supernatural. Each branch of Christianity reflects a different life experience, but that experience and its articulation in theology have had the tendency to fragment Christianity so that no common culture transcending the loyalties to the nation-state are present. The general elaboration and diffusion of belief over time is such that any real centrality in Christ is subordinated to those movements that would later interpret His nature and significance. Perhaps this process had already begun soon after the death and resurrection of Jesus. Who for instance can compare the early writings of the early Pauline and Johannine Traditions and not see already the tension existing between these earliest schools of Christian thought.

St. Paul never really left his Judaism far behind. The Christ directed towards the gentiles of St. Paul has an elaborated and generalized quality as the universal Messiah that is far from the minute and more particular details of the person of Christ appearing in the Gospel of Mark. The humanity of Christ and his pre-resurrection life are subordinated in Paul's views on grace and the law, which have a more cosmic quality. One gets the impression at times that Jesus the man is used as a vehicle to answer the Jewish Paul's questions and that the figure of Jesus as the Christ seems at times to be a creation of the mind of St. Paul.

The visionary Gospel of St. John on the other hand is more complete still in its unique theological vision, in a variety of mysticism that approaches that of the Gnostics. It combines intimate quotations from Jesus with an emphasis upon love and the imagery of light as betokening both the essence of God and as a sign of faith in believers. The Gospel of St. John is the most intimate of all the gospel narratives for it allows Christ to speak to us at length. The Johannine School has a Gospel and Epistles and finally a vision of Christ in Revelation that is even more abstract than that of St. Paul in the epistles to the Hebrews.

It seems as though only in the last two centuries from Voltaire to Renan have scholars questioned the texts of the Bible by seeing them both within their historical context of composition and as vehicles of complex communication that can be critiqued for internal consistency rather than simply being seen as the direct word-for-word dictation of God Himself. This approach would have been seen and still is seen as impious and misguided by many church leaders. However this very intransigence has opened the gateway to scientific atheism by failing to address certain theological problems that gnaw away at faith. It seems to me that to ignore the biases and partial views of history is to confuse the human and the divine.

The early theologies present in the schools of thought of St. Paul and of St. John were followed by the great early battles of Christology with the Arians, the Nestorians, and the Monophysites to finally define the dual nature of Christ in the hypostatic union. For Christ to be God yet not to be all of God, for had we not also the Father and the Holy Spirit, is still a scandal to Islam and a complication in divine/human relations. Islam in contrast avoided the traps of Zoroastrianism with its duality of gods. Islam took the God of the Jews and made Him, if anything, more monotheistic than He was, even in Jewish belief. The God of the Jews was always an intimate God, deeply and passionately concerned with the fate of the Jewish people. There is even at times a physical presence of God, a voice is heard, a whisper of sound, or a burning bush. These are not present in Islam. God in Islam is utterly unknowable and even his prior words in the Bible would be deemed inadequate if the Koran was not already present in heaven as the embodiment of a final revelation to Mohammed. The Koran then is a substitute for the Jewish Messiah and the Christian Incarnate Word of God, revealed in the person of Jesus. The Koran is a sort of "textual Jesus" without the burdens of flesh and blood, and the Prophet Mohammed, though honored, is certainly not God. The true believer of Islam then is not incorporated by grace into the very substance of God as Christianity teaches by union with Christ. The believer is always outside of God. He someday may inhabit paradise, but does God walk there intimately with him? The believer is promised a great reward, but does that reward consist of God Himself? Allah may be merciful, but He does not step down from His thrown to greet the believer as a son or a daughter and one does not address him in familiar speech as Abba.

The function of Islam was to replace the Jewish notion of sacrifice and temple offerings with the verbal worship of prayer and of direct service to the community through almsgiving. Islam disposed of the law of the Torah as completely as Christianity had before it, but spared itself the complex questions of the operations of divine grace that later divided Christianity. Islam had a message that even the simple nomadic tribes could understand: believe on the one God and follow the teachings of the Prophet or risk a great chastisement. Islam was a civilizing force. By mandating strict external belief and its demonstration it avoided the deeper questions of the human heart until the Sufi movement related Islam to individual religious consciousness once again. The Sufis have always been resisted however, for their vision is too close to the great Christian mystics and to the teachings of the great Hasidic Rabbis of Judaism such as the Baal Shem Tov. There has always been a tension between the communal functions of religion and the search for individual salvation through direct experience of God.

The teachings of the Koran show their practical effect above all in the political forces of Asia. Islam is a force that gives a vocabulary to a civilization that has traversed many ethnic and national boundaries. In this way, Islam potentially is a force for peace in central Asia. One must consider how fragmented the many tribes and ethnicities would be without it. The Islamic tide reaches as far as Indonesia and even the islands of the Philippines, but it has never reached beyond the Great Wall of China nor did it take root in Japan as did Buddhism imported from India. I fear though that its western expansion into Europe will always leave a bitter taste.

Christianity at last lost both Constantinople and Jerusalem to the Arabic religion. This consigned Christianity into the arms of Rome in the west, while leaving eastern Christianity to the isolation of Orthodoxy and created a divided Christendom even before the Protestant Reformation. Indeed without the arms of colonialism to carry it, one wonders whether Christianity might not today be a declining religion. As the masses of the world population grow in Asia, will they not leave Europe behind as a region of insular hatreds and warfare, a region of fragmented languages and declining empires based upon colonial wealth and slavery? When the colonial possessions at long last find their own voices will they espouse a Christianity that preaches renunciation when they remember that their experience of the Christian nations of Europe was one of oppression, insult, and plunder? Perhaps Christianity will need to begin again at its roots, which if it is truly of Christ and rooted in God, should not lack sustenance through divine grace.

Historically speaking, Christianity has never done well when it yields to triumphalism. It is always in an intimate and humble relationship of the soul to its God, in full awareness of its own defects, that Christian beliefs are truly admirable. True Christianity is in the last analysis too intimate to ever be a successful political force. Its spread is to the individual heart and to the small communities that may nurture the complex virtues of its teachings. The Crusades were an anomaly. In spite of Emperor Constantine's convictions, Christianity may not use the cross as a sword without betraying its own nature, for the cross is the symbol of the willing acceptance of defeat and of death itself if need be. Christ died to show the folly of arms. The glory of the church is in its martyrs who took the shortest path to sainthood.

The spread of Islam in contrast owed much to the sword, for the believer was taught to fight in the way of Allah. In this they were Arab heirs to the early versions of the Jewish God who mandated the slaughter of all those espousing conflicting beliefs such as the followers of the fertility rites of Baal. It appears to be a constant of human nature to kill when one cannot convince. For this reason, the Enlightenment philosophers spoke of the value of free inquiry and of rational debate. The spirit of inquiry had suffered for centuries under the threats of the inquisition. Once given its head though that spirit of free inquiry ran like a horse that has long been tethered. There developed an idea of an earthly paradise which became the new orthodoxy of materialistic mankind. Perhaps the great German philosopher Schopenhauer was right. He says that each individual is tied to the Will, which is the source of all illusion. Only when a man resists the blind Will by the realization that he is part of all things, and in fact is all things, that he abandons selfishness and allows the General Will to act though him to the betterment of all, not as a fragment, but as the whole. Isn't this way of religious thought that which prevails in Islam, in Buddhism, and in the teachings of Confucius?

To this belief Nietzsche opposed a radical individualism whereby a few individuals become the purpose for life. The Ubermensch becomes the great exception to the masses. He wills his own being and his own morals; but it must always be asked, from whence comes such an individual? Does any man create himself? Is he not the product of the community that forms and nurtures him? Does he not owe his language, his culture, and his values to the world that is his context? And does he not finally perish?

Nietzsche deified the Ubermensch to take the place of the God in whom he could no longer believe. But if individualized man was to become an end in himself, then he would have to be eternal. Nietzsche solved this problem by his doctrine of the Eternal Return. A man would live his life over again in each detail an infinite number of times and by so willing his fate take upon himself full responsibility, not simply for his acts, but for the nature that he creates for himself. Each man thus may define human nature anew if he is an Ubermensch. May this experiment never be tried, for the result will be a barbarism such as the world has never yet seen! This philosophy rests finally upon a great solipsism and was the fruit of Nietzsche's loneliness. Even his former idol Wagner had to be opposed, for his vision found expression in the grandeur of music which is always more convincing than the bareness of mere poetry or the arguments of philosophy.

Islam is the polar opposite of this overweening belief in the individual. It preaches the submission of all things to Allah. Islamic dress is the ultimate in uniformity and Islamic design is proportionate but never stoops to incarnate itself in objects. It is form without coalescence into body. It avoids representation as a pseudo-creation of man. Who is man to seek to rival God by creating images of his own? Man may adorn but not create. It is blasphemy to mirror creation, for there is but one God. The believer is taught to eclipse his individual identity and to be part of the great mass that mills about the Kaaba on the Pilgrimage to Mecca. He is taught to walk, not in his own way, but in the way that Allah has prepared for him. The place of man is prepared by God from before his birth, but if he submits, he will find that way. This alone of freedom is gifted to men and women that they may lay it down as soon as the realize it. In this way they mount no opposition and this is the best way. Not to oppose God.

Man begins to oppose God by simply being an individual and in this way he is already in sin in Islamic belief. To this great problem Islam offers mercy, for Allah is merciful and compassionate and he offers that mercy to those who submit. This is the Islamic way to salvation, not through the mediation and sacrificial death of Christ, but as a direct offering from Allah who is the only God in Islamic belief. This direct gift is mediated by the Koran which was proclaimed by Mohammed the Prophet. As a direct gift it requires neither the law of the Torah nor the sacraments of the Church, or any other guide beyond the Koran's message and the mandates supplemented by the Hadith. This belief has unified much of Asia. European civilization will now need to be more grounded in its Christian roots in order to confront it. I fear that the mere greed and power of colonial rule will not suffice in this struggle. Nor will a sterile Enlightenment rationalism, nor will a blind individualism that makes each man his own God. It will take a belief system that can unite all people and nations to resist the onrushing tide of Islam; for if it succeeds in uniting Asia, it will then control the key resources of the world.

The Americans may be the last cauldron for the distillation and refinement of the various belief systems. Perhaps America can tolerate conflicting beliefs side-by-side, for in America belief in God is a mere adjunct to material progress. The overriding belief of Americans is that their system of freedom can abstract from earthly contingency as such. Americans believe that they may create anew the heart of man through the influence of democratic government. In accepting all they reduce all to one common

American level. It is the pursuit of happiness here and now that defines American aspirations. It is the fount of American material progress, but has it left Americans with a soul? For all of their genius have they created anything new? America is still coasting on what remains of European civilization.

Now that America has achieved its aspiration of a Pacific coast continental limit, it will no doubt attempt to reach to Asia where it may find effective resistance at last. In the face of that resistance America will need to pause and reconsider the path it has followed from the Atlantic colonies onward across the Great Plains and to the Pacific Ocean. It will there encounter the other colonial powers of England, France, Russia, and the Netherlands barring its quest for annexation. The desire for conquest is not confined to the Americans however. May not even Japan someday seek to expand outward from its home islands? Then there is particularly the German threat. Germany has been united only since the age of Bismarck. As a great power though, it lags behind the other nations. How long will Germany accept its subservient lot? In the struggle for export markets and for trade in raw materials will a sustained peace be possible or will the Christian nations someday come to a final struggle for colonial supremacy? May I not live to witness that struggle, for it will be the end of the great defining monuments of European Civilization.

October 26, 1991
Tehran, Persia

From my present position, so far to the east in a Persia that barely knows the influence of England, let alone America, I am allowed to see the splendid isolation and pride of its people. How long can it be though before Persia too is only a colonial outpost, as Colonel Moran has predicted to me it will become. For one who has been a soldier of the British Empire, he seems to have finally found sympathy towards those whom he opposed in his youth. Perhaps the function of age is to prepare us for final repentance. My own isolation in London has always given me the comfortable perspective that we British were acting as advance guards of enlightenment to the dark regions of the world. It is the prerogative of power to believe that its intentions are always in some way beneficent and just. The thought that we might be mere intruders, if not barbarians, is something I could never yet credit or conceive. Will there ever be a set of international norms that will define the borders of nations? If there is, what evidence will be taken as dispositive of just claims?

The great tides of human struggle have left so many exigent claims that no nation of the present exists that does not have some colorable claim to the territory of a neighbor. Conquest is built into the human equation and what is history but the long bloody trail of human conflict? Greed and fear seem to breed the great perennial growth of human aspirations. Greed is the desire to expand our property and fear the desire to retain what is at least temporarily in our possession. Even the Old Testament is finally a history of warfare with its victories or restoration after defeat. Our gods are co-opted into our struggles. Surely a god who is all powerful will favor the victor, so that we pray that as we consider ourselves to be the more worthy contestant, God will take our side in the struggle. This attitude spares us the burden of guilt when we face the inevitable destruction of our actions.

Christianity of course in its universal message of love and in the utter surrender of Christ to death on a cross was meant to end forever the cycle of violence in human affairs, but this part of the Gospel is seldom taken seriously. Endless theological speculation has yet to hear the words, "Put up your sword for everyone who takes up the sword will perish by the sword." Perhaps only a common condition of shared tragedy such as the Black Death of the 14th century will cause a general repentance and stop the mutual slaughter of peoples. Perhaps the earth will move further along its tether to the sun and a vast ice age begin or perhaps the earth will slow in its speed about the sun and begin to fall gradually toward that fiery sphere.

How strange it is after all that we exist in the harmonious balance that makes life even possible. I never wander in an orchard but I marvel at the fruit that takes the place of the early blooms of spring and ripens toward its fall. I often think that we have never left the Garden of Eden. The angel with the burning sword that keeps us from the tree of life is death itself. To grasp eternal life rather than to have it bestowed upon us is but a repetition of the act of pride that we could be as gods ourselves. Surely it is enough that we strut about in our humble station without knowing in each instant that we hover over our graves and immanent dissolution. How much more would our evils flourish if our lives knew no end? We would surely, all of us, then be like the devils and beyond any hope of redemption. God in his mercy gave us death so that we might finally turn again to Him again.

The great insight of Western religion is involved with our own awareness of sin, that something is amiss, not with the universe but with us, and the fault is ours. This makes all western religious activity an effort to return to the presence of God and to fulfill God's original intent in creating us. Buddhist thought in contrast finds that the universe is evil and we are simply and unaccountably in it, not through our fault but for no reason, not even by an exercise of God's arbitrary will. The task in Buddhism becomes to escape our condition, not by finding fulfillment but by obliteration, to not return again. Whereas Hindu thought finds comfort in the all, the state of Brahma or God-likeness, so that we return into God, Buddhist thought is abstracted from God completely and assumes that nothingness is to be preferred to sharing in the life of Brahma. So deep is the horror of life for the Buddhist, in the face of human suffering, that it will be enough to cease, to draw the universe back down to a pinprick of light and then to extinguish even that forever, such is the dream of nirvana. Between these two great poles: to join God and merge with Him or to destroy and eclipse all being are the doctrines of every religion of mankind.

Western religion begins with God saying, "Let there be light and there was light," which He then finds to be good. Buddhist thought finds the first noble truth to be that all is suffering and to this great despair it advises a discipline that will wean the heart of man from any betraying hope of ultimate happiness based upon desire and to accept, indeed to covet its own extinction. In a sense it asks the individual man or woman, if it may be translated into Edenic terminology, to go back to the decision in the garden of Eden and to return the fruit of the knowledge of good and evil to the tree, for was it not the desire to be like God that condemned all of creation to suffering? Had we not in our contingency envied God's absolute being and attempted vainly to bridge the insuperable gap between contingent and non-contingent being, would there ever have been a fall? If it were possible for we ourselves to undo our primal act and to accept again whatever God willed for us, would that not be salvation?

But alas, our act was irrevocable and the world of death and suffering that we created out of our contingency has so marred that initial explosion of light kindled at the very "finger-ends of God" that only God himself may restore us and that, not by fleeing suffering and death, but by suffering it also as God, and at our own hands. This is the mystery of the Passion of Christ, the one unique event since the fall in Eden, the very center-point of creation, an event so apocalyptic that it turns the world of suffering upside down and makes it the path to God, not to be avoided but embraced, not escaped into nirvana but brought into the Godhead itself in the form of the Resurrected Christ who still bears the wounds in his hands, feet, and side. Not nirvana then but the general resurrection of the bodies of all the faithful is the universal hope of man and of woman from the Christian perspective; a perspective that is meant to explain all phenomena and to make absolute claims upon every moment of our lives.

Human flesh, the fragments strewn over the fields of battle shall be gathered, purified, made whole, and brought before God and in God to find rest at last. Is this difficult to believe? Yes, but so is the idea of returning always in some new form to this same troubled existence, only to know again the cycles of suffering until Nirvana? Which is the more hopeful choice for the individual man or woman? Or should we rather cease at last to question, take these seventy-odd years of life and fill them as we may, as the

Epicureans taught (who at least enjoy the margin of good allotted to them in this life); or facing disappointment, act as the Buddhists and Stoics and simply detach from pleasure and desire enjoying only one's capacity to endure? Or should we be as Nietzsche and accept original sin in all its parameters and say that we are as Gods, that it is our burden to create good and evil, and to endure whatever life we have made for ourselves forever and ever in an Eternal Return? (This last is for me a perfect vision of hell for what would eternity be if not lived in God). To be one's own God as a contingent being is to create hell out of our own final nothingness. We already are, ontologically speaking, in a state of nirvana; we need not seek or await it. To be enlightened is to realize that if we are left to our own devices eternally, then it would be better never to have been at all. To truly understand human life is to yearn for God with all the passion of the Psalms and to seek every fragment of hope that God may in fact exist. My quest to the east then is an effort to articulate this conviction, not for Moriarty alone, but also for myself as a man, I, Sherlock Holmes.

October 28, 1891
Tehran, Persia

My last entry was in a way a summation of the current state of my thoughts. One of the benefits and dangers of travel is that it provides one with a perspective upon the costs of the maintenance of routine in daily life. My settled habits in Baker Street have provided me with a refuge through many years, but that very refuge has often blinded me to the larger tides of events that have swept about me. My attention to the minute facts of my cases has allowed me to develop an intense focus upon a unique set of circumstances and by doing so I developed what might be called my method. My excellence as a detective, if I may so flatter myself, came from unbiased observation. I would avoid premature calculations until I had all of the facts before me, just as they were. The primary data would suggest various lines of inquiry. It was then that I discovered the value of imagination to the criminal investigator.

I found that I could place myself in the position of various persons and to imagine their motives from within that assumed position. I could then elaborate a connected course of events that would flow from those motivations that would still square with the facts as I knew them. Finally, I would apply a deductive method based on my special knowledge of the crimes of the past to see if the case at hand was a replication of a tried-and-true method or formula that had been used before in other crimes. My most instructive cases were those that promised to be unique in their fact patterns or in their methods. These cases were coincidentally often also those that provided Watson with a chance to mystify his readers. My more routine cases that for years provided me with bread and butter were of little value as demonstrations, so they were not reported by my biographer.

Applying this method to my present metaphysical speculations leads to uneven results. My last entry shows the complexity of all metaphysical thought. The attempt to account for the problems posed by our existence forces one to assume a motive for creation, imagining , to begin with, that God, as the origin of all things, could as it were debate the act of creation before exercising His option. The question begged by this imagination is that it assumes that God would ever engage in comparing alternative courses of action. Surely, the nature of God's will must be such that merely to conceive is already to intend and to intend is already to act upon that intent. But let us pursue this exercise in imagination and see what it may yield.

We must begin this mental experiment by assuming that there is an order of being that is God Himself who is uncreated. This order simply always was. The name Yahweh implies as much for its transliteration means, "I am that I am." In other words, God's first characteristic is simply that He exists independent of outside causation from another source. The same phrase could however be used in another way. It could have been addressed to us in terms of our first duty to God which is simply to affirm the absoluteness otherness of God. The phrase could mean then, "That

I am must be enough for you, I will not be questioned, my name as existing is all that you may possess in your present state and capacity of receptivity."

In other words, we cannot get a handle upon God. His name allows us no control, nor does it explain God. In this sense to debate the motives of God is pointless, so let us turn to creation. Could creation itself be uncreated? This would mean that all that we see is simply order emerging out of the dance of forces in contention but with no overriding central purpose or conscious intent. At this point the word "creation" becomes inappropriate because creation implies reflective intent in the creator. If what we observe about us is merely the present constellation of forms arising from an unending process then the very idea of utility for a transcendent purpose intended by God disappears. Yet a purposeless chain of mere causality seems to the mind of man to be much ado about nothing. Certainly a purposeless state of being must be as pointless as nothingness itself in which case it makes no difference that there is something rather than nothing. This is of course a philosophical dead-end. Therefore the mind of man assumes purpose as a first postulate to all things.

What would a transcendent purpose be; what would be adequate to a causeless cause of all other causes? This purpose, first of all must serve the function of validating the nature of the human mind, which is oriented towards truth. We observe phenomena and by so doing create order, for our minds are ordered to seeking regularities and patterns in phenomena. Does this mean though that the very idea of a transcendent purpose is itself a human construct? If there were no observer of events, we must imagine that those phenomena would still occur, but then they would have no integral meaning, let alone purpose.

Is human knowledge confined then to seeing things only in relation to each other, so that no one fact may ever be seen as primary and essential, as a starting point for all further speculation? Does this mean that the idea of order is simply a human imposition flowing from the mind itself? Are all things simply a mute set of data without the synthetic function provided by the rules set up by the nervous system of an obstreperous primate? If this should be true, then the mind of man creates the need of God in order to complete its analysis of the problem posed by man's very existence, viz. to posit a source and purpose for our existence, our unique human dilemma. It might be contended that man is his own choice and purpose, that the condition of man is to be first an "I am" and only later to discover from within himself his own nature.

The problem with this proposition of course is that it may answer the question of man's inner subjective self-awareness, but it does not answer the question of why the non-man, the context of our lives, all that exists and would still exist without our observation, exists also. (Unless we assume that we create the world in the act of observing it, we must conclude that it exists independently of us). Shall we assume that this brute fact of silent and unobserved existence, this great lump as it were, is what we would call God and simply always was or spontaneously burst without cause into being out of non-being? Would this not require a greater act of faith than any religious tradition has ever dared ask of the believer? In addition, if this great lump of creation, that would now not be called creation anymore, since it would take the place of God, be worthy of worship or reverence?

It is here in our thought experiment that the questions of time and succession appear. This great lump of being then proceeds to simply evolve over time an animal that can turn about as it were and reflect back upon the process and path of its own evolution and in doing so it finds itself alone in a silent universe. Would that be an adequate explanation for all things? It would be as though a sleeper was to awaken from a dream and not only forget that he had gone to bed, but that he even had a bed, or a house either, or a nature. Suddenly there would be a being with a brain that can organize experience, even on a primitive level of sensing a world beyond itself that might supply its needs, but with no antecedent mind with which to engage in dialogue about the manner of its own functioning. Thus the first problem in philosophy is why we exist and are able to philosophize at all.

Could brute inorganic existence ever create out of its own un-sensing being, first consciousness, and then finally reflective self-consciousness? Could non-thought ever create thought? Is thought simply a physical event like a boiling of water contained in the cauldron of the skull and caused by some remote physical causation?

Or take our intentions as an example. Do we will to will or does will simple manifest an inner dynamic of causation traceable finally to its remotest causes in some bursting star? Are we merely an ornament to the universe, a trimming of lace at the edge of being? If so, then our existence, far from being a central matter and deserving of a God, is trivial and non-essential to the whole and should we vanish at some future date and our mode of knowing and of recording our thoughts perish with us, would another order of beings arise in time and would they think as we think?

Might their mode of knowing be more immediate and intuitive and not stoop in order to grasp cause and effect or ever imagine sequences and numbers. Would that unknown intelligence grasp things as wholes and in themselves rather than first abstracting words, ideas, and characteristics?

If then God is God simply because of the way we think and we cannot think otherwise but in the way that we do, then we are lost in the God problem and in the problem of mankind and there is no escape into that clear cerulean sky of postulate-less thought! If the entire existence and significance of our lives is ever to have meaning a meaning for us, and if any meaning is even to be possible, the question of God must arise and we are far better advised to posit a God than to imagine a world of purposeless forces without God, for in that world our own thought-processes would become invalid as we conceive them and never lead to any conclusions, for all conclusions would then be illusions bred out of the shallow substance of our own brains.

But let us then, just to continue our thought-experiment, imagine a condition where God had simply chosen not to create anything at all. The result would not be conceivable as a deprivation, for what has never existed cannot be deprived of being? It cannot be robbed of what never was? Then, had there been no creation, only God would remain. God would then have no non-God to which to relate. The celestial choirs would be empty. There would only remain God relating within the three poles of the Trinity; or worse, if Islam is correct in its view of the absolute unity and singularity of God, then we would have only God relating to God in an eternal self-reflection. What would that be but God celebrating God in eternal self-worship? This would be as if the following dialogue was always taking place: "I see that I am God and I worship myself as God and I see that I am God and worship the Godness of my Godness, etc." The absurdity and futility of such an image is immediately evident. We cannot therefore, now that we exist, imagine the pre-existent inner life of God without us. We dare not think of creation alone without reference to God, or of God as he would have been if isolated from His creation. The gift of subservient being seems to be irrevocable!

This is why it is said that we are made in the image and likeness of God, for now it is also we who cannot be destroyed; we may only die. Death is the final humiliation that keeps us from reaching out prematurely for the gift of the Tree of Life that would burden us with immortality, if immortality was to be endured without love. We might then choose to relate to ourselves as an end in ourselves which we can never be. The order of our creation is to know good and evil, to escape the mere contingency of non-self-reflective being into thought. Our thought processes though are ones of seeking a state of relatedness. We cannot exist alone and still be human, so we turn to other self-reflective beings and seek relations with them, and we turn finally back to God and desire Him as our ultimate end.

By doing all of this in a spirit of love, we may then be safely allowed to finally eat from the second tree, the one more deadly than the first which plunged us into making moral choices; this tree is the Tree of Life. It will now be safe to do so because we will now not use that gift to emulate God, but to conform to our natures as being Godlike-but-not-God. Heaven is to be in relationship, because it perfects our own being. Hell would be having all things except God, to be a petty dictator without a populace to cheer us on; to exist, sour and rotting in our own self-conception of our own God-likeness with none to relate to but ourselves for eternity. Even the devil cannot endure this condition and thus he is forced into evil as a mode of inverse relating to creation and to God.

Evil is what remains after God, who is in all things, is subtracted. Evil is the great zero, hovering on the edges of non-being into which it would plunge itself if it could, to erase forever the imprint of its origin in God. What we call evil is a comparative judgment among relative goods. But Evil with a capital "E" is precisely this futile effort to assert being contrary to being, to be a god in the face of God. It is the lie that enthrones itself in lying, yet knows all the time that it is a lie. It creates its own logic out of illogic. It twists about all things like a snake eating its own tail. For this reason evil is finally incomprehensible, for it does not desire to be comprehended.

Only God can know evil without in turn becoming evil. Evil will only make sense to us when and insofar as we ourselves become evil, but even then we will know at some level that it is not the good. We have eaten from the Tree of the Knowledge of Good and Evil and thus exist between these two poles. The tension of our being can never be assuaged by running into the arms of evil (which would reject us even as we entered their domain, with a sort of nausea at our reflection of themselves). We should there be brought up short against the repelling-force of all similar "god-not-gods" who seek to be absolute in themselves. That collectivity of non-relation is hell, and the worm that dies not is our awareness that somewhere goodness still exists, but we have forever excluded ourselves from it.

The wailing and gnashing of teeth spoken of in the Gospels then becomes an outward symbolic expression of our own eternal self-division now enthroned for eternity, for only God is life, and only living in God is the happiness of the soul which is the state of heaven. To eat of the fruit of the Tree of Life brings life-eternal, but to eat of it and not be in God and to take it as a gift is to be a robber. To eat that fruit and not be in God is to be condemned to Hell, for only in God may we bear its taste and its effects!

This much appears to have been revealed to us, and more than revealed, for our own thoughts reveal that we hunger for more than this life may ever provide on its own terms. Even to the most fortunate such as King Coholeth for he said truly that all was finally vanity and a search after wind. Our brief and bitter days allow us but this alone, to take a final position vis-à-vis our own life. We may put off that hour until the end of life but if so we will be put to the test on the very brink of eternity and who will say which way we will then fall?

We pray in the Our Father Prayer that we be led not into temptation but delivered from evil. That final deliverance comes when the soul, in a manner that we cannot know, confronts what it has made of itself through the course of its entire life as seen from the vantage point of God who is love. That final test will be most severe upon the one who has been most alien from good acts throughout his life. To change course at the end will be to deny what his particular acts of freedom have long embraced. Far better for the soul it will be to enter heaven by the narrow gate and to bring a life-time of efforts to discover and to embrace the good to that dread moment of decision, for there will be that much less baggage to hinder entry from which the soul must then rid itself.

The soul stands finally naked of all adhering elements of creation that were meant to be only aids to its own self-development under the tutelage of Divine Grace. It will then judge itself (in relation to God) and will by that final act of freedom, now rid of all contingent influences, decide whether to turn towards or away from the beckoning arms of its Creator. If the light of God remains within us, what the Church has always termed a state of Sanctifying Grace, then that grace will draw from us all that is not God, for as we enter into the embrace of God all else will fall away like ancient scabs from the many wounds of our lives leaving only the fresh, healed, and now eternal skin of a Resurrected Body. Thus will end the great story of not merely an epic tale of the Jewish scriptures but what we Christians believe to be the very internal foundation of the visible universe.

If the religious instinct is true, then all that we see is but the setting for the vast theological drama that accounts for everything at last. No particle of dust in some far-distant galaxy but owes its existence to the drama of the redemption of man. No dinosaur stomping through the ooze of an ancient swamp, but it owes its plight of suffering to the fall of man, for did not Saint Paul state that all creation is in a sense awaiting redemption also with the final revelation of the Sons of God? A redeemed creation will be a new heaven and a new earth, all that is will pass away, along with the reason for its being what it is, what it has been since the primal fall of man. As all things were meant for man and he had dominion over them, so all fell when man fell. A great disorder spread its black wings over creation and the result is the violence and the pain and the death that not only man knows, but all of creation with him.

Later—I am satisfied by this present synthesis of my thought experiment but many questions still remain. For instance, was it in this universe or another that the primal fall of Eden occurred? Was the nature of mankind determined in some adjunct or annex to the realm where the angels reside or did it occur on this all-to-material planet? How to we explain the nexus and anatomical similarities between human life and the animal life that we so much resemble? Is the order of creation given us in Genesis correct with man and woman created last? Did the early creeping things and birds already gnaw at each other and die prior to our arrival in the order of evolution? If death entered the world due to sin, then how are we to understand that in nature death serves the refinement of species characteristics over time?

It is the succession of individuals that perfects the species even in human beings. In our development in the womb we recapitulate prior stages of life. Human beings are part of the animal kingdom and we share, if not always common ancestors, at least branches of the same families. Or does the sin of man have retroactive effects? Why do the animals suffer? Is animal pain not also an evil? Is every higher order spiritual being when it turns to evil a curse to the next lower rung on the ladder of creation? Or perhaps there were no beasts and birds in the Garden of Eden, but only the two great trees and our first parents. Was the garden a state of mind and not a place after all? Were the twin trees put there to tempt Adam and Eve or were they gifts to be enjoyed in due season?

What was the initial attitude of God to us other than a mere familiarity? How close after all was the similarity to God implied by being created in His image? What was the purpose of the warning about eating from the Tree of the Knowledge of Good and Evil seeing that it was so ineffective? Was this warning merely a test? Did God already mistrust our first parents, or was God surprised, innocent and caught in wonder that the man and the woman would reach out and take that which could never make them happy or to obtain for them actual equality with God? Was Divine Grace only available after the fall as a corrective and a promise?

In the Genesis account creation had gone amiss before (unless that is all creation is simultaneous in all of its possible relations from the point of view of eternity), in the fall of the angelic orders, so that God must have been on notice of the possible spontaneous eruption of evil. Perhaps this had put God on guard as it were and awaiting betrayal. Was the serpent put into the garden by God, or did it subtly insinuate itself there? Does evil leap upon creation and take it unaware and by disguise even from the beginning, or did God know that it would do so and consent to it for reasons of His own? So many theological questions remain unanswered and the believer must be content that they remain so. We have only subsequent salvation history as our guide. Perhaps no text can explain what really happened because its point of view is limited to dealing with human beings as they are and might again become.

After the metaphysical fall, begins the long and elaborate story of redemption by the means of choosing a people whose national history finally becomes dispositive for all of humankind. Is this to reason backward from contingent events to search for a universal meaning? What is the status to be afforded to a text that often serves unworthy ends by justifying aggression? Must secular knowledge shift aside as it were to make room for this theological account of all things? Is the Christian explanation universal and hence mandatory for reason to accept, not only before the initial trier of fact (to use a legal analogy) but even before an appellate tribunal so that sustained inquiry must always leave the Judeo-Christian explanation alone standing? Or should reason as well approve the religious insights that only other cultures would allow to emerge? An example is the Hindu point of view that sees instead of unity, a multitude of gods with divergent aims, yet still part of one great silent and inscrutable being, Brahma. Then there is the great appeal of submission to Allah which promises to silence all divergent views, which melt before the absolute otherness of a god who will not be questioned, but only reveals itelf (and that finally and forever) in the Koran.

Where does the yet-to-be-committed-believer turn if he or she would be certain in their faith and not succumb to mere indoctrination or hereditary belief? Am I to be a teacher on these matters to such a man as Professor Moriarty whose entire outlook stems from a precisely contrarian set of assumptions as to the value of all things or do I announce them here only for my own security?

November 1, 1891
Tehran, Persia

In my last entry I was able to summarize to myself the conclusions of my faith (such as it is), but I often wonder, not at my own faith, but at the nature of faith itself. Why should it be so necessary? The account of the Garden of Eden implies that God's original intent was to walk side-by-side with man in familiar intercourse. It is the hunger for wholeness and completion, in relation to a force that would remedy all things, that explains the religious nature of man.

From whence then comes this hunger if it is not to be

filled? This hunger of man is what I see represented each day in the Mosques. At the times of prayer all activity ceases and man returns to that primal moment with God, no longer seeking to be like God knowing Good and evil, man bows down in utter submission to God and makes a personal abandonment of that primal sin in Eden. By submitting man takes on again that role designed for him and under the terms defined by God and blindly awaits God's mercy (for is not Allah above all merciful and compassionate). The god of the Moslems demands no sacrifice, no elaborate Levite priesthood, and no cross in Gethsemane to cancel the sins originating in the Garden of Eden. Each man, in a sense, is again Adam who may choose between good and evil and not be saved by mediated Grace, as in Christianity, but directly and by his own choice; to submit to the teaching of the Koran or to refuse and suffer the chastisement due to that refusal on the last day.

There is a dignity in this Islamic position which elevates man beyond the weakness of ongoing sin that Christianity recognizes as primal and ongoing. The early Church admits only one Baptism to remit all sin by joining us to Christ who does for us what no mere mortal submission may ever accomplish. This Baptism would so change and efface our prior natures that we would be something entirely new. The Baptized soul would in effect be more in God than the primal couple of Eden (who were but themselves) for the Baptized would be part and parcel with Christ in one essence with Jesus. Collectively they would be a Church, which itself would be One Body, with its destiny to be united forever in the fullness of time with Christ as the Divine Spouse who would then present us to God the Father as a now finished creation that could partake of a greater intimacy then simply walking with God in the Garden of Eden ever could be. The Baptized would now be in and of God. Despite this extraordinary dignity to be conferred by Baptism, Christianity advises a role of simplicity to the faithful and a familiarity that dares look to God in an almost playful frivolity as Abba. Christianity asks that we become like little children in order to enter the Kingdom of Heaven. This admonition implies that God delights in his children and listens to their petty needs addressed to Him as Abba.

The world of Islam would find this attitude of the believer to be degrading to God and perhaps even to man. Islam grants to its stern-faced followers their full stature as man and is never more itself than when seen in the spectacle of a great bearded warrior laying down his scimitar and lying on his face to show his submission at the sacred hours of the day. He is no child, helpless in sin, saved only by Baptism and grace; rather, the devout Mohammedan owes his version of Baptism to the echoing of a great proclamation: that there is no God but Allah and Mohammed is His Prophet. The faithful Islamic believer's every action thereafter becomes a service and a following of the Koran and of the Hadith and finally in the collectivity he follows the laws of Sharia and should he fail in all of this he returns to God many times a day and asks for mercy.

Shall these versions of the one same God between the three faiths tracing their validity back to Abraham ever be reconciled? Will Torah, Baptism, and Submission ever be one? Will all Believers find, in their respective ways, the fruit of their separate paths to find God again, and yield again to God and so foreswear forever that sin that first set us on a path apart from God in bloodshed?

So we must hope, for a sincere heart God will not abandon. It must be our guide in such inscrutable areas as these. The teachings of each belief-system claim to be revealed: yet are they not still, by the mere fact of verbal formulation and by being addressed to the human mind, limited as our conceptions are, capable of distortion by the very act of definition and of reception? We see, as St. Paul once said so well, in a glass darkly. Will a time ever come when we may hope to know God even as we are already known? Ah, but how much conflict must there be until that day, which may only dawn with the Day of Judgment that is anticipated by all three faiths...

Dr. Watson's Narrative Continues

I set the volume containing Holmes' journal down on the table at my side and looked out of the window. I had read the account slowly, pausing now and again to think deeply about what I was reading. I realized that Holmes was writing his thoughts as they came to him and that the fruits of his meditations were not the result of that moment only but were the result of months and years of internal speculation. His great mind had not ceased to ponder the problems of the ages that so many dismiss so easily. Our ultimate fate must trouble us all and perhaps this is why we so seldom wish to confront it.

I have often walked down Pall Mall in London or through Piccadilly Circus and noticed the press of humanity all about me. I would stare into the faces and wonder at the lines inscribed upon those many visages. Any crowd is really a collection of individuals after all. Each sails the barque of his own troubles and hopes through the great sea of other minds, each a silent universe as they pass. It takes an effort to freeze a given moment, but I would imagine at such times that if the general press and flow would cease but for an instant so that each might look into one another's face and glimpse the common humanity that is so often lost in the urgent course of events, a great revolution would occur. The pressures of time often reduce us to mere human molecules and our particular humanity is lost in the mass. We flow past each other as though we had no real sense of ourselves, as though there was no candle within us but only a darkened phosphorescence, like those tiny sparks of light that appear in the stirred waters of the sea on a summer night at Brighton, where I often took my wife on our holidays. I would bend over and stir the waters with my walking stick and the path traced by my stick would remain for an instant in the light given off as these small organisms were agitated in turn. Their bright glow appeared for just an instant and was as swiftly gone and only the general path was shown by the brief succession of their lights. The path was discernible, but the individuals who traced it had already fallen back into the blackness of the darkened sea.

My wife was amused, as I had intended her to be, but I as a doctor could think only that my patients were like these creatures. As a physician I had learned to adopt an attitude of basic objectivity. It is the habit of doctors to say, "I have an interesting case of a gangrenous limb in room 32," or "I operated on a cancer this morning in the patient in room 47, quite deeply rooted it was, but I believe the patient may respond well." Names are often lost in the general welter of diseased tissues that one observes over a lifetime as a doctor. It requires an effort to see that each represents a unique personal situation and that I, the doctor, am not myself immortal, but carry the same body about with me as my patients and that we all float daily over the abyss of death. I often marvel that I have survived so long after the many dangers that I have faced.

My days with Sherlock Holmes and his intense concentration on solving individual cases would often restore me to health after a particularly intense time in my practice. His own cases took place in the open air after all, far distant from the smell of dank corridors with their smell of sickness, of idaform, alcohol, and formaldehyde. My readers no doubt have noted that I would often appear not to be engaged in practice at all, since I so often had time to spare to accompany Holmes at a moment's notice. This was because I grew gradually to loathe the practice of medicine. So much damage occurs in lives before a doctor can ever intervene. People come to us when they are already dying from the abuses of a life-time. I think often of my poor brother who was a drunkard and of his horrible end. He was far advanced in cirrhosis of the liver and I can recall how upon his deathbed he grasped my hand pleading with me to stop the pain as the blood gurgled in his throat. He died of a severe hemorrhage incident upon liver damage. I recall that afterwards Holmes took me away to Deauville for a week of rest on the channel. He tried then to help me to forget, as well as I could, that last terrible scene. I look leave at that time from the hospital where I was doing rounds as a surgeon prior to establishing a small practice of my own, one restricted to ocular patients after my marriage.

On the aforementioned occasion we would walk along the sands each day and Holmes would beguile me with his various discourses on diverse subjects. How wrong I had been in my early initial assessment of Holmes' education. I had once stated that his knowledge of literature and philosophy was nil when we first met. Holmes had hidden well his knowledge of these subjects. It later appeared that he had attended Cambridge and taken a first in French. He had studied for years the poems of the early troubadours and his knowledge of medieval melodies and Provencal songs was second to none. It was only later that he turned to chemistry at the University of London. As the third Holmes son, he was of the class of the landed gentry. Sherringford, his eldest brother, had inherited the estate in Yorkshire, although both Mycroft and Sherlock were given excellent opportunities in life and a stipend from the estate so as to live as gentlemen.

The usual practice of this class was to send the younger sons of noble families into the military or law, or into diplomacy or into the ministry. Mycroft had chosen a unique service to the government of England, while Sherlock, his younger brother by some five years, had surprised the family by his artistic leanings. They had thought at the time that perhaps he would retire to a life as a fellow at the university and at last become a professor. Holmes had rebelled at this of course. He hungered for life in the raw. He felt that the idealism of his youth must be tempered by a stern encounter with the facts of common life.

He lived for a time in one of those border regions that separate Westminster from the East-end. It was there that he acquired those skills in observation and imitation of the manners and voice of various parts of the English working-class that were to serve him so well later when he would adopt various convincing disguises in his work as a detective. He had entertained some revolutionary political leanings at the time of a Chartist nature. He once confessed this to me, but they were swiftly extinguished by his observation of the mediocrity of the men elected to the House of Commons. In politics he finally adopted the views of the Confucians. The Chinese system of tribute is one whereby each party and level of the social structure knows his or its place and pursues virtue in emulation of the Emperor, seemed most likely to ensure social order. This system of thought sees virtue as the fruit of an ordered hierarchy. Democracy was to Holmes simply a version of Thomas Hobbes' vision in which all men exist in a brutal state of nature with the hand of each raised against his fellows. The pursuit of individual good, if only restrained by law, never forces the individual to internalize the law's demands. In fact the task of the self-seeking individual is always to see the law as an impediment to action. This means that a democracy is always held together by force more than by enlightened conviction. Holmes would often point to the example of America with its vast inequities (which had grown only more pronounced in the 1870's and the 1880's in spite of all pretentions to political equality in that country). I would bristle at this attitude of his for I had once entertained dreams of going to Nevada to try my hand as a doctor on the great Comstock Silver Lode. Holmes would chide me about this fanciful idea from time to time, but do we not all have romantic visions in our youth?

My own family was not well off during my youth and my education came to me as an army physician trained at the expense of the Queen's Northumberland Fusiliers. I had seen first-hand the disappointments of the British tradesman that had finally led my elder brother into drink. I can still recall his youthful dreams of doing well in the linen export trade, of his many trips to Ireland and to America when I was a lad. He was many years my senior. He had begun his business in the late 1850's after the ravages of the famine years of the 1840's and the height of the Irish immigration to England and to America. He started out in Glasgow and established a branch of the firm he was with in Belfast and for awhile things looked as though he would prosper there. It was only in later years that with increasing competition from larger export firms that he began to retreat into a gin-soaked stupor at night after work. He did well to hide his secret pain as well as he did from me. My parents had long passed on with the comfort that their eldest son had escaped the threats of poverty that had so darkened their own years and prematurely aged them. My parents had hoped that my brother would be able to provide for my education.

My father was a mining superintendent for a time, but the squalor of the collieries was such and his heart too tender to watch the young lads coughing their lives away with the black-lung disease that killed so many while they were yet in the vigor of middle-life. He went into a grocery business, but it did not prosper because he often fed the hollow-eyed women whose husbands had been killed in the mines. England was a Christian nation of course, but that Christianity had never prevented the growth of the great fortunes nor ensured sufficient largess to succor England's poor, let alone the Scots and the Irish. Parliamentary democracy was a cloak that ill-the fitted our own aristocracy that had known its darkest hours in the 1790's when many feared that the French Revolution might reach even our own shores. It might so have done so had Napoleon been more of a republican and less of a king in disguise.

All of these experiences and reflections told upon me and I began my life as a disillusioned young man. As a result I served my countrymen more than I served my country. One might have thought that from our divergent antecedents that Holmes and I would not have been a likely pair to strike up a friendship as deep as it became after our accidental acquaintance. Holmes' eldest brother, Sherringford, had sat for a time as a member of the House of Lords but had grown disillusioned at last and returned to the Holmes estate in Yorkshire that was called Sigerside where the tenants raised a particularly hearty breed of sheep as the source of the fine woolen goods of the district. There were also mineral interests on the estate. I knew little more than this of his domestic background at the time because Holmes did not often speak of personal matters.

A certain degree of coolness existed between the Holmes brothers that while not amounting to any dislike for one another was more of a testimony to the independence of each of them in the lives that they had chosen. Mycroft, whom I had met on occasion, may have been the most conservative of the Holmes brothers at one time. He noticed little to object to on principle in his role of service to the British Empire. When Holmes would suggest that he was a Shogun in disguise and should be wearing a kimono as in Japan, Mycroft was not amused. He had learned to tolerate the humor of my friend without enjoying it. Holmes had once given Mycroft a copy of the I-Ching, but Mycroft said that if he must have his fortune told he preferred tea-leaf reading. He had thought this a great sally of wit and his rumbling laugh shook him as though it were an eruption buried deep below the surface of the earth. Between the three of us, Mycroft, Sherlock, and I, we summed up the great options of political order: Empire, Aristocratic rule of the most virtuous, or the popular sharing of the franchise in a democracy.

Anarchy, in contrast to the various forms of government, is the predictable result of excess by any one system which breeds revolt at last if it should be out of tune with the requirements of the great un-political masses of mankind. Each form of government is stable in its way and each has known different manifestations of injustice. Perhaps justice is after all a vain pursuit, but we have no choice but to do so, for without at least a perception of legitimacy, there can be no effective rule. Perhaps it was the failure to obtain justice in any lasting way through any form of political governance and order that first turned Holmes' thoughts towards religion and to metaphysics. He desired that complete and rounded conception of the universe that motivates all of the great theoreticians.

The hunger for the comprehensive leads to the creation of the great epics in both literature and religion. One need think only of the songs of the Vedas or the great summary of Hindu thought in the Upanishads to see this impulse. In our own literature there is for instance that epic poem by John Milton, "Paradise Lost," the intent of which was to justify the ways of God to man. So in these last journal entries of Sherlock Holmes, made on his eastern journey, I could see the makings of Holmes' own effort to justify the ways of God to men, but first of course, he would need to justify God's ways to himself, for does not every religious author first need himself to be convinced that he is on the right path after all. I found myself wondering if Mohammed felt that the words of his recitations were his own or did they come from some source speaking through him. We must find it hard to imagine duplicity in the founder of any religion, yet doubt remains. Do they rely upon mere interior assurance for their assertions, or does God in fact speak through them?

Joseph Smith for instance, as a product of American revivalism, claimed to have transcribed a text already written upon tablets. In this claim he resembles Mohammed whose own text, "The Koran," is said to exist in heaven. What a strange evolution of the word is shown in both religions and how at variance they are with the understanding of prophesy in the Bible whose prophets were far more humble. It is no longer merely a matter of a prophet being commissioned by means of a burning coal touched to the lips, but a prospective prophet must now possess a word that must be identical with a finished text: one written, edited, and bound in heaven itself and only now delivered intact.

Is this phenomenon to be traced to a doubt of whether our prophets are mere human conduits for a message entrusted to their fragile care or are they originators akin to other literary artists? There are, after all, so many prophets. Has this plethora of religious alternatives led to a purely worldly desire for a consolidation of doctrines? Each new religion seems now to require a new revelation, if only to dust off the accretions of reflection upon established revelations made over the centuries.

But what prophet's work can hope to stand alone without the support of a community, of ritual, and of commentary? Where would contemporary Judaism be without the Talmud to keep the Torah alive and vital? I have often asked myself, as one who does not follow the prescriptions and proscriptions of the Papacy and his Magisterium of the Bishops in union with the Pope, whether Catholicism would have survived without the grandeur of art to support it? The Great Dome of Saint Peter's Basilica and the aspiring music of polyphonic chant in the works of the great Palestrina make the majesty of God visible to the senses of man. Can mere doctrine standing alone ever capture the imagination and compel conviction?

Religion is at one and the same time the preoccupation of the human race and that which it most ignores. For myself, I am glad of any belief-system that may serve to make men better and to act in some way to enforce our pretentions to be other than animals (but of a particularly cunning type). Without religion all becomes with time but the exertion of power based upon competitive desire. What altruism can else ever hope to survive the awareness in the individual of the shortness of time and the limitation of all human resources? My first instinct then where religion is concerned is to be tolerant, not because I am indifferent, but because I expect so little from my fellow man. If at the same time, I am somewhat conventional in my outlook, it is because I was raised in the Church of England. Membership therein was the one gesture of my humble parents towards obtaining for their sons the aristocratic status so often desired by the middle-classes. It was there that my brother and I grew acquainted with the finely-dressed and well-bred British upper-class gentlemen and ladies, whom my brother long sought to imitate, but without success. I possess still the fine watch that had once been his most prized possession. It descended to me upon his death. Whenever I wind it I think of him and of the tragedy of misplaced ambitions...

It was from such musings that I was suddenly interrupted by a knock on my door. It was Sir Henry. The afternoon was well advanced and the light beyond my window was fading over the moors. Sir Henry entered at once and said, "Dr. Watson... what? Why are you sitting here in the gloaming? You might have joined me in the library. I have been reading the Iliad, as Mr.

Holmes suggested, and seeking to discover some clue as to Holmes' plan to apprehend, or at least interfere with the efforts of our foes. I confess that the process of my own reasoning has been most unsatisfactory though and I can only trust that you may have greater insight than I how he will proceed."

I answered him by advising patience and by telling him that I had often remained in the dark during the course of his investigations only to find that all was made clear at last when matters had reached the point where a final confrontation might occur. Holmes often preferred to keep his own counsel at the early stages of a case, but whether the purpose of this was not to break his thread of concentration by setting down premature conclusions that might bias his judgment in the light of further revelations, or whether it was to enhance his own pleasure when, with the skill of a magician, he would cast aside the veil and reveal the finished product of his efforts, I could never resolve in my mind. I think that both factors played a part in his method and I had too much respect for his artistic nature to ask that he vary it simply to gratify my own curiosity. His method only made it easier to write up my own accounts later, for I could recall my own bewilderment at the time and thus share its nature with my readers.

Holmes had always been averse though to publicity. No doubt this came from his aristocratic breeding which inclined him to despise anything as cheap as public acclaim. Still there was the artist in his blood to contend with and what artist does not desire a wider audience rather than that his work should languish in some private collection? The result was that he could satisfy his conscience by deprecating my work while secretly enjoying its effect, preferring as he did that the extent of my reading audience and his own admirers remain in the darkness beyond the footlights. He took sufficient interior joy in solving the cases presented to him that little else was necessary, but he would not turn aside from occasional public praise for the results that he obtained.

I forgave him everything, for I knew how delicate the balance of his own complex personality was. His times of brooding silence often alarmed me, for I could not know to what depths of desperation these black moods might lead him. He would often emerge from them though, suddenly and with a sort of desperate energy. At such times he would spend himself without counting the cost. He seemed to take a delight at times in dangerous exertion, as if by so acting he might defy the limits that nature imposes upon us all. I will even go so far as to say that he treated each case as if its solution might restore some sort of primal order to the universe as a whole, which for him was seemed always to be falling into obsolescence and decay.

There was always something of the heroic figure in him as though the world rested upon his shoulders like Atlas and whatever position he took towards the value of life itself would determine whether the world as he knew it would continue to exist. I will not say that he was delusional in this attitude for which of us does not see the world as in some way our own daily creation? We rise each day and the earth spreads about us and our primary concern lies not with the plights of distant lands, but rather with the state of our digestion and what the articles may say in our paper as we sit down over our eggs and coffee. Holmes' own preoccupations though often went to the other extreme. He would seek an order in the world that it does not present and demand justice as the price of living. It was as though he needed first to justify the world to himself before he would consent to living in it.

This was more than blasphemous pride however. It was that he felt that there must be a world of greater reality behind that which presents itself to us. Life often appears in a distorting mirror, for who can imagine such tales of horror as we read of daily? To perceive evil at all is to feel gradually that it is universal in extent. It seeps into us until all of life becomes unsatisfactory. Holmes had this perception often and to an extreme degree. I would insist that he seek solace in the many things that did in fact bring him joy such as music, good food at Simpsons, and occasional travel. I often wondered that he did not take a wife, for in my own life the solace and care of a woman had made my own life bearable. I even suggested as much to him from time to time but he would then trot out his old story of Irene Adler, confused between his admiration for her wit and possibly with a deeper and undefined set of feelings that were in any case far short of love.

I often thought that he dreaded having children for fear that he would neglect them. His work and the calls made upon him for aid were all-consuming and his love of the order provided by his own small universe was, for all the seeming disorder of his rooms, still precious to him. His pipes, his chemical apparatus, his books of reference, and even his small but select wardrobe were part of his abstemious and cat-like nature. When I pointed out that I myself was childless yet my marriage was still satisfactory, he would point out that he had been raised to believe in the duty to keep the lineage going and that marriage for him would entail children also. In his black moods he would view with trepidation the thought of bringing children into a world that had yet to protect the children already born. Holmes also feared that the mood and general outlook of the parent is often visited upon the child and he feared to impose upon a new generation the same burdens of doubt and fear in the face of mortal existence that were often too much for even he himself to bear.

For all of these reasons and not from the lack of a most passionate nature, as was manifest in his occasional poetic appreciations that showed that he was not insensible to beauty, that Holmes turned aside from marriage and from women. Many men eventually discover after living together for some years that they begin to see life through the perspective of their wives. It is the province of women to have certain unquestioned and unquestionable set-ideas on certain matters and not to budge from them. Most men learn to coil about in some manner and to accommodate whatever set of preconceived values their wives possess. In return they are often the recipients of that fierce love and protectiveness that the lioness exhibits. This loyalty and protectiveness is directed towards the husband and their children, for women are the great conservators of culture and of the wisdom of the human race. Men are often, even in old-age rather like children, always busy with some toy or other of their imaginations and the good woman will both allow this and provide that sturdy support that a man so often needs in order to preserve his own heroic image as he goes forth into battle. Marriage then is largely the art of finding a balance or an equilibrium and yet maintaining some element of adventure and growth as well.

For Sherlock Holmes such equilibrium was a goal that even within himself was difficult to achieve. His intractable nature would certainly have made marriage a trying task. The man without a family cannot evade the questions of his life by passing that burden on to his posterity in the family saga, which according to one theory of Holmes leaves a pattern for the path of the individual life. The single man must accept the fact that he must resolve all of the great questions alone and in his own life reach some sense of completion or admit that he has failed in his life task. Perhaps it was this very desperation that accounted for Holmes' great religious quest and for his choice of his profession as a Consulting Detective. All of this and more I knew about my friend and I tried in my own way to explain and answer the questions posed by Sir Henry, by saying that Holmes often kept his own counsel until the end and only revealed what was absolutely necessary. There were always good reasons for this and I had learned to trust the wisdom of this manner of proceeding.

Holmes returned as he said he would by the train that evening. We had chosen to await his coming before dining and were in the library each with a glass of amontillado when he at last arrived. He entered, still flushed with the chill of the night and rubbing his hands briskly.

"Ah gentlemen, I must thank you for awaiting me to join you for dinner. I trust that you are not yourselves famished. As for me, I have had nothing to eat all day, unless it was a most unsatisfactory steak and kidney pie served in the dining-car this morning. Yes, I shall have some wine." He took a seat before the fire and I could tell by his air of suppressed excitement that all had gone well in Exeter.

Both Sir Henry and I looked at him expectantly and he

laughed. "Come Gentlemen, let us first address ourselves to the fine table that Sir Henry's hospitality has provided, and then over a restful pipe, we may discuss our plans."

After an excellent meal featuring a leg of Devon lamb, cooked in claret with rosemary, we adjourned to the library with our port and sitting around the blazing fire were able at last to hear a particularized account of Holmes' day in Exeter.

"I was able to explain our situation to a firm of solicitors in Exeter, our plan to exchange the Murillo papers for the person of Lady Beryl. They will see to it that a deposit box is prepared and will arrange all matters with the bank. They have also drawn up a contract that explains that in return for One Pound Sterling, plus other valuable consideration, that Sir Henry Baskerville and Lady Beryl Baskerville agree to transfer various papers in their possession to the representatives of Rodger Baskerville upon the dully witnessed execution of the contract by both Sir Henry Baskerville and Lady Beryl Baskerville, such signing to occur on a date certain upon the premises of the Royal Devonshire Bank and Trust Company the in the first week of November 1896. I anticipate hearing by telegram from Rodger Baskerville that he has consented to the exchange. His representative will have picked up the note left on High Tor as he requested that we do. The exchange will take some time yet, since the representatives will first want to be sure of the nature of the papers and that they are complete. The day of exchange will involve some additional reading and effort on their part. Lady Beryl will of course be brought there in person to sign over the document of transfer and once having signed will be free to return to Baskerville Hall with us."

"Then why should we even include the papers once Lady Beryl is safely in our hands," I inquired.

"I am afraid that we must, Watson. The solicitors will no doubt ask for a preliminary inspection prior to the date of transfer. The Bank will then act in an escrow capacity to ensure that we have made no withdrawals or substitutions after the inspection. Each visit to the vault is recorded. Lady Beryl will not be brought round until on the day of the transfer an agent has ascertained that all is as it should be on our side."

"And we cannot then have these men arrested?" asked Sir Henry.

"They are merely legal representatives. No party to this transaction will announce that Lady Beryl has been abducted. We were quite wise to keep this matter out of the newspapers. Doing the transfer in this dry and businesslike way is the very security that Rodger Baskerville would expect from us and explains why he trusted me to make the arrangements. At the same time he will no doubt expect that I have some stratagem in effect that will attempt to follow the papers back to him."

"And what is that stratagem?" asked Sir Henry with anticipation.

"Alas, Gentlemen, I have none," said Holmes. "Rodger Baskerville will receive the papers and he will not be traced, nor will we attempt to re-secure the papers."

Sir Henry and I stared at each other aghast at Holmes' words. I felt a profound embarrassment for my friend at that moment. I could only think that the strain of the recent events had drained even his resources of their usual reserve of imagination. Rodger Baskerville would obtain the papers and be able to use them to obtain money or concessions from some of the most powerful men in America. He would use the money obtained, no doubt, to advance any number of other criminal endeavors. Worst of all he would escape any just retribution for the abduction of Lady Beryl and the attempt long ago on the life of Sir Henry and the actual murder of Sir Henry's uncle, Sir Charles Baskerville.

"But this is intolerable Holmes, is there nothing you can do?" I cried.

Holmes smiled. "Well I am not infallible, but I do have one thing in mind. I propose to make the papers that we deliver to him worthless."

"How will you do that?" I inquired overcome by my surprise.

"I shall do so by the simple measure of publishing them myself in America before he can use them for blackmail. One can hardly obtain money as a blackmailer when the news is already out of the bag as it were. The papers will then be of only historical interest. Rodger Baskerville will be most perturbed of course. In fact I will go so far as to say that he will be furious. All of the ancient blood of his old ancestor, Sir Hugo Baskerville, will come roaring out of him, that ancestor who rode to his death that night in the 1600's when after a similar abduction (in that case it was a local peasant lass who escaped his clutches) he left the great Hall of Baskerville roaring that he would trade his very soul if he might still apprehend the girl. Such was the beginning of the curse of the Baskervilles and the origin of the great hound that pursued the heirs of that bloodline for generations. I count upon it that Rodger Baskerville will then throw all caution to the winds and seek revenge upon those who have fooled him. He will make a bold attempt upon the life of Sir Henry and Lady Beryl and it is then that we will finally pounce upon him and end his long reign of terror."

As listeners we were both dumbfounded at hearing of this audacious plan.

"But how will you accomplish this?" asked Sir Henry after a long pause during which we both considered these startling revelations.

"We will do so by guarding you most closely, Sir Henry. We will adopt the most strenuous precautions and by that very means draw him in. He will not be able to resist the challenge. You will recall that his last attempt upon your life was made when we allowed you to appear unguarded so that he could put the hound upon your scent. This time we will adopt the opposite tactic. We will guard you closely. His own pride will cause him to assume that he can penetrate our defenses and we will finally allow him to do so. The gap we will leave will be our place of ambush. We will use his own character against him and by seeming to be caught ourselves unaware, we shall catch him in a device of his own making. It is the only way to apprehend a man as resourceful as he is."

"The man himself gave me the hint when he requested that

I devise the means for the transfer of Lady Beryl. It was his way of mocking me and of forcing me to devise the means of our own defeat by surrendering the papers. This told me that there is still a war of wits going on between us and that he relishes the game as much as the candle. I had my very first hint as to his character when, as you will recall after your first arrival in London Sir Henry, he followed you in a cab intending to kill you on the spot. When we traced that cab and inquired of the driver who his fare was, we found that the name that he had given the driver was my own name of Sherlock Holmes. It was definitely a coup on his part. The man loves the pursuit, witness his chase of the elusive but fragile butterflies and moths in his collection. He would drop everything in a trice upon spotting one and go running about with his net. The man is like a sight-hound that once having sighted its prey it will break its heart in the pursuit until it runs it down. I am dangling, what I hope will be an irresistible lure of vengeance, before him. It will place him at last in our hands. For years he has awaited the day when he might use the power that the possession of these papers represents. He knew that his wife would retain them, for in the days when he had exercised power over her he had impressed her with their importance to her people, that they might even be used one day to ensure the independence of her country from the northern imperial power. She therefore acted as a virtual conservator for them, while he was free to wander about at will, knowing them to be safe at the estate of Baskerville, for a future reclamation at a time of his choosing."

"Why then," asked Sir Henry, "did she not speak of them to me? I knew only that she possessed a curious box and that she placed great value upon it. Why did she not tell me of the contents? I might have read them and discovered their secrets and have been of some aid to her people long before this."

Holmes answered him. "She may have felt that it was by keeping silent about the papers that she could ensure the independence of her country, not understanding how best to use them. Who can say? Perhaps, over the years they assumed a sort of talismanic importance for her or perhaps they were so closely associated with her own painful past that she desired to forget about them. She could not determine to destroy them, but neither could she devote time to deciphering the cryptic importance placed upon them by her former husband."

I had been thinking of Holmes' plan to publish the papers. "But Holmes is there not some other danger inherent in your plan? Might there not be a libel suit in America after you publish these papers or at least strenuous protests and denials that might embarrass our own government? We will not have the original papers to prove our case."

"But we will, Watson. The box will contain the copies, not the originals, which we will retain. Our wily foe will no doubt give his solicitors an accurate description of the contents of the writings, but the actual details of the signatures, quality of paper, and seals will require the services of an expert to authenticate them. I am counting on his eagerness to regain possession as soon as possible, plus the fact that, since we are not blackmailers as he is, he will imagine that the papers are of no intrinsic use to us which will make him careless as to details of authentication. Have no fear, Sir Henry, his representatives will have only time for a cursory inspection prior to the actual transfer when they will have a longer period, but by then Lady Beryl will be at the bank and we will have her again under our protection."

Sir Henry looked troubled. "But why not simply give them the original documents, what are they to us?"

"Ah, there we must consider the unspoken wishes of Lady Beryl. Why did she insist so long on retaining the box and its precious contents? Was it not for the good of her countrymen who have suffered so much? Was it not to vindicate the death of her brother, when he attempted at last to hold Don Juan Murillo responsible for his crimes, that she has guarded them so well and kept their nature a secret even from you, Sir Henry? She watched as her father, one of the highest dignitaries of San Pedro, saw himself used, no doubt doing what he could to ameliorate the harsh rule of the dictator by persuading the people to make concessions, only to watch promise after promise betrayed. No, Sir

Henry, these papers are not ours to give away, least of all to this vicious man. They belong to the people of Costa Rica and Lady Beryl has kept their trust. Had she wished to simply surrender them she need not have placed herself again in the hands of her former husband. Even now, knowing the spirit of the lady, I have no doubt that she would meet any fate at his hands rather than surrender these papers to him. The originals will have every mark of authenticity to experts with the time to decipher them and to see how they form a seamless whole, a web of the systematic betrayal of her country to foreign speculators."

During Holmes' speech I could see the tears spring to the eyes of Sir Henry who stood up now and grasping the hand of my friend spoke in a choked voice. "How well you know her Holmes. You are right of course. Through these years I have watched as her beauty has known the first kiss of autumn. She might have gone with me anywhere in the world and spent with a clear conscience the money of the estate of the Baskervilles that I would so gladly have showered upon her to make up for the pain of her past. She might have had a glorious mansion in Montmartre in Paris with the city of light spread out before us or a villa in the foothills above Rome or to come with me back to Canada and have a ranch in the very shadow of the great Rocky Mountains, there to build an estate worthy of her in the great pine and fir forests of that region. But she would not have it so. She thought only of the name of Baskerville and of its vindication. She desired that as the estate had for so long drawn from the people of the community of Grimpen and the surrounding lands, that the time had come to restore a healthy yeomanry, to educate the children, to see that the cottagers had some joy in the bleak life afforded them upon these desolate moors. She had never lost that joy she had once known as a girl in the great festivals of her native Costa Rica, when every great feast of the Church would have its ferias. She desired above all to share her faith, so that a new Catholic chapel was to be built in Grimpen, for the people of the village cannot live upon bread alone. It would take the heart from her now to surrender to this evil man and though it be a great pain to me to risk her loss, I will not deprive her of that chance to see that these papers at last yield some good to the land of her youth."

Holmes nodded solemnly. "You are worthy of the Lady, Sir Henry. I assure you that we will use these papers to draw a belated justice down upon these men who hide behind batteries of attorneys and accountants and do as corporations and trusts what they would not be able to do in a democracy if its very dream had not faltered and failed to carry out the sanguine hopes of its founders. The voice of the people has now been dimmed and muted by a tide of commerce, a tide that spilling over even the vast borders of America, now reaches into even foreign lands to subvert the very natal democracies that look to America for guidance. In every system there are cynical men who know the means to subvert even noble structures and institutions to serve their own ends. America is no exception to this."

"But if these men have such power," I inquired, "will these papers not be simply claimed to be forgeries?"

Holmes smiled. "In the normal of course of events, yes. There would be lawsuits for libel and slander or attempts to buy us off, but it is here that the timing is critical. America has only just emerged from the great financial panic of 1893. Even now the nation is divided along the issue of coinage, whether it shall be of silver or of gold. The political stakes are immense. America is about to flex its muscles in the international arena. There is even talk of building a canal through Central America. Such a canal would secure America in its dominance of the Pacific region and of the islands of Hawaii and give America a first-claim status upon trade with Japan. The canal, which will no doubt remain under American control and administration, will also entail control over all of the Central American States as mere vassals of American policy. Such a canal will of course be one of the largest physical enterprises ever attempted by men. Nothing must detract from its great purposes. Vast sums are at stake. The faith of the American people, bled by civil war and depression, who must agree to see their nation's finances going forth to enrich many private enterprises, is essential to its completion. Should the project fail, the losses would be irreparable. The risks are great. At such a time, the people must have faith in their government of the people and by the people and for the people. It is at precisely this time that papers that will unmask the clandestine enterprises of the past in Costa Rica would do the most damage. Rodger Baskerville knows this of course. That is the reason why he has allowed Lady Beryl to keep these papers safe for so long. He himself chose years of obscurity, the better to throw off any pursuit, and meanwhile the value of these papers has been mellowing as a potent wine of international intrigue. Now he has chosen the very hour when their threatened publication will reap the greatest benefits. But he shall never see that harvest."

Again I spoke up. "But Holmes, is it prudent for us to publish them? What may the effect of public outrage be? Might it not even bring down the American government?"

"Oh I do not believe that the effect will be as great as that, Watson. These papers are very old now and the successors to the unjust benefits that were then received will count upon the short memory of the citizens to eventually exculpate them. The citizens of the United States will be told that Costa Rica was a country upon the frontier and that in its gallant march of manifest destiny, that America had no choice but to exercise selective brutality in order to develop the nation's resources, that the titans of industry know best the paths of destiny. It will not have been the first time that the Monroe Doctrine has opened the doors to the expansion of American borders and influence."

"The citizens of America will be asked whether, if given the chance, they would restore the lands stolen from the native peoples of America. Would they rip up the tracks of the great railroads that opened the farms that came in the wake of the buffalo slaughterers? Would they give back to Mexico the lands won in the war of 1849? What then is Costa Rica and the brutal cost of the railroad built there with slave labor, or the fate of the laborers on the great banana plantations now owned by American business interests throughout the tropics? But do not jump from this defense and justification to assume that the Murillo Papers are valueless. They are an embarrassment to American illusions as to their own virtuous intentions. It is always in the nature of great power to seek to avoid embarrassments at all costs. The uses of power must always appear to be benevolent. It must gradually attain the faith of a people, so that its endless depredations, born at the public expense, will go unnoticed. A nation does not surrender its freedoms all at once you see, but rather by degrees. The trick of the rulers is to distribute to the people the minimum requisite to satisfy their justifiable needs while taking from them that greater measure of their national wealth by channeling it selectively into the vast reservoirs of select private interests. If this policy is done over the course of years and adroitly, the people will never notice. They will work harder for a goal that is always just beyond their reach. They will sacrifice all to maintain an ideal image of the nation that is no longer sustained by the laws. The very word 'law' will become like a god for them. The phrase is, I believe, that no citizen shall be deprived of life, liberty, or property without due process of law."

"These words are at first glance most reassuring, but all hinges on the words "due process." Those small words are all that stands between a citizen and a vast governmental apparatus that can crush him as thoroughly as any great Baron might have crushed a peasant in the Middle Ages. Feudalism you see has never really ended. There are still lords, vassals, and serfs as determined by net worth if not by the ownership of feudal freeholds. I have spent some little time investigating the history of property relationships in early English charters and have found that they are similar to many modern trust agreements and corporate charters."

"But surely," said I, "in a democracy elected by a free people the elected representatives must know that they are finally answerable to the people and that their power is not theirs but resides in the people as sovereign?"

Holmes shook his head when I stopped speaking. "You have put your finger right upon the great problem of representative democracies, Watson. America from its inception was an act of faith in the wisdom of men who understood the dangers of power. To their credit, they did what they could to prevent great power from amassing itself, even within the government. There was even a debate at the time of the Constitutional Convention as to whether there should not be a council of three rather than a single unitary executive in the person of the President. One must remember always that the original colonies were left, after the American Revolution, in a most humble and impoverished position. Years of war with the greatest sea power in the world had left great loss of life, trade was in a shambles, and it was just in this hour of peril that a divided Confederation of independent states desired to turn itself into a single republic by a means not tried since the days of the ancient city-states of Greece or that of Rome. We must not speak too harshly of the men who formed the government of the confederation that later became a republic. The great Constitution that they later visited upon the world withstood even the trials of a great civil war. Who could then foretell that when in the very hour of victory the nation that had been sundered and yet had reconstituted itself, would face a still greater threat to liberty than any heretofore encountered? This threat may even now be causing that great nation to rot from within. The disease is the great arising power of massed wealth gathered into a few hands. With this concentration comes an ancillary power to subvert even the great institutions of democratic government and to turn it from its service of the people to become a means for the exploitation of foreign nations for private gain."

"But that is intolerable," I cried.

What Holmes had just said was not a complete surprise to me, for I had watched as the members of a new American aristocracy came over each year for the London season and had witnessed how even Europe now seemed to be a colony for the richest Americans. I had gone to auction houses such as Sothebys and had watched as priceless items went with increasing frequency to the rich American bidders who were building for themselves great estates along the Hudson River or in Newport or in Lenox. It had always surprised me that in America, the land of opportunity and equality in which the taxing power still remained formally with the people, such vast agglomerations of wealth were even possible. The very scale of these enterprises dwarfed the worker who was now less a citizen than he was a mere cog in the great wheels of the industrial machine. Literacy and citizenship demand leisure and how few could spare the time to engage in a general debate of significant issues. The gap between rhetoric and reality had widened with the years. Many western farms were in debt and dependent upon the free coinage of silver from the Comstock Lode so as to so prevent the deflation of agricultural products in order that the immigrant farmers might repay their loans and not lose the farms carved out of a wilderness. If prices deflated, then the sale of their produce could never generate the funds to pay their debts and the mortgage on their farms, many of them in the arid western regions with small yields to the acre, would be subject to foreclosure by the wealthy eastern banking interests. My outburst to Holmes was then, less an evidence of my surprise than it was of my indignation that what I feared to be true was in fact the case: that a vast tyranny of wealth had dawned upon the world and had even affected America and its noble spirit, an America, which had symbolized for many the last, best hope of mankind to found a structure of justice upon the earth.

"Yes it is as you say intolerable," answered Holmes. "But we, in our small way may strike a blow for freedom and leave a small record that we have not passed here in vain. We shall go to America and see firsthand what may be done."

"But have you forgotten the outstanding matter of Baron Maupertuis?" asked Sir Henry who had remained silent during our spirited exchange as his thoughts were no doubt abstracted by the future fate of his wife.

"Not at all, Sir Henry," answered Holmes. "Indeed, I believe that our proposed actions on our mission to America may be the source of the very means that I have required to enable me to deal with that gentleman. You have, I trust, been reading the Iliad as I recommended? Excellent, I trust that it has engaged both your interest and more your imagination for it is there that all crimes are finally solved. We must imagine before we may construct. What endeavor or discovery but first exists in the mind? The mind is always as it were beyond itself in those distant places into which it has yet to venture."

Both Sir Henry and I were anxious that he should continue his discourse, but that was all that Holmes would say at the time and in spite of our questions he withdrew again into that silence that I knew from long experience would be impenetrable. He was like a teacher who knew always when the lesson of the day had been completed, but who always left sufficient hints to leave his students with a passion for what had yet to be revealed.

During the entirety of the above related exchange, Professor Moriarty had remained remarkably quiet. Such was my own involvement in the discussion that I had failed to remark on the unusualness of his lack of comment. That he had also followed Holmes closely though, I could not doubt. He had sat, deep within his own armchair, while his piercing hooded-eyes showed that deep and unique intelligence that had so long enabled him to dominate the criminal underworld of London, and indeed of all England.

As Holmes concluded his remarkable statement I could see a brief exchange of glances between the two men that seemed to convey something of importance. This impression was only strengthened when Holmes proceeded to beckon to the Professor and the two men rose together and proceeded to leave the room. I could not but think that Holmes needed to reassure the Professor that his own concerns would not be neglected and that he was making some progress in the search for the horse, Silverstar.

Sir Henry and I were therefore left alone in the room. I walked to the window and gazed out into the darkness. It was at just such times that I felt the great forces that flow continually about us, forces for good or for evil. How finely balanced are the threads of circumstance. I had read much of the works of Thomas Hardy, that grim Somerset novelist and poet, who had brooded more than most men upon the role of chance in human life. It had often so appeared to me that our lives are but the patterns of falling grains of sand. Had the windblown but for an instant from a different direction, had we chanced to catch a different tram-car on a Paris afternoon, had we but awoken an hour later upon a summer day, then all might have been different in our lives!

The very course of our lives is momentarily deflected by the slightest turbulence. Some whisper in the dark may be spoken of tomorrow in the news of the day and thus be heard while a wise man may shout into the great sea-wind of public indifference and receive no audience. Happiness, that but yesterday seemed to be within our grasp, is lost today forever as the result of a mere trifle. A harsh word, a bitter phrase that leaps unbidden to the lips, and suddenly a chasm may emerge between friends, while a stranger's mere nod or kindly word may reacquaint one with the reality of human solidarity and restore our hopes.

Does nature pity us at all? As I gazed then into the bleak late-autumn night and heard, as I had so often heard since my arrival, the moaning of the trees in the yew alley, I thought of these things and wondered if men will ever be equal to the demands made upon them by life. How often had I not wished to find a place of repose and certainty from which in my later years to sift the evidence and to arrive at a final assessment of life. Was the game worth the candle? But it is not for us to judge this life that we live. It is not possible for man as man to stand as it were outside and to gaze into the spectral globe of his own existence, to peer beneath the mists, and to discover the ley-lines of the forces that govern all things. We are encased by life from the moment of our birth until our final breath when the great hand of oblivion sponges away both our memories and our regrets and only a fleshly effigy remains that will soon crumble away into dust.

I decided that it was time to retire and to seek what solace I might find in a reading from Holmes' Journal which still occupied my thoughts, even in the midst of the many complex problems that now beset us. I therefore bid Sir Henry goodnight and left the room. The great staircase was illuminated by the oil-lamp that burned upon the landing mid-way up. My footsteps were clearly audible upon the granite steps. At the top of the stairs a carpet finally relieved the chill austerity of the stone passage and some newly acquired teak furniture and paintings broke the bleakness of the long expanse of the hallways.

As I passed the study door, the door to my room, and then that of Sir Henry, I came finally to the room that was occupied by Holmes. I could hear the low murmur of voices. I perceived as well that a yellow light was escaping from beneath the door. Holmes was clearly still up and engaged in discussing matters with the Professor. I retreated though to my own room and closing the great door with its sturdy iron-latch, I went over to the table where I had left the journal. I went over to the fireplace and stirred the coals in the grate. I then lit a match and applied it to the oil lamp and soon a cozy glow relieved the gloom. I filled and lit my bulldog pipe with my usual Cavendish mixture and after a few grateful puffs I began to read.

From the Journal of Sherlock Holmes

November 5, 1891
Tehran

I had not seen Colonel Sebastian Moran for some time since our arrival. He had spent his days looking up acquaintances of his family and from his younger years. He had left me to my own resources. I had not resented this because I had my own translator from the British Embassy and was much engaged in catching up with my correspondence with Mycroft in London. Besides, I preferred my own company and to form my own impressions in this majestic land. Colonel Moran's saturnine demeanor had the effect of casting a pall over things and I preferred to retain some of the excitement that I had retained from my boyhood when encountering at long last the mysterious and romantic oriental clime. I had been nurtured, as had many an English boy, on tales from the Arabian Nights and on the Morte Darthur. The mind of Europe has always turned to the east for its ideas of glamour and excitement. Why this is so, I cannot say. Perhaps it is the inconvenience of travel as much as anything else that is the source of this fascination, but surely it also involves the language, the poetry, and even the design features of the greater Arabic and Persian worlds.

These two exist Islamic worlds exist in uneasy alliance. Within Islam this division is between the Shia and the Sunni versions of Islam. Even within a religion, history leaves its furrows and divisions multiply where there might have been unity but for the inevitable struggle for power. Is power so dear that everything must be sacrificed to maintain it? But from power come the prerogatives of wealth and luxury and some measure of power must exist merely for one to stay alive. The plight of the average human being has always been the struggle to avoid the costs imposed by the competing claims of despots for his loyalty. The serf existed simply to please and to serve the needs of his master. It is a prerogative of masters that they create power out of weakness, for surely it is a weakness to need the servitude of others. I have often thought that the nature of power is determined, not so much from domination per se, but rather stems from the fact that nature abhors a vacuum.

Goodness itself rushes in to fill the vacuum left by evil in order to restore a primal order. From this stems the universal mandate to exercise charity. But evil awaits its own opportunity to fill a vacuum. Many truly vicious people never seem to lack love or the means of subsistence, while many a virtuous man or woman knows want and sorrow throughout the course of their lives. Christ dies upon the cross, while the voluptuary and the tyrant dies at last in his bed. Still, the gospels say that it profits a man nothing to gain the world but to lose his soul. The Koran also warns of the Day of Judgment when all must give an account of their actions. There is an awareness of moral responsibility in every culture that gives the lie to power. It is of the very substance of human life to assume that there is some moral order underlying all events, but since this is the case, how strange it is that those who most spurn that moral order seem, at least in the sense of power, to escape paying the human costs of evil.

It is this fact I believe that explains a man like Colonel Sebastian Moran who, in his desire for the triumph of the good will use even evil means in order to attain it, rather than await the gradual turning of the universe under the tutelage of grace. How patient must be those who believe and therefore choose to await in patience the coming of the Kingdom of God! The centuries pass and the many are ground into the dust to secure the welfare of the few, the innocent die and murderers go free, and still, at least in the religions of the west, there is the unfading hope that a final day will come where all shall be set right. There must be something in evil that demands of God this great patience also, otherwise why should He not come quickly as is prayed for at the end of the book of Revelation? Why this delay, unless it be merely to fill the harvest of heaven.

Why are we all still the slaves of time? Why this gradual unfolding? Could we not all have existed as did the angels apparently who were created en masse and in their first bright flame of existence decided their fates for all eternity? If we all existed at once there would be no need of waiting, for everyone would gravitate at once to the respective poles of good or evil as ions dissolved in a liquid do under electrolysis leaving a great space in between. But since we being human cannot exist outside of time we are doomed to work out our salvation throughout our lives. Indeed, it is in time and by our actions that we define the type of beings that we shall be forever. We create ourselves layer by layer throughout our long and bitter days and we pray that we may not die facing away from the face of God.

Is God able to wrench us back from the abyss at the final moment if, having lived a good life in the main, we should turn in the later hours of our days to an evil long resisted but never finally denied either? It is this dread possibility that grace will fail to move us in our final hour that is the source of the fear and trembling that besets even the good man in contemplating his salvation. His danger is always before him. The evil man on the contrary, convinced of his own goodness despite his vices, delays even to the end a time when he hopes that by an act of clear and manifest adherence to the good as shown by his final actions that he may reverse the course of a lifetime. Goodness appears to be easily won and the evil man imagines that a mere gesture at the end will suffice.

God has so ordained matters that we must labor to obtain anything of worth. We must know pain even to enjoy the good which should be our natural domain. The prayer of the good man is always the same; having glimpsed evil, he prays that he may be spared the test, for he knows the call of evil deep within him. It is for this reason that the saints, never counting their many virtues or presuming upon the credit of their past actions, constantly pray that they may not give way to evil. Only the man who laboriously climbs the cliff face of virtue is aware of how far he has to fall, while those who remain in the swamps of the lower regions imagine that they have nothing to fear, even as they sink deeper into the mire. The greatest danger is that we can become accustomed to evil, and even to imagine that duplicity, greed, and violence are the way of life natural to man. If man ever loses sight of eternity he becomes worse than a beast. All of creation abhors him, as in his secret depths he abhors himself, and out of that loathing he creates a realm for himself apart from God. It is this that is the judgment of God: to allow man to decide for himself the nature of his own being.

It is a fearful responsibility that the soul possesses and one that we might dearly wish was not ours, but this gift of God is constitutive of our nature and is hence irrevocable. We took too soon and without the guardianship of grace from the Tree of the Knowledge of Good and Evil. That fruit condemns us now to decide daily and at the end forever, what we shall be. How blessed we are to be condemned to time! Time allows us the blessed gap between each action and its final effect. It leaves space for us to see the results of what we do or forbear doing. Had an angel with a flaming sword not been set to guard us from the Tree of Life and had we prematurely known its fruit we should forever have been closed to God just as are the fallen angels. It is time that allows us to observe the burdens of history, so that we may know better how foolish is the heart of man. It is time that allows us to know the folly of our own acts as well, so that we may repent of them and have mercy upon others like ourselves.

November 7, 1891
Tehran, Persia

I have been ill for several days with a fever. The winter is coming on swiftly now and the cold that we had thought to leave behind in the mountains has finally reached us here. The peaks that rim the city are already deep in snow. This has brought home to me that I cannot think of moving west until the first thaw of spring. I could of course move south and if I am needed in England take a boat for home, but I am determined to see Mecca, Cairo, Alexandria, and perhaps Jerusalem. I have even entertained hopes of going further into Africa to the Sudan. Mycroft has hinted the latter to me as a possible destination in his messages. Africa and the Far Eastern regions are where the colonial aspirations of the great European powers may eventually lead to armed conflict. The political mood of the times embraces a great scramble for territories. The days of the European wars seem, thank God, to be over. The balance achieved between the great powers is so nearly equal that war can only be destructive of essential commerce. Thus there is a great incentive to preserve the peace. The only possible exception may be between England and Germany over the issue of naval power. Now that Germany is a unified nation thanks to Bismarck, it desires to have free access out of the Baltic Sea. The ability of the British fleet to blockade the Germans will always be a thorn in their sides. The Germans are behind even the Dutch in the race for colonies and in order to catch up they will no doubt take many risks in the future, but hopefully those risks will stop far short of war.

Mycroft believes that the unexplored lands of Africa will be the decisive factor in the coming colonial crisis. To that end he has had his eye on the Sudan region as the key for some time; ever since the defeat at Khartoum of General Gordon, the entire region of the Sudan has been dominated by the followers of the Mahdi, who was a self-appointed successor to the prophet, Mohammed. The slave trade was revived under his rule and atrocities have been reported by those few traders who have dared to penetrate the area. Mycroft hints to me in his dispatches that I might enjoy some African exploration. These hints are thinly veiled assignments that I might aid the British government by venturing into the region to assess the situation.

I fear that Mycroft has mistaken the purpose of my journey, which is personal and not political in nature. I have tried to escape anything that might be termed, particular visions, and to speculate upon the greater nature and fate of mankind without those adhesions of nation, religion, and personal aspirations that blind us to our common destiny. In short, I am attempting to be a philosopher. It is the task of philosophy to address itself to the universals. This may have made my journal kept thus far in many ways impenetrable except to myself. However, I trust that others may also have speculated along these lines as I have done into the strangeness of life and may find, should extracts from my journal ever reach eyes other than my own, a common theme or echo.

To test this theory I have read some extracts from it to Colonel Moran. To aid in my convalescence he has taken me daily to a nearby river and waterfall, a site of beauty and Oriental charm. The Persians are renowned for their love of beauty. One need think only of the exquisite poetry of Rumi, whose marvelous stanzas illuminate the world with his particular vision. They are as dear to me as the marvelous Chinese poetry of the Tang Dynasty. Both show a marvelous observation of nature. There is a concrete and immediate quality to the poems, as though they were not the words of men, but rather unique objects, balanced and pure, created by nature itself. It is at such moments that art and nature so collaborate that they seem to blend their respective powers towards one great end. Such poems approach the universals of Plato and might cause even that most skeptical philosopher to abandon his deep mistrust of art. There are times indeed when nature seems itself to be art and to display an element of design.

Such was the river scene that lay before me yesterday. I sat upon some stones gazing at the remaining green of the trees upon the opposite bank, while Colonel Moran read my journal. We were quite alone and the solitude was a pleasure to me. I have long since abandoned any apprehensions directed towards Colonel Moran. He might have made away with me in the lonely regions that we have already traversed if he wished to do so. He clearly has absolute loyalty to the Professor and intends to guard me until I shall return to the presence of that great personage. Professor Moriarty, according to Mycroft, has led a most retired life since his return to England, although he has apparently had certain meetings with representatives of men who represent some large commercial banks and trading companies. This is natural, since the Professor has funds to invest, but with the Professor nothing should be treated as accidental. There is a purpose in his slightest gesture and I have requested that Mycroft and Scotland Yard will pay particular attention even to conduct that may appear harmless. At last Colonel Moran set my manuscript aside and after lighting a cigar he spoke to me.

"I really cannot congratulate you, Mr. Holmes. Indeed, had the Professor and I realized the extent of your scruples, we need not have feared you. I must say that I expected your morbid religiosity after watching your evident fascination with the monastic life of Tibet. It is all very well for you to speak of God, but surely you realize that religions are merely excuses to impose and exercise power over others. The history of religion is finally reducible to the history of war. Show me a religion that is content to merely enlighten the individual! No, religion is nothing without its missionary zeal. Even the oracle at Delphi was used to show those who consulted it the best means to extend and prosecute the lines of battle. There is no man who is content to be only a local ruler. Even Athens and Sparta could not maintain peace with each other though both were merely small city-states."

"But what I am discussing my dear Colonel is inner peace," I explained. "A man must live finally within the silence of his own cranium and in the face of his own death he must reach some definitive position on these matters," I stated in my own defense.

"If one has the time, but you must realize that the vast majority does not reflect at all, or if they do so, then only in the mute manner of oxen being led to the slaughter. I am not unacquainted with philosophy myself, Mr. Holmes. I prefer of course August Compte, Herbert Spencer, and Thomas Huxley. These men describe the nature of man as he is and has always been. They accept, as do Hobbes and Machiavelli, the struggle for power as supreme. The earth is populated by masters and slaves. What were the first actions of men like Cortes and Pizarro when they encountered the Indians of South America? Was it to love them as brothers? No, it was to enslave them and put them to work in the great silver and gold mines as slave laborers. The golden chalice that offers the wine in the Holy Mass is made of gold, wrung from the sorrow and death of those laborers, converted solely so that they might serve their masters in Europe. The Papacy divided the whole of the New World between Spain and Portugal and look at the result. They have brought to the people of the Americas only our contempt and our greed, both hidden under the guise of spreading the true faith to the savages."

"That may be so, Colonel, but those actions are condemned by the very religion that they professed to share. If vice and the lure of power are universal in mankind, would the native people have been better off under a philosophy of Natural Positivism that accepts struggle as the very nature of man according to the philosophers that you favor? Men like Pizarro lie condemned by the very religion they bore with them and their misuse of it does not invalidate its claims."

"Why then were their actions not condemned at least by those who profited at home from their depredations? Behind every rapacious empire, there are always the silent, decent people who enjoy a way of life bought at the cost of the suffering of others on the frontiers. Do they care to investigate and witness the results of their political inertia? It is the quiet shopkeepers and those who may at least read of these things who wave the flags and cheer the conquerors on the perimeter. Bah, I despair of them. Show me a middle-class Englishman and I will show you a great moral swamp of humanity. I forbear to contemn the lower classes. They are colonized within their own nation. It is the members of the middle-classes that I despise; the ones who will accept the cheaper goods that are the price of violence committed elsewhere to ensure their quiet and enjoyable lives."

"What then of the upper classes?" I inquired.

"You mean the men I play with at cards?" smiled the Colonel with a sinister leer. "Why do you think that I enjoy fleecing them? It is because I know them intimately. They are the most narrow and unimaginative of men. Pride, greed, and boredom are their prime characteristics. They are empty shells of men. Their only ability is cunning. They follow the path of least resistance toward predetermined ends. They are not even predators for they lack the courage and individuality to do their own dirty work. They manage the great trusts and corporations as cells work in the Portuguese Man of War. They leave the sting to those on the periphery. Their task is merely to administer according to the iron rule of growth and of acquisition. They behave with an instinct as blind as it is vicious. As such they are predictable and I have made a fortune in playing with them and have acquired an education in affairs of state while listening as they pose before one another. How often did I not take the knowledge that I obtained from them to the Professor who knew best how to take money from those who alone possessed it in sufficient quantities to repay our efforts! The Professor always knew best how to devise the plans that would defeat them. For the Professor it was merely a matter of schematics, of a system. The rich were for him like those asteroids whose courses he followed in the skies. I often marveled at how quickly he could devise a plan. I of course knew the people who could put the plan into motion. I always stood between the Professor and his troops. I was the one that they looked to for their assignments. There were separate legions, each assigned unique tasks. Each legion had its own particular location and expertise. Long periods might elapse between engagements, and during these times the men would follow quiet and unexceptionable lives. Our organization could strike and then virtually disappear. I dare say that there has never been a criminal organization like it."

"You must resent me then for dismantling it," I said quietly. He was quiet for a time and looked not at me but at the flowing stream and a great weariness came into his face. He spoke at last.

"So I should, Mr. Sherlock Holmes, for if you but knew it, you have left many at large who should be in chains while concerning yourself with us. We were one of the great forces of nature that keeps power in line. For fear of us, many of the rich and powerful were forced to examine their actions, if only to avoid our retribution. By destroying us you, Mr. Holmes, have become responsible for their continuance. You have yet to learn the difference between personal and political morality. By changing the balance of affairs you have allowed the growth of far more dangerous microbes to flourish. Will all of your kindness and good-will and trust in God stop these men? I think not! Their crimes are hidden in the normal course of events. It requires crime to defeat crime. You have meddled where you were not wanted. Why do you think you are still alive? Because the Professor as well as myself are deeply curious about how you will now conduct yourself to make amends for your own past actions in stopping us."

Colonel Moran tossed by journal back at me with contempt.

"I hope you can soon do better," said he. "I should hate to make a poor report of you to the Professor when our journey is over. He might then have instructions to give to me regarding you. Until then you are safe of course. I will guard you as well as even Doctor Watson would, but rather than substituting my efforts for his blind devotion it is my desire only to serve the Professor well and perhaps to satisfy my own curiosity. How will you, who claim to have defeated Professor Moriarty, deal with a world of evil that has been unleashed by your own goodness? How, shall you Mr. Holmes? You have not defeated evil by defeating Professor Moriarty; you have merely plugged one hole so that greater evils may emerge somewhere else!"

This was all that he would say about the contents selected from my journal. His words had stung me deeply, for they seemed to cut into my own mind, and to awaken my own doubts. I will not say that I doubted my own course, nor would I retract my own convictions, but I could see the risk that I ran by turning from the struggle of life and desiring instead that the Kingdom of God should reign upon the earth. It threw me back upon what St. Paul has called the scandal of the cross: that out of the defeat of all our normal conceptions of success, God brings about our victory.

Even within the Church this scandal is still present. Was the greatest age of the Church not after all in the first centuries, when the followers of Christ were seen as criminals and slaughtered *en masse* by a succession of Roman Emperors? Or was the greatest age that of triumph and crusade in the 12th century, when Christianity dominated all of Europe under Pope Innocent XII? It was then and in the following centuries that the Church could command utter obedience and persecute heretics. When the Christians became themselves the executioners and power and grandeur built the great cathedrals, had not the Church already lost the Christ who had no nest, no lair, and nowhere to lay His head? I sometimes think that the Christ of the Gospels ceased to be revered by the end of the first century of Christendom.

Still, I oppose the point of view of Professor Moriarty's general in the field. Colonel Moran represents the view that success must crown all virtuous efforts, that virtue is measured by the results of manifest good achieved. Against this view is the one that states that if evil means are required to achieve a good, then the end itself is tainted with evil regardless of any apparent success. But does goodness so rarified and pure not deny our mixed condition upon the earth? We are surely not sheep and cattle to be led to the slaughter, and even if we might choose martyrdom for ourselves, can we allow the innocents and the helpless to be slaughtered before our eyes and not take up arms to prevent it? In this way evil draws us back into itself. Before long it is we who are the aggressors. For this reason we pray not to be led into temptation and to be put to the test, for to avoid evil in some measure seems impossible for man.

The one great question is the superlative demand of Christ that we sell what we have, give to the poor and come and follow him, even unto death; this great unanswered demand has yet to be fulfilled. Which of us does not take up arms to preserve our little island of happiness? Who would see his wife ravaged, his children dashed to pieces before his eyes, and not turn against the foe the very acme of his wrath? Cain asked God if he was his brother's keeper, but only God had mercy upon Cain. It may be virtue to bind up the wounds of the Samaritan set upon by thieves on the road, but perhaps God alone can have mercy on the thieves themselves. To render mercy to the merciless, who can ever hope to do so? Does the command of love go so far as to demand forgiveness even for those who mocked Christ upon the cross?

To live life as though the final day had already dawned may be the only means whereby mankind may be saved from the wrath of that day, when the stars will fall from the heavens, and men will ask that the mountains may cover them, when women will say that blessed are the wombs that never bore. Must history embrace eternity then for virtue to prevail or will it take until the day when eternity embraces time for the life of the world to begin? Until then, Sainthood would appear to be the great exception to the weary ranks of the generations, each succeeding the others with new atrocities. But if this is so, then who and how many of this vast number of the indifferent and imperfect will be saved at last?

Dr. Watson's Narrative Continues

olmes' last words haunted me even after I had turned down the lamp and retired. I could hear the bare strands of the ivy rattling against the walls of the old manor house like dead men's bones. In my retirement years I had hoped to escape from the clamor of the times in which I lived. I had hoped to soothe my conscience in this retreat by reflecting that as a man of medicine, I had done all that I might to heal the world and in a most intimate fashion. I did not ask the virtue or vice of those that I had treated through the years, but simply tried to restore health to damaged tissues. Yet is not life more than tissue? Is not good health finally a habit of the soul? But as a doctor I could only just touch upon the surface, to heal the wounds of life, if not life itself. Even Sherlock Holmes could only solve the immediate mysteries presented to him on a case by case basis. I often thought of his words at the end of "The Adventure of the Cardboard Box" when he had asked what the meaning of it all was. I could see why his journal probed so deeply. I could see that in it he was asking and attempting to find some answer for the great silent questions that gnaw at the hearts of all men and women. Most people finally cease asking these questions and as in my own case they seek some tiny corner of repose.

My protracted absence had led me to wire to my housekeeper to see if all was well at my own humble domicile by the sea. From her reply I learned that my cottage on the bay was secure and that she was keeping it clean and well-aired as usual. This set my mind at ease. The short visit that I had imagined had now grown beyond all bounds and it was as though I was again in Baker Street. The problems that beset us were still far from a solution. I wondered about the conversation that had taken place in the late hours between Holmes and Moriarty. Were these two improbable allies laying plans together? What a collaboration it must be when two such minds are bent to but a single end! I could not but hope that victory would soon be ours and that Baron Maupertuis would be laid low at last.

And what of Rodger Baskerville, that snake-like man who enjoyed gradually creeping insidiously upon his prey and finally striking when least expected? Would he also be called to account at last and rendered harmless? And what of Lady Beryl, would her family who had so long displayed the courage and passion of the Latin races at last see her brother's sacrifice vindicated? It was with thoughts such as these that I finally drifted off into an uneasy slumber.

I was awakened the next morning by a knock upon my door. I bade the early caller to enter and was soon in the presence of Sherlock Holmes, already dressed and looking vigorous as of old when he was upon the scent. He pushed a chair up to my bed and regarded me with an amused look upon his face.

"Well, Watson, you little knew when you came to visit that you would be involved in what may well be an extended campaign, did you? Ah well, but you should have known should you not, knowing me as you do?"

I answered that I would not wish to be absent from him at any time when I might be needed and that I could not imagine missing what might be two of his greatest cases.

"Excellent Watson, I expected no less from my old comrade in arms. How glad I am to see you in such spirits, for much lies ahead. Our abilities will never have been more called upon than now."

I looked at him with concern, for beneath his energetic demeanor there was evidence of his old affliction, the lung ailment that he had so neglected. I did not like the febrile flush in his complexion and I noticed a slight tremor of the hand despite his evident effort to hide it.

"Holmes, I trust that the fever of last summer has not

returned. Let me assure you that consumption is not to be treated lightly. How often it lies in the body and then advances suddenly at the slightest sign of weakness. You have been using yourself up too freely. These bitter and damp moors are hardly the best for one with a lung ailment. You should be in Switzerland, you know."

"And so we may be soon, my dear fellow, if we are called again to the continent. No, you must not be alarmed; the fever has not returned and I am doing my best to follow your instructions. I slept very well last night after parting with the Professor."

"You were making plans?"

"Indeed."

"Will you share them with me?"

"Well there are still details to be worked out, but I can give you some idea of our intentions. To begin, we must define the problem. Baron Maupertuis is a man of unparalleled wealth and power who is so immune from ordinary justice that even Mycroft cannot touch him. He may at any time use that wealth to foment another scheme that, if not as catastrophic in its effects as that of the plague that he threatened to unleash upon England, may still cause immense harm. This realization was my first key. The Baron does nothing small or by degrees. He is never satisfied with his position in the world. Money for him is always about power and control."

"We must thwart him in those designs whatever they may be," I cried.

"On the contrary my dear fellow, we must help him."

"Holmes!"

"Oh, do not mistake me. The ultimate end will be his undoing, but we must not resist him but take his force and lead it. It is a principle of the ancient art of Aikido of which I have some knowledge in addition to Baritsu. When one is in the presence of a great force, one should not oppose it. Force has the quality that it becomes difficult to control the greater it becomes. Think of the hurricane Watson; its great force is not easy to turn. Now compare this to the light breezes of a day in spring that may change direction momentarily. Baron Maupertuis is like the hurricane. His is a great force and therefore all the more predictable. He will always act to increase his power and his wealth. There is a great monotony about the man. I took this initial insight to the Professor last night and he agreed with me."

"And had he any suggestions of his own suggestions to make?" I asked.

"He did. He suggested that we supply the Baron with an enterprise that will exceed in possible gains even what he hoped to reap by the fall in the value of British securities caused by the plague carried aboard the ship, Friesland. This new enterprise will appear quite legal. We must though not arouse the suspicions of the Baron. After the murder of Cardinal Tosca, which precipitate action I dare say he already regrets; he knows now that he will be closely watched. He will not attempt another such crime again soon. He feels safe for the present for he knows that the Professor will not testify against him as long as he possesses Silver Star as a hostage."

"Can we do nothing to restore the horse then? Perhaps the Baron has had the horse killed after all."

"I think not. The horse is of immense value for breeding purposes and the Baron, who judges all things by market value, will not senselessly kill the animal. Scotland Yard is still making inquiries and I have hopes that they may succeed in finding a lead."

"What then, Holmes, is this device of the Professor?"

"You choose your words wisely, Watson, for it is indeed a device, a Trojan horse in fact as I suggested that we plan to use. I did so in order to set the Professor's great mind working upon the problem. It is for this reason that I called Sir Henry's attention to the passage in the Iliad. Our Trojan horse will be an investment company which we shall call, 'The Greater-Dutch Canal Company,' which will soon be offering its stock to the public."

"I have never heard of it," I objected."

"Nor has anyone else. It has just been created last night in the minds of Sherlock Holmes and Professor James Moriarty."

He laughed heartily at my puzzled face.

"You see, Watson, how great will be the lure and how well it ties in with this matter of the man we knew as Stapleton and his papers of the dictator Don Juan Murillo. You do not? Well do not be discouraged, for the matter is somewhat complex. Let us return to what we know of the papers. You never did read them carefully, but I spent some days perusing them. They show a pattern of duplicity regarding the building of a great railroad in Costa Rica and the granting of immense subsidies toward that end by Juan Murillo given in the form of land-grants purchased by accepting bribes from American investors. The intent was to make Costa Rica a virtual possession of the moneyed interests in America. All of this would be well within the normal if oppressive corporate practices in American business, as displayed in the so-called 'Gilded Age' as it has been named, by the American author, Mark Twain. Unfortunately these men were so greedy and corrupt that they would stop at nothing to insure profits."

"Their excesses were truly draconian, Watson. They even resorted to slave labor. Men were brought in, not merely from China, but from Italy as well, men who died by the hundreds from yellow fever, typhus, dysentery, and cholera. They lived as virtual animals under the tyranny of this Don Juan Murillo, known at the time and referred to quite accurately as 'the Tiger of San Pedro.' San Pedro was the village in the central highlands where a revolt was mounted by the laborers who sought to escape south into Columbia. It was put down in a most brutal fashion by the troops of Juan Murillo who were armed with American weapons, provided by the American government to pacify the region under his harsh rule. The American President was attempting to curry favor with Juan Murillo at the time. The American investors intended that American control of the railroad and of the country itself might eventually open a pathway to a canal through the Americas. Juan Murillo would be retained as a figure-head of supposed independence and all investment aid would wear the garment of American generosity. This would make all of these machinations appear in the best light possible to the American press. However, if the true story is published of the atrocities committed at the time, it might easily sway the balance of votes in the next election at a critical time. America is working even now to expand its influence in the Caribbean and in Central America. This muted venture of building a canal will be extremely costly and Americans will not easily consent to the risks and expense involved in so ambitious an undertaking if a parallel reference can be drawn to past actions untaken in that same region in the late 1880's in building the Costa Rican railroad, which at least already exists and can serve roughly the same functions as the proposed canal."

"Yes Holmes, but how will this involve Baron Maupertuis? If the Americans are going to build the canal already, then there will be no need for a Dutch venture in the same direction."

"That is true Watson, but what if the Americans might be prevented from ever building the canal and thus obtaining critical control over any ships from Europe that are seeking a shorter route to trade with China and Japan? The Baron will see immediately that a European Company might, if not similarly tainted by prior slave practices in the region, beat the Americans to the game. What a coup it would be! Why the man behind it would become a national hero and need never fear any action from us to hold him to account for his crimes in the affair of the Friesland. In addition, as a primary stockholder in the company, he would reap a fortune."

"Yes, but Holmes, you said that you would yourself publish the papers of Juan Murillo in order to defeat the blackmail aspirations of Rodger Baskerville, formerly the man we knew as Stapleton. Will you then not do so after all?"

"Well, I think that we must keep open all of our options in that regard. Timing will be everything. There are details in the plan that I must withhold for now, at least until the Baron has invested immense sums in our proposed company."

"But why will he invest in a venture that will prove so risky. After all, the American plans would be prohibitive of any outside interference. How can he hope as a private investor to compete?"

"He will not need to venture forth blindly because he will be contacted by the possessor of the papers or his agent, who will propose to sell him the papers of Juan Murillo. Baron Maupertuis will see at once their importance and how he can use them to destroy the plans of the Americans at an opportune moment. Once America retires from the scene, the Dutch company will make their own offer to the government of whichever nation or region, such as the Panama region of Columbia, is chosen as the final site for the canal. If those governments accept his offer (and why should they not) then the value of his stock will increase and the Baron will make a fortune. He will not be able to resist such a prospect. That, old fellow, is our Trojan horse.”

I thought for a time, trying to take it all in. The conception was indeed a bold one, as were the ramifications of such an amazing plan. It was truly an immense undertaking as befitted the foes against whom we were matched. I did see a problem, though.

“Holmes, I believe there is a flaw in your calculations.”

“My blushes Watson!” he demurred.

“Yes, I believe you have forgotten something.”

“Pray Watson, what is it?” he asked with a show of some concern.

I continued. “As I see it you have two goals in this affair. First, you wish to cause the Baron to invest in this scheme a considerable share of his wealth and to purchase the papers of Juan Murillo from Rodger Baskerville. But both goals will only insure profit to both of our foes. It is true that the American investors who took part in the building of the railroad will finally have their crimes made public before the citizens of America, but will that belated justice be worth the cost of aiding these two arch-foes?”

Holmes looked downward with a most crestfallen expression. “Your points are well taken, Watson; indeed, you have excelled yourself.”

I had, during the course of our discussion, arisen from bed and sat now wrapped in a dressing gown in a chair facing the great detective. Strangely it was no satisfaction to me to see Holmes so troubled. My sense of momentary victory was therefore already fading when he spoke.

"I must tell you that I raised the same point with Professor Moriarty last night."

"And what was his response?" I inquired.

"That the entire plan depends upon the most careful timing. The Trojan horse must be within the gates you see, before the hidden soldiers burst out. Let me put the entire matter before you sequentially. Rodger Baskerville will discover at once, that though he has the papers of Juan Murillo, that they are only copies. We, as I have mentioned before, will retain the originals. He will be upset of course at the revelation, but he will conclude that the matter is hardly fatal, since the copies bear a great resemblance to the originals and only an expert would be able to tell the difference. I am afraid that we engaged in a certain amount of forgery during the preparation of the copies. In any case, he can only proceed with what he has and do the best that he can. His original plan would be to blackmail the principals themselves, the men who built the railroad, and perhaps some officials of the American government who aided them. They of course will have time to examine the papers and will hardly pay out for documents that can be proven to be forgeries. But blackmail is only one way that the papers may prove useful. If the contents of the papers are published, it will sour many Americans on the entire scheme of building a canal. That threat alone will cause concern in high places. The result would be immediate and it would take time to quibble about authenticity. The mere realization that these papers have been preserved and have resurfaced after so many years will give them value. You must remember my dear fellow that this project of a canal will require a great concerted effort of private and public capital and its achievement will take many years to complete once it has begun. However stock speculation is a quick and impulsive affair and in that world he who hesitates is lost. Rodger Baskerville will hear, for we shall see that he does hear, of the formation of a rival company to build a canal. The formation of the company and its underwriting will be arranged by Mycroft. The Baron will only buy-in later and will of course eventually desire to possess a controlling interest in the company."

"But let us continue in due order. This man Stapleton will see at once the value of these papers to that company's success as a rival to build a canal first while the Americans are forced to deal with the scandal that exposure of the Murillo Papers could cause. He will seek out the Dutch company investors and offer the Murillo Papers for sale so that they can be produced at precisely the time when they could most compromise the American endeavor."

"The Baron meanwhile, who watches for all new public offerings closely particularly those in Holland, will hear (for we shall again see that he shall hear) about an offer of the papers and their contents. He will see if he is the man that I believe him to be, how they might be used by the newly formed company to its advantage and therefore his own. He will offer to purchase them and simultaneously buy up a controlling interest of the new company before word spreads further of the existence of the Murillo papers. As he makes his bid for control of the new company, the price of the stock will begin to climb. Markets soon sense when there is something in the wind. He will no doubt make his purchases through various agents to keep his name out of it. Still, a point will come when the price of the remaining extant shares will begin to rise rapidly. He will then abandon his usual caution. Word will circulate that the Baron is seeking to corner the shares and obtain control of the company. The prices will then increase even faster, but still he will pay any price to obtain control before other investors can obtain the lion's share. His own competitive nature will compel it, you see. We in turn shall follow the course of these events closely. Once he is fully invested, or to use our metaphor, once the Trojan horse is securely within the city, we will act."

"We will see that a story is placed in the press that a gigantic hoax has been contemplated to blackmail some of the most respectable businessmen in America based upon forged papers that claim to be those of the former ruler of Costa Rica. The Baron will then have no choice but to produce the papers in order to discredit the resulting American claims of innocence. Experts will be consulted. The public will follow events closely awaiting the outcome. I expect that the newspapers for days will be able to discuss nothing else. When it is announced that the papers are in fact forgeries, there will be rejoicing in America. It will now be seen as a vindication of the national honor. The Americans will rally round the canal project and demand that it be built. You see of course what this will do to the price of the shares in the Dutch company. Their value will plummet and the Baron as a result will be ruined. You may be sure that he will then look about him for the man who sold him the forged papers. You will remember that in a similar instance, the Baron risked procuring even the death of Cardinal Tosca. We may logically assume then that he will make some attempt upon the life of one Rodger Baskerville. He will seek him out to the very ends of the earth."

I could see now the immense genius behind the plan and why even now Professor Moriarty could be so great a foe. The kidnapping of Silver Star had stimulated all of the remaining malice in the Professor with the result that he had devised a truly extraordinary plan. If all went well, Baron Maupertuis, who could not be convicted in a court of law, would at least be ruined in that wherein he placed the most value, his money. There was also justice and a possible solution to the problem posed by our second foe in that the murderer, Rodger Baskerville, might end by being a victim of the wrath of Baron Maupertuis.

"But Holmes, you said that you would publish the papers. If you do not publish them and the story prevails that these men were innocent, then they will end by being seen as national heroes maligned by foreign financiers. You will have defeated the Baron and also Rodger Baskerville, but what of Lady Beryl's desire that these men in America should finally be held to account for their former crimes in Costa Rica?"

"We will not disappoint her, Watson. As the Baron attempts to sell his shares and their value plummets we will be buying them, we will use the Baskerville fortune to buy up shares for a pittance. We will then announce that the real papers have been located after all. There will again be a great public furor, but we will use Mycroft's influence to see that the papers are carefully examined. When they are authenticated, there will be an immense reaction, even greater because the matter will now be firmly rooted in the public mind and what might have been ignored as crimes committed over twenty years ago will have all the force of currency. These men in America will be utterly ruined and exposed as the ruthless slave-holders that they once were. The deaths of thousands will be thus avenged. Of course the Dutch stock will then rise and we will sell to those who understand securities and international affairs better then we. The money earned in the sale of the stock will reward the initial underwriters whose funds will have been supplied by grants from secret sources known to Mycroft alone, and will also enable Sir Henry and Lady Beryl to continue their good works."

"But, Holmes, which nation then will finally build the canal, the Dutch or the Americans?" I asked.

Holmes shrugged. "It is a matter of little concern to us, Watson. We are but little people and the affairs of great nations are beyond our poor powers."

He smiled and I saw a mischievous glint in his eye that I remembered well. "Let us go down to breakfast now, old friend. These plans will demand action and all of the cunning and resource that we possess, but for now we may only take the first steps that lie before us, knowing that as with all plans, we must be prepared for alterations as events unfold about us."

The breakfast in Baskerville Hall that morning was our last together in the mansion. Events were crowding down upon us now with great rapidity; Holmes had called for a general conference after breakfast in the library, after we had fortified ourselves with English bacon, eggs, and crumpets. We took our breakfast tea with us to the library. There we positioned ourselves in the comfortable chairs. Perkins had built up the fire so that a roaring blaze went up the ancient chimney. It was well that he had done so for a bitter chill had settled down upon the land. I could see from the window that each spear of grass was coated in frost and the landscape was a glaring white as far as the eye could see. The wet ground would be hard as stone and even the Great Grimpen Mire might be frozen over. The ducks and pheasants would be in close shelter. I turned my eyes from the window to Holmes where he stood before us with his back to the fire. I glanced over at the others. There was an air of expectancy in us all. Sir Henry perhaps felt again the energy of his youth on the Canadian plains. The Professor of course retained that inscrutable aura of a spider just before it descends upon its prey. Holmes and I of course felt as of old that comradeship that had grown between us through the years which could often speak without words.

Holmes began quietly, "Gentlemen, the hour has arrived when we must divide our forces. Events must be set in motion. I have received a confirmation from your cousin, Rodger Baskerville," he said addressing Sir Henry. "He agrees to the exchange as proposed. I will take the copies of the Murillo papers to Exeter where they can be examined by Rodger Baskerville's solicitors. It will be a critical moment. If the forgery is discovered we will need to adapt upon the instant. I am trusting to one key fact. Rodger Baskerville is a lone and secretive man and prefers his own counsel. He is also a man who has been known to display sudden impulses, one who might leave a conversation and go racing off over the moor to catch a butterfly, or as he once did in London to assume for an instant the name of Sherlock Holmes as he told his cabby when he shadowed Sir Henry after his first arrival in London. He is also a bully by nature. He will imagine that he has so cowed us that we will take no risks with Lady Beryl at stake. For this set of reasons, I believe that he will fail to have an expert at document identification present. In any case, I was able to match the character of the paper exactly and I am pleased to say that our copyist was able to match the typefaces and signatures with great accuracy. I am something of an expert upon fonts and instructed him what would be required. An ordinary inspection by the solicitors will reveal nothing. If they are satisfied, then the exchange should proceed easily."

Turning then specifically to Sir Henry, Holmes said, "You,

Sir Henry, will proceed to Exeter in a few days time. Watson will remain with you to see that all goes well with the actual exchange. Meanwhile, I shall proceed to London. I will arrange with Mycroft for the underwriting of a company to be called 'The Greater Dutch Canal Company.' Mycroft has retained agents in Amsterdam who will see to the details involved in the formation of the company. When the shares of stock become available to the public, we shall see that a substantial block of the stock is purchased by Sir Henry through a private trust account and I may even make a small anonymous investment myself. I am afraid that this whole matter is a rather criminal endeavor, for of course we have no intention of ever building a canal at this time, but we will make a great fuss over the matter anyway. There will be a great deal of speculation in the press as to our fortunes. Mycroft will see to the hiring of geologists and engineers and has committed government funds to buy up further shares under the names of various proxies."

"We will give the impression of a veritable gold rush in the stock. Once we are well launched, it will be a more delicate matter to induce Rodger Baskerville to sell the Murillo Papers to Baron Maupertuis. I am counting on his rage when he discovers that the papers are forgeries. He will realize that they are worthless to the original target of his blackmail scheme. He will then have two choices. He will either have to obtain the originals or he will need to find a third party who might purchase the copies as they are if they might conceivably to be used later for purposes of blackmail. In his darkest hour such a man will emerge."

"But how can you be so sure of that?" asked Sir Henry.

Holmes smiled. "I am certain of it because we shall provide him. The world of first-class blackmailers and their market is a small one. It demands specialized skills in order to acquire compromising documents in the first place and later to negotiate the amount required to ensure their continued secrecy. I believe I know just the man."

It suddenly dawned upon me who Holmes had in mind. "That man is Charles Augustus Milverton!"

I had often heard Holmes speak of this man. He was to the

world of blackmail what Professor Moriarty had been to fraud and violence. Charles Augustus Milverton was the great drain toward which all of the secret information in the city would inevitably drift. He was a virtual wholesaler in secrets. If there was a compromising set of letters, an obscene diary, or anything that might wring the pocketbook of the man or woman who fell into his clutches, he would purchase it and was able to afford to pay a premium price for the articles in question. He knew best the subtle ways to hint at possession without making actual claims that would leave him liable to prosecution, so that though the authorities knew of his activities, they could prove nothing. In addition, he always delivered the papers intact and complete if payment was finally made. He had a reputation for complete integrity in that regard. He even claimed that he performed a public service by sweeping up evidences of past offenses and indiscretions and removing them from circulation. His semi-legal status did not make him beloved by lesser blackmailers who could not afford to match his prices. His name was well known in upper society, and although he was universally loathed, he was regarded as a virtual guarantor of the authenticity of the causes that he pursued. His name was undoubtedly known to Baron Maupertuis. He would be the perfect intermediary for our copies once they were in the hands of Rodger Baskerville, formerly known as Stapleton.

Holmes continued. "It would not be an easy task for a man as unknown as Rodger Baskerville you see to suddenly emerge with these papers. It is not impossible that he planned all along to retain the services of Charles Augustus Milverton as an intermediary with the Americans, but upon discovering that he has been fooled by us and been given only forged copies of the documents, he will be desperate. He will find a way to contact the one man who may save his chestnuts from the fire. A sale will be concluded and it is Milverton who will contact Baron Maupertuis. While I am in London I will have it bruited about that a man in Devonshire is about to come into possession of some very valuable papers. Milverton will hear of this and his appetite will be whetted.

I expect that he will in his own quiet and sinister fashion find a way to trace the papers to Rodger Baskerville even if Rodger Baskerville does yet not know of him. We will leave as few things to chance as possible. Milverton will then make contact at the very hour of Rodger Baskerville's dismay and the deal will be concluded. Rodger Baskerville will feel a need to flee the country of course after the sale of the papers, for he may still fear our pursuit. Under the pressure of these circumstances I believe he will accept a smaller price than he would under less urgent circumstances and Milverton will take advantage of the situation and make a hasty purchase at a bargain price without first taking measures to authenticate them. However, even if he should discover the forgery, I believe that he will still go ahead with the transaction anyway and then rely upon his reputation to further the exchange with Baron Maupertuis who will assume that the papers must be genuine for Milverton to have ever purchased them in the first place. The money that the Baron will be prepared to pay Milverton will make Milverton take the risk this once of selling articles of doubtful authenticity."

"The Baron in turn will have been chafing at the bit and wondering whether to invest in this new company that has appeared on the scene, the shares of which are being bought up with such rapidity. The thought that these Murillo Papers might contain information not generally known that may be used against the Americans will be irresistible to him. He will offer an unprecedented sum to obtain them and to better know their character. The very size of the offering will persuade a man like Milverton to make one last big recovery and the papers will be sold. The Baron will then begin to purchase the shares in the company that remain outstanding and in consequence he will also bid up the shares that we will have purchased while the fortunes of the company remained uncertain. It is then that we shall spring the trap. When the Baron attempts to contact the principals in America to get them to withdraw their support for the canal, or even if he goes so far as to publish them and to rely on public indignation to achieve the same effect of delaying the American bid to build the canal, the end result will be the same. The papers will then be revealed to be forgeries at the key moment, as I explained earlier today to Watson, and the price that the Baron has paid for his stock will be as a rock about his neck when the price of his shares tumbles. The prices of the stock will plummet! We will by then have sold our own shares of course at the prevailing market price so as to augment Baron Maupertuis' number of shares that he obtained in a frenzy from all the other sources so as to give the Baron a controlling interest in the company."

"He will suddenly find himself with a controlling interest in a worthless company. He will immediately try to cover his losses and will put his own shares up for sale in a frantic effort to avoid a catastrophic loss. But then his very notoriety will work against him. Others will take note that the Baron is selling and the remaining speculative holders will also see their shares begin to collapse. The Baron will be ruined and with him any men who might have invested with him in the affair of the rat born plague had that plan ever succeeded. When the shares reach a bottom of course, we will step in again and buy into the company. Only then will we reveal that the actual papers do in fact exist after all. They will be authenticated in due course and the price of shares in the company will rise. The Baron's initial position will of course be vindicated, but alas too late for him, for he will have sold-out most of his shares in panic when he realized his overexposure. He will hardly look at the same stock twice after being convinced that he had in the first instance been the victim of a gigantic confidence game. As the old saying goes, once burned twice shy."

"We will therefore gentlemen achieve all of our goals. We will expose, after some slight delay, the men in America who in cooperation with the President, Don Juan Murillo, were guilty of such immense crimes in Costa Rica years ago. We will frustrate Rodger Baskerville who will only obtain a small share of what he had hoped to make from the use of the Murillo papers, and we will leave him vulnerable, along with Milverton his go-between, to the rage and vindictiveness of Baron Maupertuis. Finally, we shall bring about the financial ruin of a man who values wealth above all other considerations and prevent him from having the power to misuse that wealth again. Though he may not be prosecuted, unless perhaps for defamation, which is unlikely for he will undoubtedly threaten the principals through agents, he will lose both money and power. For such a man to lose power while still alive is worse than death."

We had all of us followed this amazing exposition with some interest. The chain of events and probabilities, though attenuated, seemed likely to proceed as Holmes had outlined them. The entire mechanism was like some vast machine built by Sherlock Holmes and by Professor Moriarty and I could see the Professor nod in agreement several times during the course of the explanations.

Sir Henry stood up shaking his head. "Well it is all beyond me Holmes, but I have placed my life in your hands once before and I have complete trust in you now. I will make the investment as you suggest and you may have my draft for the funds which I render gladly. I was once a poor miner in Canada and I may be so again when all of this is through, but I learned to gamble my life on a winter's grub stake in those days and I trust that the spirit of adventure has not deserted me in my middle years." He clasped hands with Holmes heartily.

I could see that Holmes was moved by this show of confidence. "Thank you, Sir Henry. We are certainly playing the long odds this time but I feel certain that Lady Beryl if she was here would stand with us in what we have determined to do. Let me proceed then if I may. We all know our stations during these next days. After you obtain Lady Beryl you will return here, Sir Henry, and you will make of Baskerville Hall a veritable fortress to protect the original documents of the papers of ex-President Murillo. You will be aided in that regard by a visible ring of constabulary under the supervision from London of Inspector Lestrade who will see that you are both safe in the days to come."

I had wondered what Holmes had in store for me, so I questioned him at this time. "And what should I do after we recover Lady Beryl? Will I accompany the Professor and where shall we go?"

"I shall ask that you join me in London in our old rooms at Baker Street, Watson. I think it would be as well that we both remain in London to see matters through when the stock in our new company is offered on the London exchange. Our old rooms will be our citadel and center of operations. As for the Professor, who has contributed so much already to our endeavors, I believe that we may allow him to concentrate upon his own concerns for a time. I have called in some favors of old and Scotland Yard has assigned that most able man, Inspector Stanley Hopkins, who you will well remember from many of our past cases. I have the utmost confidence in his resourcefulness and abilities and I have no doubt that he will be able to aid the Professor in recovering Silverstar in time for the spring running of the Wessex cup. He will also guard the Professor against any late-stage attempt by Baron Maupertuis upon the Professor's life."

I nodded and acquiesced to the plans as Holmes had outlined them as did the other occupants of the room upon that momentous morning. My concern was as always for Holmes' health, but I could see how much it meant to him to be upon the chase again. I hoped that while in London I might have him re-examined by the lung specialist Dr. Moore Agar of Harley Street. He appeared healthy though that morning to my humble eyes as a general practitioner. I had no doubt that the excellent food obtained at Baskerville Hall had strengthened him. I knew that I would miss the regal fare of the country house. The recent weeks had been a renewal of many of the glad days of my youth when I had pursued adventures of detection with the man who now stood before us.

He was as ever the Sherlock Holmes I had always known, but was less the cocksure and spry man of his youth though he had still the steel resilience about him that seemed to feed upon some inner source of strength. His youth had been spent upon the bracing moors of Yorkshire and he had still that health bred in the generations of his forbears who had for so long owned the manor, Sigerside, in the North Riding of Yorkshire. One who is active in his youth may retain that constitution and the habit of preserving it throughout his life. My own wounded leg had forced upon me a more sedentary life and my domestic duties had constrained the more extreme exertions that had been Holmes' meat and drink for years. I could only hope now that, even if he was still consumptive, I would be able to keep up with him in the days that lay ahead for us both. These were my thoughts as our meeting broke up and we each retired to our respective rooms. A few hours later I saw Holmes off to Exeter from whence he would proceed to London. The Professor likewise departed for his own home at Kings Pyland where Inspector Hopkins would soon join him. Only Sir Henry and I remained in the great Baskerville Hall that now seemed so empty to await our journey in a few days down to Exeter where, if our plans succeeded as we hoped, we would be able to greet Lady Beryl Baskerville and restore her to the embrace of her dear husband, Sir Henry.

It was a time of suspense for me and I sought distraction in what had become a welcome habit by returning once again to the manuscript recounting Holmes' thoughts and actions on his great journey to the east where I had left his account of his winter spent in Persia in 1891. I had noticed that many of the thoughts that he had entertained and expressed in his journal now seemed to awaken within me similar responses. Could my own religious quest and the answers that I had thought to have reached regarding eternity so long ago be re-visited in the light of my present reading? I eagerly began to read.

From the Journal of Sherlock Holmes

November 12, 1891
Tehran, Persia

I was troubled for days after my discussion with Colonel Moran. His suggestion that it was I who needed to answer for my actions in bringing to a close the career of the Moriarty criminal organization seemed both inaccurate and impertinent to me. Though I have not been blind to the inequities of life I had always assumed that the concept of complete social equality was a utopian idea. There seemed to me to be gradations in human life and that persons naturally migrated to those stations best suited to their talents and aspirations. I had taken for granted that the vast majority of men and women existed with only a veneer of civilization. The bawdy humor of the cheap music halls, a taste for cheap gin, and a generally vulgar life seemed to content the vast majority of London's denizens.

The middle-class on the other hand could aspire to little more than a small sitting room, Sundays spent in a cold Methodist Chapel, and a joint of mutton for Sunday dinner. The husband would sport a stiff collar and the wife, if she was dissatisfied, might as a married woman at least escape from clawing-out a spare existence as a milliner or a shop girl. Such a couple might even leave a small estate of pounds sterling, but the gravitational pull back into poverty and squalor would likely be too much and their offspring would be forced finally to emigrate to America or to Australia if they wished to avoid the fate of most of their class and descend again into the anonymous labor pool of the working-class.

The fate of rural England was even worse. There a man might not so much as poach a rabbit from the great manors and estates without being answerable to the law. The genius of power in England has resided in its resistance to the republican spirit of France. The concentration of wealth that has enabled England to dominate the world has been wrung from the laboring masses that have yet to share most of the fruits of Empire.

Even in America, for all of its vaunted aspirations and claims to the freedom and equality of its citizens, the general trend has been to resist upward mobility and to treat trade unions as conspiracies in restraint of trade. This judicial practice has kept relative wages low and has made it possible for an upper class as a new aristocracy to have risen in contempt of the basic principles of democracy. The mass of the people are only given sufficient means to prevent revolution. As a nation grows in material progress therefore revolution becomes increasingly impossible.

This was proven recently by the failure of the attempted secession of the southern states from the wealthy capital-driven north. The southern states that were to form the Confederacy began to realize that they were essentially a colony of the northern states. The North had money and the factories to generate capital, while the agrarian South had cotton and tobacco and romance. Raw materials can seldom create the same degree of wealth as manufactures. The two bases of economy are vastly different. The South then, in a desperate attempt to retain a vanishing way of life, seceded from the Union. It was a doomed experiment from the start. Slavery would have failed with time in any case. The people of the North had proven that it is not necessary to have formal ownership of the workers. The wage-earners of the North in the squalid factories were and are essentially slaves. They must take the wages that are offered or quietly starve.

A life of grace and dignity is not within the means of a large population, even with the vast and unexploited resources of the virgin land of America; how much less then is this possible in overcrowded Europe. The result of this scarcity is the social order that we see about us. It is one of suppressed violence held in check by penury and want and the fear of the law. The laws will always tend to serve power and property; but without legal restraints would we not have the even greater savagery of the jungle? Besides there is always the hope of Christian charity is there not? Unfortunately, when the theology of salvation by grace alone triumphed, charity took second place. Good works were seen as vaguely impious. Surely God could take care of his own, the elect, who showed that they were the elect by the very prosperity and frugalness of their lives. Why should an industrious middle-class aid the starving widows and orphans of the working-class? These denizens of the lower depths of society were badly bred. Since nature, according to this view, is governed by a God who ordained its cruel wisdom, that the weak should die, who then is man to alter nature's disposition of resources. Virtue became for many an Englishman the science of good breeding. If one had wealth it was because one was well-bred. From this came the rigid class-structure of the British Empire.

It seemed to me appropriate then that the radical republicanism preached by Colonel Moran would come from one such as he who was raised far from England and no doubt tainted by the notion of the Mohammedans that one of the pillars of the faith is to sustain the body of believers through regular almsgiving. In Christianity the teaching is that any charity must spring from the heart to be efficacious and to bring merit. It must be founded on love, that most elusive emotion of the heart. The practical follower of Mohammed though recognizes in the giving of alms a remnant of the ancient tribal duty of hospitality to the stranger and since any believer may find himself a stranger at some day or hour his gift is simply the bond that makes civilization possible in the rugged desert regions of Asia. The life of the believer in the teachings of Mohammed is a rugged one, but it has a stark realism about it, and the teachings are simple and practical. Even prayer is not something that springs unbidden to the pious heart, but rather a daily communal discipline binding upon all at set times of the day.

There is little debate as to the nature of man in Islam. The focus is kept upon the sovereign rights of God and man turns to God in submission, not because he is convinced that he is a sinner, for what men or women ever really believe that they are sinners and do not seek above all else to justify themselves even before God. But rather, in Islam, the eye is always upon God and upon that final dread day when the book shall be opened and every man and woman will see what has been recorded and all will be answerable for what is written therein.

Colonel Moran has put the question to me, how I shall pay for my virtues, which have done nothing to set aside the order of things that prevails in England. In my own small way I know that I have profited by a social order that from the point of view of Colonel Moran is itself an affront to justice. I know not how therefore to answer him. I had always thought my life to be somewhat Spartan, spent in my humble rooms in Baker Street. I had often attempted to aid my many clients who had few funds with which to pay my fees. I had even allowed a great gap to appear between my brother Sherringford and myself, for he is of the landed gentry of England, while I as a third son am only Sherlock Holmes of Baker Street.

My relations to Mycroft have also been somewhat distant due to his immensely reclusive nature. There may be a bitterness shown in this that is common to second sons in a system of primogeniture. Mycroft may have preferred to be the Lord of a manor. Instead, he is in many ways greater than the run of English aristocrats; his unique position in the government allows him to act as a Lord of all the manors and indeed of all of England. He has for instance, daily access to the Prime Minister and even the Queen. There has been talk of making him a baronet, but Mycroft will not hear of it. It is his peculiar pride that he must be a complete original, a class unto himself. His unique role stems from his status as a commoner who is yet the superior of all in the government. He has created in a sense his own peerage rather than having it bestowed upon him. He will not condescend to the exigencies of the feudal order. He performs his services to the Crown of England directly, and simply because he chooses to do so. He is bound by no oath of loyalty. He will not even speak to other misanthropes like himself in the Diogenes Club.

I share in many ways the reserved habits of my brothers, but in me this reclusiveness has always been a painful one. How desolate my life should have been without Doctor John Watson at my side to celebrate and to witness my triumphs and to aid me in those hours of my despondency. Yet even Watson has been known to abandon me at times to undertake the incomprehensible joys of wedlock. I used to catch sight of him now and again in the London streets during his married years. He took pride in owning his own carriage and I would see him, black bag in hand, off to deliver a baby or to examine some elderly patient. His practice was always a small one, but it did provide a decent living. He could never aspire to a Harley Street address of course, but he was a professional man and the joys of the middle-class were his in abundance. His ideas were always somewhat prosaic and plebian at times and he would look with disapprobation at my own sometimes Bohemian ways with cocaine and my habit of seeking out the society of the lower-classes, so that I might understand their ways. It was of course essential to my line of work. One must know intimately the mind of the working-class in order to assume its guise convincingly, as I often was forced to do in order to solve many of the mysterious problems that were brought before me.

By identifying with the poor, I developed, over time, a certain sympathy for the destitute that remains with me to this day. This is why the words of Colonel Moran stung me so. His implication that to avoid violence, certainly a major Christian teaching since Christians are asked to turn the other cheek, is impossible in an unjust world where the rich use the laws to sustain their unjust means of extracting the labor of others and of exhausting their very lives. Therefore, an abiding Christian peace was impossible. True justice lay more in a jihad, to take up the avenging sword of Allah, which was an offense to my deepest instincts. I did not wish to agree with Colonel Moran, yet I could not imagine that the present state of affairs might continue forever in England.

I have wondered whether Colonel Moran is, after all, a secret follower of the Prophet of Islam. He has not said so, yet his ideas seem often to have been drawn from the well of some branches of Islamic thought. This entire matter has come of weigh deeply upon my mind. I had thought to tarry the winter in these Persian lands, but I can feel already a great restlessness within me. I must see the center of Islamic thought. As soon as travel permits therefore, I believe that I shall press onwards to the coast and then to Mecca. It is not enough in examining a religion to look merely at its tenets. I might have done as much without ever leaving Baker Street. It is essential to go further and to witness the culture as it is and to see the actions of the believers themselves. Yes, I must go to Mecca!

November 15, 1891
Tehran, Persia

I have made inquiries with the British Consul and told him of my plans to go to Mecca as soon as matters can be arranged. He advised me though to abandon that particular aspiration.

"I should not attempt it, Mr. Holmes," said he. "You must understand our situation out here. We are tolerated rather than welcomed. These lands are just beginning to adjust to the change in the balance of the great powers. Indeed, if the Persians did not fear Russia more than us, I doubt that we would even be allowed to maintain an embassy here. These people still view themselves as the possessors of an empire and are jealous of what they feel are the pretentions of the modern powers. Their industrial capacity and weaponry is of course mediocre at best, but due to the remoteness of the region, they possess a decisive military advantage. We learned this back in the 70's in Afghanistan and during the Punjab Revolt. Our capacity to project force is limited the further we are removed from the sea. Besides, our commitments in Egypt at the present time and our resistance to the spreading Turkish influence in the eastern Mediterranean are quite dispositive at this time of our main forces. We cannot afford to antagonize these Moslem chaps any further. Her Majesty's government is committed to a recognition and respect to all outward manifestations of these various religions and we try and give them leeway when we can. The poor blighters take it all quite seriously you know part of their culture. It was quite a job simply putting down the Tuggee Cult with their bloody worship of Goddess Kali. Religious extremism can tear India apart. India is the crown jewel you know. With our navy deployed in Bombay and patrolling the Persian Gulf though, we can still dominate sea trade in the region. As for Mecca, well, Mecca of course is a backwater, lot of sand that's all, but stir up trouble there and the whole body of Islam contracts as though on a galvanic charge. Should you get into trouble out there I assure you that there is nothing that we could do for you. No, Mr. Holmes, let me prevail upon you; do not go to Mecca."

I explained to him that I was on a valuable reconnoitering mission assigned to me by Mycroft and that I had no choice. I could see that the name of Mycroft Holmes impressed him. While not knowing the details of Mycroft's service to the British government, he had heard at least that my brother was highly placed in the diplomatic service.

"Well then," he answered after a time, "that of course puts another face upon the matter. We may at least guard you to the frontier and we shall render every manner of assistance possible should you be captured between here and the Red Sea, but I am afraid that there is little that we could do really other than registering a strong protest with the Emir. Your presence as an unbeliever at the site of the Kaaba would be seen as an affront to the Prophet and to Allah. These people do not treat perceived blasphemy lightly. Without intending to be graphic, let me simply say that they might carve you up a bit."

I assured him that I had often impersonated an Arab in eastern London and come away unharmed and uncarved from some very unsavory regions. Besides, I would have Colonel Moran at my side. I could see that he was still unsatisfied as to my soundness of mind, but he knew that my mind was made up.

"Very well then, Mr. Holmes, let me know please when you plan to leave Tehran. We will fit you up with supplies and guides as far as the Red Sea or the Arab frontier. I shall alert our embassy in Cairo so that they may provide assistance should you run into trouble in the Sinai region. We send a few patrols at times as far as Medina and they may catch word of you should there be any fracas."

I thanked him warmly for his help and returned to our villa to report the results to Colonel Moran.

He heard my story and was amused. "I dare say that you put the wind up the fellow. These embassy types want peace at all costs out here. Serve their time and return to England on a fat pension, that's what they want. There is nothing worse than some starry-eyed wanderer seeking out Ali Baba to throw a spanner into the works—lot of paperwork, awkward questions and all that. You really don't know what a bother you are with all your philosophizing and searching after God. These people believe they have found him and they have rested in that belief for over twelve hundred years. Besides, what can you learn from a lot of chaps in white robes in Mecca, milling about like workers in a beehive?"

"Well, I can feel the energy of the place if nothing else. Surely, religious emotion of such an extent must communicate itself along the nerves. I feel that I must be there to witness the phenomenon of the Pilgrimage at first hand. For many it is the high point of their lives, to be in Mecca, to fulfill that primal promise of every devout Moslem. If belief is not a matter of weighing the evidence, but rather of a mere feeling or emotion, then I shall witness it there at its height in Mecca. I must try and see if the sheer gravitational force of such belief may convince me too."

The Colonel shook his head. "You would stick your head in the lion's mouth in order to count his teeth! Oh very well, I shall come along too, for my instructions from the Professor are clear, if only to see your own reactions. I find you interesting, indeed I do. The good Dr. Watson had it wrong, the real mystery is not your cases; it is you yourself, Mr. Sherlock Holmes."

Dr. Watson's Narrative Continues

I was interrupted in my reading at this point by a sound from below. A carriage had drawn up at the door. It was a rainy, blustery day and the occupant ducked his head and ran for the door. I recognized the spare form and unusual gait at once. It was our old friend Dr. Mortimer. I set Holmes' manuscript aside and descended to greet him. Dr. Mortimer had already handed his overcoat to Perkins and was being shown into the drawing room. He turned when he heard my salutation. He came up to me at once and shook my hand warmly.

"Dr. Watson, this is excellent. I see that you have not returned to Cornwall. I have come to see Sir Henry and I hope... May I ask if Mr. Sherlock Holmes is also still here? He is not. Ah that is too bad too bad."

He shook his head with an air of deep disappointment. I could not but smile. The man inhabited a region of his own where only his own enthusiasms reigned supreme. He was not alone in this though, for we all tend to be rather egocentric about our own pet projects, but Dr. Mortimer carried about with him an air of great mission as though his researches might change the course of human history. It was impossible not to be affected by his presence. Sir Henry must also have heard the commotion below, for he joined us from where he had sought repose in the great library.

"Dr. Mortimer, this is something of a surprise on such a day. I am sorry to say that Mr. Holmes has departed if it is he that you came to consult. But come, you must be chilled to the bone. Perkins, we shall have a hot rum punch if you would be so good as to prepare one. Come into the library gentlemen. It will be warmer there."

We returned to the library where the fire had kept the room warmer than the chill hall. Sir Henry himself added a log to the blaze and taking a seat he asked Dr. Mortimer how his researches progressed. Perkins entered soon after with the rum punch and we filled the antique pewter vessels with the steaming mixture.

Dr. Mortimer recapitulated the news of his unique find of the ancient British barrow but he now added some details based upon his further excavations and told us of his attempts to date the objects that he had found. He also gave us something of the background knowledge that we would require in order to appreciate the significance of his discoveries.

"I am indeed sorry that Mr. Holmes is not present, for his advice and opinions would be invaluable to me at this time. His own research into the early pre-history of these isles has given him knowledge of the matter second to none. You are no doubt familiar with his opinions upon the matter of atavism." I mentioned in reply that Holmes had made comments to me from time to time but had not given a thorough explanation of any theory that he might entertain.

"Then gentlemen, perhaps you will me allow a brief discourse on the subject. The problem of atavism is this: is human nature evolving, as Mr. Huxley believes, or are we rather going backwards. I know that this theory must appear absurd when one considers the wonders of the age. Trains cross great distances. New steamships draw the trade of the entire world into one vast linkage. Huge buildings arise and daily we discover new things in the sciences, but shall technical progress alone be the measure of man? We must ask what makes us most human. Surely a great part is played by the emotions and those sympathetic faculties that unite communities, for what would man be if all relations though rational were based solely upon contract principles."

"I have often discussed this matter with Mr. Franklin, who as you known has a passion for the law. He prefers all undertakings to be definite and to have set consequences, for he has never trusted in the benevolent nature of man. How often has he waved in my face the three books that constitute, along with his legal books and copies of old English charters, his entire library. Those books are Thomas Hobbes' book 'The Leviathan,' Herbert Spencer's, 'Social Statics,' and Charles Darwin's, 'The The Ascent of Man.' Mr. Franklin prefers to believe that man is but a cunning animal and that he only ever enters into relations with his peers through self-interest. He would maintain that we have never really left the jungle and as such the question of atavism is moot, for we are by nature predatory beasts."

"Mr. Holmes and I on the contrary maintain the opposite opinion, that man has a spiritual nature, but that this nature is being daily compromised by forces of evil that deny that nature of man and induce us to retrogress into savagery. I assure you that we have all three had rather heated discussions upon Friday nights when we have been invited to take a late supper at Mr. Franklin's house. Those evenings usually ended with Mr. Franklin vowing to sue us both for defamation of his character and other various obscure offenses. By the following week though, we are usually invited to return to his fire and hearth. We have yet to possess conclusive evidence to back up our various assertions, but I believe that my present find may provide us with just such evidence. It is promising, indeed most promising."

Sir Henry and I smiled at each other. We could only imagine the nature of such evenings. Knowing how my friend would on occasion enjoy baiting certain men of choleric temperament, I could only imagine how he would tempt the wrath of a man like Mr. Franklin. At the same time I could vouch for the fact that Holmes considered the question of atavism to be an important one and that he would regret not being able to devote his full attention to the quest on which Dr. Mortimer was engaged. I assured Dr. Mortimer that if all went well, in a few months Holmes would again be free and that in the meantime I would bring to his attention anything that Dr. Mortimer cared to share with me.

"But I had hoped for far more, Doctor. I had hoped that you would return to the site with me. Mr. Holmes hinted you might be able to do so at my last visit."

I told him regretfully that the posture of the matter that engaged us demanded my full attention at present and that I would be soon leaving to join Holmes in London. He shook his head ruefully.

"Very well, Doctor, what cannot be changed must be endured, but perhaps you may take some of my questions and suppositions to Mr. Holmes and he may write to me when he gets a chance. So that you may be better prepared for your role as an intermediary it may help if I outline for you where we stood prior to this most momentous find."

"Mr. Holmes as you know has a fascination for obscure subjects. You are no doubt aware of his researches into early English music of the medieval period. These tunes precede in time even the chansons of France which were brought here during the Norman Conquest. They trace their origins to the ancient bards who in turn were latter-day descendants of the Druids who were the priests and judges of the ancient religion of the Keltoi or Celts who inhabited not simply these isles but also Northern Gaul at the time of the Romans. Julius Caesar wrote of the Druids somewhat disparagingly. While acknowledging their extreme bravery in battle, he claimed that they engaged in human sacrifice in tandem with their celebrations of harvest festivals and fertility rites. The question of the true nature of these people has puzzled scholars ever since."

"The Druids appear to have had a most sophisticated and even a Pythagorean conception of the immortality of the soul. Their burial rites included the practice of burning a man's possessions so that sublimated into smoke they might follow the man's soul into his new life. They were also magicians of no small note and there is some speculation that they had even had ties to Egypt, to Greece, and to the ancient Phoenicians. That latter maritime people may have conceivably rounded Gibraltar and the Pillars of Hercules and have visited these shores. Your friend Mr. Sherlock Holmes adhered to just such a theory, for it would explain the advanced metallurgy and ornamentation of the Druids and also account for certain ideas that they possessed that show some knowledge of Greek Philosophy, particularly that of the School of Pythagoras."

"The members of the priestly order of the Druids seem to have been among the most enlightened men of their age in what today we would call the sciences. But there is another side to what little we know of them from the ancient sources. There is evidence that in their sacred groves some members at least practiced human sacrifices of a most appalling kind. Their soothsayers would read the entrails of the dead or the dying or attempt to discern from the grotesque distortions of the limbs after death some sign from the other world. Their very desire to pursue knowledge beyond the boundary of death created within them an evil that is still said to haunt their sacred sites. Oh you may smile gentlemen, but I have felt it myself. Often of late I have tarried past dusk in my excavations working only by the dim light of an oil lamp. I would feel the soil slip between my fingers or see the dust blown away as I sifted through it with my brush so as to let nothing escape me, no artifact or object however humble it might be that might tell me something of those vanished lives. On such nights as I am describing I would see the moon seeming to flee beyond the clouds and the entire landscape would be bathed in that silver light that still has the power to awaken a sense of awe within us..."

He paused and a shudder convulsed his frame before continuing. "I have seen then in my mind's eye the white-robed Druid priests marching in a line over the moors. They came then to the vale in which I worked and I could see them as they led their victim to his doom. They would enter the sacred grove, for what is today barren moorland must then have been thickly covered with trees, not yet cut and harvested by our rapacious Anglo-Saxon race. In that darkness perhaps they carried lighted tapers or torches. By its light there would appear a crude stone altar stained with the blood of prior victims. To it they would bind the newest of their offerings and the young acolytes would be brought forward, those who would wish to share the Druidic priesthood. After what unholy chants and imprecations, only our own imaginations may supply, they would reach beneath their girdles for their knives of bronze and descend as harpies upon the supine figure transfixed with terror of what was to come. He would be pierced by the many knives and even in death know the further indignity of being opened like the earth so that his blood might bring life to the soil. The many eyes would stare into the steaming entrails and from them read horrid prognostications of the future year."

Sir Henry and I no doubt showed our horror upon our faces. Dr. Mortimer's description showed me that he had been perhaps too much affected by living so long upon the ancient moors. Perhaps there were indeed spirits abroad, just such spirits as might addle a man's mind who paid too much attention to these fancies. Some matters must be forgotten by the human race if only that it may begin again to recover hope. Dr. Mortimer must have discerned my thoughts for he smiled and reassured us.

"No gentlemen, I am not mad. I wished only to share with you why I require the steady mind and hand of Mr. Sherlock Holmes to aid me in my researches. As a theosophist and a follower of Madame Blavatsky I am no doubt prone to spiritualistic influences as is my wife. Our circle has during the past year summoned many an ancient one to our side to tell us of the past. But alas we live in a most skeptical age and in a materialistic country. I doubt that my findings will be given the proper weight if they are not confirmed by another, and who better to do so than the greatest private investigator of our times, a man known to many through your own writings, Dr. Watson, as a man of no romantic bent, but one who always demands and relies upon evidence for his conclusions."

I knew that my friend had at times shown an interest in these obscure matters. His choice of a site for his retirement on the bleak moors rather than along the English Channel was partially so that he might engage in this same abstruse line of inquiry into the early Britons. Holmes had a passion for unique objects that might tell a strange story. I well recall how he would use his magnifying lens to scrutinize any object belonging to a potential client in order to discern something of the character of its possessor; how much more might be revealed by the remnants of past civilizations of their habits and religions.

Alas, human history beyond a certain point is always a *terra incognita*. The most ancient of civilizations is but a few thousand years old and before that we have only a few obscure paintings upon cave walls or crude figures carved in stone. These tell us nothing really. Was human nature the same in those far off years of our nativity as a species? Perhaps we had then no real sense of ourselves as a unique type of animal at all. We must then have hunted and gathered and saw about us only other beasts like ourselves. Where then and when did we first awaken from that primal incognition and perhaps cast our eyes upwards to the heavens and dreamed that in those far off stars we beheld the gods?

From whence later came our sense of guilt and shame, those first gifts of the sin spoken of in Eden, the knowledge of good and evil? How did we first develop compassion and see in the fate of the other some hint of our own fate? Our earliest sources of knowledge already show a sophistication and insight that surely could not have emerged all in one piece. Perhaps human beings were already somewhat civilized before the means of recording their thoughts and feelings allowed for a more permanent and fixed account of those customs that were already rooted among them. Where are the precedent documents however to those now included in the Bible? Even now we have hardly supplanted the wisdom of the Bible or the insights of the early Greeks and of Plato and Aristotle. It is this very lack of knowledge from rational sources or actual writings that have led to all of the sciences of the occult, that shadow side of revealed religion, for man desires above all things to know, to be certain, and to avoid the necessity of faith if he can but actually ground that faith in direct experience.

Dr. Mortimer had fallen silent for a time. He was clearly still abstracted and absorbed in his grim vision and the need to confirm the true nature of the ancient Druid Religion. I asked him if his own dark interpretation was universally shared by other scholars.

"Oh by no means," he answered. "There are writers who

take the contrary view that the Druids were a most peaceful people until they were invaded by the Romans and that the dire speculations of the early writers were based upon their own need to justify their invasion and extermination of these ancient people. It is in the nature of the drive for power that it must justify its own incursions. No people desire to be condemned in the light of posterity for their brutality. War must always seem to be an inevitable struggle of self-defense or an effort to spread an enlightened civilization to the barbarians. The barbarians of course may never speak, for they are among the silent dead; even their languages must vanish with them or be incorporated over time into the dominant tongue. What is our English language today but a conglomerate tongue made of the languages of those people whose poetry has died with the bards who once chanted their ancient lays? But I believe that their spirits still remain grounded in the soil that they once inhabited; they may even still be summoned forth. The ancient art of necromancy is alive in modern England. Indeed I invite you both to attend one of our circles. You may be surprised to discover ... well, there have been signs only recently..."

Sir Henry shook his head and interrupted him. "I am afraid, Dr. Mortimer, that the preternatural has left upon me a most unpleasant set of memories. I am yet to fully recover from the dread that was once imposed upon me from the spectral hound said to haunt our family. I have no desire to awaken any other ghosts. I pray daily for their peace. Let it go at that. I have of course no influence with Dr. Watson and I am sure that Mr. Holmes will, if you think it essential, comply with your wishes when he returns should his current professional commitments allow him to resume his own private inquiries at your side."

I could not but agree with Sir Henry. Surely it is enough to deal with the manifest and obvious evils of the world or as Holmes had often said to me, "The world is big enough for us, no ghosts need apply." I have among my friends though a diverse set of writers and other men who have speculated about 'the other side' as it is termed. Some even go so far as to believe in the fair folk or as they are sometimes called the fairy people, those legendary beings, at least so I hope to believe, who occupy a station below the angels but above that of human beings. These races are called the Jinn in the Arabic world, the leprechauns in Ireland, and go by other names in other places. They come in all manner and varieties of shapes and natures: the fearsome Kelpies of Scotland, the Bogeys of Germany, the Trolls of Norway, and the Gnomes and Brownies of England. Are these beings only figments of the universal imagination of man or do they really exist? I have often debated the matter with my colleague, Dr. Arthur Conan Doyle, and my young Catholic friend of late, Mr. Gilbert Keith Chesterton.

The three of us span the spectrum of the available positions that might be taken on these matters. Dr. Doyle, as befits his Irish ancestry, adamantly believes in them. Mr. Chesterton, whose subtle mind admits of many gradations, sees in them an affirmation of the limits of human reason. In his efforts to dispose of that bland and cocksure materialism that is now so fashionable, he has argued that when the mind loses its capacity for fancy it is no longer a human mind but a pure mechanism. He believes in the creatures of fancy in a qualified manner, for faith seems to him to be the natural posture of a human life, and faith is nurtured by all that does not quell the human imagination. I on the other hand neither believe nor disbelieve, but take the position imbibed though my years with Holmes, that it is a capital mistake to theorize without data.

I can recall one occasion when at mid-summer and after perhaps imbibing too freely of an excellent claret we three stayed up until dawn around one of the so-called fairy mounds to see if we might spy one of the wee folk. We were armed with iron so that we should come to no harm, for the various branches of the unseen world are said to dread that metal above all things. Whether the fairies ever appeared, I cannot say, for each of us fell asleep upon the ground during the course of the night. When the dawn came and the mists began to melt away I rose with stiff-joints and with aching muscles. When I remarked in an ill-temper that we had at least that night's witness that there were no fair folk, I was vehemently contradicted by Doctor Doyle who said that my various pains were the result of having been ridden all night by the fairies who resenting our presumption in lying in ambush for them had placed us in a trance and ridden us like horses in their nocturnal hunt. Such was the force of his suggestion that I developed during that very day red marks upon my sides that might have been left by their tiny spurs. I remember that it left a most unpleasant impression upon me at the time and when I had confessed my folly to Holmes, he had laughed heartily and said that it had been my just deserts for the odd company that I kept.

To hear Dr. Mortimer now, as he discoursed about the Druids, recalled that previous occasion and I had no desire to return with him to the barrow, there to dig into what might be the very graves of that ancient people who had once dared to resist Roman rule. I recalled an account of a battle in which the Roman legions were almost routed due to the presence of the women of the Celts who went about among the warriors clothed in black and keening in shrill voices. The mind of man quails in terror before the unknown and for that very reason many to this day fear the power of the witches and the other wise ones. We stand in awe before madness, perhaps discerning in those said to be mad those lost faculties that are part of our own instinctual nature and which may have allowed us to survive when we lived, not in the brusque business of our world of cities, but in small communities and tribes. Indeed, I wonder whether we are not now in a way creating ourselves an emulation of our creations rather than dominating them in a human way. Will man someday become a mere appendage to the forces of his own production? Will he simply serve the machines rather than being served by them?

Perhaps it is the fear of this prospective future that induces Mr. Chesterton to place such store upon fancy and why Mr. Samuel Taylor Coleridge in his remarkable book, 'The Biographia Literaria,' speaks of the fancy as the unifying force of the mind and its understanding. He discusses the synthetic function of the understanding which must in some manner integrate that strange dread and awe before beauty that is celebrated in William Wordsworth's remarkable poem, 'The Prelude.'

Where would the mind of man be without our poets? Truly, if we ever feel that we can dispense with the heart and its images, ah then what would be left of the type of being that we are? Can we ever be saved without poetry? Perhaps the highest theology lies not in the detailed provisions of the Torah but in the Psalms, those songs of God. Even in India, the 'Rig Veda' which is a collection of divine songs preceded the more philosophical Upanishads. Man always makes a mistake when he aspires too far beyond the unique and the incidental in life in order to grasp the universals. Aristotle knew this and his more concrete philosophy turned from the Platonic emphasis upon the comparative unreality of all that we know here on earth and did not spurn the unique and the concrete nature of the real.

In Christian teaching this respect for the concrete is shown by the scandal of the doctrine of the Divine Incarnation of Christ, which states that the Godhead so far embraced the world that God descended and embraced our limited nature and made Itself subject to time and to all the minute particularity that comes with a temporal existence. Surely this realization vindicates our troubled hours and sustains the Christian in his pain and sorrow. All of life is lived now within the shadow of eternity. We are no longer mere animals. I had imbibed as much from discussions with Mr. Chesterton and from my reflections thus far upon the journal of his travels kept by my friend.

I cannot leave the question of man's engagement with the supernatural without returning to the question of the so-called evolving nature of man. As a physician it has always seemed to me that our bodies may contribute as much to our advancement as our minds. If man is redeemed, it is not as a mind alone. Indeed I will go so far as to say that the body serves to humble what might otherwise be an overwhelming pride in our cerebral faculties. So it is that primitive man may be closer to the human and therefore less savage than his supposedly highly evolved cousin with all of his tools and machines. Who can say whether survival is always the supreme virtue?

The spawning source of every religion is the sense of awe that we feel before all of the ineluctable facets of human existence: birth, maturation, and death combined with their attendant joys and sufferings. Planting, fruition, and harvest, the alternation of the seasons, all of these find their place in religion as does the role of blood of sacrifice, and above all else the need to find an ally through propitiatory rituals in our struggle for survival. Even at its most primitive level religion invokes invisible forces that will take an interest for good or ill in human affairs. That interest may even take the form of imagining that the universe itself possesses moral underpinnings that only emerge in conscious beings. The great cataclysmic events of aging and exploding stars, of numberless galaxies that are utterly indifferent to our affairs, or are even aware of our existence seem not to trouble the religious consciousness that never ceases to draw all things into the ambit of its few and inadequate categories.

They are inadequate precisely because they take one sort of statement clothed in mythological garb and then seek to apply that perspective in a universal manner to all phenomena whatsoever. The religious consciousness goes further still however when it equates the physical universe in which we live and the impulses of our own moral feelings, always seeking some outer basis for the impetuous demands of the conscience. We need to believe that good will be rewarded and that evil will be punished rather than accepting the responsibility and the dignity of our own inner conviction that morality has a just claim upon human nature. By locating the source and nexus of morality outside of our own experience we create a distant God, one divorced from our own history. By denying the historical basis of religion we imply that we can translate the intentions of the absolute into the realm where contingency rules all things. Religion then becomes a source of exclusivity and even of oppression as one group implies that another group should pay the price of blood for offending what is finally a projection of our own wishes and ideals. To speak intelligibly about God therefore implies the very height of human arrogance.

These thoughts came to me later in my room. Sir Henry's objection had turned the conversation to other matters than the possible sacrifices of the Druids. Dr. Mortimer had agreed to be patient until the time when Holmes might be able to join him at the site of his excavations. We spent the rest of our time together discussing the local events of the village and the county. Sir Henry said that he hoped to continue the tradition that he had inaugurated of holding a Christmas ball and to supply toys and sweets for the village children to be handed out by Father Christmas on St. Nicholas Day. Father Christmas is said to owe something to the English pagan tradition as Dr. Mortimer quickly reminded us. I had learned in my time in the southwest counties of England, where many of the ancient Pagan practices still endure, to embrace those remnants of another belief system such as the lighting of bale-fires upon the hills in spring and to enjoy the loaves of bread at Lammas. The interpenetration of Christianity with the native folk-religions and customs of the lands to which it has spread is well known. The desire to be reborn from the underworld is innate in the Pagan traditions in culture after culture, so it was a message to be welcomed when Christianity claimed the ultimate rebirth, not to a new life of the sorrows that we know, but to a life changed and made perfect, a life no longer tainted by sin.

How different is this conception from that of the Buddhist doctrine of nirvana. To the follower of the Buddha it is rebirth and resurrection that he dreads as the worst fate imaginable. The entire practice of eastern meditation has as its goal a state of insensibility, to silence thought, to end consciousness of the particular by merging into the universal. It attempts to achieve by mental discipline a foretaste of non-being. Christian prayer on the contrary exalts the particular. Christ asked that we approach God in our needs and even in our sin, that even the hairs upon our head are numbered. The Western religious tradition never despairs of life in the particular so that the advent of the universal is seen as an increase in being but not as an extinction of what is unique in us; heaven then is a full participation in the divine order, but a participation in which all that we are as unique individuals is to be preserved.

In Buddhist conceptions it is individuality and desire that bring about sorrow and pain and suffering. Only by ceasing to exist as individuals do we realize that we have always been part of the greater whole that alone exists. Our separation and uniqueness is held to be an illusion born of some unknown cause but not without remedy. By means of virtuous actions and mental disciplines such as Yogic breathing and exercises, the believer may hope to regain the truth through 'mindfulness.' But this belief denies the ultimate dualism implied by creation. There is to the Buddhist mind only God; there has always been only God. But as to how God came to dream, what we in the west call the separate order of creation and how it is that we can even be free to take a position toward that life to which we have been doomed is never explained. If there is only God then how did God fragment into parts? If we are not real but only deluded by our separate natures then our being as we know it is not being at all but an illusion based upon a something that must be reminded that it is even dreaming. If there is only Brahman, God, then it should be impossible that we could exist at all, even in delusion. This essential contradiction does not appear to have been resolved by the eastern mind. Certain concepts can only appear when philosophy and language find the means to express them. The western mind cannot refuse to draw distinctions once having discovered them. Thought takes precedence over meditation among us and even prayer is said to have a goal.

As a western man who is also a doctor and a man of science, I cannot think myself out of existence nor find virtue by cultivating and hoping to become perfected in indifference. I have buried two wives and it is no comfort to me that they no longer suffer if they do not also still exist in some manner. In their final hours they prayed that they might remain because they found life precious still even if flawed by history and tainted by age and sickness. Each loved her life and would have gladly paid the price of pain for one more hour and would always have paid it to continue to exist. I have risked my life on many occasions, but I could not have done so were it not for the inherent sense that I had at the time that I would be preserved and that I might trust to God, that having once been I could never again not be.

I turned that day (so long ago now as I write this) to look at Dr. Mortimer. I saw in the man a happy Pagan who sought among the bones of the Druids for his own origins in that obscure religion that has left no cohesive doctrine behind in written accounts. The struggle of natural man to seek religion in the good things of this earth seems preferable to me to the dry and cerebral doctrine of nirvana. Christianity does not despise this life. It is only in finding the partial good that we may imagine a perfect good. God leaves his signs upon all things. We dare not turn from them in contempt but should rather seek within them for their ultimate origin in God. This much I knew and had come to believe with the years, for what man knows more of life than a doctor, one who brings life into the world and escorts it to the very gates of eternity.

The talk of Christmas had occupied my friends while my own thoughts had drifted. I had thought more of these matters since I had been reading Holmes' own thoughts on religion. It is no easy task to examine and to take a firm position upon ultimate values and to articulate the base from which one moves out into the world each day. Many live lives of comparative religious insensibility, but the human stirs within us all and though these thoughts may never find words, they do recur from time to time in all men and women I am sure. So I remain a Christian through all of my doubts even when discomfited by my own affirmation of faith.

As the afternoon waned I could see that Sir Henry had profited by our company. I could see that we had distracted him from the daring task that lay before us. While we had been speaking together, Perkins had entered with a telegram that had been delivered from the village. Sir Henry opened it quickly and read its brief contents avidly. "It has come, Watson. We are to deliver the papers as agreed to the bank in Exeter two days hence at 1:00 P.M." Dr, Mortimer looked at me with a puzzled expression and I gestured that he should ask no questions. Dr. Mortimer was discreet enough to obey this sign. He finished what remained of the punch in his glass and stood up to depart. With that we adjourned our afternoon gathering. We escorted Dr. Mortimer to the door and watched as his carriage drove away down the yew alley. We closed the door then to the gathering night and I returned to my room for a brief rest prior to the serving of dinner.

It was indeed a great responsibility with which Holmes had entrusted me. The short interval allowed us between the notification that Rodger Baskerville had accepted our method of exchange and its actual accomplishment showed the man's eagerness to regain possession of the papers. I could only hope that his agents will have inspected the documents delivered by Holmes to the bank and that they in turn will have given Stapleton a favorable report on their authenticity and completeness. I decided that it would be best if we would leave by the mid-day train on the following day to Exeter so as to be on hand the following morning. We would stay in a hotel that night. At Holmes' request we were to go alone and without any aid from Scotland Yard. Holmes was determined that Rodger Baskerville must believe that he had scored a complete victory over us. He would of course soon discover after resuming custody that the papers that we planned to deliver were only copies.

He would then look about him for an alternative market, knowing that he could not obtain blackmail money from the principals in America unless they had a chance to examine the papers for themselves. Such was the reputation of Charles Augustus Milverton that even many English domestics knew that he provided a ready market for the purchase of private papers. So cunning was the man in his contacts and so careful about the means of payment that the authorities had never been able to prosecute him, nor would the men and women of importance whose affairs were involved testify against him for fear of bringing about the very publicity that they had sought to avoid. Indeed it was possible that Rodger Baskerville had always intended to use the services of Milverton as a go-between and to profit by the man's international reputation.

In any case, Rodger Baskerville would need him now, for only Charles Augustus Milverton might still be able to extract reparations, even with copies that in his hands at least were certainly not valueless. The copies were accurate in every detail and contained information unlikely to be obtainable elsewhere. Milverton would use his unique talents to descry the one man who could best profit by the inside information contained in these papers and he would think immediately of Baron Maupertuis, the great international financier. I could only hope that all would go forward as Holmes had planned. My rest that late afternoon was troubled. I could not put out of my mind the dangers that still beset us. At last I dismissed these thoughts and did as Holmes had often advised me to do when we were on the chase. I attempted to lose myself in a comfortable dinner and cigar. I descended to the dining room as the evening shadows gathered across the moors to join Sir Henry.

Book Five

The Journey to Mecca

From the Journal of Sherlock Holmes

November 21, 1891
Tehran, Persia

These last days have been spent in elaborate preparations for our journey. It is no small matter to venture forth across the desert and Cairo seems far away. Few Englishmen have ever visited Mecca let alone dared to seek to join the masses of pilgrims and to enter the sacred places. I must do so alone I fear, for although my own aquiline nose and features may allow me to impersonate an Arab, I fear that the bluff and hearty visage of Colonel Moran will hardly pass. His face is quintessentially English. If I am discovered, I fear that even Colonel Moran will not be able to free me and my fate may even be my death, for what will be regarded by the Arabs as blasphemy rather than as respectful interest in their religion. Allah may be a God of compassion but his followers in their zeal to preserve the prerogatives and dignity of God are seldom as understanding as the deity they worship. There is no humble and gentle figure of Jesus Christ in their religion, but only the august and unapproachable Supreme Deity, Allah.

Besides, theirs is a stern culture in other respects as well. The hostile environment where Islam originated is unforgiving of human error. It is no accident that the Moslem version of heaven bears a great resemblance to an oasis. To the Arab mind it is the ultimate luxury simply to have food and drink in abundance. To the English of course, who live in the fat and fertile English midlands, the prodigality of nature alone suffices and we seldom think daily of God to supply our needs. I have often wondered if the reason why the great Semitic religions took the shape that they did was because in the desert man is constantly reminded of his own inadequacy. In addition, the gods were often seen as tribal deities that traveled with the nomads who wandered over these lands.

Only the Egyptians elaborated a pantheon worthy of that of the Greeks and the Romans. They were a settled people along the rich course and at the mouth of the Nile. It must be remembered that the intricate law of the Torah did not exist when the Jews were slaves in Egypt. Their only claim at that time to an identity as a people at all was a remembered promise to Abraham and to his son Isaac. No wonder that they received only gradually the deeper impression of the Passover events and the reception of the law and the covenant at Sinai to confirm their identity and their difference from the beliefs of the neighboring nomadic tribes.

It took the stern leadership of Moses and the intricacy of the Levitical laws to form the wandering former slaves into a people. I use the term "stern leadership" for Moses because he seems to me not to have been a patient man. In the Old Testament we see a gradual change in the perception of God, from the early God of warfare as the Israelites conquered the land of Canaan from the original inhabitants, to the God of the Prophet Isaiah whose gentleness prepared the way for Jesus and his message of a loving Father.

The religious growth of man seems to be as slow as it is in the individual with long periods of sliding backwards into sin and into forgetfulness of God's past favors. Islam may be envisioned, it seems to me, as a vast tutelage in the ways of God. The message may be simple, but the effort to spread it requires the daily rounds of enforced prayer, mandatory almsgiving, and the ever present witness of the Koran which is held to be the definitive statement of God to man. Finally there is the Pilgrimage, an event so costly and arduous that some are even excused from making it. It is an event that sums up the whole in the life of the believer. By making the Pilgrimage the believer renounces in the most dramatic manner once and forever all allegiance to the Shaitan and he affirms his solidarity with all those who will be saved according to the will of

Allah. It is less a going forth than a homecoming and a foretaste of the garden prepared for those written in the book of God as worthy of the rewards that have been prepared.

For the Christian there is less one supreme moment or event of faith, unless it is Baptism; there is only the daily carrying of the cross until death. A Christian pilgrimage to the Holy Land is simply not an equivalent to the Moslem Pilgrimage. The sites in the Holy Land, though reminiscent of the life of Christ are not Christ himself. The resurrected Christ is known instead in the humble bread and wine of Sacramental Communion which may be received daily in one's own parish church. The result is that the Christian seldom realizes the gravitational pull present in the masses of believers at Mecca. Though the Catholic may go to Lourdes, France where the humble peasant girl Bernadette witnessed the apparitions of the Holy Virgin Mary, this experience is not mandated by the faith nor is it essential to salvation.

Faith for the Christian thus may become a far too individual matter and finally be degraded to the level of simply one more allegiance of choice such as joining one or another of the London clubs. Islam as a culture has never lost the corporate and societal sense that religion is a matter of life and death and utterly dispositive of one's eternal destiny as well as the best basis of the polis. It is not that worldly affairs never eclipse religious duty in the Islamic world, for many a Sultan has been as renowned for his opulence and lechery as for his role as a leader in the Islamic world. The point remains though that religion touches all aspects of Moslem life through the laws of Sharia, whereas in the Christian west we seem even to have trouble enforcing some slight prohibitions against simple usury. Christianity has become a minor adjunct to our lives in Europe, while in America, except in the somewhat comical hysteria of the tent meetings of the revivalists, those traveling religious circuses that serve to break the monotony of rural life, worship is largely a matter of a weekly visit to a Church or chapel. Indeed, in America it may be remarked that only the Quakers and the Amish seem really to practice their faith constantly and communally as do the few pious Catholics who go beyond merely the avoidance of mortal sin and seek to grow towards sainthood.

There are of course the followers of Joseph Smith in the desert regions of the American west who have their own book and like the followers of Islam have been molded by their own desert experience in the trek across the American desert where they have put down roots. Mormon religious practices also touch all aspects of life and they are to be commended for their zeal. Surely God must observe the heart and I trust that all differences of doctrine will finally be melted into insignificance in the face of the wonder of God himself who must surpass all of our words and concepts. This is not to say that all doctrines are equivalent but that sincerity of heart is all that man may offer to his god.

As the time for our departure from Tehran is near, I can only reflect that the time that I have been able to devote to these meandering thoughts may be coming to an end. I will soon again feel the pressure of events upon me once again. How I wish that I might remain here or return to Tibet, but then I would merely create in time an eastern version of my long residence in Baker Street. My time of secluded brooding must end at last and I must go forth to encounter the world with all of my doubts and fears yet intact. I have sought in these meditations thus far some measure of certainty, some articulation of what would be a worthy belief. I have tried whenever possible though to maintain a position of theological neutrality and to weigh factors without bias, but I am sure that I have failed in this. No one can abstract from the culture out of which he comes. I can be certain that I have absorbed elements of Christianity simply by being an Englishman of the 19th century. Should these notes ever be read by another, perhaps they will be read only by my friend Watson and my brother Mycroft, I would ask that they make some use of them.

Perhaps some theologian may take phrases from this work and create a systematic elucidation for a wider audience and so fill in the gaps of what for me were only random insights and not a systemic treatise. It would give me pleasure to read such a work some day. I pray that I may live to read it and find the certainty that so often has eluded me and may do so until the end. Perhaps I will end my life with no final articulation. Will anything that I have yet said convince the Professor when I return? Have I even convinced myself? No sooner do I dilate upon a subject than I turn back upon myself and say that it is inadequate. It is said that even St. Thomas Aquinas after writing his immense *Summa Theologica* referred to it as chaff. Was this assessment due to his immense humility, or was it rather that he realized that all human distinctions and formulations melt away, not only in time, but before the Presence of the God that he had glimpsed in prayer.

Will my own journal find its repose somewhere in the desert should we be attacked by wandering tribal warriors? Will Mycroft finally climb those fabled stairs, for now they seem such to me, in Baker Street to tell Watson that I did not die at Reichenbach but that my bones lie bleaching in the desert sun in far-off Arabia? Will Mycroft be able to deal with Moriarty and his plans without me there to convince the Professor, as our wager mandates, that I have found the primal way for a human life to proceed? Perhaps Colonel Moran alone will escape and tell the Professor of my end and of how I spent my final days. If so, will he echo the closing of that great American book, "Moby Dick" in the passage where its narrator says, that the sunken ship Pequod is no more and that "I alone am escaped to tell thee."

December 1, 1891
On the Road

We are underway at last for Mecca. Our party makes up quite a caravan. We have been provided with an escort thanks to the generosity of the British Consul. We carry with us the last remnants of the season's produce, dried meats, and other items likely to make our journey less subject to privation. We have expert guides now, for in the vast sea of the desert it is no small matter to navigate one's way. At first of course we will be passing through the endless mountain defiles of central Persia. The tops of the mountains are dusted with snow. The wells that we will encounter along the way are being slowly replenished by the late autumn rains. We will of course need to avail ourselves of the cooperation and hospitality of the tribes that we encounter along the way and we have brought gifts and trade items with us for that purpose.

I have sent my last messages to Mycroft and told him to expect word from me upon my arrival in Cairo, but to not be alarmed if he does not hear from me for some months. From Mecca I hope to cross to Abyssinia and from thence to enter the region of Sudan and visit Khartoum. After that I will proceed down the Nile to Cairo and take a ship from Alexandria for Marseilles. Thus far in my journey I have been in regions that afford to the European some closeness to India where British rule offers a means of retreat and a restoration to the customs, language, and manner of life that an Englishman craves. There is a special instinct for comfort in the British heart. One need only think of the gardens that surround the country estates, the warm London Clubs with the ever ready games of whist and the Pimm's Cup or single-malt Scotch, or the cheerful tents at Brighton by the Sea.

How different is the spare and fearful prospect that lies before me. Rugged mountain peaks stretch as far as the eye can see with vast sandy stretches in between. Where are the rich green fields of Surrey? Where the white villages of Wales? Even the rugged Scottish Highlands are a virtual land of plenty when compared to what I have seen thus far. What must Arabia or the Sahara be then? I can feel not only the limitations of my views as an Englishman but my own physical limitations as well. Travel by camel demands a certain type of fluidity in the body and adaptability to motion that my own knowledge of proper riding techniques acquired in my Yorkshire youth never taught me. By evening I become a mass of pain. My own pride in my Spartan nature is often frustrated and I cannot but take offence at the smirk on the face of Colonel Moran. He occasionally is so indelicate as to remind me that this entire journey with all of its privations is my own choice and that if I wished to find God, I might just as well be sitting in a comfortable drawing-room before a plump Bishop of the Church of England.

I can well imagine the nature of that imagined discussion. I would lay my doubts and fears before him and he would nod sagely. At last he would push his chair back and sighing, say, "Ah you remind me of my youth, Mr. Holmes. I was swayed for a time by Cardinal Newman and the Oxford movement, Keble and all that. My sister, I am sorry to say, fell prey to religious enthusiasm in her youth and joined the Methodists. Let me advise you to cast aside those twin dangers to the English Christian represented by Romanism and the vulgar Evangelicals. Faith, my dear sir, is a habit of mind. One acquires it in youth and with prayer and fortitude one may maintain it to the end. We are fortunate not to live in an age that requires the miraculous nor even a strenuous apologetics. I assure you that all is well. Victoria is upon her throne and God has established his own throne securely in the bosom of the Church of England. Never do I hear our marvelous British choirs but I am overwhelmed with joy at its resemblance to the heavenly choirs. May I offer you a glass of Amontiado?"

"There now, well as I was saying you must cast aside these doubts of yours. I must caution you against any too-close reading of the religious classics of other religions. We must always recall that they are without the benefits of revelation. Whatever their aesthetic beauty may be, they are of no more use to the pious Christian believer than the mythologies of Greece or Rome. What to us are the eastern gods, Shiva or Kali, or even Allah? We possess the truth in all its fullness. I would also advise you against any reading of that American blighter Emerson. It is all fluff and froth. Fluff and froth! Faith is simply adherence to a series of clear propositions. Once the assent is made, one must not turn back. Our Lord warned us about the man who puts his hand to the plow and then looks back. There is no preliminary to faith. It springs forth suddenly for those so unfortunate as not to be raised in its embrace. If one has been raised, as I trust you have been, in the correct faith, why would you now look outside of it for truth? You say that you do so in order to ensure the salvation of all? So! Would you be a Universalist or another Origen? My dear sir, read your Augustine. It is impossible that all will be saved. Why would Christ have winnowed the grain if there was no chaff? Would you have heaven to be a vast dumping ground for every man and woman? Would you care to share eternity with every swine and vile fellow, with every bawd and every opium addict? I think not; surely not! Think of the disorder! Indeed I often ask my dear wife, who labors in my behalf among the poor at the local workhouse, how she can endure the stench."

"I wrote a paper last year against our supposed duty to practice charity to the non-Christian. When our Lord was speaking of the little ones he was speaking of his own flock. Why even the early Christian communities lived in the world but not of it. This world is going down to perdition as it was foretold. The Church is a frail bark sailing upon the flood. Recall the words of the Old Testament that only a remnant will be saved. Or recall the Gospel admonition that, 'Many are called but few are chosen.' Place those words of our Lord before you, Mr. Holmes, before you seek to throw the doors of heaven open to all and sundry."

"No I can hardly see a purpose for your great journey. I should advise instead an hour spent at Vespers followed by a good dinner of English beef and a good night's sleep followed by a breakfast of strong tea and kippers and a long strenuous walk. There's a good man. Try that regimen for a week and see if it doesn't help this faith-crisis of yours. Will you do that? Excellent! Excellent! And now you really must excuse me, for there is an address that I must give to our Church floral society; gardening you know is next to godliness. A fine hobby, it keeps one close to the earth and supplies labor for idle hands. Don't think too much, Mr. Holmes, it is never a good idea. You might end up as one of those casuistical Jesuits if you do. And I shouldn't read too much of Aristotle or Plato or the rest of those lascivious Greeks. Stick to Milton my boy and Butler. 'The Pilgrims Progress,' now there is a fine book for you. Quite enough there to keep the mind occupied. There now, thanks for this most interesting visit. By the way, I read one of your cases the other day by your friend Doctor Watson. Apply yourself there, my dear fellow, keep your observations and deductions upon the things of this world and do not venture forth onto the seas of God. That way leads only to blasphemy. Goodbye now, goodbye."

But it is too late now for these hypothetical warnings, for I have made the journey. I am indeed in the middle of it and my imaginary Bishop and his wise counsel are far away. I am now in the position of the ancient prophets who gazed out upon the barren sands. Did they imagine a God out of this empty desert loneliness? Did they look to the blackened skies on these clear and cold desert nights and see Thrones and Dominations in the stars? Shall I in turn hear direct testimony of God, if only in a gentle wind, or must my relationship to God be always derivative, a matter of texts and the clergy who administer them, interpret them, and apply them to the unruly masses of men and women upon the earth?

Dr. Watson's Narrative Continues

I spent that evening after dinner at Baskerville Hall reading Holmes' journal. It had become a habit with me. I left off at the point where he had begun his trek to Mecca. Though I was tempted to press on I stopped for I knew that each new entry gave me much to think about and to digest. I knew that I was following an arduous process of thought and resolution and that I could not hope to swiftly incorporate and resolve ideas that had come to Holmes with such labor and pain. I was reading it, as any journal of a private nature must be read, as a privileged insight into another's deepest soul.

That last dinner, before I turned again to the journal, had been subdued. I could see that Sir Henry was worried about the condition of his wife and whether our elaborate plans would succeed. I therefore endeavored as well as I could to distract his thoughts by telling him of Holmes' researches into early English charters. His interest in them began with our involvement some years ago in the famous Smith-Mortimer Succession case. The question involved the title to lands in Yorkshire between one of the richest families in England and the religious order of the Cistercians. It was on that occasion that I had met for the first and only time Holmes' eldest brother, Sherringford Holmes. He had requested that Holmes lend his aid in the matter, for the members of the family in question were among his friends. He portrayed the issue to us as one that presented a desperate and futile claim on the part of a French religious order to reclaim lands that had passed to the Smith-Mortimer family at the time of King Henry VIII, a time when the lands of many monasteries in England were confiscated by the nobility.

Holmes had agreed to investigate, but he warned his

brother in advance that his investigation would be an unbiased one. The entire matter hinged upon a charter given by King Henry's forebears granting the title to the order in perpetuity. This grant exceeded the normal feudal grants that still reserved to the crown certain rights of taxation and in the case of lay persons, feudal military service from the vassals of the estate. The exact phrase used escapes me, but it was an example of the interpenetration of Roman law into Britain and the phrase remained in English law long after the Norman Conquest.

Of course the obvious course was to show the document to be a forgery, thus obviating any consideration of the legal questions presented. Holmes was asked to examine the charter which had lain in a vault in the Cistercian Monastery among many other manuscripts for centuries. Its significance was only discovered when a scholar from the Sorbonne had attempted to order the documents as part of a doctoral thesis. He had immediately pointed out the antiquated phrase to the abbot with a summary of its possible significance for the fortunes of the abbey. The abbot in turn had contacted a firm of solicitors in London who began an action for the recovery of title in the lands in question. The family in turn turned to Sherlock Holmes in the hope that he could discover documents that would compromise the integrity of the claim by proving that either the charter itself was a forgery or that the lands granted had been entailed at a later date, thus forfeiting the special protection of the phrase "in perpetuity."

We had gone up to Yorkshire by the express train from Paddington Station as I recall. Holmes was silent during the journey and I could see that he felt compromised by the investigation. Holmes always preferred to keep a free hand and to follow wherever the trail led. Even after finding a solution he preferred to allow his own conscience to dictate how he would proceed. In this case he was being treated in what I felt was a most high-handed fashion by his elder brother and I must confess that I felt a dislike of the man even prior to meeting him that day in the drawing-room of the elegant Tudor Manor-house that was his home and the place where Holmes had spent significant periods of his boyhood when he was not away at school. I could see the distant nature of the relationship between the two brothers when they shook hands briefly after what must have been a long period between visits. Holmes and I sat down by the fire while Sherringford paced the room before finally condescending to take a seat and to light a cigar. Holmes and I had already quietly lit our pipes and prepared to listen to an exposition of the case.

"Of course the matter is perfectly simple," Sherringford expostulated. "The French have never adapted well to losing their claims on British soil. As the head of the Church of England the King wisely united both temporal and spiritual power. He could thus command any religious order to relinquish its claims and simultaneously bestow those claims on whomsoever he chose. To take a contrary position denies the entire efficacy of the English Reformation. The charter has no say in the matter. The lands in question belong to the Smith-Mortimers and there is an end to the matter!"

Holmes spoke up quietly. "Perhaps, Sherringford, I have misunderstood the matter. I believe that it hinges not upon power, but rather upon execution of that power. Has the family been able to show how they first obtained the lands in question?"

"There is a line of probated wills extending back for several centuries granting the title to the heirs in fee simple absolute and furthermore there is an initial charter granting the same title from the Lord High Chancellor and from the Court of King's Bench according to law. The claim could not be clearer, Sherlock. These obstreperous monks are simply trying to use a technicality to spread their odious doctrines here by gaining a more extensive claim on good English soil. I hear that they plan to use the land to restore a monastic foundation here in our very neighborhood. An occasional Roman chapel may be tolerated but this is too much!"

Holmes smiled. His brother's vehemence invited what I have often noted in his character, a desire to play with his opponent. "Your summary of the case has been most succinct, Sherringford. It makes me wonder why you ever felt the need to consult me. I am as you know a criminal investigator and since no crime…"

"But it is most certainly a crime, Sherlock, a crime under the pretension of godliness. These monks are trying to encroach upon the lands of one of the finest families in England, a family, I might add, that has done much to extend the benefits of civilization to South Africa by putting the natives to work in our mines there. The rents of the lands in question here are essential to pay for the costs of expansion for new and promising claims in the Zulu regions of Natal. Gold and diamond discoveries are appearing daily. The Smith-Mortimer family has made a decided contribution to the British Empire through the ages and continues to do so today."

"As I was saying," Holmes continued imperturbably. "I investigate crimes and try, in my poor manner, to advance the cause of justice in any way that I can. If I take an interest in this matter, I must be given a free hand to proceed as I see fit."

Sherringford drew himself up with some dignity. "I see that a certain republican spirit has come to prevail in you Sherlock. I should think that your breeding would be all that you need to consult. The Smith-Mortimer lands adjoin our own and we have been neighbors for centuries. While they may not be kinsmen, our relations have always been cordial. Think of your place as a son of the Holmes' line and do your duty."

Holmes had answered him, "My duty is to my conscience. I regret my dear Sherringford that it has some qualms about aiding you in the manner that you direct. On the other hand I believe that in this case the law will provide the solution and that no scruples of my own will be required to yield the proper result."

That was, as I recall, how our initial interview ended. The brothers parted that day with some coolness. We spent some weeks in Yorkshire reviewing a succession of documents including wills, letters, and receipts. We were however unable to obtain any document from a court of equity. The Smith-Mortimer family could show only legal title and even that was subject to any prior charter, but since only a court of equity can exercise jurisdiction over ecclesial matters and since the initial title had been granted not by the chancellor but by the King himself and in perpetuity, that haunting phrase, it appeared that the title thus granted to the Cistercians and their assigns had not been extinguished through the many long years and that the attempted legal conveyance was therefore insufficient to defeat the superior title. This was not to say that under British Law the King or a court of equity might not have commanded the Cistercians to relinquish title, but there was no evidence that any King had ever done so. In the hurry and excitement to grasp Church lands, the Chancellor had simply opted for a legal proclamation read and adjudicated in a law court when law and equity were administered by different courts. The long drawn out process of equity courts could not procure the immediate results desired. The Smith-Mortimer family must now pay the price of that impatience. When this became clear to Holmes, I could see that he was secretly pleased.

"It spares me some domestic bitterness, Watson. Sherringford will have to admit that I did my best to uncover the needed documents and to give them a fair reading. He can hardly blame me when documents that might support his own position are not there to be found. I am afraid that the Smith-Mortimers will have to carry out their task of civilizing the poor natives of South Africa by other means and relying upon other resources, so that they may labor in the bowels of the earth to enrich the family further without the rents on the lands in question."

Thereafter we returned to the family estate at Sigerside and Holmes proceeded with a grim and crestfallen air to endeavor to explain the whole matter to Sherringford. The latter listened I recall with growing asperity and impatience. At last he leapt to his feet.

"This is a most unsatisfactory result, Sherlock. Most unsatisfactory! In the current posture of our relations with France it will hardly do to bring the matter to the Queen's attention or to seek summary action by the Privy Council. The House of Lords will defer to the courts, which you say are likely to rule for the French due to this charter and the absurd law and equity distinction. I must say that as your brother I have been guilty of a gross overestimation of your abilities."

I was about to rise to Holmes' defense, but Holmes placed a finger on his lips and I sat down again. "Well you may appeal to Mycroft of course. He may be able to render an assistance that I cannot as a private citizen provide."

"Bah, my relations with Mycroft are not of the best, as you well know Sherlock. Quite frankly, I think the fellow is mad. There he sits in that beastly club of his where no one ever talks. I have never seen such a group of misanthropes in my life. The man needs to get out into the fresh air. A brisk hunt would do him a world of good, chase down a fox over the moors. I hear he has put on weight due to his sedentary ways. He would need a Clydesdale simply to bear him about the estate, but I would gladly supply one in order to see him here on an occasional visit. He is next in line you know should anything happen to me. Thank God my health is brisk. You on the other hand look pale Sherlock and too thin as always, that nervous energy yours and if I may so your artistic temperament are no doubt at fault. You were always a bit too close to our mother and the French side of the family while I favored Father's side. As for Mycroft, he always went in too much for study. He practically grew up in the library as you will recall and the results are there to see. He is a vast repository of knowledge yes, but to what end, a chair in a dusty club and his bachelor rooms in Pall Mall!"

"I believe that he is of some service to the government." Holmes interrupted blandly.

"No doubt he is. Well, I may write him a letter, I can do no more. He will undoubtedly point out that it is hardly the time to antagonize France. Very well, I will speak to the Smith-Mortimers and give them your results though I am embarrassed to do so. They will have to decide what to do. I do not believe that they will relish the publicity of a current action in equity. A defeat there would be a terrible humiliation. I shall advise that they therefore make a gesture and offer to donate some of the lands to the religious order in question and to seek confirmation of that advice from some qualified barristers."

We left soon after, a parting if anything more stiff and

formal than our greeting had been. A few weeks later, Holmes tossed a copy of the London Times into my lap.

"The Cistercians received the entirety of the lands, Watson. They refused the settlement offer, very properly in my opinion, for their title was secure from the beginning. The Smith-Mortimers then made a great show of fairness by claiming to have suddenly discovered documents proving that the lands did indeed belong to the Cistercians. They have been hailed, even on the continent, as honest men and religious benefactors. The Pope has even sent a Cardinal to accept the gift, for so it is being portrayed, and to carry news to the Cistercian Abbey in France. My name of course will not appear in the matter, nor will the basis for my conclusions."

Thus ended the Smith-Mortimer Succession Case; however, some word leaked out and the monks of the Cistercian Monastery that is located outside Montpellier in France celebrate daily masses for the intentions and benefit of one Mr. Sherlock Holmes.

Sir Henry had I recall enjoyed my story immensely. I had seen him shake his head from time to time when he recognized the character of many of the members of the House of Lords of his acquaintance in Holmes' brother, Sherringford. Sir Henry had a right to sit in that chamber, but after several terms he had realized the inability of his dissenting voice to make much of a difference in the policies pursued by the majority. He was viewed, I am sad to say, as a traitor to his class, though he was popular among the progressive wing of the House of Commons and many lamented the fact that after several years he had concentrated his efforts upon local reforms and had left the larger questions of national policy to decide themselves without his aid.

After dining that evening we returned to the library and discussed the trip to Exeter that lay before us. At last matters would be resolved for good or ill. If the time had seemed long to us, we could only imagine the horror, which we tried to put out of mind that the good Lady Beryl Baskerville had endured since her abduction. We hoped that when she was home and safe at last that she would quickly recover from her ordeal. We agreed to take her secretary, Mrs. Castillo with us to provide the comfort for her that only another woman might provide. We could do no more that night, so we agreed to seek what repose we could find so as to be ready and prepared for whatever might await us on the morrow.

We were up early the following day. Perkins was left in charge along with several men sent down from Scotland Yard at Holmes' request to help guard the house and its occupants. We were driven to the station through a misty rain that obscured the bleak hillsides. We unloaded our luggage and were soon aboard the slow and ancient train that served northern Devonshire. We spoke little on the journey south to Tavistock. I looked out of the window of our carriage at the swelling expanse of the moorlands that now assumed the aspect of a desolate and mossy green. The trees were bare and I found myself wondering why I did not live in Italy and enjoy the hillsides of olive trees around Perugia or the lovely bays on the seacoast of the Italian Riviera or at the Amalfi area surrounding Naples.

What was it about England that kept me there still? Perhaps it is simply the pleasures of the familiar that root us to a place. There is a scent of England that cannot but grasp at the heart of every Englishman when he returns from abroad to one of our ports. How often I have enjoyed the comforts of an English pub with its snug and warm atmosphere and the familiar laughter of the barmaids as they serve up pints of lager, bitter, or stout. To walk down the line of row-houses and to stop in for some fish and chips wrapped in newspaper and drenched in malt-vinegar or to bite into a Cornish pasty with a cup of strong tea by one's side as I read a copy of Punch was to me a familiar joy. To feel the solid weight of English money in my hands as I pay is as solid and respectable and reassuring as a safe bank account. Even the weight and color of the coins seems to speak of security and comfort. Even the English class-system gives one a sense of place and identity. There is here a cap to social aspirations that prevents a sense of personal failure such as exists in America where the classes are really as divided as they are here while the national hypocrisy of a pretended social equality that does not exist prevails and breeds bitterness. In England a man only competes with his peers and there is a satisfaction in arriving at a comfortable acceptance of one's station in life. This allows the Englishman or Englishwoman to be able to enjoy life's few and simple pleasures and not to be forever dreaming of a fortune that will never come.

My memories of Sherringford Holmes only reinforced the belief that the lot of the ordinary citizen may be freer in England than even the lot of the titled gentry. Sherringford, with his rigid adherence to form had isolated himself upon his lonely estate. Even his position in the local hunt did not relieve the need to maintain a dignity and austerity that his younger brother Sherlock possessed naturally but could lay aside at will. Holmes was able to exercise humor at the expense of any stiff client who dared to doubt Holmes' abilities. It was one of the great gifts of Sherlock Holmes to have penetrated all of the diverse professions and classes of England and I have often thought that if any man could write the true history of his country in all its aspects it would be he. I once commented to Holmes that his diverse interests and huge library would require more than a single life. He answered me by saying that one must live life as though one had infinite time or one would not make even a beginning at the wondrous tasks that lie about us. The effort to trim a life to fit within the single margin of the years at our disposal is futile. It is for that reason alone, if nothing else, that we must dream of eternity.

I found that I had dozed off in these contemplations and I awoke with a start to feel Sir Henry's grasp upon my arm. "We are just coming into Exeter, Dr. Watson." I opened my eyes to a forest of bleak chimney-pots as we passed through the suburbs and before long we were at the train station where we disembarked and hailed a hansom cab to take us to our hotel. The streets were wet and shining and the stench of coal filled the air.

Our hotel was small but elegant. We had engaged the best suite of rooms in the hotel and the owner took us up himself in the new and modern lift to see that all was well and to our satisfaction. The bank where the exchange was to take place was just across town and it felt good to be at last upon the scene of battle. My nerves were keenly awake as I tried to anticipate any last-minute devices that might frustrate our intentions, but I could think of none. I could only trust that the plans outlined by Holmes would succeed. I wondered how he was progressing in London and looked forward to rejoining him there.

We had lunch in the hotel dining-room together before parting. Sir Henry decided to pay a call upon the bank, to see that all was in readiness and to see how we were to proceed on the following day. I offered to accompany him, but he preferred to go alone so as to make the matter appear to be an ordinary business transaction. I therefore returned to my own room and to my reading of Holmes' journal while I awaited Sir Henry's return.

From the Journal of Sherlock Holmes

December 8, 189
En route to Mecca

We have decided to pursue the sea-route to Mecca rather than to cross the great Arabian Desert from the east. We will therefore proceed southwards through the central Persian desert to the opening of the Persian Gulf and where we shall catch a boat for Mecca. It will take us around the tip of the Arabian Peninsula and through the Red Sea to the port of Jeddah. From there it will be but a comparatively short overland journey to Mecca. In many ways, the journeys ahead of us may be the most dangerous part of our journey. We will be beyond the protection of British influence in Mecca and we will be even more isolated in the mountains of Abyssinia and in that great central region of Africa, the Sudan. In my dispatches to Mycroft disguised under the name of Sigerson, I have indulged a fancy that is a legacy of my youth in Yorkshire by somewhat romanticizing my travels. It is a quality of the human mind that it cannot endure too much truth. Strip us of our illusions and a type of vertigo sets in. For this reason I wrote what I feel is an excellent fictional account of my journey to Lhassa and of a year wandering through Tibet. I have seen enough of the country to have added the right local color to my accounts. I flatter myself that even Watson, that master of the romantic, could not have done better. I will of course be forced to stick to my story upon my return, but since my entire persona of the Norwegian explorer Sigerson is fanciful in the extreme, some degree of fiction is no doubt inevitable and may be forgiven. I have done what authors do. I have shaped the actuality of experience to give it form. It is said that even the eye could not see if it were not for the interpretive faculty of the brain. We see in categories. Mere optic nerve-impulses cannot give us a proper sense of form. In a similar fashion, every act of exposition involves a simultaneous act of interpretation. There is no way of avoiding bias and selectivity in what we write. We all remain children at heart and I hope that my public dispatches have mixed truth with fancy in such a way that I will move my readers to consider new possibilities for life put forward in the guise of adventure.

We live in an age of verisimilitude where the reader of a novel must believe that all that he reads has actually happened and that there is no author standing in the wings watching as his actors move about the stage. Thackeray did not feel so constrained. The author dares to emerge now and again from behind the scenes of "Vanity Fair" to address the reader directly and to remind him that after all, he holds a book in his hands. Whether this is wise for an explorer as well as a novelist I cannot say. Perhaps it would be a case of mere scrupulosity on his part, to be completely honest and to dispel the illusions that he has created with such labor and exertion. Or perhaps it may be mere whimsy or a desire for a greater intimacy with his unseen readers than the written word alone may convey. But then I am only a poor consulting detective the memory of whom memory will fade with the issues of The Strand containing my adventures.

Perhaps I may be forgiven for attempting in the guise of Sigerson to pose as a great explorer, another Doctor Livingstone, another Gordon of Khartoum. Which of us does not wish to be a hero of his own story as Dickens says in the first chapter of David Copperfield? To accept one's minor place in history is at times bitter. How I pity those with the power to change the lives of millions yet who fail to act justly. I should hate to leave this earth with the burden of thousands of deaths upon my conscience through inaction or through the vanity of tyranny. What man of power can avoid carrying behind him a cortege of innocent victims? To play a great role in events is finally to disappoint even those who loved and trusted us as well as the great anonymous populations who must bear the cost of the decisions of those who are called great. How blessed then is the man whose influence is so slight that he may keep track of his actions through daily intercourse with only his local associations within the ambit of his power rather than to require history to be the ultimate witness of the value of his life.

December 18, 1891
Great Persian Desert

We are making remarkable progress and have left the most difficult of the mountains behind us. To avoid the constant ascent and descent spares our camels and reduces the constant motion that brings such pain and fatigue at night. Even these efforts to ameliorate the rigors of our course have left me after a long day with such pain in every joint that I doubt if I shall ever be quite the same. My long lean frame is not suitable to travel by camel. Even Colonel Moran shows signs of fatigue which only adds to his usual gruffness and silence. It appears that his years in swank card-clubs and casinos have taken a bit off the edge of even his iron endurance. That he has done as well as he has, considering that he is some years older than I, neither of us being youths anymore, shows what a remarkable man he must have been in his young manhood. His language abilities and his general and intuitive knowledge of the Persian mind have enabled us to deal well with the local sheiks without any untoward incident occurring. We are neither obsequious nor are we proud in our bearing, but simply direct and forthright in a land where judgments are formed quickly and character and strength are quickly assessed and falsehood immediately punished.

There is little room for hypocrisy and illusion in so unforgiving a landscape as this. I do not know how the moonscape must appear, but it cannot be more brutal than this land. I begin to think that the Professor, however matters shall turn out, has definitely had the best of our wager thus far. Even the moors of Devon, though often desolate in their aspect, are a garden compared to these bitter lands of central Asia. Had we not been able to depend upon rail travel, however primitive during parts of our journey, I doubt that I could have come this far. I can see now how vain are the attempts to draw borders and to assign nations in this infinite sea of forbidding geography. The map-maker has no function in Asia but only the topographer and the geologist. This is not a land of established laws but only of custom, religion, and the force of arms. It will never be truly civilized, if by that we mean groups of men in legislatures and courts of law exercising power quietly through established forms. Had Islam not swept through these lands to provide a common view of existence, this vast expanse would be one great gladiator arena. Mohammed's visions convinced these proud warlords that there was One greater than even they that had in store for them a great day when all their actions would be examined and that fate was governed in all its aspects by the Lord of the Koran.

It is hard for us in Europe to imagine the impact of Islamic thought on daily action here. We have surrendered many of the tasks of worship to women. It is the women with their rosaries who fill the Catholic Churches and the ladies of Bible Societies that fill the low-Church chapels of the Methodists and the Baptists. Here it is the men who follow the way of Allah and the women occupy a virtual separate caste of wives and concubines. They do most of the menial labor and as a result grow old before their time. If Europe has barely begun to address the inequities meted out to women, who have neither the vote nor full property rights, how much worse their status remains in Asia where women are seen as merely a type of domestic beast of burden or as a source of pleasure. Mohammed may not be blamed for this though, for Islam at least has recognized the dignity of woman in the Koran. It is rather the harsh reality of tribal-living that has condemned women to such a harsh life.

The earth has yet to recognize the dignity of all men; will it ever recognize the dignity and the right to live a full and complete life for women? Too see the freshness in the young and the great sorrow and wisdom of the old in women here is to see the erosion of all of life with the passage of time. The human race looks always to woman as it does to spring and to the budding trees. It celebrates a beauty that is at times too great and abundant to be comprehended in youth, only to see it wither and be wasted by our sordid and sorry world. Perhaps I have never married, because I sought first to obtain a world that would be worthy of the one that I would love before I could ever consent to visit upon her the duties and sacrifices demanded of a wife. I have never yet found such a world. I consider my life thus far to have been one great effort at amelioration, to clean up the rubbish and the squalor of life so that when I would finally venture forth into taking a definitive position and to take a stand for more than just myself but for a wife and children as well that I could lead her forth and trust that should I die all would be well for them.

I seldom speak of the death of my mother at a young age, but it destroyed in me that basic trust in life that must sustain the young as they venture forth into adulthood. Her passing took away for many years all my sense of life and beauty. I turned therefore to the abstract and the rational and away from the musical career that she had once hoped that I might pursue as a violinist. How often in Baker Street did I play, not melodies, but mere sonorous chords in those hours when I would mournfully recall all my youthful hopes. I finally learned to enjoy in Paganini and in Wagner abilities that I did not myself possess as a mere improviser. To accept that out of the hundreds of lives that we imagine for ourselves that this, this tiny thing, is the life that one has actually lived is the most bitter task that we face. How grand is the prelude of the opera of our lives so that when the curtain opens at last one discovers only a cheap set with a juggler or a gaudy minstrel upon the stage. The audience is sparse and the lights dim. An old man with a mop and pail stands visible in the wings just waiting to clean the stage and to lock the doors for the night.

But enough of this maudlin remonstrance at fate! I have at least seen the great Himalayas in far off Tibet and now I go to Mecca where for many a follower of Mohammed it is enough to give life meaning that he or she has completed the great Pilgrimage. In modern Europe we must each design his particular

Mecca and that task is often too much for us. Our crossing over, if it does not result in actual martyrdom, in the final apotheosis of the Cross, must be empty and without meaning. Death is no less than the final pilgrimage, the last journey. We dread it, even as professing Christians we dread it. We may not glimpse behind the veil before it is upon us, stern and unyielding as the desert sun. Where then is the Christian equivalent of the shining minarets of Mecca and the glorious Kaaba, the black stone that awaits the devout believer's kiss? I like to believe that the Cross as the sign of the ultimate defeat and humiliation of death with all of its bitterness, and our willingness to enter into that same defeat, is to make a personal return in the company of Christ for all of the arrogance of mankind and by doing so to accept from God an entirely derivative existence, one that cannot stand on its own. Our life is only from God and we have no life without Him.

I often think that if we but gazed at the ground each day and realized that we are more akin to the feeble grass and the mud from which it springs than we are to the eternal wandering clouds and the sunlit day that illumines them, that we would fold up all of our flags and take down our triumphal monuments. We would stand with downcast heads in the submission that is the posture of the devout follower of Islam. When the Cross became our battle emblem, at the time of the Crusades, it lost its true meaning. When Christians took up the sword they became like the very people who once slaughtered Jesus the Christ. We have been doing thus ever since in every European War. I like to believe though that General Chinese Gordon of Khartoum died unarmed and that he simply faced his death in the sole belief that slavery was wrong and that for the northern Arabic traders to kill and to traffic in the slavery of the black tribes of Sudan was a great evil. Evil is made most manifest when it is allowed to triumph and to stand in the bitter rags of its seeming victory. This for me is the meaning of the Cross.

December 25, 1891
Christmas Day

Daily we press southwards. The desert grows quite cold at night and the stars blanket the heavens so thickly that I can see why the religions have placed God in the sky. That God may lie instead within all things and have chosen to make his domicile right here among us seems at times to diminish God's majesty. Is this not the scandal of the Incarnation? God became not only man but a mere child, a baby! Is this not the mystery of Christmas Day? How shall we celebrate the coming of God into time, a God who is timeless? This idea is utter folly to Islam which proclaims an ardent monotheism and holds the Trinity in contempt, for how may the one God be three persons? Christianity on the other hand rejoices in, not only the wonder, but in the very violation of our most basic sense of numerical difference and distinction represented by the concept of a Blessed Trinity.

There is a great literalness in the Islamic mind. It is no accident that the Arabs were the great mathematicians of the ancient world. Christian thought on the other hand is not troubled by absurdity and contradiction. In this it resembles Zen Buddhism as practiced in Japan. Christianity strains belief to the breaking point, for it is precisely in that breaking that God can break through, to shatter all of our conceptions, our desire to be like God knowing good and evil. Man is left at last with empty hands, not merely supine before God, but ripped into pieces, as we will be at death, and utterly dispersed! It is for God alone to be our base and refuge. Only in God do we exist at all.

This is why non-belief is condemned in scripture as being worthy of hell. Non-belief for the Christian is not to be punished by hell; it is to remain in it, for hell is any existence without God. It is the setting up of an idol of self as an independent entity set up in-itself and for-itself. It is our desire to be our own God. It is the eternal frozenness in that stance, which was initially chosen by our first parents, the stance chosen again daily in every sin; that is hell.

The metaphysics of salvation requires a great wrenching about of that fundamental stance of sin. It requires that we willingly surrender and accept death as the price of sin. It is by humbly accepting death in all of its bitterness that man consents to accept whatever God is willing to bestow upon us. This is why Jesus advocates, even in this life a great poverty, for poverty is like death. Poverty and powerlessness place us in danger of death. We need only look to the poor who die among us each day of cold, disease, and starvation to absorb this fundamental truth.

I think often of the Irish Famine of the 1840's that occurred just before my own birth in 1854. As a youth I heard of it often, for many Irish emigrants found work upon my father's estate. Many could never understand how England would prefer the deaths of so many rather than to surrender its economic system. The great fear at the time was that England would be forced to sustain what many English leaders felt was the great indolent mass of the Irish people in a form of perpetuity of relief. The famine as a result persisted year after year and continued from 1845 into 1847. The workhouses were filled and even the feeding stations were finally closed. By 1848 Ireland was commanded to be self-sufficient, but by then a third of the Irish people had left Ireland and 700,000 were dead of starvation and disease. How could this happen in a Christian country? This is the price of our need for power and for property, for our empire.

Christ goes so far as to define the narrow gate as one that would put each of us in the very position of the poorest of the poor, which is to risk death. Strangely, if everyone risked a propertyless death, then that greatest of expenses, the cost of the arms spent to defend life and property, could be turned to guarantee life for all and the cultivation of a common humanity; then there might indeed be enough for all. Does it really matter when we die, if we die with the right disposition of soul? But we have not followed Christ our Savior but have instead followed the Egyptians who were quite content to build pyramids to deify the few deaths of the Divine Pharaohs while the slaves died beneath their burdens. So it is that we have two approaches to religion in the last analysis: we have the Jewish religion that ended in Christ, who is God becoming man; and on the other hand, we have the religion of Egypt, where a few men exalt themselves above the mass of other men and claim to be like gods themselves.

Between these two poles of course we have the path of the average man in a capital-ridden society who hopes to obtain the good life here on earth and simultaneously to save his soul. It is like the desert we are now traversing between the mountains that lie to the west and to the east of us. We occupy a desolate plain between these two extremes of the great central Persian desert. We go from oasis to oasis as humans in life go from joy to joy. We pick our way through life pursuing various visions of happiness, yet never finding lasting contentment and always with the prospect of death before us. Even our bodies, our precious flesh, must be surrendered at last, yet we do not surrender! We cling to our goods, to our beauty, and to the illusions of youth even in the very shadow of the grave until finally, oh vanity of vanities, we build great silent tombs to celebrate what we once were, long after we are dead and beyond the ability to savor our former status and fame.

Such is the nonsensical life of man and woman and it all goes on age after age. It makes the entire question of atavism irrelevant of course, for we are like monkeys finally, strutting about in borrowed finery. I think at times that the reason that God allowed the great apes to exist is to remind us how close we are to them. The apes mock our humanity for they are so close to us in aspect and in behavior. I wonder how long we will allow them to continue to exist. They are like relatives of whom we are ashamed. I recall sitting in parliament one day listening to Sherringford and his peers as they addressed other members of the House of Lords on the issue of Chartism and the plight of the English working class. I couldn't stand it after awhile and I took myself off to the London Zoo. I went to the baboon exhibit and spent an hour watching them as they posed and preened themselves. I found little difference between the two assemblies.

But these are unworthy thoughts for so joyous a day. God

tolerates our weaknesses and as in the wedding feast at Cana does not despise all lavishness and celebration among us. He advises though the narrow gate, "Take what you have and give to the poor and you will have treasure in heaven and come follow me." When his disciples once asked if the rich man may still be saved, they were assured that with God all things are possible. Still there is the warning to try and enter by the narrow gate, for many will try the other ways into heaven and will be unable to do so. Ah, it is all a great mystery.

Later—I see that I am beset by doubts regarding my own salvation. It is not easy for an Englishman to be absent from home and to miss an English Christmas by being abroad. It is the peculiar genius of the English to have added to Christmas a unique celebration of the bounties of nature. The feast of Christmas is perhaps as much a Druid festival of re-birth as it is a Christian celebration of the unique birth of Christ. The most familiar Christmas narrative only figures after all in the Gospel of St. Luke. If anything it is a story of exile and privation showing that the Christ was born in great poverty, but that His birth was a sign of great hope to both the simple and to the wise. There is a particular charm in the idea of the Nativity of God. We find the humanity of Christ most at the extremes of his life, in His humble birth in a cold stable and in His brutal death on the Cross. Since the message of Christianity is finally not a set of doctrines alone but rather one of formation in the believer of a unique relationship to God the Father through incorporation into the very body of Christ, it is essential that we know something of the humanity of Jesus. There must be a set of particulars to copy, for our own lives are made up of our unique histories, of those that we have loved, and of the things that have happened to us.

Christmas then gives us a unique set of particulars present before Jesus as God could even begin to teach us. There is a unique value in this. The English Christmas is at best a celebration of charity and of rejoicing in abundance. The holly and the ivy and the mistletoe of course are the evergreen signs of life. The mistletoe in particular, that grows upon the sacred oak tree, must have appeared to be a reservoir of life that brought life back to the great and sacred oak trees that fascinated the Druids. They believed that its power of life and fertility could similarly restore life to the human and even now it is a sign of fertility and romance. How strange that a parasitic and poisonous plant should be so honored! Then there is the roast goose, the port wine, and the plum puddings.

How I miss being at home in Baker Street at Christmas time! I would go customarily to a midnight service at Westminster Cathedral and then later the following morning to a Catholic mass at the tiny Catholic Chapel on Oxford Street. Mrs. Hudson would cook a brace of pheasants and perhaps even Mycroft would stop by for some plum pudding and a glass of brandy after dining alone at Simpsons. I would have a note from Inspectors Lestrade or Gregson wishing me the compliments of the season and hinting that they might have a little problem or two to place before me soon since my opinion and my own unique methods might have something to contribute.

Watson might present me with a new pipe to join my malodorous collection and I in turn would give him a walking-stick or a book of sea stories or some adventure tale by H. Rider Haggard or even by that American chap, Mark Twain. Watson I always thought might have gone to sea, but for his leg wound, the effects of which he continues to suffer from still. It would have made the constant motion on deck difficult to bear. He does speak though at times of retiring to a cottage by the sea someday and when he takes a holiday he usually runs down to Cornwall or to Brighton. Ah well, old friend, I wish you the compliments of the season from where I stand today. You little know that your friend still lives and that his Christmas dinner this year will be some dried dates rather than a plum pudding and that there is no brandy in be found in this Moslem land. I vow that upon my return that I will do a proper penance for putting you through all of this sorrow. But none may know until I return that Moriarty still lives, the terms of the wager that exists between us are strict indeed, and my own supposed death will at least allow my enemies to be dispersed before I return. I have requested that Mycroft will see to it that the Yard guards Watson lest he fall prey to my enemies' displaced vengeance. I trust that I shall find my old comrade safe and sound upon my eventual return and that his dear wife may provide some comfort to him in his present sorrow at my supposed death.

Dr. Watson's Narrative Continues

I placed the manuscript down with a tear in my eye. It meant more to me than I could say to know that his thoughts were with me in the danger that he had faced in those far off lands. I well recall that Christmas. My wife's long illness had already begun which was to take her from me two years later. She attempted to distract me from the sorrow that I had known though the year of 1891 after my solitary return to England. Mycroft had assured me that I had done all that I could do, but I was still haunted by the fact that I had not been there to guard Holmes in his final moments. Mycroft said that Moriarty undoubtedly had brought a confederate along who might have seen to my death as well had I been present and what a blow that would have been to my wife. The entire matter was portrayed in his cool way as a virtual sacrificial offering. Holmes and Moriarty canceling each other out like two bonded ions in a single molecule there at the Reichenbach Falls.

I was affronted at first at this version of what had occurred, but I saw in Mycroft's eyes sympathy for my own sorrow so that I could have no doubt that in private moments he had also been deeply affected by Holmes' demise. Mycroft further proved his devotion by seeing to it that Holmes' residence in Baker Street was preserved intact and as he had left it. He paid the rent to Mrs. Hudson through the years of Holmes' absence. The place became a virtual shrine and it was not unusual for me to pass the street and to climb the well remembered stairs, when from the sidewalk I would see that the rooms were lit up as of old. I would sometimes find Inspectors Lestrade or Gregson or Stanley Hopkins sitting in the room silently with bare heads looking at the chair from which Holmes had once held court as though they might still drink inspiration or insight by simply being again at that place where they had so often consulted the master detective in times gone by. We would on those occasions exchange reminiscences and it was in the sharing of our loss that I found comfort during those bitter days and hours after my solitary return from Switzerland. It was painful for me in the present to journey backwards in time to that desolate period. I knew now that if all went well upon the morrow that I would soon join Holmes in London for it was now almost the year of 1898.

Holmes returned in 1894 as I have recorded in another place and it was my wife who had passed at the beginning of the previous year and it was she who would never return. The cases with Holmes in the intervening years since her death had helped to keep me occupied and to somewhat ameliorate my loss over time. I may truly say that Sherlock Holmes could not have been more devoted to me after his return. He made every effort to make it up to me for all of my pain and it was he who came up with the money to purchase my medical practice when I retired in the name of a cousin of his, a Dr. Verner, so that I might at last retire to Cornwall with perfect security for life. Holmes may have even put his own financial position in danger in order to accomplish this. In any case he continued to practice as a detective for several years thereafter until 1903. My more faithful readers already know these facts regarding his history after his return, but it is only now that I feel free to explain in detail the hitherto hidden events that may be considered to have represented the summit of his career.

His many labors at the time had led inevitably to a virtual collapse in the summer of the year of 1896. I had become increasingly alarmed at the time by his growing symptoms and insisted at last that he consult the famous lung specialist, Dr. Moore Agar of Harley Street, if he doubted my own preliminary diagnosis. Holmes had already consulted him on a prior occasion and he trusted the man, while Dr. Agar had once in turn consulted Holmes on a most delicate matter. After the consultation in 1896 he had prescribed absolute rest. I now vowed to have Holmes seek him out again on this present trip to London in order to assess his progress. Holmes would be engaged in arranging details of the plan that would bring justice to bear upon Baron Maupertuis.

Sir Henry returned in the afternoon and assured me that all was in readiness at the bank and that the prior inspection of the documents by the solicitors had apparently met with their complete approval. We dined early at the hotel and we each went to our separate rooms in the suite that took up the entire top floor of the hotel. I received a telegram from Holmes that assured me that all was going well in London and that I was to join him in Baker Street to report the results of the Baskerville matter as soon as I could see that all was well with Sir Henry and Lady Beryl. I went to bed early with great hopes for our success on the morrow.

We both awakened early and after a hasty but excellent breakfast repaired to the bank. I think that we were both in fear that at the last minute something would go wrong and that we would be informed that Lady Beryl could not be produced. Should that be the event, we were both resolved that the papers would not only not be surrendered but that no further examination of them would be allowed. I would of course need to contact Holmes immediately should this occur as he had agreed to be present at Baker Street that day in order to receive any necessary communication. He would then bring with him the full force of Scotland Yard to get the solicitors to reveal the whereabouts of their client. We doubted however that we would be forced to take such extreme measures. Rodger Baskerville clearly valued his wife only insofar as she could lead him to the papers and his own self-interest would not allow him to retain her, if by so-doing he would only succeed in forfeiting the Murillo papers. We had brought along Mrs. Castillo who would immediately take Lady Beryl in charge.

We were met that morning by a plain-clothes officer sent from London by Holmes to act as an additional body guard. Sir Henry and I had been instructed that the solicitors were not to be followed or harassed in any way, since it was essential to our further plans that Rodger Baskerville be assured of his safety so that he would attempt to sell the letters immediately to Charles

Augustus Milverton rather than taking them with him and escaping to America. We could not be sure that he did not have a private means of crossing the channel to France or Ireland so it would not be easy to prevent his escape even had we desired to do so.

Holmes and I were resolved to travel to America ourselves as soon as possible, so that if Rodger Baskerville did escape or refuse to deal with Milverton we could contact the principals ourselves and assure them that it was we who possessed the authentic papers and not Rodger Baskerville. We could only hope that when he discovered upon gaining possession of the copies that he had only obtained forgeries, and knowing and respecting the talents of Sherlock Holmes as he did, that Rodger Baskerville would take the first opportunity to obtain, if not all that he had hoped for from the papers, at least a substantial return. Charles Augustus Milverton would no doubt pay a hefty price for them, knowing that he in turn could sell them for a substantial amount to Baron Maupertuis. The Baron in turn would attempt to use them to demand concessions from the Americans under threat of making them public. This would have the probable effect of delaying or preventing the plans of the Americans to build a canal and it would open a prime opportunity for the Dutch to build the canal instead, thus giving the Europeans the priceless benefit of control of this new pathway to the oriental trade through the barrier long posed by the Americas.

The ultimate prize of course was to be the rich markets of Asia. The greatest economic battle of the coming century would no doubt be between the economies of the European empires and the rising star of America's own expansionism. Unless the Europeans engaged in some sort of mutually destructive war, which seemed madness, a madness that seemed inconceivable to the wiser minds of that day; they could combine and by doing so equal the swift growth of the American power as the century drew to a close.

Since the English and the French already possessed a head-start over the Dutch in the Pacific region and considering the American dominance in the islands of Hawaii, it was essential that the Dutch as a maritime power should regain some point of influence if they were not to be overtaken in the race for Pacific dominance in trade. The colonies of the Netherlands in the Dutch East Indies would soon be lost if an alternate route to trade with them were not soon supplied. The best avenue for this would be a canal and who better to know all of this and to desire to profit from it then that man of colossal schemes who already headed the largest trading company in the East Indies, Baron Maupertuis! Holmes had explained these nuances to me prior to his departure and I trust that I have been able to explain them here adequately in all of their complexity.

As the time for the exchange drew near I could see that Sir Henry's nerves were reaching the breaking point. All of us were concerned of course for the Murillo papers had come to play a central role in a larger European drama. But for Sir Henry his wife's safety was everything and I prayed that his trust in Holmes would not at this late hour be disappointed. The president of the bank had kindly opened his private chambers to us where the meeting would take place. He could see that we were distressed and it was no doubt a surprise to him that a mere exchange of papers should elicit so grave a response. He had kindly seen to it that we were served some brandy which helped in some measure to calm Sir Henry. The bank president endeavored to keep us entertained since Sir Henry kept a large deposit in the bank and his peerage title commanded respect as well. The president no doubt wondered why this particular business transaction was so important to us that its accomplishment could not have been delegated without the actual presence of the Lord of the Baskerville Estate.

We had succeeded against all odds at keeping the abduction of Lady Beryl a secret from the general public, helped in large measure by the isolated location of Baskerville Hall. We had given out the story that Lady Beryl was visiting friends in Inverness, Scotland and by so doing had explained her absence to those in the county who enjoyed her many personal ministrations.

Sir Henry had been kept busy performing himself many of the services to the community that his wife usually provided during these last days, aided of course by Mrs. Maria Castillo. The woman knew every detail of her mistress's affairs and how best to keep a cheerful expression and an ordinary demeanor in the face of Lady Beryl's absence. This manner of proceeding had convinced all and sundry of the local gentry and the farmers alike that all was indeed well at Baskerville Hall.

As the final hour approached, we could all feel the tension in the room. I looked at Sir Henry and smiled and nodded by head to convey my confidence that all would go well. At last the doors of the bank opened and two gentlemen entered leading a woman clothed in black and heavily veiled. We could see her through the windows of the office to which we had adjourned as the hour drew near. She walked slowly and unsteadily and the men on either side of her appeared to be supporting her. We all stood up at once and left the office to greet the small group. The bank president recognized the two solicitors and he led all of us back to his chambers in the rear of the bank. He then excused himself and proceeded to the vault with a guard to obtain the papers. The rest of us had taken seats in silence. Sir Henry had rushed forward at once and taken charge of the woman who now leaned her full weight upon him. He helped her to her chair and in a quiet voice said, "Beryl, Beryl, my dear is it you? Is it you my darling?"

The shrouded figure proceeded to raise her veil for just a moment before letting it fall back. She grasped her husband's hand with both of hers as she did so in a convulsive grip and I heard one swiftly repressed sob. Her back was to us, but I could see Sir Henry's face and the mingled horror and sorrow on his face as he was able at last to observe his wife's condition after her long confinement. I could see that it was indeed she, Lady Beryl, who sat now before us, but I could see that she had undergone a most horrid ordeal by the grim expression on Sir Henry's face, with a supreme effort though he mastered his powerful emotions while the two solicitors looked at each other with concern.

Sir Henry went over at once to the sideboard and poured a

glass of brandy, which he gave to Lady Beryl. She reached up feebly and took the glass. She raised her veil slightly and took a sip before setting it down on the table before her. Sir Henry had brought a chair over and he sat now before his wife holding her two small hands in his own. Not a further word was spoken by any of us until the bank president returned. He entered briskly bearing the intricate box that had for so long contained the Murillo papers. Sir Henry rose and took it from him and using the unique method necessary to gain entrance to its contents soon had it open. He removed the papers and placed them all on the desk before the two solicitors and surrendered the box to them for inspection after explaining its mechanism and showing them that it was now empty. The two gentlemen then proceeded to examine the papers to ascertain that they were complete and that all was indeed in order.

The bank president laid before Sir Henry and Lady Beryl a prepared document that both would be required to sign to transfer the title to the papers to the solicitors acting for Rodger Baskerville after reading its terms and a description of the contents which the solicitors were then to sign in turn. I observed the entire process in silence. The quiet and businesslike manner of the procedure was belied by the undercurrent of tension that pervaded the room. Sir Henry had not ceased to hold Lady Beryl and to support her. He only relinquished his grip upon her for a moment to sign the document and to pass it over to her. Her feeble hand grasped the pen and signed her name in a shaky hand. The papers then passed to the two solicitors who had produced a signed power of attorney from Rodger Baskerville under the name of Stapleton, which was examined by the bank president. They in turn signed, one as agent and the other as a witness. The Murillo papers were transferred to a secure briefcase that was carried by one of them, while the other took charge of the now empty box that had contained them. We were all then invited to partake of a brandy to celebrate the transaction. It was while we were thus engaged that Lady Beryl attempted to speak.

"You should know," said she speaking to the solicitors, "the manner of man who has engaged you and the use that he will make of these papers."

Sir Henry stood up. "No Beryl, do not speak further. You will recall the gentleman who helped us both once before. He has sanctioned this transfer and we are both in his hands."

The good lady paused. But the bank president spoke up.

"Gentlemen, if there is anything irregular in this matter, it would be better that you speak now."

The two solicitors reassured him that since the identification was complete and since the papers had been produced and all details of the process had been followed scrupulously, that all was in order. Their client had a prior claim upon the papers as the documents of transfer stated."

Sir Henry spoke again. "We in turn in are quite satisfied and as my wife appears to be faint I desire that we shall return to the hotel immediately." Then turning to the solicitors he said grimly, "Thank you, gentlemen, for escorting my wife this morning. I will not inquire as to the place of your meeting with Mr. Stapleton, but you may assure that gentleman that I hope to see him again soon and to repay him for the hospitality shown to my dear wife during her visit. I believe that he will understand."

The two solicitors rose then and bowed to us all before withdrawing and being escorted to the outer door by the banker, a man named Hawkins, if my memory serves me correctly. The instant that we were left alone, Sir Henry had raised the veil of Lady Beryl further than he had at first and a ghastly sight was presented to me. The great beautiful eyes gazed out at us filled with tears. There remained a swelling along the jaw and a discoloration and bruising of the flesh about the eyes. The woman had clearly met with ill-treatment from her former husband. Sir Henry had leapt to his feet and was about to pursue the two solicitors in a fury as the full extent of her injuries was presented to our view, but I grasped his arm and arrested his progress.

"No, no, Sir Henry. Pursuit now will avail us nothing. Lady Beryl's injuries are not of a permanent nature; let me assure you. See, the process of healing has already begun. Dear Lady, may I ask if you have sustained any further injuries of a physical nature that do not appear to us with your lifted veil?"

She shook her head in silence.

"Then, Sir Henry, I believe that this is a matter wherein we may rely upon your wife's secretary and friend, Mrs. Castillo for confirmation and healing, you are too overwrought. Let us return to the hotel at once," I advised.

We left soon after without further discussion or explanation to Mr. Hawkins. Mrs. Castillo was re-united with her employer and the two women were only restrained from a tearful reunion by their well-bred natures and the habits of dignity of the Latin race. We placed Lady Beryl in charge of that good woman upon arriving at the hotel. She would see that her mistress was bathed and put to bed without any further demonstrations that could only distress Lady Beryl and further enrage Sir Henry. I was indeed grateful for the woman's aid at this most difficult time. Between us we were able to take charge of the distressed couple on that most distressing yet joyful day of their reunion.

I immediately wired Holmes that the exchange was completed and that he was free now to take any action that he cared to pursue in accordance with our plans and that I would join him as soon as I knew that all was well with Sir Henry and Lady Beryl. The man from Scotland Yard who was to escort them back to Baskerville Hall arrived that same evening. He proved to be none other than the former lad, Wiggins, now quite grown up, the head of the Baker Street Irregulars. He was now in a position with Scotland Yard, thanks to Sherlock Holmes. The former street urchin had grown into a strapping young fellow and Holmes as always trusted him implicitly. As the eventful day waned we were in the drawing room of the suite of rooms at our hotel when Mrs. Castillo joined us. Our eyes expressed all of our questions and Mrs. Castillo sat down and began to speak.

"Take courage, Sir," said she. "The good lady has been roughly handled to be sure and her dear arms show the grip of strong hands. There is still a marked discoloration but she has not sustained any beating in the trunk of her body. Her dear face shows the most abuse, but she will heal in time. I did not ask indelicate questions of her, but my eyes asked for me. Lady Beryl shook her head firmly. I believe that is as much as she will ever say upon the subject and you, her husband, will not ask anything more of her. She is sleeping now, for she is quite exhausted. Be patient, Sir Henry, and know that the courage that has sustained her thus far will not abandon her now. She will recover and you will find again the joys of your past."

Those few brief words upon that occasion proved prophetic as my readers will see and they brought peace that night to the troubled Sir Henry who soon retired to sleep. Mrs. Castillo left to watch by the bedside of Lady Beryl while I descended to the hotel dining room to have a word with young Wiggins. The evening had come on cold. Winter would soon be upon us. There was little doubt that Rodger Baskerville would be well advised to delay his departure for America, as would we rather than attempt a winter passage. We would have to be prepared though for a reckless move on the part of our foe if he wished to exchange the papers in America immediately through fear of apprehension. Blackmail is a delicate operation and it is best handled in person. On the other hand, if Baron Maupertuis gained possession of the papers, he might simply publish them at once, just as they were, in the continental newspapers. It would not be essential that the papers be the originals since any delay, doubt, or controversy that arose prior to the production of the papers in a court of law for authentication would be adequate to arouse public opinion when word reached America of the contents of the Murillo Papers. This would have the effect of delaying the American funding of any canal project and give the competing Dutch Company a chance to negotiate a favorable site. The company and the country behind it that could gain a lead in obtaining finances would be most likely to be able to complete the project.

Our waiter soon brought us each a whiskey and soda and I was able to give Wiggins what I believed would be some helpful information that might aid him in his task of guarding the two Baskervilles with any of the additional help at his deposal. He listened carefully as I described the landscape and the house and told him something of the household staff.

"Thank you, Dr. Watson," said he at last. "Let me assure you that they will be quite safe and you and Mr. Holmes can devote your efforts to the other matter. Yes, I am familiar with the matter of Baron Maupertuis. I am only sorry that I cannot be there for the chase, but I am still working my way up at the Yard and this assignment is by no means a small one. I read with great interest your account of the former case that you entitled, 'The Hound of the Baskervilles.' If this man Rodger Baskerville should try a direct assault, I am well-armed and quite ready to bring the fox down. I was instructed to inform you that with the help of Mr. Mycroft Holmes and some connections in Holland, Mr. Holmes has been able to expedite the usual procedures of underwriting a corporate venture. An initial offering to the public of stock in the Dutch Company will be published next week. All is in readiness. If you bring to London a note authorizing any sum of money that Sir Henry chooses to invest, he may join the early bidders. We expect interest to be marginal at first, for the scheme will seem unlikely to succeed in the face of American ambitions in the area and the failure of the prior French attempt. The bidding of course will pick up quickly if Baron Maupertuis obtains the Murillo papers and joins the fray. Mr. Holmes is also counting on an emerging nationalist sentiment in Holland and upon a Dutch desire to service the possessions in the Dutch East Indies without any interference from control of the canal, which would surely be the case should the American plans succeed."

I noted, not for the first time, how educated and intelligent this young fellow Wiggins had become. Holmes had seen to it they he obtained a first-rate education in London. The lad was in many ways the adopted son of Sherlock Holmes. Holmes had also funded a trust, which enabled the other lads who had served in the private investigative force that he had termed the 'Baker Street Irregulars,' to borrow money from the trust as need arose in order to set themselves up in small businesses in the city. As men, their loyalty to Holmes had never wavered. He knew that he could call them forth at a moment's notice even now should their help be needed. Wiggins of course was now official, but knowing Sherlock Holmes as he did, he was aware that Holmes' methods were sometimes unorthodox and he would look the other way when that course proved advisable. He chose not to notice the occasions when Holmes, and even I as his assistant, would skate quite close to the thin edge of the law's prohibitions. Holmes always managed to pull back in time though and neither of us had ever stood before a magistrate.

"How does Mr. Holmes appear to you, Wiggins?"I inquired. "His health as you know has not been quite up to the mark in this last year."

The young fellow looked concerned as though my words had strengthened his own secret fears. "Well, I can't say that he looks ill, Dr. Watson. Perhaps a bit thinner and he coughs a bit now and then, but he doesn't look feverish as he did on occasion this time last year, which is a blessing. I didn't like to see him running about the city all day though, meeting these financial fellows, but I hope that when you arrive you can take charge a bit and see that he gets his rest."

I of course resolved to do just that and with a few parting words and a steady shake of his hand and a clap to the shoulder I took an early leave. I was confident that I could now surrender my mission in Devonshire. We would all go together to the train station on the morrow. The Baskervilles and Wiggins would head north to Tavistock and Grimpen while I would go east to London through Bath and Oxford.

I slept well that night and joined the others at breakfast the next morning in the drawing room of the suite. It was something of a celebration for all of us for the safe return of Lady Beryl. She remained in bed taking her rest after her long ordeal where she was served by Mrs. Castillo. Sir Henry, Wiggins, and I were free therefore to discuss the plans for the return journey and the precautions that were to be taken once they arrived at Baskerville Hall. It was a pleasure to me to see that Sir

Henry no longer wore the haunted look of recent weeks. I could see that he was still deeply concerned for his wife's health and had arranged a consultation with his Exeter physician for that morning before we were to take our respective afternoon trains. He was anxious to return soon to the security of his own home. We all trusted that being again in her familiar surroundings would be the best medicine for the dear lady. I could not but marvel at her fortitude. I could see that beneath her many bruises, she was still a remarkable beauty, with a loveliness matched only by her inner nobility and virtue.

The physician's report proved to be satisfactory though he did express some concern and curiosity as to the source of her injuries. We explained the kidnapping to him and he agreed out of professional discretion and in consideration of Sir Henry's title to see that no word of the matter would reach the local officials. When Sir Henry and Lady Beryl returned to the hotel Wiggins and I had already seen to it that their luggage was packed. The bill for our lodging was soon paid and the hotel manager escorted us to the curb with all solicitation and courtesy where we caught a hansom for the station. It was there that I parted from the little group after receiving sincere thanks from Sir Henry for the part that I had played in the affair. I saw them safely away on the wheezing and ancient train that served northern Dartmoor while I took the express to London. I thought of how pleasant it would be for me to see the old rooms again in Baker Street where I had spent so many years of my young manhood. I still hoped that it would not be necessary for us to take a ship that winter for America. A transoceanic voyage is not easy at the best of times, but in the winter it can be an insufferable ordeal and would hardly be conducive to the return to health for one such as Holmes suffering as he possibly did from incipient consumption.

I had always kept a picture of Henry Ward Beecher on the wall of our rooms to signify my respect for the great preacher and abolitionist as well as a picture of General Gordon of Khartoum. The one had fought slavery in America, the other at its source in Africa. Both Holmes and I abhorred the institution of slavery. I can recall reading dispatches from America in my boyhood days and following with great interest the progress of the great civil war between the states. I came at times to doubt if any struggle, even one so clothed in religious rhetoric, could ever justify such internecine slaughter. Is war a tidal phenomenon in which men get swept up out of loyalty to their communities and fear of what their neighbors might say if they were to hesitate? Surely each man should have the right to determine in complete freedom the cost to be placed upon so great a sacrifice as to give his life in war before being asked to make that sacrifice. Yet such is the nature of war that it is fought with masses and not with individuals. One becomes at last in war a mere commodity, a part of a company or a regiment. One's individual fate is no longer determined by one's own actions but by the accidents of war. When the smoke finally clears and the peace is made and the noble dead are buried the world goes on much as it did before but with one great difference to the individual who has died, shedding the bodily raiment of his one, sole, and only life that now is no more. He may not even have died in the glory of battle but instead have perished from the many scourges of camp life such as dysentery or typhoid. The effects of war are always less than satisfactory.

America's late civil war only succeeded in freeing the black men so as to be terrorized by the Ku Klux Klan. Ironically, the great benefit of being recognized as a full legal person under the constitution was later granted in 1877 with a single judicial decision and extended not to men at all but to any business taking the form of a corporation. If the decade of the 1860's in America saw the height of American idealism and sacrifice, then the decades of the 1870's and the 1880's witnessed the triumph of American venality and greed. The last resistance of the American Indians in defense of their lands came in 1890, which reduced them to utter beggary. The Union troops that had fought so black men could be free soon turned their efforts toward ensuring that red men would be forever slaves!

The triumph of the northern states meant the triumph of business interests throughout America. The state of black men changed little, while the South was left forever bitter, lynching black men now that they were free and had no master to object to the destruction of his property. No, I did not think that I wanted to see the new America. I longed for the days of Emerson, Thoreau, and Whitman, though those days were long past, with all that they had hoped for from democracy, for America, and for the dignity of man. Instead the great writers of the new age: Twain, Howells, and Norris, have seen the triumph of power and of size over principles. The America of Chateaubriand which once beckoned as a virgin land to the highest aspirations of all mankind has merely become a parable of how swiftly a paradise may be ruined by sheer greed. The dead buffalo rotting upon the plains might be the national symbol for America instead of the proud and voracious Bald Eagle. But then again perhaps it is that predatory bird that battens upon the weak that is the proper symbol for America after all. I am older now and the ready enthusiasms of my youth no longer hide from me the nature of life and its many sorrows and hypocrisies. I myself once thought that in Afghanistan, that bleak and brutal land, that I was furthering the honor of England. Instead, the imagined civilizing armies of British civilization and Christian rectitude proved to be little better than the barbarian spirit of Genghis Khan.

As the train sped on towards London, which together with New York, represent the great powerhouses of this industrial age of trade, I wondered whether I had always felt thus or whether I was subtly absorbing the influence of the journal of Sherlock Holmes that now lay before me on my lap. I opened again Holmes' journal to continue what had become a habit with me, this reading of his adventures and meditations from so long ago made during his Asiatic odyssey.

From the Journal of Sherlock Holmes

January 1, 189
The New Year

We have now left the desert behind us and are following the Persian Gulf to its head where we shall take a dhow for Mecca. It is imperative that we arrive in an Arabic craft and with other pilgrims to lessen as far as possible our impact as interlopers. We may not pass as Arabs but we may at least pass as Circassian or other foreign believers of a lighter skin color, although both Colonel Moran and I are now quite bronzed from our late desert sojourn.

The Persian Gulf is a desolate region and of little interest to the world at large now that the Persian Empire is but a distant historical fact. The people have learned to live within the limitations imposed by the arid climate. The sea is rich with fish that the tribal peoples dry on great racks along the shore. There are tent makers and weavers of carpets showing the elaborate designs that have made these creations famous. What the Persian and Arabic lands lack in natural endowments they supplement by their native resilience and hard work. Nothing is taken for granted as in more prosperous locales. A common poverty creates a dignity and self-reliance that even the Americans would envy. We will celebrate the New Year with a meal of fish and rice and take a few days to rest before moving on down the gulf. I intend to make some purchases which we will then consign to an agent for delivery to Mycroft who will store them until my return. Among other items that I have collected there are several valuable manuscripts and illuminated texts to which I hope to be able devote time when

I return.

It is a lovely day; soft breezes are blowing below me on the blue expanse of the gulf. The many boats form swiftly moving flotillas with their great sails spread, towing their nets behind. On the shore many white-clothed men with their robes skirted up behind them wade into the sea to help unload the fish. They are then unloaded on the shore and placed in great carts after being gutted and cleaned. They are immediately salted-down to preserve them and some are smoked over fires of brush gathered by the women in the hills surrounding the village. The market stalls sell eggplants, peppers, and countless other vegetables. Great bins hold the rice and lentils that are staple items of the diet here.

I ask myself, as is my wont, what this year will bring. I could not have imagined last year at this time that I would no longer be in my old rooms in Baker Street awaiting whatever problem should come to my door, but would instead be in Persia eating fish by a distant sea. Such is the fate of human foresight and resolution; they are always met by the unexpected. Perhaps this is why I have such great devotion to the Greek philosopher Heraclitus who proclaimed that all is change. I have also studied over the years with interest that Chinese book of augury, "The I-Ching or Book of Changes."

It is not hard to visualize change in the desert where the ever-shifting sands show that the tides do not stop with the sea. The wind also carves the land as do glaciers the mountains. The land that we inhabit might once have been at the bottom of ancient seas and swamps. Do the gods also change I have asked myself? Are religions only massive, tidal movements of the ever-questing spirit of mankind that wash over the peoples of the earth, triumph for a time, and then recede to give place to others? Dying beliefs leave their detritus along the shore in the form of abandoned temples and outworn doctrines that no longer appeal to the hearts of men and women. The legacy of ritual finally becomes mere sterile form and its emissaries lose the ardor that can only come from being nourished from below by the faith of the people. Such anyway is the assertion of the sociological students of religion who see in belief-systems only an exterior phenomenon of group behavior.

But what of the individual, as Kierkegaard said, in whom alone exists the infinite passion of belief, for it is the individual who wills to entrust not only his life but his eternity as well to the choice of belief versus unbelief. It is a matter of inconsequence how many follow him or her, or whether the forms have grown threadbare through neglect or habit. Such a one reaches out to God out of the depths of his very soul as a refuge from all that passes in this world of change and sorrow. Individuals may even go so far as to leave as I have done their home and culture to pursue God in far-off lands and seek the brotherhood of mankind where it may be least found, among those most alien in speech and manner to oneself. This is why I am going to Mecca, not because I hope to become a Moslem, but because I wish to find what in the faith of Islam speaks to so many. One cannot bear a contrary witness to those one does not understand. If the name of Allah cannot stir me in some way, then I must also hold Yahweh and Jesus in contempt. God cannot be domesticated as though he were our own possession. God possesses us; we do not possess Him.

It is for this reason that I have long felt uneasy with a hymn such as, "A Mighty Fortress is Our God," for he is not "our God" rather it is we that are encompassed by Him. The moment that any people believe that they possess God, at that very moment idolatry and magic begin. The task of the believer is not to own God but to proclaim Him in all humility. Our witness is confined to our own small fragment of experience and the faith that flows from it.

To claim anything more is the beginning of an imperialism of religion even as the concept of Jihad if it is wrongly interpreted or the zealotry of the crusader and all others who would oppress others into belief. God is quite capable of vindicating His own interests; He needs not our violence or our pride to do so. It is enough to wage the struggle within the individual heart and to confront our own sins. Religion is not an outer force but an inner disposition of transformation. This is what Jesus meant when he said, "The Kingdom of God is within you." It is not of this world.

There is no triumph for the Christian then but the Cross. And what is even that but a share in the defeat and the sorrow of the One who hung upon the Cross?

January 6, 1892
Persian Gulf

We are at sea again! I do not believe that I could face another mile of travel over land. The livelihood of these people is sparse but as a denizen of London with its coal-fumes, its dank fogs, and the ever-present crowding of humanity, I have reveled in the luxury of pure space. I have come to wonder if man was ever meant to live in the great cities of the world. Is it not a strange thing that the great ideas, those that continue to govern mankind, have not come from the masses, but rather from individuals and those individuals have not come up with their insights in the press of the metropolis, but in desert regions and from those lands that still dwarf the aspirations and the pride of human constructions? Man only attains his true stature when he is put in his proper place by confronting the naked sky, the barren mountains, or the indifferent sea. To live in an atmosphere of human creations is finally to drown in the human. Even our detritus, our waste, all that which we slough-off, become finally form a great membrane filled with poisons and disease. One need only think of the recurrent plagues of cholera that can bring sudden death to whole neighborhoods in London or Rome or Venice. It is not the germ that is to blame, but the conditions of life that bring about contagion.

What is war for instance but the great periodic blood-letting of nations whereby they dispose of their surplus of young men? The fate of the individual is dictated by the tides and currents of history that sweep down and scatter the barren leaves of our lives in the midst of the sophisticated systems in which we live. Which of us can claim to control his fate? Who is not subject at least to the whims of his employer or of his government? To stand at the great intersections of trade and commerce is to feel that one is watching the pulsations of a great beast the heart and sinew of which owe nothing to our individual dreams. We are the mere cells of a larger organism with a consciousness that is so distributed and varied that it has no consciousness let alone any collective conscience. We may not even take a position towards our own deaths in such a world, for our death is to it the mere wearing out of parts in the interconnected mechanism to which we are chained.

Against this pulsing urban spectacle there is the life I have seen here in the desert, one that gives what it does while exacting little. If the prospect of plenty breeds cities and industry, then it is to the barren desert that one must turn to discover his own proper measure and dignity. To die in the desert is at least to die as a man. In his last hour a man may search into the overarching dome of heaven and imagine for himself a witness to his pain, face to face with the eternity of sky and sand and sea; but in the city his death will likely come in some barren lodging-house with the rent overdue. He will die a pauper in someone else's house. No, if I must die, as all men must, let it be naked to the glaring sun, the harsh rocks, the endless sands of the desert, there to feel my pulse expire with the ground that will contain my remains close at hand. Let me be dried and bleached by the sands that will cover me and not turn to corruption wet and sodden in a coffin buried in some English field.

I recall the leaning headstones at the cemetery at Whitby located on the hillside beside the ruined abbey. The names and epitaphs are blurred and the headstones stand all awry. It is as though one were witnessing a great macabre dance in which the stones are more alive than those beneath them. These monuments only mock the dead, for they are no longer signs of permanence but show in their blurred letters and obscured names that even stone breaks down before the assault of weather, lichen, and moss. All is passing away. The commerce of yesterday is a mockery of prices, bills of lading, and contracts. The law books are but a record of old quarrels, resolved by some sour judge at the behest of some wizened advocate. They are all no more. But in their day how great did all these matters seem; what contest of wills and passion... and now all is silence.

Today is the feast-day of the Epiphany when Jesus was presented in the Temple at Jerusalem. The child was taken from the obscurity of his first days and was witnessed to even in that early hour as the arbiter of the destiny of his people. It is a momentous day in the liturgical year, a day of revelation of the hidden. The word epiphany has come to mean any sudden revelation or insight. We live for such moments, even when they are bitter, for from them we discern the truth and for truth we are made. So this day, the anniversary of my own birth, more years ago now than I would like to recall, I am thinking of life and of death and of God as I have during these last months, seeking to turn the leaves of the great unread volume of circumstance in order to discern at last the hidden text that will restore all things in this passing world.

January 10, 1892
The Red Sea

We have rounded the lower tip of the Arabian Peninsula and entered the Red Sea. I spend the days on deck, relishing again the great expanse of waters that lie before me. Raised as I was in Yorkshire where the horizon is always constrained by the great mounded hills of heather and bracken, my vision of the possible was constrained by the landscape. To know constraint in youth either through a physical handicap or through living under domestic circumstances that curtail freedom and instill fear is to desire freedom above all else. It is that urge for freedom that leads people into the desert.

I have often thought of Moses who not so much led his people from Egypt as he dragged them out of it. The constant desire of the people during the Exodus was not for the Promised Land but to return to slavery where their needs were at least met each day and life was predictable if limited. This was proved by their doubts and rebellion against him at Sinai. How much easier it was to worship a golden calf than to adhere to a set of abstract moral principles and to be commanded to perform odd rituals, both delivered to them by an invisible presence!

The task of all false religion is to domesticate God. It is to reduce the challenge of the unseen, the uncertain, the unknown, to certainty, predictability, and finally to ownership; once God is reduced to a possession: localized, systematized, and finally simplified, then the power of a religious vision is lost. This can be seen so well in the Old Testament where the priests redacted the early texts and supplemented them so that vision and prophecy were reduced to law and ritual. It was not until the great prophets arose under the threat and experience of exile that God was freed again from the restrictions and prohibitions that destroyed all intimate relations between God and the human heart.

The genius of Christianity is that it places God literally within the believer. It destroys once and for all the idea that God is out there and to be found in externals. The Christian soul is as it were condemned to interiority, to subjectivity, as Soren Kierkegaard has explained so well. Christianity and Christian empire-building are contradictory by nature. Christianity is such a naked faith that even a temple is unnecessary, indeed it is superfluous. Christianity is at its most profound when Jesus says that if a man takes up his cross and follows Him that the Father and the Son will come to him and make their dwelling place within him. To know the kingdom of God and to enter it is to prepare within one's own heart the conditions that will allow God to exist there. When those conditions are present then God will be found within him. The believer will then not seek God, but God will come to him and so transform and fulfill his nature that a similar unity and intimacy will exist between that man and God as the relation existing for all eternity between the Father and the Son. What that condition will mean after death has yet to be revealed: "Beloved, we are God's children now, what we shall be has yet to be revealed."

If my journey thus far has taught me anything it is that though I may witness the different cultures of faith by travel, God in Himself is not found by excursion but by incursion. God is inwardness, but not in the self-idolatry of the man who makes of himself a God, but rather in the man who seeing his own emptiness, the desert within him, turns to the Cross in all humility, knowing that no servant is better than his master and if the Cross was the way for Christ it is even more the way for us.

Jesus enacted a direct reversal of the initial disposition to sin: where human nature desires power and recognition, he fled from them; where human nature desires possessions, home, and comforts, He, the Son of Man, had nowhere to lay his head; where man desires to test God, Jesus refused to put God to the test, to demand that God prove first that he existed and would protect Him. Even the words, "This is my beloved Son, listen to Him," spoken by God the Father was heard by bystanders as thunder rather than intelligible discourse. Jesus lived a hidden life, obscure, humble, far from the august council of the Sanhedrin and further still from Augustan Rome. To stand all of human aspirations from Babel onwards on its head was the task of Christ, the last of the Prophets, who far from delivering man from original sin, confronts man with it; God seems in fact to allow it to stand unchallenged. Man is in original sin to the degree that he demands equality with God as an independent right. Yet God allows us precisely that by stooping to our level and even becoming one of us. God allows man to approach him with demands simply to reveal the final absurdity of such an approach to God.

For the absolutely contingent to confront the absolutely non-contingent on an equal basis is ridiculous. It is the one and everlasting supreme disorder, so disordered as to disturb the very pre-existence of God before creation, God by definition stands forever as the basis and root cause of all that we know of the material order, but its quality and aspect are dependent as well upon us. In that sense, human sinfulness is a precondition for the order of creation as we know it, for absent original sin would creation as we know it have been necessary at all except as a temporary setting, one soon to be supplanted by something higher? Might the present order of creation with its historical contingencies absent the deflection introduced by humankind in Eden have already yielded to the onward pressure of eternity so that the Parousia to which all Christians aspire would be already present among us in its entirety? Genesis has it, that man was created last with the rest of the material universe existing before us. The function of the human is confined to naming what already exists. There are however two accounts of creation in Genesis. I have always favored the version that depicts the intimate relations of man and of God in the Garden. In that account man's nature is not yet specified. I believe that this indicates that man's nature, metaphysically speaking, was once closer to the angels than it was to the animals. I have often noted that in Christianity God became man but there is no indication of a similar incarnation of God into the form of an angel. Might some of the angelic orders, as far superior to us as we are to an insect, have resented that Divine slight and preference and by this means have fallen from grace into their own realm of hell, a place as far removed from God as they could hope to engineer for themselves, and then not satisfied with that had attempted to proceed further in opposition and to destroy and corrupt the dull but innocent beings in whom God took such delight in the cool of the day? To attempt to fill in the gaps of the story may be a fanciful speculation after all, since the details of this primal drama may predate our own historicity, but this insight seems, as I used to say to Watson, to coincide with the facts as we know them. When one has exhausted the impossible, whatever remains however improbable must be the truth. In any case the Genesis story is not complete or adequate as it stands.

January 14, 1892
The Red Sea

We have met some head-winds that have slowed our progress. The days are clear and fresh and all the dust and smell of our camel caravan seems to have been blown away from us in these last days at sea. We are not alone for a host of sails crowd these waters. The tiny crafts of fishermen skim about like the water-gliders on the ponds at home in England, those unique insects that use the tension of the water to support them. They often appear to be on a collision course and then suddenly they sway and bob and pass safely to starboard or port at the last instant. It is a sort of water-ballet that we witness and I spend many hours on deck under a makeshift sunshade watching them.

We have given over the ruse that we are Moslems ourselves while on board the boat since I found the postures of the daily prayers impossible to perform with a back injury sustained through the long hours of riding in our long journey over the desert. It is well that we have done so, for an inadequate performance would draw more attention to us than our British origins have. Our time aboard is not being misspent however. I am using every opportunity to observe the minutiae of movement and attitude at prayer in the many pilgrims who surround us daily who are forced to pray in the open on deck. The whole boat has become a stage and I at least, who am less familiar with the customs and the language than Colonel Moran, have become a most avid audience observing the performance.

When we arrive at Jeddah we will allow a few days to pass for those who know us well to proceed on their way. We will then join a later group and travel overland to Mecca. We are still taking a chance of course that we will be recognized later, but I am trusting to the presence of the many pilgrims and to the intense religious emotions present among the people at the time of the pilgrimage to prevent the close scrutiny that might reveal our presence as infidels in the Holy City of Mecca. It is a great chance to take I know, but I cannot face having come so far without attempting the final ascent as it were to Mecca. Certainly there were times on our journey through the Himalayan Mountains when we had to cross ice-chasms or wind our way along narrow defiles with nothing but space and a thousand foot drop between us and the jagged rocks below when I was tempted to abandon our quest; yet we pressed on then and so we shall do now.

Colonel Moran is his usual silent presence aboard, but I can see that he too is enjoying this time at sea. He has spoken of his desire to return to the islands of the Dutch East-Indies with only occasional trips back home to England. He loves that region of the world, not least of all because of the intricate passages between the islands which lie as he tells me like lush green gems upon the surface of a sapphire-blue sea.

The Colonel is much revered in that region as a tiger-hunter. In his more genial hours the Colonel lightened the burden of our journey among the immense solitudes that we have traversed with tales of elephants and narrow escapes from the treacherous and immense salt-water crocodiles that infest the region and make any trip to the riverbanks a potential source of danger. The beast emerges suddenly to grasp with their huge jaws a native washing his clothes by the river dragging him swiftly into the depths where by rotating rapidly it first drowns and then dismembers its victim. In addition there are countless snakes such as the cobra to the constant presence of which one must adapt in those otherwise lovely isles. Perhaps worst of all, there is the ever-present menace of disease. Malaria, cholera, elephantiasis, and dysentery are endemic as well as a most gruesome disease called the Black Formosa Corruption that appears mysteriously now and again in the spring of the year when the population of rats soars in the region.

This latter disease appears to be carried by a huge species of rat known to infest the cane plantations which are torched periodically to reduce their pestiferous numbers. The horrible screech of their dying in the flames is said by the natives to be the release of demons. The natives shudder even to speak of them. I think that those isles will remain one of the lands that I shall not visit in my lifetime. I can still recall the ghastly night I spent many years ago awaiting the serpent responsible for the death of Helen Stoner in the case Watson has entitled, "The Adventure of the Speckled- Band." That experience had left a most unpleasant impression upon me and it is with difficulty even now that I recline near a heating-grate in a hotel. I have often wakened in the night after dreaming yet again of the sibilant whistle that heralded its approach to the bed where I awaited its nocturnal appearance sending it back to the man who had used it to commit the murder of his niece.

I realize of course that the ancients did not dread snakes, but saw in them a sign of the fertility of life and even of the presence of the divine, but I am much influenced by their sinister reputation in the Bible and cannot claim that I do not loathe the brutes. I am also not fond of the black scorpions that we met on our journey through Persia. The Colonel taught me to shake my boots each morning and my bed-roll each evening thus sparing me on more than one occasion from the ghastly sting of these hideous creatures. I fear that the urban life that I have hitherto led has ill-suited me to live very far beyond the confines of Europe for any extended period.

Already I am dreaming of a return to those comforts. I believe that I shall reside for a time in France after visiting Alexandria. I know the French language well and there is a unique comfort for me in the prospect of visiting a patisserie in the morning for my baguette and café and perhaps whiling away the afternoon in the green parks. In the evening I might join the good folk at mass followed by an evening meal of brochettes of veal or a buttery quiche. I might read again the tales of the Morte Darthur and the poems of the troubadours and in the autumn watch the laborers bring the rich squashes in from the fields and to thresh the harvested grains. Dare I say that I miss the opera and the sounds of a full orchestra after being driven to distraction by the repetitive rhythms, sounds without any real discernible melody, of the stringed instruments of the Orient that have assaulted my ears during this journey?

I am not without my prejudices and limitations of taste. To be grounded in some set of particulars is not to be despised. It is our uniqueness that makes for the variety and wonder of the human tapestry. I am not as hidebound as my brother Sherringford or as rigid as Mycroft, but as Watson has pointed out on more than one occasion, I often dispense brusque and ill-considered outbursts and opinions. I can be impatient with dullards. Sometimes, I must confess, I do so simply to nettle the poor fellow. There is something about his persistent admiration and devotion to me that induces a desire to try his patience at times. He is so very stolid and so, if I may so term it, British. He is no visitor of music-halls and I seldom can recall his laughing. He is the axis, as are most truly stable persons, around which the world turns. He is always eminently respectable. The usual indiscretions accompanying army life were never for him and it must therefore have been a great trial for him to observe their ubiquity. Yet for all of these reasons I trust Watson with my very life. I doubt if I should have survived many a bout of melancholy but for his loyalty and reassuring presence and his occasional medical interventions. I owe him more than I can say and I trust that the dear fellow is doing well at home in England. I shall endeavor upon my return by every means at my disposal to make it up to him for keeping him in darkness about my present situation and for all the pains that his association with me have caused him through the years. He is as true as steel and as orderly as a compass or a Swiss watch. He has been the sextant of my life in moments at sea and should he ever read these lines I hope he will know the gratefulness and respect in which he is held by one Mr. Sherlock Holmes.

Dr. Watson's Narrative Continues

I placed the manuscript down on my lap as I again reached, I must confess, for my handkerchief. I recalled well those bitter years of his absence and of how often I thought of our former days together in Baker Street. I had indeed been convinced of his death so that when he at last returned to London in 1894, I had been so overwhelmed by what had seemed miraculous in his returning at all that all of the pain that I had known vanished. I harbored no resentment within me, but I had wondered at the time what Holmes' thoughts had been during his long sojourn, if he in turn had mourned the fact that circumstances had so forced his hand that he had to undertake this desperate and arduous exile from England. Here at last was proof that he had felt, even at a great distance, the pain that he had caused me and that contrition was his constant companion.

Holmes liked to appear beyond human emotions, but I at least knew that his past was responsible for this. The early loss of his beloved mother and the experience of being raised as the third-son of an aristocrat who had acquired all of the bleak characteristics of the chill and austere moors of Yorkshire accounted for much in Holmes' own emotional makeup. For this reason I was willing to forgive much in him. In addition there was the masterly manner and the sheer moral force of the man which, whatever personal weakness he may have had at one time for drugs, never touched any of his outward dealings with clients or with the world at large. While I cannot say that he manifested the disposition of a saint, he at least always showed a forthright and noble character that might be the very model of the British Gentleman.

After wiping tears from my eyes I looked out of the window

and saw that we were even now drawing into London's far-flung suburbs. The city lay like a great cephalopod before me. Within the confines of London one might find not only all of the races of mankind but every type and condition of human being. For this reason it was the ultimate laboratory for one such as Holmes who sought the truth of human nature. He may have needed to go to the east to clarify his opinions upon the questions of divinity, but for an equal grasp of the mere human condition, he needed only to remain at home. London was and is, if any metropolis may so claim, a microcosm of the entire earth. A hundred lifetimes of effort would not be sufficient in order to explore London's height and depth, nor would one historical period be adequate to sum up its continuing influence upon the rest of mankind. The most abject poverty existed here in the very face of luxury and power. Here the world's goods were brought by ships that circled the globe. Here the plans were laid that would determine the political destiny of nations. A hundred tongues were spoken in its streets by merchants, seamen, immigrants, and servants. In all of this variety and congestion there was a surfeit of impressions and influences.

The cities of the earth overwhelm us with options. We are solicited by too many demands for our charity and given too many options for our greed and desire to choose among them. For this reason it took our native Balzac, William Makepeace Thackeray, in his book "Vanity Fair" to make a stab at putting it all within the covers of a single book. Perhaps Charles Dickens did this best in his book, "Our Mutual Friend," for it is money that rules here, money in its coldest form as that which makes all men mere abstractions to one another. Exchange is the very opposite of generosity. What is not given freely must be coerced and money is the means of that coercion.

What appears to be a free exchange of benefits in trade is more often a testimony to the unequal bargaining powers of men. Most sell their lives and even their virtue for a pittance and women often are forced to sell even more in this great city of London. They sell their youth and their beauty. How many gin-soaked hags were once young maidens who might have lived better, even in the penury of the country districts? How much better to labor upon the land than to be choked in the fumes and grit of London? But then I am betraying my current prejudices as a resident of Cornwall am I not? I have found country life so congenial that I would not return even if it were to take up a prosperous Harley Street medical practice. I even wonder why I remained in London so long if it was not simply to be near Holmes and to share his adventures. Still, I did have some fondness for Baker Street as well.

It was for that familiar destination that I embarked in a hansom cab after my arrival at Paddington Station. The cab soon deposited me on our very doorstep. I looked up at the windows and saw the lean form of my companion looking down into the street. He nodded to me and made an urgent beckoning gesture. I opened the well-remembered door below the fan-light windows marked with 221 Baker Street. Mrs. Hudson, whose husband had once been a prosperous ship captain and who occupied the ground floor apartment, number 221A, admitted me and gave me a warm embrace.

She is a jolly and portly woman who had needed to have a good disposition to put up with her fractious tenant through the years. Holmes had been a tenant whose habits would have tried many a landlady to distraction. She was blessed by being somewhat deaf and so had not objected to the mournful violin music that might commence at any hour of the day or night when Holmes would find sleep elusive or to the occasional target practice with a small pistol, which had been for a time a most revolting habit to have practiced in the small confines of an urban flat. Her cooking had improved through the years, from her early Scottish days of porridge and oat-cakes, until she was now quite a passable cook. Alas, her expertise had come too late to benefit me, but had she been a better cook in her youth I would have missed many an excellent meal at Simpsons to which we often resorted for variety.

After greeting Mrs. Hudson and assuring her that I was well and receiving her admonitions to look after my friend who appeared as ever to her to be as lean as beanpole, I climbed the seventeen steps to the landing and proceeded down the hallway to the door to our old sitting room. I opened it and encountered an immediate cloud of tobacco smoke, his most pungent Latakia mixture. I immediately protested, for smoking had been forbidden in the most stringent terms to Holmes by Dr. Agar. Holmes demurred and bade me to take a seat after urging me to help myself to a whiskey and soda.

A brisk coal fire was burning in the grate and I could see at a glance that all was as I remembered it in our old lodgings. I was surprised to find that they still felt like home to me. I reflected that we might be arriving for the first time to inspect them as we had done at young Stamford's instigation so many years ago. He, poor lad, had perished since in South Africa. I owe him much and think of him to this day. Though I have aged no doubt since then, I still feel within me the young soldier just back from Afghanistan who met that day a young chemist who had just discovered a new test for blood-stains. Where had the years gone?

Holmes greeted me warmly as I entered. "Ah Watson, here you are. Excellent! I must hear in detail how things are with Sir Henry and Lady Beryl and your account of the details of the exchange of the papers."

He noticed at once my expression of disapproval to find him smoking again from his collection of malodorous pipes. "I assure you that I have not been idle myself. The matter of the Dutch canal venture is proceeding with remarkable speed. Come now Watson, you need not look at me with such remonstrance. After all, when the cat's away the mice will play. I am sure that a few days with my old pipes will not produce irrevocable harm. The old place was quite forlorn without its accustomed clouds of tobacco smoke. Pray sit down by the fire in your chair of old and tell me all that happened in Exeter."

I sat down and immediately and in detail told him everything of what had occurred and of how the much relieved couple had been sent back to Baskerville Hall. Holmes seemed relieved that the transfer had been accomplished without a hitch. I could see however that he was disturbed to hear of the condition of

Lady Beryl and I saw the resolution in his eyes that a time would come when the villain, Rodger Baskerville, formerly known as Rodger Stapleton, would be made to answer for his crimes.

"The man is a brute Watson, a most cunning brute. But he is by now a disappointed brute as well, for he holds in his hands only careful imitations of the papers. I have placed myself in his shoes here while watching the clouds of tobacco smoke climb and eddy about forming their unique patterns. They drift in the slightest draft and show by their impermanence that all events are always in a process of change. I deduced that his mind will be forced to grasp at alternative courses of action. The men he hoped to blackmail will hardly hand over great sums of money unless they are given the originals and they will be in the best position to be able to authenticate them. Rodger Baskerville will know at once that the papers are forgeries because he will no doubt have perused them often through the years and noted minor matters of uniqueness in the papers, accidental folds, watermarks, ink smears, etc. Anyone not familiar with the papers though, such as his solicitors, would be unable to notice these things. He will marvel at the accuracy of the forgeries and no doubt be cursing me, for he will see my hand in the whole matter. He will not though easily accept defeat if he is the man that I think he is. He will think that what has fooled his solicitors could easily fool a secondary party, perhaps another blackmailer acting as an intermediary who would be willing to take on the complexities of the matter out of his hands and complete the entire project. But such a one sufficient to meet his needs would no doubt also be cunning. Such a master blackmailer would wonder why Baskerville would be willing to turn over such valuable papers to another rather than reaping the full reward himself. He might offer to do the whole thing on commission it is true rather than buying them outright. This would of course mean that Baskerville would have to trust an admitted criminal though and doing so might entail undue delay. He would prefer the money for the papers immediately so as to escape from any possibility of our pursuit."

Holmes reflected for a few moments before continuing.

"We can accuse him of little at this time. In order to allay suspicion Rodger Baskerville will conclude that he cannot go directly to America to deal with the men in question. He will realize that he requires a confederate who will be part of the plot, one who is willing and able to engage in the delicate series of negotiations that such a blackmail scheme will require. If he plays his part well the master blackmailer will present his own reputation and skill as the qualifications for such an extensive operation. These will be a sort of negative *curriculum vitae* and suggest that no other confederate could hope to possess the delicacy, the rare touch of ... shall we name him at one, Charles Augustus Milverton."

"But Holmes, how will Milverton find Rodger Baskerville? Why we ourselves have no idea where he is. If we knew we could arrest him directly for a battery upon Lady Beryl and spare Sir Henry the pain and fear that he will exact some sort of further horrible vengeance upon them. This is why I am so happy that the couple are well-guarded by young Constable Wiggins. Yet even knowing that he is well guarded, it was hard for me to leave Sir Henry to return to you here in London without remaining personally on guard."

"Ah, good old Watson, you are always a bulldog for courage; but you need not have worried. You see, my dear fellow, we have known for at least a week where Baskerville is to be found. Pray allow me to explain. You evidently underestimate the abilities of Scotland Yard. That organization is quite able to perform such a simple task as engaging in surveillance. The solicitors have been watched and every man bearing the slightest resemblance to Baskerville who has called on their offices has been followed. It took many men to do so, but Scotland Yard considered the case to be of the highest priority. At last a man was followed who returned, not to the elegant lodgings that one might expect for a man capable of paying the rather high fees of the solicitors in question, but to a squalid garret. Further discrete inquiries have been made in the locale. It appears that this man has recently been visited by a woman who always took her meals upstairs during her visit because she is rumored to be an invalid. We are certain that we have found our man."

"Then why has he not been arrested on the spot?"

"You forget that the Murillo Papers are our only means of bringing matters home to Baron Maupertuis."

"I do not," I said somewhat indignantly. "I realize that Milverton must receive the papers at last, but why not arrest Rodger Baskerville and simply have a substitute impersonate him at the time of the transfer to the Baron?"

"Pardon me, my very dear fellow, I had no wish to slight your own rather considerable abilities by explaining too much. I wonder whether you have considered how suspicious Milverton is of his informants. We cannot rely upon actors. We must use the real thing. Only the real Rodger Baskerville will be able to answer questions of detail about Costa Rica at the time in question. No substitute, even with tutelage, would know and be able to explain certain details in the papers and how they relate to each other that will be essential for the prospective blackmailer to know in order to proceed. Milverton will act for Baskerville and Baskerville will unintentionally be acting for us. Rodger Baskerville is in effect acting as our unconscious agent in a scheme to trap Baron Maupertuis. It may in fact objectively speaking make some amends for his many past evil actions."

I was silent for some time as I sought to absorb this information. I could only marvel once again at the subtleness and genius of the web that was being woven about the Baron. It would take just such a ruse to trap such a powerful a man.

"Very well Holmes. But do you intend to let this man, Rodger Baskerville, make his escape simply in order to capture the greater foe?"

"Oh hardly that Watson, once Milverton has purchased the papers there will be every reason for Rodger Baskerville to leave England and no doubt attempt to return to some place in Central America to seek refuge where he no doubt has imagined himself chasing butterflies in freedom. Need I assure you that he will never succeed in that delusion? It is then that Scotland Yard will effect what I believe they term, 'collaring the bloke.' Inspectors Lestrade and Gregson of venerable memory will swoop in like harpies and fix their talons upon our man and we shall have the pleasure of having him stand before us and Sir Henry also and to give an account of his actions in an English court.

Charles Augustus Milverton meanwhile will proceed to the continent and attempt to sell the papers to Baron Maupertuis. I have complete faith in his ability to do so and we shall not meddle in the deal that may be struck between them. Milverton will no doubt reap a substantial return, but that cannot be helped. We must allow the little fish to slip through our nets in order to catch the larger fish. Milverton's time will come, I assure you."

"But as you just mentioned, perhaps he will choose to act as a mere agent rather than purchasing the papers outright," I suggested.

"I doubt that will be the case because Milverton always prefers to act as an independent agent without any partners or associates," Holmes answered. "Milverton does not like opening himself to the power of any confederate who might someday appear against him in a court of law."

"But how will Milverton find our man, or alternatively how will Baskerville find him? Surely Rodger Baskerville, who has all along expected to possess the actual papers and to take them with him to Central America and to act from there cannot know all of the intricacies of European blackmail," I protested.

"You underestimate Charles Augustus Milverton. He is like a naturalist and all of Europe is his garden. Wherever scandal blooms, he is there as if by magic. Wherever innuendo surfaces, he makes inquiries. His long legs and antennae note the slightest variance in the surface tension of the social waters. He is the master of his dark arts, the central exchange of the communication of secrets. We will need to only bait the waters by letting drop a few hints here and there in select circles. We will leave the assembly of the facts to him. As it is, he knew a few days ago that the delivery of the papers was to be made and he has reportedly left London already for a visit to Devonshire. Our hints supplied the address of the bank and the date of the proposed transfer.

These hints were left with different persons and it took some effort to assemble the whole, but Milverton was just the man to do it. All is well in that quarter I assure you. In a day or two at most he will return to London with the papers and go from here to Amsterdam."

"And we will follow?" I inquired.

"Not at all, my dear fellow; it will not be necessary. We will simply watch the stock market returns. I expect that within a week there will be a sudden increase in the value of our shares under the increased volume of shares traded. The Baron will start slowly at first, but with increasing momentum he will buy a larger number of shares in order to eventually obtain a controlling interest in the company. The initial offering of shares to the public will already occur tomorrow; the prospectus has been run through with lightening speed. We will obtain an early position and establish a modest portfolio. Government agents here and on the continent will also be bidding. I have also arranged for some notice to be taken of the offering in select financial circles and in the newspapers on the continent. The Baron will notice this at once and be intrigued. He will make inquiries, but all of the initial bids for the stock will come from impeccable individuals and through the usual brokerage houses. He will not plunge in though until he is contacted by Milverton and has secured the papers. He will then believe that he has just the inside information that will enable him to make a killing and in the process, as I explained to you in Devonshire, he will destroy himself. He will find a means, after he has bought in and secured a solid interest in the company, to have the existence of the Murillo Papers' revealed and to give hints about their contents to the men most affected. An international furor will be threatened and for a time it will appear that any American canal scheme will be jeopardized. The stock in the Dutch company will soar and we will quietly sell our shares. We will then reveal that the papers are a hoax, the stock will plunge, and the Baron will be ruined."

"But Holmes, think of the small investors. Won't they be ruined as well?" I objected.

"Well Watson, this entire matter is speculative in the extreme. After all, no canal of this magnitude and difficulty has yet to be successfully built by anyone. I doubt that widows and pensioners will speculate on such a scheme. The wealthy however can afford to speculate and to absorb any losses incurred. Besides, I believe that the Baron will eventually control the majority of shares offered at any price in order to obtain absolute dominion over the fate of the company and many people who are in an intermediary position in the stock will do quite well if they sell in time."

"And after the stock price collapses, what then?" I asked.

"We will produce the original papers that are still in our possession in order to discredit at the perfect moment the Baron's claims that the Murillo Papers were forgeries and we will do so where we can do that most effectively, in America," Holmes said grimly.

"But the authenticated contents will mirror the ones that were the basis of the Baron's initial claims! How will we explain the similarity?" I protested.

"Ah, that will be the real coup, will it not? We begin by discrediting the position that was based upon rumors of the contents as well as the ownership of the spurious physical papers purchased from Charles Augustus Milverton and then once Baron Maupertuis has been ruined by the revelation that the accusations against the Americans were based on forgeries we will finally publish the contents of the papers in their entirety based upon the actual papers that we possess so as to bring to account many of the men in America who stood behind Don Juan Murillo and the mining and fruit interests of America. The confirmation will come too late however to help the Baron because he will have already sold his shares at a loss in a desperate attempt to escape from the trap that we have set for him. He will not know for certain that the contents of the papers are true until they are revealed and he will not dare to take a chance that they will support his own assertions based as they were initially on mere forgeries. How would he explain his possession of the forgeries if he makes an issue of the matter? Would that not reveal his inside knowledge of the whole affair and the stock-jobbing manipulations of which he was a central figure? What would become of his reputation in financial circles?"

I was silent for a time before inquiring, "Then you still plan on going to America in order to accomplish all of this?"

"I see no other choice, my dear fellow. We must eventually present the papers at the proper time to editors of the great newspapers of America and have them published after they have been thoroughly authenticated. There will of course be a great row over the matter. The Americans will have come to view the entire matter of the Murillo papers as a scurrilous scandal thought up by the Europeans. We will point out that we are not Dutch, but rather British subjects as our bona fides. We will come with a message from the Prime Minister saying that the papers were recovered by Scotland Yard as part of a criminal investigation. As they contained material implicating our foreign policy, they were forwarded through the inner ministries before being entrusted to a private citizen acting as the agent of the British government, one Mr. Sherlock Holmes, who has been commissioned to see that they be returned to America in any manner that he sees fit to pursue."

"It will all be quite formal and diplomatic you see. We in turn will be so indiscrete as to let it be known to a few editors upon our arrival that we come with a commission to the President of the United States. We will say no more at first so as to build interest. At least I will not. However you, Watson (in a startling breech of confidence for which I will admonish you most severely) will let it be known that the purpose of our presence in America involves those very Murillo Papers, which in fact may not be forgeries after all, for we possess the originals and are even ready to produce them before the proper authorities!"

"There will be a huge competition of course among the newspapers to wheedle out of us further revelations while we remain in New York before catching a train to Washington D.C. We will wait until the storm reaches fever pitch and offers are flying about our ears. I will resist of course manfully, ever mindful of my duty, but you alas will be prey to greed and will sell the papers to the highest bidder. You will perhaps even abscond with the proceeds of the sale and I as the greatest private investigator of our time will be forced to undertake the unpleasant duty of tracking down one Dr. John H. Watson!"

I had listened to this entire discourse with my mouth open in astonishment. "But Holmes, the whole thing is farcical!"

"Of course it is Watson, but evidently you underestimate the appetite of Americans for the sensational. If we simply presented the papers they would garner only a back page if they were published at all. But, by surrounding them with mystery and shocking events we will make their production and publication worthy of headlines across the country."

"But Holmes, my reputation must be considered; after all I am a distinguished doctor and..."

"Tush, my dear fellow, reparations will be made to you after the fact. Besides, you will have committed no crime since the paper's owner at that time will be the British foreign ministry and I assure you that they will not prosecute. The Americans will have no jurisdiction at all. In fact you will be something of a hero in America in populist circles at least for exposing the truth at last: that a few greedy businessmen having once decimated a small nation with the help of a dictator now intend to borrow vast sums from the American citizens through taxation to support a ridiculous scheme to build a canal through Central America. The citizens will recall that it has not been long since the financial panic of 1893 and will conclude that it is hardly the time to undertake such an ambitious project. The news of the American hesitation and conflict will reach Europe and the shares of stock in the rival Dutch Company, which after the panic-selling of the Baron will now be largely in the hands of those who invented the company in the first place. The prices of the stock shares will rise as the American scheme retreats under public pressure. The Baron of course will be out of the picture by then. Indeed, his own Bank may be in receivership if all goes well for us. It will only add to his chagrin that had he hung on to his shares, he might have profited after all. Instead the name of the company may be changed in order to reflect the interests of the new British holders. Of course who can say with certainty what course the Americans will finally pursue; after all they are only wild colonials!"

"The whole plot is a bit outlandish and even fiendish, I must say, Holmes," I commented after trying to put it all together in my mind.

Holmes smiled ruefully. "Ah well Watson, when one is dealing with a devil in human form such as Baron Maupertuis some liberties must be allowed. Besides, we must remember that much of this strange plan has originated in the mind of Professor Moriarty, whose gears of malice though no longer in daily use, are not yet rusted. You see now why I once referred to him as the very Napoleon of Crime and appreciate what his country has gained by his reformation."

"And you really expect events to unfold as you have outlined them?" I queried him.

"It is a complex plan of course with many parts, but we shall be on hand at every phase to adjust to circumstances as they arise," he answered.

I was silent for a time but knew in my heart that I would bear as always with any personal inconvenience and embarrassment if by doing so I could aid Holmes. Still, I worried that the journey to America might prove too much for him in his present state of health. A winter journey across the Atlantic alone would entail great strains. I must be sure that he could bear up.

"Then Holmes, you will come with me tomorrow to see Dr. Agar."

"You forget that we will then be present as observers at the stock exchange."

"The next day then," I insisted.

"Oh very well Watson, I can see that I am at last in your custody again, but for now let us be off. I have reservations at Simpsons tonight for dinner and after that a box awaits us at the Albert Hall for it is a Wagner night."

The dinner at Simpsons was exquisite. Holmes ordered a braised rack of lamb and I had a brace of grouse cooked in Curacao and topped with chestnuts. We then caught a cab to the Albert Hall. I looked over at Holmes often during the performance. The music was, as I often find Wagner, a bit overwrought, and considering Holmes' health I should have preferred a symphony by Brahms. There was no avoiding though the excitement of the times. The century was ending and the world itself seemed overwrought as though gathering its strength for some great effort. The place of each of us in history dictates more than we might wish the nature of our lives. The world moves forward or backward in sudden jolts while the life of each man is more like the seasons moving from spring to winter and hence is predictable.

I am at present situated in life's autumn. I feel about me the late green of my years yet the snows cannot be far behind. I feel already the receding of the tides of energy within me. I shall not witness another high-tide before, like the century in which I have spent the majority of my years, I too shall pass into the greater ocean of past lives, as insentient as its great waters. But then perhaps I am being too melancholy, perhaps my life having trailed over the edge into the new century will still endure for an indefinite length. I shall be one of the few living witnesses remaining of what has been accomplished during the long and hectic years of the reign of Queen Victoria. Will Holmes be at my side? Perhaps, but I do not like the excess of the sudden enthusiasms that always beset him. He will not give up the chase, but like an old sight-hound will pursue the quarry though his heart may burst in the effort.

After the opera I hurried Holmes back to our lodgings. I asked Mrs. Hudson to bring some hot water and we both had a hot whiskey-toddy before sleep. I heard his cough several times though during the night. That fact and the noise of the great city made for a restless slumber on my first night back in London. Holmes of course was up before me on the following morning, neatly dressed, and had a fire blazing in the hearth when I came out of my own room. He greeted me warmly. A short time later Mrs. Hudson entered with bacon, banger sausages, and kippers along with the usual eggs and hot tea for our breakfast. Holmes ate heartily and while doing so commented on his plans for the day that lay before us.

"Of course the entire project would have been impossible without Mycroft's help. His advice now has all of the authority of commands. He is in personal contact with persons at every level of the government. It was the work of only a few hours to set all in place and to overcome all of the usual hurdles. His reach is amazing. He is, if I may say so, the Napoleon of bureaucrats. It is a paradox of government but the leaders are actually governed from below. In every area there are structural imperatives and vested interests that can stifle real political initiative through sheer inertia. For this reason the world never changes and the most unaccountable follies persist from age to age. To look to governments for change is to look to the dragon that is ravishing the countryside for succor."

He continued. "Mycroft is the great exception to this rule. Established channels mean nothing to him. He sees the path that action should take and all obstacles fall before him. He could well be a dictator rather than an advisor, but he has no power in himself but that which is grounded upon reason and the ability to assemble facts and to place them in the proper order so as to make a certain course of conduct seem to be inevitable. He rules without paper. The entire fabric of events exists within his brain. Each fact is properly catalogued and assigned a weight and measure. But it is in his capacity to see the problem presented from multiple angles simultaneously that his real genius lies. His mind exists at that fulcrum point between strategy and tactics, a perspective that only the best generals possess."

"To observe him sitting in his chair at the Diogenes Club would be to see only a great physical bulk with a bland expression on his countenance no different than the supine characters who surround him with their pipes and newspapers, but within, ah there could we look within, is a vast and busy exchange going on, a mighty system, a very metropolis of knowledge. The result in this instance is that today we will see the public offering of stock in the Greater Dutch Canal Company. There will be agents bidding with government funds but we will see that our own small offerings get in at the bottom. I have seen to the formation of a partnership that will invest our funds with the fanciful title of Hudson Investment Associates, in honor of our good landlady. It will invest Sir Henry's funds and I am adding a bit of my own small capital that I was holding in reserve for a wager on the outcome of the Wessex Cup Race. You are welcome to take the plunge with us Watson for I assure you that I have every confidence in the security of the investment."

He was smiling with that air of mischief in his eyes that I found difficult at times to square with his moral obsessions. I spoke up with some temerity. "But see here, Holmes, is not this whole affair somewhat irregular, to profit using government funds and by using our intimate inner knowledge of events? What of the innocent purchasers of these shares? Some may be ruined."

"Ah the ever scrupulous man of honor, you raise a most delicate point. We are indeed playing upon a field of battle that will leave some damages. The luxury of moral choices is often confined to the narrowness of the private arena. Meanwhile, on the world stage of armed force and of international finance the many permutations of the chains of causality break down and one must accept greater latitude of decision in order to do the least harm possible. It is true that we are playing a role in setting a large trap for a particularly dangerous beast of a man, Baron Maupertuis, who can only be effectively thwarted at the level of the game that he customarily plays. We are setting up a mechanism that will not be able to achieve its effect without working some subsidiary harm. We cannot prevent certain innocent parties from entering the trap as well, but even they have elected to play a game that on its face is somewhat daring and speculative. If we were setting up this company as a mere shell and only for a motive of profit, the ethical choice would be clear; but it is the only means available to us to defeat the Baron and even then we will attempt to minimize the harm to other parties. That is all that we can do. The company that we are forming will be quite real. The underwriters are prepared to hire geologists and engineers and when all is done a perfectly viable company will remain. The stockholders at that time will be at perfect liberty to pursue other endeavors. The Baron will be destroyed by his attempt to gain sole control and by riding the wave that he himself will create due to his enthusiasm and his greed. When we lay our dynamite charges to the excessive share price we will not be destroying the company but only the exaggerated value of the shares."

Holmes lay back in his chair with his fingertips together. "However since you have raised the point we may probe deeper still. To understand value is to understand that it is at best always an imperfect calculation and therefore a risk. What for instance should a painting sell for? It has no par value, it is only paint and canvas embodying an idea in the artist's mind; yet works of art are auctioned off at Sotheby's for millions. Why? Is it not because a sufficient number of bidders have emerged to bid up the price based upon the subjective desire to own the work? But where is the value? Is it in the mere form, the lines and shadings? No, it is in the act of valuing that value is created."

"What for instance is the value of gold to a starving man on a desert island? He would trade a bar of gold for the last coconut. Do you see? We are entering today into one of the great irrationalities of human life on earth, the behavior of masses of people engaged in making value judgments. What makes sense at the individual level is nonsense to the herd. Once one joins the herd he must take his chances. The true philosopher will know that the price of anything is set by markets and that individual assessment is finally irrelevant. The wise man only invests his time and effort in what is within his control and there is nothing as chaotic and uncontrollable as herd behavior. So, you see Watson, the moral issues here are far from clear. We will attempt to create a viable company. The waves of speculation should only draw speculators, if it also draws investors, ah that is a pity, but it may serve to show them what they are actually about when they seek extravagant returns in excess rather than relying upon the daily grind of business and exchange at the most local level possible to generate income to live. All excess is finally immoral for it dwarfs the proper measure of men and women."

"We cannot advance ahead of our own steps can we? Our leg length sets the furthest margin of our steps. When does man exceed himself? It is when he forgets his human measure and uses devices to extend his reach. He creates abstractions and claims that they are real: money, corporations, even nation-states; all alike are merely creations of the human mind. They have no real existence except there. Outside there is only our naked bodies, no titles, no aristocracies, no not even laws. Show me a contract for instance. It is not a paper? Paper is only the evidence that a contract exists. The contract itself is an abstraction. It is a formalized agreement with consequences for breach that can be enforced. Do you see? How much of our lives are trades of mere symbols? We are divorced from the things in themselves. We are in fact ruled by our own creations!"

Holmes continued with his demonstration. "Even our sense of time is skewed. We live in a tomorrow that may never come. We lament a past that has vanished. We honor the dead and despise the living. We pray to Christ and forget that he is present in the least of our brothers and sisters who are now living before us. What will it take for man to know his proper measure, to gaze about him and to know that he is a creature of flesh and blood on this all too material earth and to seek God where he is to be found, not in the world of physics but only in our own hearts where alone He has chosen to dwell."

"But Holmes, if this is the case, then the truly Holy man would of necessity live in the desert where abstractions fade into the most real sense of human limitations."

"Yes Watson, and many do indeed live in this manner as history has shown, but for the many, those who still live and must live in the ordinary world, they can at best limit the harms of living in what is in most respects an illusory world. They must seek though to constantly remind themselves that all that they see about them is a Vanity Fair, or as the Buddha has said, all is suffering and suffering also is part of a world of illusion. In any case, my most dear friend, we do what we can. This plot to catch Baron Maupertuis definitely sails us close to the wind. It is nearer to evil than I care to usually venture. May we soon resume that peaceful retirement more conducive to health and to peace of mind and soul that we both desire at this time of our lives. Come now, finish your plate of kippers, for the market will soon open and we may as well witness in fact the birth of the monster that we have created."

After our excellent breakfast we emerged in good time for the short hansom ride to the stock exchange. We were met by the president of the exchange who bowed deeply and escorted us to the gallery above the exchange from which location we had an excellent view of the beehive of activity below us and the boards that recorded the prices. We were joined before the opening bell by Mycroft Holmes, who after shaking hands with us settled his great bulk into the chair provided for him. I found the chairs less than comfortable, so I can imagine that Mycroft Holmes found his to be a positive torture. Mycroft informed us that his agents were on the exchange floor to register trades with one of the major brokers. We in turn had deposited our own funds and received a letter of credit from Sir Henry's London bank that would be accepted on the exchange and we had a courier in the gallery with us to carry any last minute orders to the floor below.

All was in readiness. At the designated hour the exchange opened and trading began. It was some time before our stock issue, which had already been underwritten and subscribed, was introduced on the floor. There were only a few initial bidders at first and the price dropped below the assigned par value. Holmes passed a note to our courier who ran with it to the floor. In a series of rapid transactions Sir Henry's purchase order was in and filled and I marveled at how fast increasingly larger sums of money could be pledged. Sir Henry's purchases caused a minor rally and the price of the stock rose. Clearly, other investors were willing to

take a chance on the new company in small amounts. These were
for the most part speculators who like to bid-up initial issues of
stock regardless of the merits of the company. They invest little but
they keep the stock alive in the first days giving the company name
time to grow and become familiar to investors.

The government agents were well supplied with money to
keep the stock near par value and to prevent any precipitate sell-
offs for the first few days while the stock became established. The
goal was to obtain a gradual increase in the price over the initial
weeks. This would show Baron Maupertuis that the stock was an
earnest endeavor and make it more expensive for him to buy in
later. It would also reward those early speculators who helped us
sustain the early momentum. The cash supplied by outsiders
would gradually let the government agents, who had initially
underwritten the stock, to get their money back, and leave the
general public to invest as the company became a thriving
enterprise.

The company would of course be listed on the British
exchange, but its place of operations was to be Rotterdam. Offices
had been leased there and an initial Board of Directors had been
set up by the underwriters. Initial studies of the terrain in Central
America were soon to be conducted and plans would eventually be
accepted for canal designs from international engineering firms.
Everything gave the indication of a major national endeavor by our
creation, a Dutch company with substantial British backing. It
could not fail to be noticed by the continental press. The bait was
in the water and our great shark would no doubt soon begin to
circle.

Holmes hoped that the Baron would hear within several
weeks from Charles Augustus Milverton and would see how the
Murillo Papers could be used to cause a rapid increase in the price
of the stock in this new company. The Baron would make a fortune
if he could obtain a controlling interest before they were published
or news of their existence leaked out. The prices to be obtained on
the exchange would reveal the course of events. If the stock began
to climb rapidly we would know that a major new buyer had

entered the lists and if the rise continued unabated we would know that our great fish was on the line.

The next step would be the publication of the copies of the Murillo Papers. It was imperative that Holmes and I leave for America with the original copies of the papers as soon as we knew that the Baron had taken the bait. As soon as news of the threatened publication of the copies reached America and the resulting explosion in the price of the stock took place, we would allow the Baron his moment of glory. He would now have his desired controlling interest in the company. The initial board of directors would be replaced by one of his choosing and the initial investors would have sold out. We could not then be sure if the Baron would take his own profit and withdraw, but Holmes was counting on the Baron to retain ownership in the hope of getting a jump on the Americans and actually starting on the canal. In any case we would be in America and ready to pull the plug on the whole affair by revealing that the papers soon to be published in Europe were forgeries.

We would whip up public indignation there and the Baron would need to establish that the papers were in fact what they claimed to be. Holmes had carefully inserted a few obvious variances in dates and other critical details that would show upon careful examination by experts that the papers contained substantial inaccuracies. The press of two continents would wage a war and the national honor of the Dutch and of the Americans would be at stake. Upon reaching the conclusion that the papers were false, there would be rejoicing in America and a rising of confidence in the prospect of an American canal. The price of the shares in the Dutch Company would fall and the Baron would suffer the results of the collapse of the speculative bubble that he had created in the attempt to obtain sole control of the Greater Dutch Canal Company. He would then realize his position and attempt a strategic retreat, but the shares of stock would fall rapidly in value and he would be at least wounded severely if not ruined in the process.

We in turn would then wait a respectable time and when

the Baron had substantially sold out and control of the company had passed to the remaining government-sponsored British interests and to the remaining good-faith investors, we could purchase the shares at bargain prices as they declined. We would then see that the true papers were brought to light in America. The publication in the face of the American national triumph would be met with jeers and incredulity at first, but when the papers were authenticated the dismay and outrage of the Americans would be doubled by their disappointment. Support for the American canal would dissipate and the foresight of the Dutch Company would be vindicated, but unfortunately too late for Baron Maupertuis to reap his long anticipated reward. After that we would leave the field of battle and let the fate of the canal rest in more capable hands than ours.

Such was our plan that was set in motion that first day on the London stock exchange. Holmes and I returned that afternoon to Baker Street. Holmes lay down at my insistence for a rest after his efforts of many days while I again sought refuge from these exciting events in the eastern meditations and adventures of Holmes' journal.

From the Journal of Sherlock Holmes

January 25, 1892
Approaching the Port of Jeddah

Our progress to the north in our sea passage up the Red Sea has been satisfactory. I am happy to say that since we are a boat filled with pilgrims we have not been boarded by the pirates that frequent these waters. We have also been fortunate in not having any cases of fever aboard. Many a pilgrim has been known to die of cholera or typhoid on the way to Mecca and many ships arrive in Jeddah bearing more dead than living passengers. I have picked up a smattering of Arabic on the journey and Colonel Moran already had a small but workable knowledge in the language. He is fluent in Farsi and several Indonesian dialects as well as Hindustani. We are quite alone now and have no guard or escort from the home country to sustain us or to come to our aid should we encounter any difficulties. We are well-armed though, thank heaven. I trust to the resource and courage of Colonel Moran to see us through. He of course is of the opinion that this excursion to Mecca and my planned journey to the Sudan are utter madness.

"Is it part of your great religious quest to court trouble?" he asked me yesterday as we sought some relief from the shipboard smells by going forward to the bow.

The fresh breezes there dispersed the inevitable odors of a vessel overcrowded with a human cargo. "Or is it that you need material for your dispatches home as Sigerson? You could make up the whole thing you know. I am quite willing to share any number of anecdotes which you could use as material."

"Well, "I answered, "I have already taken a few liberties in that direction already by not quite making it as far as Lhassa to visit the Dalai Lama. Still I did make it as far as Tibet and did speak with a head lama and I trust that I have done justice to the eastern experience in my fashion. You must remember, Colonel Moran, that there are scholars of all of these religions at Oxford whom I might have consulted if I was looking for mere objective knowledge. What I am after is more than knowledge of doctrine. I am seeking the religious experience of the people. It is not enough in evaluating a religion to see it as a mere text. One must also see the effect upon people's lives and the imprint that it leaves upon a culture. There is of course the opposite error of assuming that religion is a mere cultural artifact along with art, literature, and architecture. Once the transcendent element disappears, then so does actual contact with God. Religions are in a sense bridges beyond the contingencies of life to the absolute, to God. They are effective or ineffective to the degree that they reveal or obscure God's intentions towards us."

Colonel Moran smiled. "Ah that is your great assumption, Holmes. Why should God, if He exists, have any intentions towards us at all? Even assuming that you might prove a need to posit a creator of all that we see, why should he reserve for us alone some measure of special solicitude and concern Himself with our conduct? Does not the violence and arbitrary nature of life prove that there is no God who cares for us as persons? Have you not, even on this journey, seen enough starvation, wasted limbs, and premature age and blindness to show that God has no real concern for man? We are beasts, cunning beasts I grant you, but beasts still, and should expect nothing in the way of any help or guidance from beyond."

"Well then, Colonel, how do you explain our notions of virtue, heroism, charity, and duty if the world, as such is a world would be, is one of unrelieved savagery where we are reduced to being as you say cunning beasts?"

"These idealized notions are all the creations of man," he answered. "They are what we would like to believe about ourselves, but look at history, look at the disgusting conditions of life that prevail in the east end of London or in Manchester or Liverpool.

What do you see if not the use of man by man? It is all a vast factory, a ghastly slavery. Have your read Engels or Marx? It is the nature of man to seek excess. Morality is the food of debutantes purchased for them by their industrialist fathers and their fat mothers. No society can survive that believes in the illusions of a seventeen or eighteen year old girl, my dear Mr. Holmes. We seek to preserve the young from what the old know all too well and to preserve them from the struggles of the pit."

"Have you for instance ever gone to a bull-pit and seen the cigar chewing men taking wagers on the dogs? There is an image for you of life, a few men taking profit from the many losers, while the dogs fight to the death. Even the winning dog is never the same again. He may get a kick or an old bone to gnaw on for all his trouble. After all, there is always another dog. Well just so to the employer there is always another employee. The task of a stable society is to keep the minimum wages just high enough and the prison terms just long enough to make crime unprofitable. The whole social calculus is a mere equation of violence summed against violence. The task is to keep dropping wages until the cost of running prisons becomes too great or until a revolution threatens. With a large enough prison, like Siberia, wages can drop to almost zero as in Russia. Serfdom is the natural condition of mankind. For this reason every man must be a rebel. Good management and labor relations simply mean that management has yet to find a way to cheat its domestic labor force by bringing in foreign labor or doing the manufacturing overseas. Why do you think that the great bitch Victoria hangs on to India?"

I told him that I found his language objectionable.

"Look here," said he. He opened his cloak and revealed his torso which showed the scars of several great wounds. "All obtained in Her Majesty's service in my youth. Many a brave man have I killed, fighting in his own land and for his own freedom. And where is the Empress? She is sitting on her throne in her benighted isles with diamonds cascading down upon her bosom, diamonds wrested by the once proud black men of South Africa by that fiend in human shape Cecil Rhodes, one that I place only second to King Leopold of Belgium as a plague to the continent of Africa. No, Mr. Sherlock Holmes, speak not to me of decency and patriotism, for they are but the hypocrisy of nations to justify their exertion of the iron law of mankind: for the few to impoverish the many."

"History is my witness. And, since you enjoy your philosophy so much, read 'The Leviathan' by Thomas Hobbes. It tells that the many are like the dogs in the pit. They themselves put up with exploitation and even honor their masters and why, because like dogs they fear each other more than they fear their masters. The function of the masters is to keep the dogs apart. You may ask of course what if the dogs should kill their master. This last great alternative gave me hope for years in my youth. I dreamt of revolution when I came home from India. But let me assure you, the course taken by the French Revolution answered that once and for all. It was the great experiment! What began as liberty, equality, and fraternity was the prelude to a bloodbath and finally exalted Napoleon who proceeded to kill more men than had ever been slaughtered up until that time in war. What happened then in Europe? For mere self-preservation the Kings and Queens were welcomed back and Europe was divided into rival Empires while the rest of the world was forced open to become colonies of the great powers."

I had become silent before this torrent of rhetoric from a man who in all our days together thus far had been so reticent. It was clear that he found my quest a great comedy or a vain pursuit. He spoke again after a time spent gazing out to sea.

"Would you like to know the future, Mr. Sherlock Holmes? Perhaps you imagine that man has at last reached a state of civilization. Many believed so in the time of the great illusions of the 18th century, that age of grace and order, the age of Dr, Samuel Johnson and his friend Boswell, the so-called age of reason. It was all a prelude to the great industrial expansion that has taken place in the 19th century. Ours is the age of power and of empires. What then must follow? Do you not know? The 20th century will be an age where all the forces that we have gathered, both of ideas and of power, will be unleashed upon our own heads. The empires are themselves only dogs in the pit. They will spend the century in the struggle for power and it will all probably begin with the scions of the great bitch Victoria for it is they who rule over the empires of Europe. The wars that will come will use all of the panoply of civilization and of morality to clothe themselves in virtue, and young lads will die by the hundreds of thousands to uphold these eternal illusions. No, I do not believe in a moral universe, Mr. Holmes."

How could I answer him then? How could I hope to grope deep into so well-reasoned a state of despair? Yet I made the attempt.

"Do you not see though Colonel that your very outrage proves the need for the transcendent, for God? You would not feel such disappointment and outrage if the world and the history that you describe was the way that things were meant to be or if that existence were proper to man, for as you say the dogs in the pit do not object to their condition, but what is the history of religion, of philosophy, and of literature and art as well, but one long protest at the condition of men and women and the hope for something better. If to despair and die was the only option left to the man of reason and compassion or to be a stoic with grinding teeth gnawing at his own entrails, then I would agree with you, but we have a witness of protest in all of these, however weak and feeble, and to that tradition wherever it is to be found I affix my hopes for a better world. It will not be a world of triumph and improved conditions from age to age, things may always be much the same, but there are moments of light, fragments of grace and of beauty that litter the charnel fields, and to gather these fragments and to treasure them is the task of the moral man or woman and it is in that task I am engaged in on this quest of mine."

With that I turned and left him to rejoin the pilgrims clothed in their white garb and their hopes amidst all the smell and stench of the ship upon which we sailed.

Dr. Watson's Narrative Continues

On the following morning I was interrupted in my reading by the sound of a fit of coughing from Holmes' room. The mists were rising from the Thames as the bleak winter light penetrated the room. I leaped at once to my feet, flung open the door of his bedroom, and was at his side in a moment. He was bent over, halfway out of bed. He clasped a handkerchief to his mouth while the wracking spasm continued. At last he was able to get control and lay back upon the pillows gasping for breath. I had hold of his wrist and noted that his pulse was weak and threaded. My eyes no doubt showed my concern and my incipient reproaches for the excesses of recent days for Holmes smiled weakly and spoke as soon as he could catch his breath.

"You needn't say anything, Watson. Yes, there have been similar episodes such as this one lately, but they are not regular or sustained like they were last spring. There has been no sign of bleeding, just a dry cough and a slight fever at night. I shall be quite alright by next morning. There is still much to do you see and..."

"You will have sufficient strength for a cab ride to Harley Street, but you shall do no more today," I said severely. "I shall see that you lie in bed for a week and then I shall see that you leave London. It's these beastly fumes of coal and the damp air. It is just as I warned you months ago. When your first symptoms appeared, I advised complete rest. You may even need to go to Switzerland to a sanatorium for years. If you keep on as you are you may require a protracted period of the restorative air of the mountains."

"Oh that would hardly do since we must leave for America within a month," he protested.

"You may need to devise a new strategy if you persist in

burning the candle at both ends as you have done. I am not sure that you ever fully recovered from the rigors involved in your long sojourn between 1891 and 1894. It was then that the seeds of this ghastly illness were no doubt nurtured. If you combine the demands that you placed upon your resources then with the demands of the many cases of the last two years, the result is before you. If you intend to live to see the new century, you will have to adapt to the special needs of a convalescent. This entire year was to have been spent quietly studying various manuscripts in Devonshire, with at most a short daily walk upon the moors in the clear and bracing air. If you do not wish to leave England and be forced into permanent treatment in a dry, cold climate, you simply must follow orders, Holmes."

"Ah, Watson," Holmes said at last after an inward struggle that was painful for me to witness. "You are still the old army surgeon are you not? But I ask you to believe that I had no choice. Besides, what if I do perish in the lists? Surely this work against the Baron is worth the life of a poor consulting detective."

"That, Holmes, is language that I have heard before. You once spoke in similar terms of your struggle to bring an end to the career of Professor Moriarty."

Holmes sat up in bed in protest.

"Well, I succeeded did I not? You will not witness though a conversion in the case of the Baron. We may of course entrust him to the mercy of God, but he has sold his soul to mammon. He is a man without principle and such a man cannot be brought round by mere argument as was the case of Moriarty who, for all of his ill-will, was not a man divorced from reason. I have not asked where you are in your reading of my journal, but when you come to the end you will hear in detail of my final conversations with Professor Moriarty after I returned from France and before I came to London and met you in the guise of an old bookseller. You have not reached that part yet? Well that is hardly surprising since my journal is more than a mere travel account. It contains a record of my own interior struggles and reflections on issues of the very greatest moment!"

"In any case I shall not spoil the continuity of my journal by any untimely revelation." He made a sudden effort and sat up in bed.

"I am feeling somewhat better now. I think if you will help me up, I can at least make it to our sitting room. We shall dine in tonight. Pray ring for Mrs. Hudson and give her our preference for dinner. Would you be so good as to do so? I fancy that some good Sussex lamb, some buttered parsnips, and an apple compote might just give me the strength to visit the good Doctor Agar tomorrow. Today I shall abstain from any tobacco until I am quite restored. You have my word upon it. There, that's a good fellow. I shall not risk again that censorious brow."

I proceeded to help him to his feet where he swayed for a moment. I then led him to our sitting room and helped him into his chair. I rang for Mrs. Hudson and described the menu. She looked at Holmes from the doorway with a worried look upon her good honest face. Holmes did indeed look pale and exhausted where he sat limply in his chair before the fire. I walked with her to the hall and closing the door behind us assured her that Holmes would be quite alright and that her excellent cooking would soon bring him round. I told her that we were bound for Harley Street upon the morrow. Though still hesitant, the good woman accepted my reassurances and bustled down the stairs to have her manservant head to the local market for the necessary items.

I opened the door and returned to Holmes who had in my absence procured a copy of a book on the Chaldeans which he was reading with careful attention. I went over to the fire and added some coal to warm the room and closed the velvet drapes. Baker Street was busy with the traffic and I could hear the sounds of the street-boys hawking the latest edition of the Times. Fortunately, Holmes was quietly absorbed in his book. He could read the results of the market report in the late afternoon editions of the newspapers.

We were both silent for the next hours with each of us absorbed in his own studies. Our dinner was excellent. Mrs. Hudson's cooking had improved through the years until she was a master of the cuisine that best suited Holmes' tastes. She had even condescended to learn some elements of French provincial dishes. Holmes had become more particular as he grew older about the type and quality of his meals. No longer would a cold joint on the sideboard and some bread prove satisfactory. His time in Montpellier, France had been congenial to him. It had not been easy for him to adjust again upon his return to the stolid and practical British cuisine. I noticed that his political views had shifted in the republican direction as well and that he chafed under our monarchical form of government in a way that he had not done formerly. This is not to say that he favored American democratic notions though. I had once inquired directly how he felt about democracy in America and Holmes had said that he felt it would be a good idea if the Americans ever decided to undertake the experiment. His implication was clear. I had asked him I recall about his rather arch and cryptic comment.

"Well, Watson, in order for democracy to work one must give the people a choice among options, is that not true?"

I agreed that it was most certainly true and that the American party system appeared to do so admirably.

"Oh, do you think so then?" he had inquired at the time with an air of surprise. "Then it is strange is it not that America has moved from being a collection of states based on the commonwealth model to become a mighty octopus in which the states are now merely suppliants for federal largess. I must confess that except for the slavery component I favored the views of the Confederacy in the American War Between the States. It cannot be called a civil war you see in my view for the Confederate position never presumed to tell the entire nation what form of government to adopt. The Northern States were quite welcome to remain in the Union if they so wished. The Southern States merely chose to withdraw from an arrangement that they no longer found met the needs of their citizens. For this assertion of their presumptive residual sovereignty they were defeated and pillaged. Slavery of course was appalling, but its time had come and gone. It would soon have fallen of its own accord without war. Cotton was no longer king. The moral reproaches dished out to the Confederacy completely ignore the latent commercial aspects motivating the war. What were the industrial workers of the North if not slaves in all significant aspects of their lives? For that matter what are they still?"

I had become accustomed to statements from Holmes that seemed designed by him to try my patience from time to time, but I usually found that if given sufficient consideration his views made more sense than they did on their first presentation. It was that night, after our excellent lamb dinner I recall that Holmes startled me once again. He lay down his book down suddenly announced. "No, there can be little doubt about the matter; there are certainly signs that the fairy-folk of England once existed."

I started where I had been sitting musing in my own comfortable chair and enjoying a glass of brandy. "Well Holmes, I shall not comment upon that extraordinary statement since I am sure that Dr. Agar will soon diagnose the cause of these delusions when he concludes his examination tomorrow."

"A touch Watson, a decided touch," said Holmes. "But I assure you that I am not in jest. I am referring of course to my long-held theory that the Chaldeans visited these shores and that they encountered a race of diminutive people who were served by the Druid priests. That they do not exist today is simply the result of inter-breeding with the Roman settlers and other invading peoples such as the Saxons. I have no doubt that Dr. Mortimer's discoveries in the barrow will further support these views of mine. I have by the way received notes today from both Dr. Mortimer and one as well from Sir Henry. Perhaps you would care to read them and favor me with your opinion."

So saying, he opened the drawer in the end-table at his side and withdrew two letters with Devonshire postmarks and reaching over he passed them both to me. He then placed his finger tips together and sat back in his chair. I opened both letters and after unfolding them I leaned towards the lamp on the nearby table and proceeded to read them.

The first was from Sir Henry and it went as follows:

"My Dear Mr. Holmes, I am writing on behalf of my dear wife and myself to thank both you and Doctor Watson for your aid without which I am convinced that I should never again have seen my Beryl's dear face. She is at home now and under the constant care of Mrs. Castillo, her companion and friend. I have installed Constable Wiggins in the room formerly occupied by Doctor Watson. He has been in consultation with the local constabulary for any additional aid and we feel now quite secure. It will of course be some time before my wife will be able to carry out her various missions in the neighborhood as of old. Beyond a few short walks on the immediate grounds, she has remained indoors since her return and is content to do so. I have asked her gently if any observations she might have made might aid your further investigations or help in the capture of her husband, for alas now that we know that he is alive, she is bound to him once again in the eyes of the Roman Church until she receives a judgment of annulment from an ecclesiastical court. She only looks down when asked about this and shakes her head. I fear that you alone will know how best to capture this evil man. I urge you to do so for should he abscond to some forgotten corner of the world we shall never know whether he is dead or alive and Beryl will forever feel bound in conscience to the tie of her former marriage, which will prevent us from resuming the happiness of our union. I beg you to keep me informed of your progress and I in turn shall keep you informed of all that passes on the moors. As a first effort in that direction I am enclosing a letter to you from Dr. Mortimer who has called several times along with Mr. Franklin and other neighbors to support us at this trying time. Many were shocked to hear of the abduction and I explained that utmost secrecy had been required in order to secure Beryl's safety. They are making up now for any prior negligence in our regard by the aid and sympathy that they would have shown to me at the time were they aware of my grievous loss. Please find enclosed the letter from Dr. Mortimer and believe me to be, my very good sir, your devoted friend, Henry Baskerville, Baronet."

"You see, Watson, all is as well as can be expected at

Baskerville Hall," said Holmes folding the letter.

"But Holmes, what of this marriage obligation; can it possibly be that the Church of Rome would bind this woman to such a man as Stapleton?" I protested.

"Ah well, but these matters are not within our jurisdiction, old fellow. Marriage partakes of the nature of a contract. Both parties must consent in conscience. I believe there are valid grounds for an annulment in this case. I am not without close ties to various persons at the Vatican. I shall take the liberty of making inquiries and will inform Sir Henry of the processes and documents required."

"But let us turn now to Dr. Mortimer's letter. Will you be so good as to read it out loud?"

"Dear Mr. Holmes," it began. "You really must conclude whatever other investigation is distracting you at this time. If I may be so bold as to say so, the future has little to offer in the way of romance. It is to the past that we must turn for life's true mysteries. I have been engaged for some time as you know well in efforts to trace a certain confluence of religious beliefs in the regions of Devonshire and Cornwall. I have attempted to find evidence of the content of the beliefs of the Druids and you in turn have been following your theory that the isles of Britain and Ireland were prepared as it were for Christianity by an advance seeding of the soil with Middle-Eastern beliefs carried to these shores by Chaldean tin traders from Phoenician shores. I believe that the barrow that I have found contains evidence that will be welcome to both of us. The find is rich and most promising. The site was evidently used for years and only the fact that so little of the abbey erected over the original Druid site remained explains its neglect to date by other scholars. I discovered the site by searching among various hillocks surrounding the former abbey which had already been abandoned by the tenth century. The region is obscure, even in this remote region. The local village still manages to preserve, insofar as that is possible, most of the local superstitions. The locals believe adamantly in the existence of fairies and dread and avoid, with a belief that you might find

comical, the various supposed fairy-mounds that dot the region. You may imagine then, the fear that they showed when I explained that I wished to begin digging in those various mounds and had permission from the owner of the land who now resides in France to do so. They would on no account aid me and gave me to understand that I did so at my peril for the forces of the Evil One lie just below the surface of the ground. Many even went so far as to beg me to desist, fearing that should I awaken the fairies to revenge, that there would be a plague of changelings in the village as a consequence of my temerity. I, as you know, share many of the same beliefs with these people, but I assured them that I would practice all of the requisite Druid rites and sacrifices and would choose the days and hours of my excavations with great care in order to placate the fair-folk and avoid their ire as I sought for the remnants of the Celtic and early Christian remnants that I hoped to discover there. They were not to be placated by any means though, so great is their fear, but I have at least avoided the prospect to date of any active opposition or danger of assault from the villagers and the surrounding herdsmen and farmers. Still, your presence and persuasiveness would be of the utmost use to me down here and I beg you to complete with all speed your present investigations and to join me here. If I could tell you of the vision of the full moon in the heavens, the silvered moor grasses, and the moaning of the wind as I sift the soil, only to find with each dig further confirmation of the richness of this site, I know that you would hurry at once to my side. Do so then, Mr. Holmes, and believe me to be your very humble servant, Dr. Mortimer."

Holmes folded up both of the letters after I returned them to him, chuckling. "Well old fellow, what do you make of that? I have often said that this world is big enough for us and that no ghosts need apply, but what of fairies, pixies, witches, and Druids? Can we with all of our rationality, and of course with a proper respect for orthodox opinion securely in place, still make room for any other preternatural denizens that may exist upon this benighted earth of ours? Certainly in my travels in Arabia I heard of the Jinn. Might not these fair-folk of Cornwall and Devonshire be but Jinn under a different name? Certainly the superstitions of the world show many remarkable similarities. Can we say with certainty that these things do not exist? Ah well, in any case we may be honest archeologists, may we not, and turn our efforts in that way when once we have dealt with the dry and unromantic case of mere greed presented by Baron Maupertuis and his audacious schemes? But I see again that admonitory look in your eye, Watson. I shall then be off to bed, all the more to impress the good Dr. Agar in his examination room on the morrow and to allay your fears into the bargain. I assure you that I am quite up to the tasks that lie ahead."

With that we bade each other goodnight. I decided to stay up for a while. My time guarding Sir Henry had made sleep elusive. Often in the night I had seemed to hear again the mournful sound of the great hound that had once haunted the moors. Now it was the sounds of London that kept me awake. The great city sprawled about us in all directions. Among its millions how many crimes and tragedies might be taking place at any hour? No wonder Holmes had been willing to place his efforts here at the center of the greatest empire that the world had yet known in order to have the largest possible effect and scope with the great powers that he possessed.

The cases that I have recorded give only a sample of the most curious and bizarre of his many cases. My intent was always both to celebrate my friend's gifts and to amuse the public. In doing so I tried to be as accurate to the facts as possible, but I often needed to omit or to change the dates of various incidents in order to prevent inquiries that might have embarrassed living persons or violated pledges of professional confidence.

In spite of that my narratives sometimes touched a nerve and various attempts have been made to invade our lodgings from time to time and to destroy essential records. The result is that I now keep my more sensitive records with Cox & Company for safekeeping. Our rooms still contain Holmes' commonplace books and reference materials, but all records of actual cases and the attendant documents are now kept under guard. This has relieved me of fears of burglary to some extent, but I have never assumed that Holmes and I were safe from assault. Our outer doors have great bolts which are slid home at night and even Mrs. Hudson has been provided with similar security to prevent her being held as a hostage. Holmes and I are both armed and Mrs. Hudson has been provided with a mastiff that she was fanciful enough to name after her late husband Henry.

The result of all these preparations is that I usually feel safe in Baker Street from the usual band of assailants. But all of my foresight had failed to guard Holmes from the greatest killer in London, the scourge of tuberculosis, the white plague. It was no wonder that Holmes would encounter the disease. His time spent in unsavory environments in the East-end of London among the fogs and damps of Whitechapel, his youth on the tuberculosis-ridden Yorkshire moors, and even his travels must have exposed him to the deadly microbe.

As is customary with this dreadful illness, its assaults are often interrupted by long periods of seeming recovery when the scarred lungs are given a respite. The disease is insidious though and often waits for a time of constitutional weakness or emotional upheaval to assert its claims again upon the life of the sufferer. A point may be reached when the walls of recovery are breached and the disease becomes fulminating in nature and kills its victim within a year. Medicine has yet to provide an effective specific or a cure. Isolation of the more active cases and rest in a wholesome environment are the only remedies known. I could not but be overcome with remorse that I had allowed Holmes to prevail upon me to so forget my duties as a doctor as to allow him to undertake the strenuous efforts of the past months.

What had started as a quiet visit to Holmes had turned into a series of adventures, ones unprecedented in their implications and effects upon the outer world. At the very time when I believed that I had taken Holmes beyond temptation and that he would spend a year or two in recovery among his books and manuscripts upon the moors, there had come these challenging events that demanded all of his resources at a time when age and illness had already sapped the strength, if not the ingenuity of his youth. Still, what could I do? Holmes was as imperious as ever and the lives of many had been at stake. It was to escape such troubled thoughts as these that I returned to Holmes' manuscript in order to distract my thoughts by losing myself in his adventurous quest to Mecca.

From the Journal of Sherlock Holmes

February 5, 1892
Mecca

It has been some days since my last entry but events are crowding now fast upon us. We arrived in Jeddah where we spent four days recovering our land-legs after our journey by sea and in order to allow us time to hire the camels and to obtain the provisions necessary for our journey to Mecca. I wonder if I am being foolish after all in undertaking this visit to Mecca. My months of observation have at least taught me something of overt Moslem behavior at prayer and elsewhere and I have done what I can to learn of the particular ceremonies that take place during the Pilgrimage. There is no doubt that we are taking a great risk in going to Mecca as infidels.

We are daring to insert ourselves into the stronghold of a belief system that has survived for the past 1200 years, a religion that has leaped beyond ethnicities and climates and linguistic barriers, a religion that has even challenged Judaism and the Christian sect that emerged from within it, that dares to claim to be the final revelation; each of these faiths in their own way is predicated on the end of human life as we know it and the final inability to understand the human condition from within the human condition. For those of us raised in the shadow of the French Revolution and of the Enlightenment, those who have looked successively to Condorcet, to Chateaubriand, to Kant, and to Hegel to descry some purpose for human existence and some answer to the final problem of death, each of these throwing us back into ourselves to find an answer that will sustain us, the spectacle of human beings milling about a black stone as the most significant event of their lives must seem either ridiculous or frightening. By domesticating faith to the demands of ecclesiology the nations of the Christian West have set aside any urgency that the present world-order shall cease in a final day of fire and ruin and judgment. As cultures we have turned to human progress to lighten the load of existence. Science seeks to explain all phenomena of the physical order and to psychology and political theory to reconcile the hearts of men and women to the inexplicable character of our own transcendent aspirations. We fight to preserve nations rather than to vindicate God.

Islam has preserved what is so often lacking in the Christian world, a sense of the sheer power and magnificence of the deity. All of the familiarity and ease with God that is the goal of the teaching of Jesus, who even bids us to address the Father as Abba, is lacking in Islam. Between God and the believer in Allah lie always the majesty of the Koran and the dignity of the Prophet. God remains imageless, without incarnation, and only the words of the teachings reach out to the believer as an absolute demand. His response is conditioned by the majesty of God and the response is to fall upon one's face in prayer. It is only the compassion of Allah that spares mankind. We have no sacrifice that will be pleasing in the eyes of God; there is no recompense for sin brought forth from within human nature itself by Jesus Christ. God does not dwell familiarly with us, as in the case of the Holy of Holy's in the Jewish Temple or the Arc of the Covenant of Moses, or the sacramental presence in a Catholic Church. Still less does God take on human flesh and live sacramentally within the body of the universal Church while the souls of believers are filled with the Holy Spirit and with Sanctifying Grace.

No, in Islam the separation wrought at Eden remains and the most that may be said is that those who die in the favor of Allah will return to the Gardens of Paradise, there to be served by Houris, to recline upon couches, and to receive the bounties of a rich reward. But man and woman remain, even in this paradise, alien to the substance of God. God does not serve man in the person of the Divine Son. God, in the Islamic vision, remains God.

He rewards, but still keeps his own counsel, and creation remains inscrutable in its purposes and for whatever final end God may have in store for it. The world of Islam is an all-encompassing system in which a separate, secular life has no part. The great battle between the kings and the Pope for control of Christian history would not have taken place within the Islamic world. There would be but one successor to the Prophet, the Hidden Imam to rule the Ummah, the collectivity of all believers. How different this is from the working out thus far of Christian history!

Christianity began with heresy and conflict. The sword of orthodox belief was sharpened against a succession of false beliefs. Each heresy demanded that the orthodox creed be stated firmly to point out the contrast between Catholic doctrine and heretical opinion. This made Christianity a dynamic faith and one rooted in philosophy from the beginning. It forced doctrine to encounter every change of thought and terminology and word-usage for now almost two thousand years of Christian history. During all of this time there was a desire to unite the civil and the religious and thus a tension was built up between the Pope and his Bishops and the divinely anointed line of Kings. This struggle has yet to be resolved.

The primary opponent to centralized religious rule is the secular nation-state a new phenomenon has as its origin a mere accommodation imposed at the Peace of Westphalia that ended the Thirty Years War. The western claim to supremacy is still intact in the person of the Pope. The Protestant Reformation is rooted in the struggle to create national churches as opposed to the universal vision of the One Universal Church with one guardian of the common faith, the Pope. A fragmented Christianity is a contradiction from the start.

If the first age of heresy defined the nature of Christ, then the second age has gone to the struggle to define the borders of Christ's spouse, the Church. It is this struggle that brought forth the teachings of John Calvin, the French lawyer, that were the closest thing that Christian history has produced to Mohammed's purified Islamic community, the Ummah. Calvinism succeeded in making God majestic and inscrutable once again. Calvin put to death any possible dignity within man and reduced man to a mere adjunct of an inscrutable divine purpose. With predestination Calvin eliminated forever the struggle between man and God, the wrestling with the Angel by Jacob, the complaints of the prophets, the lamentations of the Psalms, and even finally the sacrificial death of Christ that brings life in the Holy Mass within the sacramental system. Instead all that was left was an imageless God and the Bible to remind us of the inhuman fate to which every person is doomed for whatever inscrutable reason may guide God in His choice of whom to predestine to heaven or hell.

Lost also is in Calvinism is the call of the ordinary graces given to sinners all through life to awaken hope again within them so that they may be turned back to God. Calvinism dispenses with all of this. We are saved or damned before we draw our first breath in Calvinist belief. The course of a human life then is consigned to the working out of the course of an irresistible grace or its absence, a mere shadow-play of the mind of God imposed on matter. It appears that man and woman are mere pawns and not allowed the dignity of experiencing and thus knowing the difference between good and evil and thus forced to distinguish the two and to wrestle with that contradiction in every act of their undetermined lives.

Instead all dignity was forfeited forever in Eden and the fate of all humanity was to fall at last upon the mercy of God and the redemption of Christ and to entrust their souls to God with no basis for certainty as to their ultimate fate. John Calvin was the first among those who are impatient for the Kingdom of God, the group that cannot tolerate sinners among them and to face sin without exalting themselves as members of the elect. Final repentance in Calvinism is a foregone fact, so to retain hope until the final hour for a conversion of heart in the sinner is replaced by confidence that only the Godly can be saved. Calvinism begins in anxiety and ends in despair.

This impatience with God's mercy and with human nature forced Calvin to imagine a perfect community here and now! It meant creating his own communal structure at Geneva in opposition to the Church instituted by Christ to sanctify the world, the Catholic Church. Calvin claimed that his group was already sanctified, they were the elect and so no further grace was necessary but instead only a mysterious and continuous proof by acts of virtue that the discrimination had been accurate, that the individual soul was not deceived in deeming itself one of those whom God had already chosen and not to be counted among the irretrievably damned.

This attitude distorts not only the concept of church but of Jesus Christ as well. It allows God to escape from the humiliation of Christ's humanity back into the fearful distance of a God whose dispensation of compassion is meted out only to the few for whom the legacy of damnation serves as the defining edge of the election of God. The image of God that emerges in Calvinism is of one who defines Himself by what is opposed to Him. The God of Calvinism is one who does not lament over the sin in the Garden, but rather intends it, sends the serpent, uses the Satanic forces the better to create a fallen race, exalting His Glory by first creating opposition and then triumphing over it. Calvinism makes God like a child with toy-soldiers, such as I had in my youth in Yorkshire. I would set up the field of battle with great care, one side Napoleon, the other side Wellington. I would then enact the battle with myself as the ruler of destiny. Shall we imagine that God plays thus with creation? Shall we take it as an act of faith that God, rather than living in love and in fact being love itself in the Trinity, is instead only a great celestial child working out in the boredom of eternity the drama of salvation with the pawns of human lives?

Nonsense! Why this perennial need to undo the work of Christ? Why attempt to drive God back into the darkness of inscrutability when He has manifested His desire to dwell among us, and even to live within us, and to take us to Himself as children? It is man who opposes God's mercy, not God who refuses to grant it! God enthrones the freedom claimed by man and woman in the Garden of Eden. He honors our dignity as the image of Himself. It is pointless to speculate upon what might have been the fate of man and woman had no sin in Eden ever occurred.

Perhaps we would have been sinless pets of God as are the animals for God surely must love them in their great innocence. Man and woman took a great if tragic step in sinning. They reached even beyond the angelic orders that exist only to serve the will of God. Man and woman demanded equality with God and alas God granted their wish but not as they wished it to be. Afterwards a new initiative of creation was required so that we can see in what we do the difference between good and evil and then when we can do nothing about the results receive grace unearned and unexpected, grace as the means of attaining the true knowledge of the difference between good and evil.

God made man and woman feel the inadequacy of their independent means to meet the task that they had set for themselves, for it is only God who can tolerate the possibility of evil without becoming it; God alone remains always what He-Is: God, the One whose very existence is to be Goodness itself! The entire purpose of life is so to expose man and woman to sin so that we may feel our position clearly and to turn to God again who is our only solution to the problem that we created ourselves through our own foolish ambition to have a hand in the limits of our own creation. God allows us this latitude because He never stopped loving us and knew that only by being presented with our emptiness could we finally know what it is to live without love. Indeed, the Incarnation must have been willed by the Father in the very hour of our doom, so that feeling, after the Death of Christ, the constant reality of sin and the constant pull of grace to resist it and if having fallen to seek forgiveness once again, we would learn to love God in return and to know that our end is in Him alone. Each form of heresy seeks to defeat this process and as such heresy is evil for it would either reduce the mercy of God or destroy the dignity of man. This is why the Church resists to this day assimilation to faulty beliefs, not to deny the good-will of other faiths, but in order to be true to its mission given it by Christ: to heal the world and to announce until the end of time the Truth of God.

How strange to have written the above account of what has

become my own faith in the face of the white towers of the holy shrine at Mecca! Yet I do not feel anything but respect for these pilgrims clothed in white who desire to submit to God. Certainly they do not lack charity, for among the precepts of the Prophet is almsgiving and the pursuit of justice. Nor is Islamic prayer, with its submission, degrading to the spirit of man. Islam is not so very distant from the design of Christ and certainly not as distant as Calvinism, that viper seed that arose from within the very bosom of the Church.

The result is that I have determined that I shall not seek to enter the shrine where lies the Kaaba. This decision, of course, is a great relief to Colonel Sebastian Moran who was not looking forward to the prospect of rescuing me should we be discovered. I in turn know that I am doing the right thing. The curiosity of even a detective in celestial matters must have limits. When faith takes upon itself and grants to any place a special significance to God, it is blasphemy to dishonor what God has clearly honored in allowing so many to believe as they do. It is not my province as a detective to unveil all of the sanctuaries of God, to seek to order or determine the outer limits of actual grace and to outline the ramparts of salvation. God must speak to all peoples in His own way. If God tolerates the vagueness of history and the opaque and dull understanding of men and women, I cannot doubt that His patience can tolerate our present state of unclarity and opposition among the many faiths of the world. If unity of belief eludes us, let us at least enact in charity what is yet distant in faith. Let us act as Christians, as children of God among men, rather than seek to impose uniformity by tactics that would only be worthy of devils.

Since it is true that I hope that God may bring all things into final conformity to His will, I trust in His ability to do so without any aid from Sherlock Holmes. Since God wills that all people shall be saved I trust that He will find the means to do so. The Church exists, not to tell the world what God might do; it exists in order to tell the world what He has already done! For the rest the Church quite prudently leaves everything to the mercy of God in both the individual life and in the destiny of peoples. It is one of the greatest of puzzles, why men seem so anxious to erect barriers between those whom they deem to be alien to God and the evident will of God to draw all men and women to a dwelling place with Him. If that were not God's will as evidenced by Holy Scripture, then we might assume it to be so; for what sense would it make for God to desire that hell, that great infected wound to creation, should be augmented at the expense of His own Kingdom?

If God must tolerate the manifest evil that hell and its presumed denizens must present, it can only be that evil must be left to design for itself its own conditions and that those conditions must be the very opposite of God's intent. Hell, if considered not as a place but as a state of Eternal Opposition, then becomes entirely self-inflicted out of the gift of choice, which considered only in itself is a great good, for without choice there can be no real love but only a slavish dependency or a brutish compliance to necessity. Love can only be fully valued when its loss becomes a possibility, not through any choice made by God to damn us, but rather through our own folly.

From this possibility arises the fear and trembling in the contemplation of our own powers that should beset us all. Our fear is that we may yield to the worst of our own dark obsessions and choose to be as once we did, to seek to be God's equal and thus capable of existing without God. It is the God within ourselves that we fear, and rightly so, for such arrogance in a contingent creature is a form of being that denies the very source of all being as such. This attitude would turn all things upside-down and inside-out to create an alternate to the only thing that is. One might picture a mill wheel running in reverse or bread un-baking itself, or nutriment obtained from refuse, or any other ghastly image of hunger for decay.

The point of course arises that this makes no sense. Why work against our own interests with the sole benefit of being able to cast God's gifts back upon Himself; yet do we not see this daily in the face of all truly evil actions? Who can rest content in Evil? Does even revenge bring anything but the great emptiness of the opportunity of forgiveness abandoned? Does man profit by surfeit or does not the wonder of life finally become cheap, unwholesome, and boring to the rich? In the rush to new sensations man simply flays his own nerves until happiness becomes a great, heavy, sodden thing that lies heavy upon the soul. Joy is known by its freshness, by its unexpected presence before us and by its undeserved quality. Heaven is known precisely because its contours are not defined by us but by God who alone can reveal what has not yet even entered our thoughts, goods unasked for by us because we have yet to even conceive them. Heaven is a furnace that takes love for its fuel. It turns even our masterpieces, our art-forms that can only bring eternal wonder to us to mere symbols of bliss, into inadequacy. God shall surely delight in unveiling at last, what was His original intent for all things, on the last day.

This means of course that evil is always guilty of stopping too soon. Evil is finally a willed infancy of the spirit, but not the infancy of an innocent child reaching towards all that life presents, but rather, if we may imagine it, a sour infant turning from nutriment and the welcome of its mother to seek comfort in the desolation of its own puling and disappointed nature. Evil creates the gulf for which it blames God, a gulf that God may not traverse without denying that spark of divinity in all of creation and violating its right to be itself. God cannot, in other words, deny God's own nature, with the single exception of the miracle of the mystery of the Incarnation. In that mystery God accepts a lower-order of being and unites it to His infinite nature in what has been termed the Hypostatic Union.

All of human history is only the prelude to that final day, called figuratively a wedding feast, where God will espouse all of humanity, caught up in the very flesh of His Son, and take all to Himself. This is the mystery of the Christian solution to evil, a solution so involved, so sophisticated, so metaphysical, and yet so homely and familiar to us, that it has captured the imagination and the inner convictions of the best minds for two thousand years. Shall any other vision so capture our hearts and still meet with our own experiences and desires? I think not.

Heaven is more than the reward promised to the faithful Moslem. Heaven is more than a mere end of suffering and rebirth as the Buddhists believe. Heaven is more than a mere balance between opposites as in the Tao. Heaven rips us away from hell and restores all things and then proceeds to what has been veiled since Eden: God's original intent. This is what is meant by our prayer that God's will be done for it is to trust that God cannot will what is not good and that we do well to trust Him, for he desires not to withhold his gifts from us, but rather to bestow them when our nature can tolerate the gift. The great problem of evil is that evil is a hunger for a premature good. It is a case of grasping a gift before the ability lies within us to know its nature and to use it to perfect our own natures.

To know all things in God and not as separate from God is the true task of the soul. Perfect order is won by patience and by consent in accepting even suffering as being most appropriate for that day and hour, in order to wrench us back to God by denying even present good so as to obtain its proper measure once again. Life's journey is an all-encompassing process of re-membering of re-establishing what was, and yet realizing that one's greatest efforts still leave a gap, and that gap is to be insurmountable unless God says, "Welcome, enter the Kingdom prepared for you from the foundation of the world."

That He wills do so is the Christian virtue of Hope. To storm heaven is a figure of speech that suggests the measure of the ardor that we should being to the task, for God says, "The Kingdom of Heaven suffers violence and the violent bear it away." This is a measure of how intense should be our desire for one true good. It turns evil upon itself, for evil is not ardent but rather lethargic, dull, tainted, rotting. To desire anything good then is to desire heaven. One cannot desire what falls apart in one's hands, a fruit rotted and pitted. One only desires the fruit that lies just out of reach, on the furthest branch, and it is God who picks that fruit for us and delivers it safely into our keeping.

These have been my thoughts here in Mecca. I have not made the Pilgrimage as commanded by Mohammed's doctrine, but

I believe that I will not leave Mecca without having met God in my beliefs as a Christian. I trust that I have honored the vision of compassion that is the core of the teaching and that the God who spoke to Moses and to Mohammed has not denied some measure of clarity to me. We have enough of revelation and have had now for over a thousand years so as to somehow find a path back to God. The essential elements have been revealed and we shall have quite enough to do to heal history. God does not drown us in minutiae. The message of salvation is not beyond even the simple to grasp and many saints have simply listened and obeyed. Alas, it takes more to convince a great consulting detective and still more perhaps a Professor Moriarty when I return, but I hope that in reading this journal, as I shall allow him to do upon my return, that he will be as convinced as I am, that I have solved the case put before me at the Falls of Reichenbach by a man who I once termed the Napoleon of Crime.

Will Professor Moriarty be one of those who prefer the rotten fruit to that from the tree from which the fruit of eternal life falls, the fruit of the One who planted the tree, nay more, the One who created both tree and the Garden that contains it? I think not, such a one as Moriarty may desire perfect knowledge and may rebel at the theorem that I propose, but even Professor Moriarty must ask if there is not an order even within disorder. Will he opt to live forever in a Euclidean universe or will he step beyond his stern geometry and imagine a higher order of things?

The answer to that question must await my return. I can but lay my case before him. He must then do as all men and women must; he must consider whether he shall believe or not. Faith is not a compulsion but a choice. What God cannot compass without violating our freedom, neither can Sherlock Holmes. I cannot command Moriarty to forego Evil, but I may unmask his pretentions and hope that he may see his proper and reserved place in the order of creation at long last.

February 10, 1892
Our Departure from Mecca

We are leaving Mecca today and returning to Jeddah. We have been able to observe with some completeness the ceremonies of the Pilgrimage while refraining from the more intimate rites where we might be exposed. Even as it is there have been moments when we have been under a more intense scrutiny and Colonel Moran has warned me repeatedly that if we linger we may end by finding our terminus here in Mecca. We were followed once or twice through the narrow lanes and only the crowds of pilgrims provided for us a means of escape from fatal questioning. I have enough material for several articles under the name of the Norwegian explorer, Sigerson, which I will dispatch from Cairo. I will be able to tell of the exquisite white minarets, the milling crowds, the rich spices of the foods, and the sky lit by many torches at night. Our last night was a peaceful one, but dawn is at hand and the Colonel is below seeing to our preparations for the return journey to Jeddah.

From Jeddah I plan on crossing the Red Sea to Port Sudan and from there crossing the desert to visit Khartoum. I can see that this choice does not please Colonel Moran. I heard him mutter something to the effect that we would soon be out of the frying pan and into the fire. He may be right, for Khartoum remains under the control of the followers of the fanatical Mahdi. The Mahdi was of the opinion that he was the successor to the Prophet Mohammed. His views are not shared by the majority of Moslems, but he was at least sufficiently convincing to unite the Moslem tribes of the Sudan behind him and to expel the British.

His regime has resumed the trade in black-African slaves. These poor people are treated with contempt and cruelty by their semi-nomadic overlords of the Northern Tribes. Sudan itself is an arid plain, an extensive region between the Sahara Desert and the more mountainous regions of Abyssinia. It is kept alive by the waters of the Nile, but the land is mostly barren, a land of whirling dust-storms and of dry scrub-trees. Famine is often present in the dry years.

I should not care to visit it were it not the site of the heroic final sacrifice of Chinese Gordon Pasha, a man for whom I have always had the greatest respect. It may be that I will be able to appraise the situation there and get word to Mycroft regarding the conditions prevailing there. I know that he trusts my judgment even though technically speaking I am not from the world of international diplomacy, an arcane realm at best where secrets of state that might shock the consciences of honest citizens are the daily fare of those who govern us.

Ethics in the traditional sense cease to operate behind the doors of power. In England we are accustomed to believing in the rule of law, but that faith wanes at precisely the point of intersection where social distinctions enter the picture. The entire social structure of any society might be thought of as possessing the ideological equivalent of tectonic plates on the surface of the earth moving past each other. It takes great earthquakes of social change in order to resolve long-standing inequities. Those social earthquakes are responsible for not only wars and revolutions but are also present in the mundane affairs of elections when in one form or another they are allowed to take place. Elections are a risky business because power always has a tendency to preserve itself unless acted upon by an outside force. This is why absolute rule is so dangerous in whatever form it takes.

Elections of course are no guarantee of the public welfare though because the very process of electioneering is prey to lies and delusions. Nothing is more attractive to a gullible public than to believe that a political savior will change everything for the better for those who desire change or will keep things precisely as they are for people who are satisfied with the status quo. For this reason elections are forms of low intensity warfare where lies often take the place of violence and where success in the end is the only criterion. A search for truth must therefore leave politics behind and the hope of the people is far more likely to be grounded in religion, until of course one realizes that in all too many cases religion is only politics in disguise.

I came to Arabia in order to assess the strength and persuasiveness of one of the great social attractors of history. It would be folly to deny the success of Islam as a geopolitical force, one that is likely to carry great weight in the future history of the world. In contrast, Christianity in its present fractured form is most influential when it is most inchoate and emotionally based. Few people are able to digest and incorporate the larger doctrinal issues raised and seldom definitively resolved by theologians, even with the full power of the Roman Catholic Church behind them. The result is a reliance upon childlike trust, one that is in awe of the great art and cathedrals of Catholicism in those who remain true to the Catholic faith; and for the rest whatever local chapel or meeting place can feed a street-level religiosity as represented by such groups as the Methodists, the Quakers, and the various more imaginative sects of more recent vintage, those still frothy with the enthusiasm of religious hysteria.

As I approach this task I carry certain documents given to me by Mycroft in London before my departure that may be of use in obtaining an audience with the Kalifa of Khartoum, the successor of the Mahdi. These papers are risky to carry, but how much more risky it would be to be without some evidence that we are men to be reckoned with before summary execution should we be taken prisoner by the zealots. I must stop now for Colonel Moran has just informed me that all is in readiness for our departure for the African continent. Farewell Mecca.

Dr. Watson's Narrative Continues

As I set the journal down that day I began to discern certain threads that made clearer than ever before why it had been essential for my friend to escape the center of gravity in London that had hitherto dominated his life. I was finding, in the journal that he kept, an abiding need for Holmes to address not only the great questions of human existence, but also questions specifically arising from the extraordinary demands of the times that we were living through. The Victorian Era was ending with the dawn of a new century. The Napoleonic Era that preceded it had ended with the Treaty of Paris in 1815.

The years that had followed ushered in the greatest technical and trade advances that the world had ever seen. What was ahead of us had yet to be determined, but the seeds of events are always present at each moment of history, even when they remain latent and undiscerned. I felt at the time the forces drawing me back into the froth and chaos of life at a time when I had been content to withdraw into solitude in my home by the sea, in order to heal from my many losses and to find there some basis to anchor my own beliefs in order to face eternity, if any existed, with peace and some measure of security, to sum up my life in that delicate balance of regret and affirmation that is all that finally remains for us as we relinquish our brief tenancy of the earth.

To Be Continued...

Note From the Author

As one who has always esteemed writers such as Graham Greene, Evelyn Waugh, and George Bernanos (each of whom was Catholic) it has been my hope that my own effort in *The Confessions of Sherlock Holmes* might be part of a venerable tradition. I would like to point out however that the position of a writer who incidentally is Catholic must be distinguished from that of a Catholic writer whose writings are meant precisely to reflect church teachings as such. There is a tension between these two positions that makes it difficult for a Catholic to be both true to his faith while remaining simultaneously true to the form and literary intent that must accompany any act of composition. It would be awkward and indeed impossible to write a cohesive narrative seeking to capture and comment upon human life and conflict if the writer had to simultaneously ensure that goodness and fidelity always emerged in clarity and triumph while its opposite was equally revealed in all of its inherent malice and folly. Fiction, even when dealing with theological reflection, as is the case with the present work, can never be a substitute for catechizes. The reader is therefore cautioned that in reading the present text no decisive conclusion be drawn that the positions of any of the characters reflect either the final views of the author or the official position of the Catholic Church. Literature embraces life according to its own limited perceptions as it is and even in its suggestions of a better world must always fall short, not only in displaying accurately whatever emerging forces may exist in human history, but in depicting all that has been revealed of a higher purpose and source to illumine us in our beleaguered world.

Thomas Mengert possesses a Masters Degree in English Literature with a special expertise in the complex works of the Irish author, James Joyce. His background in humanities and philosophy are combined in this probing novel. As a final Sherlockian synthesis, *The Confessions of Sherlock Holmes* is Mengert's attempt to understand the true depths of the best known detective in world literature, a hero to his many fans who find in his character and habits of mind an endless fascination.